A CHANGE IN TACTICS:
Maiden Voyage

Lisa Pachino

Copyright © 2017 Lisa Pachino
All rights reserved
First Edition

PAGE PUBLISHING, INC.
New York, NY

First originally published by Page Publishing, Inc. 2017

ISBN 978-1-63568-145-1 (Paperback)
ISBN 978-1-63568-146-8 (Digital)

Printed in the United States of America

For My Dad, who taught me to reach for the stars,
And My Mom, who gave me the tools to get there.

ACKNOWLEDGMENTS

To Todd, who is always only an email away and ever so insightful
To Wendy, who spent countless mornings listening to the first draft
To Rich, who started me on this course over thirty years ago
To BK, who got me back into shape and taught me how to stay safe
To Linda and Carla, who critically read the final draft
To Yael, who drove two hours to take my picture
To Page Publishing, for having belief in my work
To My husband and children, for always being supportive

PART 1: LUAC

Planetary Home of the Tāl-Kari

CHAPTER 1

There were never days without problems or questions, and she was expected to always have a solution or answer. Born to military royalty, Leba Brader never wanted for anything. It's not like anything was handed to her, though; she worked hard for everything she achieved, but the path to get there was orchestrated with military precision. Well-identified objectives with their inherent obstacles were plotted on a realistic timetable, including options for workarounds or push-throughs. Support services defined, plans refined, and decisions opined all led to where she was now, a well-liked and highly skilled trauma surgeon. So why wasn't she happy?

It had been over thirty years since the last great galactic war ended, and the Tal-Kari secured their position as the premier free-planet protection force. Her parents, Commander Reela Savar Brader, the first female Tal-Kari fighter pilot, and Commander Darian Brader, were both instrumental in defeating the Etalian Empire. The highly decorated veterans appreciated the quiet. Troopers and civilians alike enjoyed a conflict-free existence threatened only by boredom and complacency. But Leba wanted more than shift work at Luac General Medical Center. She wanted to understand who she was and her purpose in life. She needed to stretch her wings, fly out of her comfort zone, and soar to new heights.

A tiny green icon blinked in the upper-right corner of the head-mounted display that serviced the VR helmet. *Focus on the mission.* Leba Brader tried to ignore the beacon. *Don't think, jump—thwamp—fifty-eight, suck in air, jump—thwamp—fifty-nine, breathe, stop thinking and focus on the black dot on the floor. Stop looking at the call icon. Focus, breathe. One blink only. See who it is. Long right eye blink. Uh-oh, jump*—thwamp—*don't forget to jump*—thwamp—*sixty, sixty-one. Esre Brader. Breathe, focus on the spot, jump*—thwamp—*sixty-two. I really should get it. Hurry, jump*—thwamp—*sixty-three. Breathe. Long right eye blink.*

"Hi, sis." *Jump. Jump. Jump.*

"What are you doing?"

"I'm holojumping." Leba sucked in a breath and exhaled quickly. "Dammit, and I was so close to a new record." Leba stopped jumping, the simulated rope lying tangled under her feet. "Wait, let me switch the display." Exaggerating a left eye blink, the icon turned yellow, putting her sister on hold. Loosening her chinstrap, Leba purposely blinked twice in rapid succession. The holorope melted from her hands, and the display returned to her living room. Thankfully, everything appeared on first pass to be intact. Last time she attempted this workout, she forgot to move a table lamp, and it became an exercise-induced casualty. Remembering to log in the parameters with a final blink, Leba shook her head free from the confines of the helmet. Her brunette hair was sweaty and matted against her forehead. Grabbing a nearby towel, she ran it over her face, sopping up the sweat dripping into her eyes, dried her hands, and slung it around her neck. Snatching the remote off the table, Leba activated the wall unit, her younger sister's image materialized upside down on the screen.

"Where are you?" Leba asked before she recognized her sister's reverse incline angle perch.

"Cliff face, Lesser Luacian Mountains."

Pressing a few keys, Leba focused the image. "You said it was urgent," her sister puffed. The screen flashed momentarily as a short stream of exhaust fired from Esre's hover boots.

"That was a few hours ago." Esre Brader too followed her destiny along a similarly chartered course. But Leba's younger sister was able to manipulate the path, making time for a husband and children. Not only that, she found adventure as an expert in sports and wilderness medicine. Every day filled with exotic locales, exciting challenges, famous patients, and invitations to perform for the most demanding audience—professional athletes. Leba wasn't jealous; she was proud of her baby sister but wished she could experience more of life.

As the eldest of three siblings—she had a little brother, a star in his own right—Leba was expected to set the example, do her best without complaint or regret, but stay the course—make her parents proud of their number one. Misbehavior, freelancing, straying from the straight and narrow were not options. Safe and secure, staying in her comfort zone, never making her parents worry. And why should she; they gave her everything.

Leba followed the structured plan she and her parents designed and did very well—model student, top of her class, offers for distant postings. Her sibs searched out opportunities to experience more of what life offered. In her mind, they did better, were happier, and lived adventurous and exciting lives. Not that she herself hadn't helped them achieve those goals. She was right beside them every step of the way, whether it was helping with schoolwork or practicing for a competition or as simple as words of encouragement.

Adjusting her handhold and securing a toehold, Esre asked, "What's this about an ice moon?"

It was difficult to talk to her sister, who was hanging upside down from a sheer rock face, and Leba felt the need to incline her head. "Are you sure you've got time to talk?"

A sustained hiss momentarily interrupted the communication. Releasing her fingertip grip from the rocky crevice, Esre righted herself. From Leba's view, Esre now appeared to be standing on a cloud. Crossing her arms over her chest, Esre smiled. "This better?"

"I volunteered for an expeditionary mission to Vedax."

"You did what?" Esre laughed.

"I volunteered for an expeditionary mission to Vedax," Leba repeated. "Vedax, a moon in the Glirase system. Full of cool stuff like crystalline glaciers and cryo-volcanoes, and I need your help to get me there," Leba continued.

"But you don't like heights, and you don't like travel, and you don't like change, and I could go on all day…" Esre trailed off as her boot stabilizers made a small correction.

"Do you think you could teach me everything you know about surviving in the wilderness...and help me at least qualify for this mission?"

"From your voice message, it sounded like your mind's set on it," Esre paused. Inclining her head one way and then back, Esre smiled. "So sure, I'll help." Bouncing ever so slightly as a wind drift made its way past. "By the way, are Mom and Dad okay with this?"

"Well, I'll let you know when I ask them. For now, I thought if I can prove I can survive your training schedule, then I could survive anything some old frozen ice ball of a moon could send my way."

For the two sisters, this was a weird situation. It was generally Esre asking Leba what she thought of something she was about to undertake that strayed from the plan. Something they both knew would rock the boat, something Mom and Dad would be less than pleased to know about. The task to break the news, soften the blow, and at the end of the day, convince the adults it was okay ultimately fell to Leba. If she approved of it, typically, at least according to Esre and Lav, Mom and Dad would stamp it sanctioned as well.

"Now seriously, have you told Lav? You know our brother is worse than you when it comes to making changes."

"I think he'll understand, and I bet he has lots of suggestions for making the whole trip much more interesting."

"Listen, Leba, for starters you'll need to get back into physical shape. I'll set up a doable exercise and endurance beginner schedule for you, and we'll see how fast you make progress. Then we'll add in the survival stuff you'll need to know." Esre hesitated for a moment and then continued. "But the mental stuff you'll have to figure out on your own. Don't get me wrong, you have determination and perseverance, but you've got to get over some things that even survival skills won't help you with."

Leba said, "I know, and that's the part that scares me the most. That's why I need to be more than ready when the time comes."

Esre interrupted, "Thanks for asking me to help. It means a lot to me that one of the people I look to for support and guidance and rational thinking is asking me for help. In fact, this conversation usually goes the opposite way. Despite the fact you can't see your own worth, the rest of us around you do. We depend on you, trust you, and think you're totally awesome."

Six short months. Signing up for the deployment was one thing; actually making the team was another. The mission didn't leave for a year. It would take six months to find the right people for the mission. Rumor was command already handpicked the majority of the elite team, but for appearance's sake and nondiscrimination policies, they were required to at least post the mission offer to its rank and file.

And that was the other big issue. Despite her parents being military royalty, their princess was civilian working at the most prestigious military hospital, with access to all the latest and greatest technology funded by an association of free planets as gratitude for keeping the peace. The Tal-Kari was not only the premier first responder for the stars, putting out fires wherever they sparked, but also the police keepers, international guards, and babysitters for anyone who needed it. This came with a price though. Not a monetary one but a charitable one. Tal-Kari services were free, but in return, the host planet would contribute access to intelligence, resources, or personnel. The wealth of intellectual data was overwhelming, but sometimes it didn't pay the bills, and budgets sometimes ran short. Her parents got Leba an exemption to work alongside the military doctors but not have to enlist. And although she would have been willing to do so, her parents made it clear, formal access but no formal dress. Being part of an expeditionary mission would change all that.

Leba listed the things she'd need to do to get picked for this deployment. *One, get help from little sister—done. Two, get parents and brother to buy in—pending for now. Three, actually get accepted to go on the mission.* Leba continued mentally checking off the items she needed to have in place. On paper, Leba was an ideal candidate, but six months wasn't a lot of time to get her act together, both physically and mentally.

On these kinds of exploratory missions, the medical officer was always the most nonessential person. Somehow it seemed funny to Leba. The one keeping everyone functional, healthy, and fit was often the least argued appointment and therefore the most expendable. That was her in. The team member who shadowed everyone else, staying out of the way, not getting lost or into trouble, probably the most critical to everyone else's ultimate survival was last on and first off. The outsider. But normally Leba felt like an outsider. Unlike many of her colleagues or teachers, she chose to hang with the enlisted rather than the party with the establishment. This oftentimes made her rank-mates snub their noses at her for "getting dirty." What her rank-mates didn't realize was all the great information and skills, technical knowledge, and common sense "those enlisted" possessed. Leba learned all kinds of useful tidbits, setting her apart as a quick thinker, innovator, and fixer.

Affectionately known to her as Grand Uncle, Baal Tosona was the man who raised her father. He too was unceremoniously dubbed fixer. She called a select few uncle, some real, like Uncle Heli Bebcnof, a true hero of the Tal-Kari, and some adopted, like Uncle Trent Crenon, her mother's lead flight. But only one Grand Uncle. Quite old now, slow and deliberate, but still a pleasure to talk to. When prodded in just the right way, he would tell her stories of his life as a fixer, infiltrating the enemy, uncovering their deepest and darkest secrets. He not only raised her father as his own son but also helped her mother become the first female Tal-Kari fighter pilot. Like Leba, Grand Uncle was not often noticed until the job was done and the results spoke for themselves. He shied away from gaudy recognition, saying it interfered with his ability to perform his work. He counseled Leba sometimes, there was more light in the shadows; one only need open their eyes to see it. Seeking Grand Uncle's thoughts on her newly made decision might help her find a way to break the news to her parents.

"You have six long months to ponder your decision," Baal Tosona began. "In fact, you are rather lucky you have so much time. When I was chosen, or volunteered, for my mission to Etali, there were only three weeks to study details, memorize schematics, learn contacts, and plan my eventual return. Compared to your mission, which I assume has both a start and an end date, my mission was open-ended."

A CHANGE IN TACTICS: MAIDEN VOYAGE

"I don't get it," Leba probed. "I don't understand why anyone, especially someone as important and vital as you were to the ruling council, would have given it all away to go undercover, assume a new identity, live under an oppressive regime."

"When Mirella died, everything was taken away from me," he responded curtly. The forcefulness of his words, the pain and suffering and anger caught Leba by surprise. She detected something in his voice she never heard before—a loss of composure. Her life was good. Enviable to most. Maybe she should be satisfied with all she had. Maybe she should reconsider.

"Good Morning, Doc. Another early start?" the construction superintendent said as Leba Brader negotiated her way past the barricades outlining the new hospital addition.

Leba smiled and waved back. "Always."

"Hey, Doc, if you have a minute later, can I run something past you?"

"Of course, I'll be around all day." She smiled again and continued toward the building. She didn't mind the curbside consult. Besides, he was single, kinda cute, with muscles in all the right places.

Leba liked this time of the morning, so early the light of day was only a sliver piercing the darkness. The sun, with its vibrant oranges and reds, was barely peaking over the horizon, filling the sky with subtle pinks and blues. No one was around, and the clinic was dark. Leba swiped her identi-card into the scanner, opening the door. Crossing the entry portal, the timer on the alarm system began to count down, prompting her to enter a deactivation code. Tension, almost like defusing a bomb as the seconds ticked down, was the most excitement she had. What would it be to have those seconds continually ticking for everything she did? That's how she imagined an expeditionary mission to be. Always on edge, constantly thinking on your feet, lives hanging in the balance, the rush of adrenaline fueling you on, everything depending on your next decision. As the signal light turned from red to green, soft lights bathed the hallway as the med clinic came to life. Leba proceeded toward her office, sequentially activating the lights as she entered a corridor. It was almost as if the building recognized her and was welcoming her for another day.

Dr. Leba Brader knew everybody. Well, almost everybody, and not just the important people but the really important people. Those people making Luac General Medical Center tick. Outside the classroom, her training continued here, lessons learned from all the hardworking people, each uniquely suited to their role in the great hospital machine. Sometimes the answers were not in the text files. So why was she running away? She needed to experience life and death, happiness and sorrow, respect and contempt in the real world, not trapped behind fabricated borders or protected by her parents' overwatch.

As she passed by the patient care areas, she noted soft blue lights illuminating each patient cubicle. In a few hours, the stretchers would be filled, and the place would be awash in bright lights and busy people. People who needed her. For now, she enjoyed the calm and walked on. When she reached the administrative corridor of offices, she passed them and entered the stairwell.

She liked having her office on the lower level, tucked away from intrusion. This was her private sanctuary, shielded from the piped-in music, the constant buzzing of comm signaling, and the incessant never-ending conversations. Sure, when she was attending the clinic, she needed to be immersed in all the chatter and chaos, but she also needed a refuge to concentrate, think, puzzle things out, enjoy her specially brewed MX. The clinic staff called it rocket fuel. Making it was usually her first task of the new day.

She unlocked the door to her office, laid down her travel pack, slipped on her jacket, affixing the identi-card to the upper pocket. Looking around her sparsely furnished office, tucked away in the basement of the medical clinic, Leba surveyed the organized piles on her desk. Ingoing and outgoing correspondences, books, charts, things needing her certifying signature. To the left side corner was a large info station monitor and terminal. Most doctors keep it front and center, keeping a healthy barricade between them and their patients. Leba's approach was more welcoming. Every morning, she followed the same pattern, activating her info-station, emptying the overnight messages in her in-basket, refilling prescriptions, answering nonurgent patient text inquiries. Once the queue was zero, Leba could start with a clean slate and head back upstairs.

Automatically activating the lights in the longue by entering, Leba started preparing the MX. Enjoying the aroma of the brewing drink, Leba stopped. Something was wrong; something was different. Closing her eyes, trying to remember her office, she felt something different. Something changed, something was out of place. She poured herself a steaming cup of MX and hurried back down the stairs. Furiously scanning the room, her eyes zeroed in on the thing out of place. Her picture cube, displaying her family, was turned. Subtle, yes, and almost imperceptible, but turned. Turned and replaced.

Leba liked everything in its place, the same way, precise and undisturbed. Was she willing to give it all up? Every day she would turn the cube a quarter of a turn so a different picture would be displayed. It was wrong, the sequence was off. She rotated it at the end of each day so a new face would greet her every morning. Compulsive as she was, today was supposed to be the picture of her and her siblings at her parents' thirtieth anniversary celebration. What an awesome party.

Leba remembered how surprised her un-surprise-able parents were. She and her sibs planned for months and scored a giant coup, luring her mom and dad to a supposed sixtieth birthday party for her uncle Trent Crenon. Her mom was Uncle Trent's wingman, and he and Aunt Reylan were just like family. Leba remembered hanging out with the Crenons, holiday dinners, off-world family vacations. So it only made sense her busy mom and dad would both show up for the party. No excuses. Uncle Trent was more than willing to participate in the ruse. Over the years, pranks between the two couples were family legends. As time went by, each couple's respective kids tried, to no avail, to recreate some of the best ones. The cleaning service knew better than to touch things on her desk, so who violated her space?

Reviewing in her mind, Leba made a mental list of who had access. A reminder icon popped up on the desktop monitor, interrupting her concentration. Leba hated this part of her job. In fact, she hated a lot of things about her current post, but interviewing and training newbies was the worst. Rarely would any of these recruits care about anything but finishing their shift and getting on to more exciting rotations. Sitting behind her modest wooden desk, sipping a steaming cup of caffeine and reviewing the tests from her latest group of patients, Leba waited for her next monthly charge. The altered picture cube still baffled her, but further investigation would have to wait because there was a rap at her slightly open door. Leba checked her watch. *Strange,* she thought. Her candidate was not due for another forty-three minutes. This would be a first, not only on time, but early.

"Wait, what were you thinking? You hate change," Sendra Tohl, her auburn hair newly bobbed, plopped down in one of the consultation chairs and stared, breaking Leba's morning routine for a second time.

Sendra would echo her sister's concerns. "Let me guess," Leba said, her eyebrows shooting skyward so her eyes could avoid Sendra's glare. "You came in early today so you could change my mind."

Pinching her face, her eyes now only narrow slits, Sendra nodded yes. In Leba's reality, Sendra was her best friend and the clinic administrator, the one who made her life smoother. The reader of signs. Blessed with a razor wit and even sharper tongue, Sendra wasn't afraid to say what she thought. The poster child for confidence and self-esteem, she complemented Leba's reserved style, and the pair made a formidable team. That's why Leba waited to tell her. Sendra needed to understand why she was making such a drastic change, and Leba needed to be ready for all of Sendra's "what ifs?"

"Sometimes, it's not enough to be a doctor. I want more. I want to feel like I belong outside my own little world." Leba shifted in her seat, straightening her back, intertwining her fingers on the top of her desk. "It's time to live a little, have more fun. Something I missed, spending all those years in school. I want to make a difference I can see." She extended her arms and pushed back. "Like the difference my mom and dad made during the Great War."

"But you do make a difference. You've helped lots of people besides you, like knowing everyone in your own personal solar system. You are set in your ways, routine and comfortable. Right now you're all wigged out because I interrupted you before your in-box was empty, and it's driving you nuts." Sendra reached over, moved a pile of periodicals from one corner to the other.

"No." Leba let the word be drawn out then reached across, recornered the stack, and placed it back. Typing a few keys, Leba swiveled the monitor to face Sendra. "Look at how cool this mission is." Displayed on the screen was a star field Sendra didn't recognize. "If I make the mission team, I'm going to the Glirase system." She pointed to a planetary array. "The big one is Glirase, a very cold, ringed gas giant, pockmarked with craters and serviced by an underground ocean." The gray planet was covered in swirling blue-tinged clouds. "Look at her moons, each unique in their own way. See this little one here, that's Vedax, the one this mission is about. It's a small icy moon exploding with volcanic activity. Not ordinary volcanoes erupting hot magma and choking black ash clouds, but cryovolcanoes spewing ice crystals and belching freezing gas of ammonia and methane."

"And you want to enlist and freeze your butt off, why?" Sendra moved closer, almost nose to nose with her best friend.

"To keep the rest of the team in good working order." Leba tried to turn away, but Sendra kept the pressure on.

"If it's exciting you want, agree to go barhopping with me again, and I'll show you how to have a good time." Sendra leaned back in her chair, grinning. Her weekend foray in the dating world must have been productive.

"Talk about shattering my comfort zone. An expeditionary mission to an ice ball in the middle of nowhere seems rather benign to being your wingman." Leba bowed her head, typed a few more keystrokes. "After last time, you remember, I vowed never to do that again."

Sendra frowned at her. "Hey, it wasn't my fault his best friend had one big eye under a furry brow." Sendra propped herself up on her elbows. "To continue, you hate flying and space travel and sea travel too." Tapping the side of her head with her index finger, Sendra expounded, "I remember something about even thinking about watching scenery whizz by making you nauseated."

"So I'll keep my eyes shut until I get there." Leba grinned.

Sendra inclined her head. "Besides, what am I going to do when my chief confidant and stabilizing, bring-you-back-down-to-reality, superanalytical, but socially awkward best friend leaves for an extended mission?"

There was the Sendra look, and right now, Leba tried to avoid responding to it. Everyone knew it, some feared it, and some ran screaming when they saw it, but mostly what came next was a good old-fashioned talking to. Slowly Leba let her eyes lock on Sendra's. "This is something I have to do." She couldn't let Sendra talk her out of it. That's why she waited to tell her. Sure, it wasn't fair, but her best friend, better than anyone else, understood her self-doubts. It wasn't like Sendra hadn't threatened to leave the clinic every time some man swept her off her feet with a promise of domesticated bliss. This mission was something Leba needed to do. And no one, not even Sendra Tohl could talk her out of it.

"Maybe there are hotter guys than here at the hospital," Leba purposed. "Maybe that's why I want to go. I've always been partial to men in uniform."

"If there were, don't you think I would know about it?" Sendra shook out her hair, obviously forgetting shorter didn't yield the same effect. "Besides, everyone here is in uniform, and that didn't mean you got any more…" Sendra snorted. Leba turned back to her work again. Sendra was right. Maybe this was the dumbest decision she ever made just to have a little more excitement in her life. Ignoring any more advice, Leba rocked back in her leather-bound desk chair, closed her eyes, and tried to imagine life outside the four walls of the hospital.

"Kixon, ma'am," he crackled. Clearing his throat of youth, he corrected, "Neocadet Zachary J. Kixon, the second, but you can call me Zach." He stood at attention, ramrod straight as he could with his lanky frame uncooperative and his shoulders settled into a practiced slump.

Leba put out her hand in greeting, said, "Leba Brader, the first and probably the last," and then offered him a seat.

"Thank you, ma'am," he responded as he sat in one of the two empty chairs in her sparsely furnished office. While he surveyed the walls, noticing the matching framed certificates, all full of scribbled signatures designating her schooling, degrees, and credentials, Leba observed him. Zach Kixon, with close-cropped hair and deep-set dark and thoughtful eyes, was barely old enough to shave. His head swiveled the room.

"That will serve you well, you know," Leba started.

"Huh?" he replied, snapping his head back to face her. "What will, ma'am?"

"That habit of yours. The one where you investigate your surroundings so you know what you're up against. It will not only help you size up patients in this job but will keep you out of trouble when you get your deployment post," Leba trailed off for a moment to let him ponder her remarks.

"Sometimes it gets me in trouble," he answered.

"Stealth, kiddo. If you're going to stare at girls and study all their assets, you need to learn to do it covertly." She laughed. "So I see here on your dossier you're a math whiz."

"Numbers are my thing," he hesitated and restated his position less casually. "What I mean to say is, I tend to see the world as a series of equations. Every problem can be solved if you figure out its representative equation. You plug in the variables and out pops an answer, fitting all the parameters."

"Unless someone or something is working from a different base system." Leba took a sip from her drink. The steaming cup of caffeinated goodness was now lukewarm. The swallow bitter and acidic.

"Ma'am?" Zach questioned, a puzzled look on his face.

Leba continued, "First, stop with the ma'am stuff. It's either Dr. Brader or Leba. I can't work with someone who feels they are somehow subordinate. We're a team, and it has to feel like we're all equals. We have to trust each other and not withhold information. One day our patients' lives might depend on it. Not to say one day my life or yours might depend on it too." Leba leaned forward on her elbows, her palms together, and rested her chin on her fingers. She wanted to study his face, watch his reactions. "Now back to the issue of equations. Our computers now work on qubits, but did you know decades ago calculations were done on binary-based systems?"

"Binary systems used zeros and ones to designate all computations, but in quantum computing, qubits give us all the possibilities in between," Zach, puffing out his chest, reported.

"Great, a student of history as well." She clapped. "We can learn a lot from history, especially how not to repeat the same mistakes twice," Leba started. "And I expect you also know not all situations conform to the parameters you set. Patients, people in general, your colleagues, and your enemies don't always respond or react the way they're supposed to. Information is the key to preparing for the unexpected. Sometimes there is no way to test your hypothesis. Computer simulations are a wonderful way to train, but they are no substitution for real life." She reached for her drink again, remembered its staleness, and instead veered course and picked up an info-pad stylus. Pushing back slightly from the desk, Leba narrowed her gaze. "This brings me to why your commanders find it necessary for you Neos to spend time in this medical rotation." Leba tapped the stylus on the blotter. "Military service is fraught with countless opportunities to get you and your teammates hurt. There are situations where you have to think on your feet, be prepared for the unknown and unexpected, and be ready to deliver a swift and decisive response that could save the mission or your lives."

"I know," he bemoaned, but before he could continue, the door to Leba's office burst open. Both Zach and Leba quickly turned to the door.

"Hey, Leibs, I wanted to tell you about my—" Sendra stopped abruptly, stared first at Zach, and quickly shifted her gaze to Leba.

"Sorry, but these neos usually don't show up on time. I figured we had a few minutes."

"Neocadet Zachary J. Kixon, the second, I would like you to meet Sendra Tohl, world's best administrator, organizer, orchestrator, life coach, et cetera, et cetera, et cetera."

Zach stood up, surveyed Sendra, probably less stealthily than he should have, and extended a trembling hand to her.

"Nice to meet you, Neocadet Zachary J. Kixon, the second. Welcome to our little slice of heaven here in the basement level of the medical executive complex, where the caffeine is free-flowing and Dr. Brader rules with an iron fist." She giggled as she took his hand. Leba knew she wanted to recoil at its significant clamminess, but true to form, Sendra held steadfast.

Medical clinic administrator Sendra Tohl's rounded face was punctuated by a button nose and full lips that drew men in, and Zach Kixon was trapped immediately. "Remember, stealth," Leba cautioned. "We'll have to work on that." Leba continued, "Sendra, why don't you join us. I was just beginning to tell Zach what his duties will be at this station, but I'd bet he'd rather have you set his orientation straight." Sendra rubbed her hand on her tunic and ended with a slight tug at its hem. Hands dry, now Kixon-sweat-free.

"I think it's probably pretty straight already," she deadpanned. Sendra was a few years younger than Leba, but they'd known each other since early school. Although their lives intertwined when they were children, they followed divergent paths to the same final destination. Meeting initially on the athletic field, they came from different circles of friends. Sendra was very intelligent, but her popularity interfered with her schoolwork. Spunky and pert, her life was exciting, though. She was stylish and beautiful and athletic, with the trophies to prove it. Leba was studious and, as she put it herself, rather boring.

Leba worked hard to make team captain of the varsity squad at her school when a younger but very talented Sendra was promoted to varsity. The coach handpicked the younger girl to be the current and future star of the team. Leba always worked for everything she achieved, never letting obstacles get in her way. She generally figured out all the angles ahead of time, practicing far longer than any of her contemporaries. For the most part, her perseverance paid off, making her the silent delight of her coaches, the go-to girl, the team player, the reliable, boring, but consistent one. Sendra started out talented and didn't have to practice very much to excel. Leba was concerned focusing attention on the new girl would bring resentment from the others. "Hi, welcome to the team. I'm Leba Brader, senior, team captain."

Sendra looked up at the taller girl and replied, "Sendra Tohl, freshman, team star." Hands on hips, striking a dominant pose, Sendra questioned, "I thought seniors weren't allowed to talk to underclassmen?"

"Not in my world," Leba retorted and then continued, "This team needs every point, so everyone is important. We all warm up together, practice together, perform together. We need to be a cohesive unit to do our best." Leba did her homework and knew all about Sendra's track record—impressive, to say the least. Sendra was a star. She knew it, the coach knew it, and soon the rest of the school would know it. People would be impressed with Sendra's star quality and tremendous potential, so much so the rest of the team would suffer. Resentment would begin to grow, separating and dividing the team. The team, yes, the team was more important than the individuals making it up. Teams were like puzzles; not any piece would fit, and the wrong piece would make the entire structure weak. Even if that piece was Sendra Tohl.

"Liebs?" Sendra's voice in the present shook Leba from her reminiscence. "I was just explaining to Zach that his primary responsibility was to make your brand of caffeine in the a.m. You know, rocket fuel strength, 99 percent MX and 1 percent hot water."

"Huh?" came Leba's quizzical response.

"That's if he can beat you into work. So far, Zach, my friend, it's never happened." Sendra laughed.

"Well, save the MX making for me," Leba responded. Leba watched how Zach listened earnestly to Sendra. No matter how mundane or trivial, he hung on every word. Leba was continually impressed with Sendra's ability to catch the male eye. Just once, Leba wished she could turn heads the way Sendra did. Leba was every guy's friend. Sendra was every guy's dream girl. That was why Leba and Sendra remained friends for so long; they didn't compete for the important stuff. The trivial stuff was different altogether.

Once Sendra finished detailing administrative minutia and left the room, Zach turned his attention back to Dr. Brader. "Zach, if you work at this rotation, I'll be more than happy to give you as much responsibility as you're willing to take on. In fact, do well, and I'll recommend to your section leader you get promoted to cadet sooner than your academy gradmates. That's a promise!" Offering advancement in rank grade often made an excellent motivating force. In fact, Leba's neos invariably outperformed her colleagues' charges, making rotating under her guidance a prize match for any young and ambitious recruit. Zach was no exception. She knew he sought this position, figured out the equation, and showed up early at his interview.

Being one of the senior-ranking teaching clinicians, Leba often enjoyed an early choice for who rotated on her service. She and her colleagues would review the neos' intake interviews, answers to standard questions, and scores on the aptitude and agility tests, then draft their first-round pick. Like choosing sides in a schoolyard ballgame, sometimes getting the full package was better than getting the repudiated star. Not all her draft picks were stellar; in fact early on, she was fooled once or twice. Usually they would show their true colors by midmorning of their first day, or Sendra would root them out just by meeting them. In fact, Leba found having Sendra help review the potential candidate's dossiers a few days before draft day made her choices wiser. Sendra argued physical appearance, although not a legitimate selling point for a candidate, was certainly something they should take into account when deciding. This obviously did not apply to the female neos, but for them, Sendra felt they should at least exhibit some gamesmanship. That is, they should perform well as teammates and not be overly concerned with their own prominence. The candidates too submitted a list of their top choices with whom to work. This was often based on the experiences of their upper bunkmates, reputations for ease or difficulty of the work, and ability to get along with their supervisory officer.

Leba's reputation was tough but fair. There was much work to be done, lots to learn, and many hours to put in. If you were on Dr. Brader's team, you would run your butt off but be well rewarded at the end. On match day, a computer would pair recruit with rotation chief.

"Zach, about your newly formulated equation for this rotation, remember, a lot of recruits have tried to get their parentheses around Sendra only to result in negative integers."

"Well, Doc, the way I see it, if I replace the parentheses with absolute value lines, the only result that can occur is a positive integer," Zach countered.

"Excellent. Very well thought out."

CHAPTER 2

Leba was looking forward to beginning her formal, self-arranged training. Well, not really. Although she was excited about getting back into shape, learning wilderness and trauma medicine and self-defense and combat tactics, there was never enough time in the day. The paramilitary classes promised to teach her what she needed to know to survive in the big, bad universe and even make her sweat. Leba's sister, Esre, promised to school her in wilderness and trauma medicine, including climbing and rappelling, exotic rescue, and survival skills. All this she struggled to fit in at the end of the day or on her scant time off. Mom and Dad handled the news better than she thought. Her dad, Commander Darian Brader, under the watchful eye of his fastidious mentor, Grand Uncle Baal Tosona, promised to teach her all the ins and outs of space vehicles. Maybe they knew her evolution was inevitable. Maybe this was their plan all along. Maybe the decision to enlist was one only the person themselves could commit to.

"So much to do, so little time" became her mantra as the time to begin neared. Leba knew once she immersed herself in the rigorous training program Esre intended for her, she would put all her dynamism into it. Getting started was always the toughest part for her, altering her routine, forming new mental and muscular pathways. So when Leba, tired and beat from a long and physical day at the medical clinic, got back to her modest on-base quarters, she really didn't feel like doing much of anything. But that's why she had to do it. She hated losing her previous athletic form to the poor diet, long hours, and the abnormal sleep routine associated with shift work. Qualifying for this expeditionary mission was the motivation she needed to embark on a new path.

Given she was a civilian working at a military medical facility, she was at a distinct disadvantage in her chances of being chosen. Dr. JT Hobes, one of her military counterparts, was already signed on for the mission. He bragged about how exciting it was going to be. Trying to best her at every turn, mainly just for the sport of it, JT challenged Leba to outqualify him for the mission. JT and Leba competed for everything, oftentimes for fun or to keep each other's skills sharp. Now he taunted relentlessly.

He oftentimes reminded Leba of her brother, Lav. Lav was tall and handsome and very smart. Everybody's favorite. Being the youngest when growing up in the Brader family and the only male child, Lav generally got away with whatever he wanted and tested the limits of their parents' patience. "He's a boy" was a common excuse for his antics. JT got away with stuff all the time, sorely testing his superior's patience on more than one occasion. He was academy handsome, playful, brilliant, and possessed mad skills. Charisma oozed from his pores. Lav was extremely loyal, JT not so much.

Both often sought Leba's advice. She was Lav's big sister and held a special place in his heart. She was probably the only girl JT knew who would give him a straight, "not affected by his incredibly hot looks" answer. On the other hand, her brother would do anything for either of his sisters, even chase off unwanted suitors. JT not so much. Leba's list of suitors was never long enough for Lav or even JT, on the rare occasion when a patient got too friendly, to have much work in that department. Very few boys wanted to date the athletic brainiac, but they all wanted to be her friends, including JT. Not a love interest for most, Leba was able to move unobtrusively through a male-dominated medical specialty and rise to the top. The men she did date never seemed to measure up. Realistically, she never seemed to be what they were looking for in a girlfriend. But as a girl friend she was an asset, and pissing her off was not a smart move if you expected her to make your ride in life smoother.

Leba's father said her mom, Reela Savar, was still as beautiful as the first day he saw her. Leba desperately wanted someone to feel that way about her. Right now, though, there was no one in her circle fitting the bill. One of her secret hopes was she would encounter someone in her combat training classes who wasn't scared off by her. She loved men in uniform. Somehow, wearing a uniform demonstrated a commitment. It meant duty, responsibility, and hopefully strength, both mental and physical. Her mom assured her, a pilot in shining helmet would one day swoop her off her feet. Once she felt better about herself, her new radiance would attract men like miners to a gemstone.

Back to the time management problem at hand, Leba stayed after her shift was done to treat a late arrival, a young cadet vomiting copious amounts of blood. The evening shift doctor told her to take off, but Leba, not one to leave a job undone, finished the endoscopic hemostasis of the bleeding lesion. Once her patient was secured in the recovery suite, Leba looked at her chrono, panicking at how late it was. One of her pet peeves was being late. Unfortunately, now she was an hour behind, and there was barely enough time to get home, change, and get to her first defensive tactics class.

Quickly putting on pristine black combat trousers, Leba tied the cuffs at the bottom. She donned the gym-logo'd black workout shirt over a long-sleeve T-shirt. Gathering up her shoulder-length hair, she cinched it with a bright-pink band. Into an already prepared carry bag, she placed a fresh, cold water bottle among the clean white towel and sparring gloves. After securing the door to her quarters, she rushed to the base's martial arts gym. She didn't like to be late—first impressions were everything—and she entered the dojo-like room with only a few minutes to spare.

The atmosphere was surprisingly relaxed. She was greeted at the door and welcomed aboard. Everyone was eager to meet her and help her. Here, in a room where countless killing machines and supersoldiers were created, there was calm, no tension, only strict decorum and smiling faces. As she learned the skills and exercises and routines, the instructors were more than accommodating to her newness. They excused her awkwardness and offered assistance or advice at every turn. She could get used to this. Being the center of attention as the new recruit, the instructors were attuned to her specific needs. Taking keen interest in her progress, they made her feel special, and she liked that. The attitude was, if she failed, they failed. Camaraderie and teamwork ruled. She worked hard the first day and sported the bruises and sore muscles of a job well done. It felt good to feel her muscles burn with prolonged exercise. She needed to do better, though, to make her instructors proud. Hopefully with continued participation, she would see rewards very quickly. Leba liked progress, and being able to see it was even better, and feeling the evolution was the best. After thanking her instructors for a gainful session, she headed home for some needed nourishment and rest.

The next evening, she planned to meet with one of her mentors, Dr. Uart Othra. Othra was brilliant, a dedicated physician. For his age, Othra was well muscled and as limber as a tree simian. He found slow movements, stretching and breathing, a way to find balance and harmony. At first, Leba was unconvinced, but over time, she appreciated his path to inner peace. Othra often said the way to wisdom was being able to open your mind through relaxation of the body. He not only healed bodies, but he healed minds, possessing an uncanny ability to modulate people's behavior by speaking to them. His melodious tones somehow reached into their troubled minds and brought them calm. He quieted their fears and strengthened their resolve. Whenever she was troubled by a particularly tough decision, she sought his counsel. After what Esre implied about mental toughness, Leba decided a visit to Dr. Othra was in order. Earlier that day, Othra asked her if they could change their dinner plans. Something unexpectedly came up, and he would be running much later than expected. Instead of dinner, they would chat over a workout session. This meant the trip to his mountainous retreat would be undertaken at dusk. It was treacherous and difficult to reach during the daylight hours but at night, almost prohibitory.

Nestled between snowcapped mountains that seemed to serrate the bottom of the azure Luacian sky, among their forested slopes of sentinel evergreens, the lush green Vidas valley led to a terraced hill. Dr. Othra's small cottage sat at the top of this hilly rise. Very few places on Luac possessed such a magnificent view. The conifers, with their long, thin needles and cone shape grew so close together they blended into one another, protecting the hilltop chalet from biting wind and frosty coldness. The cottage's roof angulation mirrored the tree canopy, whose downward angle allowed the heavy and melting snow to slide effortlessly to the ground and form serpiginous tributaries. These rivulets reassembled into a crystal clear cyan-blue lake teeming with fish. The air here was crisp and clean and smelled of life.

The hill's rocky outcroppings fashioned into stone terraces were planted with a variety of flora, each carefully selected and lovingly tended to by Othra's wife. Approaching the cabin on foot, the only way possible short of an airborne drop, required ascension of countless steps. Othra warned only one who truly wanted to make the journey would undertake the climb, but those who succeeded would be greatly rewarded. Negotiating the winding trail up to his house was a test in itself. Leba always appreciated its irony. If it was worth visiting Othra, one would accept the challenges it took to get there. The twisting trail was precarious by day. Lit only by starlight, the path at night was perilous. Unencumbered by urban skyglow, the darkness was pervasive.

Once at the summit, when your legs ached from the climb and your lungs burned for more oxygen, you could stand for a moment, in the fog stratus hiding its presence, and feel a true sense of accomplishment. Talk about achieving a higher spiritual plane. Up here among the clouds, looking down on the majesty of life, it was hard to imagine why everyone was in such a hurry. This was a place of peace and tranquility, and if you listened carefully enough, all you could hear was natural, nothing artificial, nothing burdensome, and nothing intrusive.

Othra's wife greeted her at the heavy wooden door. "Such a long time it's been." She nodded her head. "You should visit more often." For such a petite woman, she possessed coarse features and a large round face, every inch smiling. Her wiry black hair was long and pulled back, secured with a homemade barrette, most likely a present from one of her five granddaughters. She continued, "You know you're his favorite protégé." Leba blushed. "Come in, come in," she invited. "We've just had another grandchild, a boy this time."

Wiping her shoes on the welcome mat, Leba made her way into the small front room. "Congratulations," Leba smiled. "An heir to the throne." As she removed her jacket and handed it to her host, Leba surveyed the great room. It was how she remembered it, sturdy wooden furniture, rustic decor with crafts from local artisans, and the smell of pine. Fresh cut flowers sat in a vase in the middle of a lace-doilied table.

"Yes, yes." The older women beamed as she returned from the coat closet. "Our first grandson. The boy is a welcome surprise."

"Thank you for indulging my late change of plans," a familiar voice said from the next room. Uart Othra was smiling from ear to ear, almost unable to contain his joy, as he entered the room and clasped Leba's hands in his. "So glad you could still make it." She took in his every detail, remembering when they first met, and he explained how hair refused to grow except in thick clumps, so he kept the top tightly shorn. Leba told him the baldness made him look more distinguished. He told her it was so his female students would find him more appealing given the testosterone it took to get the look. That was when she knew they'd get along great.

He was clean-shaven, his strong chin gently rounded. Only his arched choppy black eyebrows belied his original color. The bristles covering the back of his head were a strong gray. His crown was age-spotted and, despite its healthy tan color, was smooth and soft, bearing no ill signs of prolonged sun exposure. His cheekbones were high, but a thin upper lip allowed attention to be focused on his expressive almond-shaped eyes.

"Congratulations, Poppa," she said. "Any vids?"

"Yes, yes, come into the study and I will regale you with his visage." The next few minutes were spent reviewing Othra family photos and vids. "See here, Poppa and his girls." He pointed to a framed picture on his desk.

"Outstanding." She giggled, borrowing one of her mentor's favorite terms.

"Now you mentioned in your call something about an expeditionary mission to a giant ice ball of a moon, tell me more." Leba plunked down onto the threadbare cushioned couch that abutted the side wall of his study. Like a king holding court, Othra sat on his high-backed throne chair. The centerpiece of the room was hand-carved and a gift from a grateful patient.

For the better part of half an hour, Leba detailed not only the mission details but also why she needed to go. "Why must you continue to try and prove yourself?" he questioned, drawing his brows slightly together and down. He stared intently, studying her face. Leba needed an answer he would accept. "While you're working on your answer, why don't we continue this in the gym."

Beneath his small cottage was a splendid meditation room. Sounds echoed from an elaborate fountain, the smell of outdoor freshness permeated the air, and soft lights illuminated every corner. The floor was natural with soft plush soil and velvety moss underfoot.

"Changing room still over to the right?" Leba asked, motioning with her head.

"Of course, nothing changes, but everything changes." Othra stretched his arms over his head, palms opposed, and interlocked his hands. "You'll find your regular tunic freshly laundered." Othra thought of everything. One of the benefits of training with Othra was a standing invitation to experience his meditation gym. At the end of your tenure with him, if deemed worthy, you were presented with a monogrammed tunic and a designated spot in the locker room for your belongings. Not unlike having your own monogrammed CV-79 Sabre fighter, it was an elite club. Leba loved spending time reading the names above the hooks in the locker room, an impressive group of peers. When she got back to the gym room itself, Othra was almost finished with his warm-up.

"Join me," he said, breathing in and out slowly as he stretched.

Embarrassingly awkward in her movements, Leba struggled to mirror his poses. "You know my ligaments are too tight."

"Do the best you can." He waved her off. "And stop thinking so much. Relax and breathe."

One of her biggest problems, she couldn't relax. Everything made her tense. Too much analyzing, too much scrutinizing, too much. "You've slipped. Othra waved an accusing finger. "Not enough time for yourself. Not practicing the exercises I taught you. No time."

Tears welled in Leba's eyes, and she turned her head from his gaze. She didn't like disappointing him. Othra knew her too well, so Leba shied away from making any more excuses. "It is difficult to watch you struggle," Othra said.

"I should be going." Leba was frustrated with herself.

"Stop," he scolded. "Sit on the bench and listen." Leba sat, folded her arms across her chest, and pouted. He was always a sucker for her pouting. "Now close your eyes and listen. Relax your shoulders. Clear your mind of thoughts and listen." Shaking her head in disapproval, Leba slowly closed her eyes. "Now relax your neck and shoulders," he continued. She inhaled a deep breath, taking in as much air as she could, and, as she exhaled, let the tension in her shoulders fade away. "Good, much better." She concentrated on his rich and melodious voice. Feeling like she was slowly losing her stress, she continued the rhythmic breating. Othra smiled. "See, not so hopeless."

"Ah, good, put it on the table over there," Othra instructed. So focused on breathing, at first Leba was startled; she hadn't heard his wife enter the room. Peering through slitted eyes, Leba watched his wife totter over with a serving tray. The teapot was simple in design but delicate and hand-painted. It bore the signs of use, the picture fading, and a smoky residue crept along the bottom edge remnants of slow-cooking over an open flame. Leba closed her eyes again and slowly inhaled the fragranced brew as it wafted toward her. She heard Othra pour two cups. "Leba, tea?" he asked, already pouring a third.

"Of course," she said, opening her eyes wider this time. She leaped up, thankful for a moment to be out of the intense spotlight, the focus of his scrutiny, and joined them. Leba watched his wife stir in a syrupy yellow substance. She looked over at Leba for her answer. "Yes, please, and thank you. Your tea is always so delightful."

Othra's wife handed her the cup. "Be careful, it's hot." How wonderful it must be to have a grandmother. Grandmothers were unstressed mothers, at least when it came to grandchildren. Leba never knew her grandparents, although her mother often spoke affectionately about her departed parents. In her father's case, the subject was never mentioned.

A CHANGE IN TACTICS: MAIDEN VOYAGE

They were all finishing their tea when Othra began, "Now back to your lessons. Seems a refresher course is in order." He gently dismissed his wife, who obliged without hesitation. She removed the tray, teapot, and used cups. "You have to find your inner strength," he counseled. "You have to believe in yourself, not for the sake of others."

"Sometimes I feel so insignificant," she confessed.

"Look at all you have accomplished, your accolades, the countless people you have helped and continue to help," he reminded her.

"I somehow need more," she continued. "It's not enough anymore. I have something to prove. Maybe if it's only to prove to myself I can do it."

"I think you are too hard on yourself." He shook his head. "You need to let go of the negative energy, your frustrations, your feelings of inadequacy. I wouldn't have picked you for a protégé if I didn't feel you were worthy." Leba felt embarrassed, and her face betrayed her. "I'm right, you know. In fact, I'm always right." He laughed. Leba laughed too. The tension in the room slowly ebbed away. "I'm like the fountain water slowly eroding away at the rocks below. Drip, drip, drip, slow and steady, eventually exposing the beautiful crystals that lie beneath."

Leba always felt better after talking to Dr. Othra. Sometimes she struggled to figure out her relationship with Othra. He was more than a teacher. She actually believed he cared for her. Not in a romantic way, but almost as an older brother for a little sister. He was barely older than her father but didn't act that way. He always seemed so much younger than he really was. Maybe because he enjoyed and experienced life so much. She admired the way he could do things so precisely but with so little effort. He was rewarded with more time to enjoy the subtleties of each situation. "Professor, as always, I am unworthy of your teaching."

"That's your problem," he said, "always putting yourself down." He paused, sneered, and turned his back to her. "Sometimes I wonder why I bother, you never seem to listen."

"I always listen."

"Then how come you don't hear?" He started to walk away.

"Oh, don't run off mad now," she playfully pouted. "You're no fun, anymore." Othra continued toward the exit door. "You know I'm your favorite student. Smarter and more talented than all those who have come before. In fact, truth be told, if you had a little sister, you'd want her to be just like me."

"I do have a younger sister, and she's nothing like you. Pity, though." He smirked. "With your last barrage of self-centered egotism, you are becoming dangerously close to me putting chewing gum in your hair." He turned and flashed a grin. "Now go clean up and meet me in the front room."

CHAPTER 3

Weapons. Tonight began Leba's foray into the use of tools not for healing but for harming. Learning about how to use a knife as an edged weapon rather than a curative instrument was fascinating. In one sense, a scalpel could be used precisely to incise flesh, reveal a diseased organ, and skillfully eradicate a disease; but in a second sense, a shiv could be used imprecisely to slash the flesh, expose a vital organ, and no less skillfully eradicate a life. Scalpels were sleek, shiny, and almost sexy the way they felt in a surgeon's hand, but shivs, although often brutal in their assault, could be wielded with grace and exactness in the right hands. Training with an edged weapon, letting it become a flowing extension of one's hand, a crude shiv could take on many of the scalpel's characteristics. One never *drew* a scalpel; it was handed to you in an orderly and precise fashion. Its presence in the room was announced and then slapped into the doctor's waiting hand. The *thwack* it made as the surgeon gripped it made everyone in the room momentarily stop and watch as the doctor slowly and carefully split the skin. It drew a line of blood, which slowly bubbled along the wound. Escaping from the warm innards as the surgeon deepened his exploration, steam hissed along the precise edge. There was no turning back.

An edged weapon often appeared surreptitiously from its concealed location, no announcement, no fanfare, but it garnered similar attention from those standing by. Everyone would momentarily gasp as light glinted off the metallic blade. The fight would take a more deadly turn when a knife appeared. There was no doubt someone, possibly everyone, would get cut to some degree. Once a knife was pulled out, there was no turning back.

Tracing through the nine angles of attack, Leba practiced moving the knife, slicing at the air. It was not easy at first. The edged weapon was heavier and clumsier than a scalpel. She never remembered dropping a scalpel during training but dropped her training knife more times than she cared to remember. Once she got the feel for it, after many hours and days practicing in the gym or in front of a mirror, it became an extension of her hand. Her motions smooth and fluid. Leba found sparring with a knife much harder than with a stick or a staff because it was necessary to be close to your opponent to be effective. Violating the unseen personal boundary space made the attack more intimate, more brutal, and more real.

Leba made it a point to try and alternate nights between the defensive tactics classes and exercise classes. The next evening entailed one of Esre's killer calisthenics routines, an interval workout to the nth degree, mixing weight training with cardio in a never-ending cycle. Once Leba's muscles were used to isotonic movements, it was back to isometric movements. No time for recovery, only time to switch gears. Fast-twitch fibers ignited, slow-twitch fibers ignited, and repeated countless times until exhaustion set in. Worse than that, Esre made Leba do the routine wearing a heavy flak jacket. This was supposed to simulate carrying a full pack. By the time the hour-long routine was done, it was time for a stationary bike ride cooldown. Besides breathing, Leba realized hydration was the key to completing the exercises and still be able to walk out of the gym.

Despite being sore the next morning, muscles ached she didn't even know she used, Leba got through the medical clinic without a falter. She did take any opportunity she could to stretch a tight back muscle or work out a neck cramp. At least tonight, she could take a break and read up on the ecobiology and geophysiology of Glirase and its moons. Although well intentioned, she didn't last very long after a small dinner and fell fast asleep after only a few minutes of study. When she awoke, she chided herself for not being able to complete her assigned task and vowed to do double the next chance she calendared for reading.

The next night was stick class. Ungloved and armed with only a crude three-foot piece of wood, Leba sparred with her partner.

A CHANGE IN TACTICS: MAIDEN VOYAGE

Through a series of strikes and blocks, they traded blow for blow, slash, block, parry, repeat. At the end, the instructor wanted them to feel the sting of a real hit. One by one the students hung from a metal pull-up bar. Their classmates proceeded to pelt them with smack after smack to the midsection and thighs. The trick was to breathe through each whack and strengthen one's resolve with each hit. Despite some early trepidation about her ability, Leba hung tough and took each strike, challenging her partner to hit harder and faster as the absorption drill progressed.

When Leba got home and showered, four palpable large purplish welts now adorned her body. They were tender but well earned, and she was proud despite the pain. Maybe she could survive this after all and be better for it. With each physical challenge Leba faced came a certain mental toughness, a desire not to give into pain or to quit. Both mentally and physically stronger, she was ready to meet her next set of tests with renewed strength and vigor.

"Why are you walking funny?" Sendra questioned. "Hot date?"

Leba smiled. "Well, if you must know, I got hit with a stick." She tentatively lifted her shirt up a few inches to reveal two relatively symmetric fist-sized bruises on each side of her midsection.

"Ooo." Sendra winced. "Looks like they hurt."

"Only when I move or touch them or look at them." Leba gingerly tucked her shirt back then smoothed the front of her pants.

"Why do you insist on doing this to yourself?" Sendra inquired.

"I need to be ready," Leba insisted.

"You didn't even get picked yet. You may not even get to go," Sendra retorted.

"Some friend you are," Leba replied. "I thought at least you would have faith in me."

"It's not that I don't have faith in you. I know you can achieve anything you set your mind to." Sendra crossed her arms. "I know how the system works, and the system isn't fair." She took in a breath and sighed. "Besides, who am I gonna hang out with if you get deployed?" Sendra finished arms out, palms up, with her lip in an exaggerated pout.

"I'm sure they'll assign some hot, young, sexy resident in my place, and you'll forget me in no time." Leba smirked.

Sendra pondered for a minute, a full-toothed smile overtaking her face, then burst out, "Okay, hope you get picked."

Leba frowned at her. "I promise if I get to go, I'll check in every chance I get." Pausing, Leba's eyes glanced upward and then back to Sendra. "Unless I meet my own hot, young, sexy soldier, and then you're on your own."

Sendra laughed. "Listen, Liebs, don't fall for the first recruit who offers to carry your gear. Take some time to"—Sendra air quoted—"experience the military." Sendra paused. "Besides, you're gonna need to keep me on speed dial so you'll know what to do if a handsome soldier takes a fancy to you anyway. Don't want you screwing it up."

"It's not like I haven't dated before," Leba said exasperated.

"If that's what you want to call it," Sendra replied. "I don't think you've ever been in love, have you?"

"I thought that's only supposed to happen once."

"See, now there's your problem, girlfriend—" Sendra was interrupted by a call from the clinic. Leba watched the conversation, and Sendra's eyebrows rose almost to her bang line. Her lips pursed. "It seems we have an uninvited guest upstairs."

"So who is it?" Leba cocked her head and waited.

"The director is snooping around and I need to make an appearance." Waving her fingers, Sendra said, "We'll finish this later." Leba frowned. "Don't worry I'll give you a crash course in men before you leave." Sendra headed out the door only to quickly poke her head back in, the pout back. "I'm just sad because I know you're going to get picked, and it won't be the same."

Leba's progress was slow but steady, and she was thinking if she didn't get picked for the mission, she would try and keep up with both the exercise and combat classes. She met a lot of interesting people, and yes, they liked her well enough, but no, no date possibilities yet. She did like the packages some of her classmates presented, but it was too soon. The flirting was still rather low-key, and she could make conversation, but her shyness in those situations usually won out. At the moment, she was still too new and needed to concentrate on getting her tactics up to speed. Getting sidetracked would only put her further behind.

Weekend weapons class was always a surprise. Mixing weapons was another way to keep you guessing, and her DT instructor constantly reminded the class fights weren't necessarily fair. They were usually quick and dirty. The unexpected generally portended a bad outcome, sorta like when patients neglected to tell you they were allergic to something that you ordered for them or forgot they were taking a medicine that interfered with something you did. Being prepared for any possibility usually made surprises less deadly. After a few seconds grappling a new sparring partner and delivering a significant practice slash to his left torso, he pushed into her, sending her forcefully to the ground. Although a legitimate defense, Leba was not ready for it and hit hard, the impact to her head jarring. For a few moments, she tried valiantly to get up, but the room was spinning, and she was listing to one side. She wobbled to her feet, hands raised and ready to continue swinging. The instructor grasped her shoulders and stared into her eyes.

"I'm okay, let me go."

"Fight over."

"I know I don't have a concussion." Leba wriggled out of his grasp, but he grabbed her hand and made her sit on the floor. Burying her head in her hands, Leba pinched her eyes tightly, shutting out irritating stimuli, and tried to clear her mind. *I'm a doctor, and I'm okay.* A hint of nausea bubbled in her stomach.

"Take some slow deep breaths and reorient." His shadow loomed over her, helping shield the light.

Okay, okay, I'll sit, but I'm not giving up. Through squinted eyes, Leba peered at him. "Did I do okay?" It was hard to look up at him, bending her neck made her head spin more.

"You did well. Got in some good strikes." He squatted beside her.

"I must have fallen wrong." He shifted positions to face her. *I really screwed up. Embarrassed myself in front of the whole class and especially my instructor. I'm not coming back. I can't afford to get hurt. I have a job and people who depend on me. This really sucks!*

On his haunches, his shadow blocking more of the light, he whispered, "You fell correctly, but a stick shot to anyone's head usually ends the fight."

What? But we weren't supposed to hit the head. That jerk, hitting me in the head with his stick. Leba wanted to get up and in her sparring partner's face and have an up close and personal about his foul, but her main task became trying to stand without tumbling over. Having her brains scrambled was not what she planned. She could feel the instructor closer now. His breath moved up her face and past her head as he stood. He gently tugged her arms so he could steady her on her feet. Class was about over, and despite her slight disorientation, she insisted on lining up with her classmates for the instructor's final thoughts. Her head was still spinning as she made her way out of the gym. Maybe a walk in the fresh air would help.

By the time Leba made it to her vehicle, the dizziness in her head was gone, but the throbbing wasn't. Not exactly remembering getting home, once in her quarters, Leba fashioned an ice pack, placed it on top of her head, downed an anti-inflammatory painkiller, and sat on the couch. She would need to practice her follow-ups, no more getting hit in the head and ending up on the ground. Leba needed to be more aggressive and finish the fight, not rest on her last effective strike. Trusting her opponent to abide by the rules was another mistake she wouldn't repeat. The rest of her day off was spent trying to get her headache to go away. Thinking was a chore, so she avoided things needing significant concentration efforts.

By the next morning, both her head and neck ached. Although Leba took more pain medicine, wearing an ice pack at work would garner unwanted stares. Her hand instinctively rubbed the muscles of her neck but to no avail. *Try and ignore the discomfort, and don't think too much.* Hoping freshly brewed MX would reignite her neurons and override any persistent fogginess from her injury, Leba sipped at the hot drink carefully, every once in a while massaging her neck muscles to keep them from getting stiff. Thank goodness it was early and still quiet in the med clinic. The silence didn't last long as the construction crew, working on expanding the clinic space, began their rhythmic banging. Each hammer fall shot through her head like a bullet. Leba bent over her desk, rubbing her temples, trying to will away the pain. It wasn't going to be one of her best days.

By the time clinic was over and the seemingly endless stream of patients paraded through, Leba was more than ready to go home. Unfortunately not off duty, it was her turn to cover night call. No matter how hard she tried, she could never seem to get through a shower without having to answer a call. Tonight was no different. She could barely hear the annoying *beep, beep, beep* as she finished washing her hair. Squeezing out the excess water, Leba wrapped herself in a towel, slammed the lavatory door, and left a dripping trail into her bedroom. Another nonsensical call robbed her of a relaxing steam cleaning. After dealing with the caller, she headed back to wash the remaining dirt and grime off. Despite the recommendations of Esre's schedule for a long and arduous run, Leba, exhausted as she was, opted for one of Professor Othra's stretching routines. Getting her heart rate up would only fuel her pounding headache.

Worse than getting a page in the shower, a call disturbing her calm while stretching was even worse. By the time the third call disrupted her rhythm, Leba gave up trying to exercise and opted for the comfort of her bed. When she awoke the next morning, she was surprised how deeply she slept and checked her pager to make sure she hadn't slept through any calls. Entering her small kitchen, she realized how uncharacteristically hungry she was until she remembered she forgot dinner the night before. There weren't enough hours in a day. As she rummaged through her cupboards to find a suitable breakfast, all she could come up with was a protein bar. She needed to go shopping for food, but the restorative sleep intervened, eating up a large chunk of time. It didn't hurt to think anymore. She reassigned her priorities: breathe, hydrate, sleep, eat. There would hopefully be time for other things when this was all over.

CHAPTER 4

Dieuvoxyl's Fighting Academy. The placard was small and nondescript, as was the building housing the premiere martial arts dojo. Leba was lucky to get a spot in the beginner class. It didn't hurt she could afford the astronomical fee or brought references from Tal-Kari high command, specifically her father, Base Commander Darian Brader. Climbing the stairs, Leba noticed the fraying carpet and distinct wear pattern. Thunderous booming occurred above, and Leba plastered herself against the wall as a herd of bodies flew past. The smell of sweat and antiseptic combined with the humid air was nauseating. Once the pack ascended the stairs for their return trip, Leba shifted her gym bag to the other shoulder and continued upward.

"In order to understand how to win a battle," the two-headed, four-limbed instructor stated, "one"—the second head spoke, the flow unbroken—"or two must understand what drives a conflict." Leba stood at attention with the other newbies. The coordination beween the two sides of this being were perfectly in sync. Despite the physical separation, the two minds seemed to work as one. Dieuvoxyl continued, "You will not only learn about victories but also about defeats. You should never have the opportunity to make the same mistake twice." Could they also work independently? "In fact, making the mistake the first time may result in a headline in this class or on your memorial plaque."

According to Leba's mother, Dieuvoxyl once held the reputation as the toughest instructor at basic school. Prejudice and pay forced her to freelance her services and resulted in the opening of her own fighting academy. She, or they, were a curious sort, well-muscled arms and legs, two heads, and a connection at the waist. In researching her trainer, Leba noted this species was native to a distant red planet leaving a lasting blue sheen to their skin. When her home world was overrun, millennia ago, Dieuvoxyl's race, the Greth, scattered among the stars. Given her species extended lifespan, small communities sprang up in wide and varied places. To their credit, the Greth established links between brethren, and their intertwined network prevented their extinction. Their mating and ability to produce offspring only with those of their own kind kept the species intact. Distances between tribe members were overcome with proper planning and exact timing. Leba also knew this Greth was marooned after an explosion jettisoned her spacecraft off-course into an unknown sector. She was injured and alone, unfortunately unable to sense her own kind. The Tal-Kari rescued her from a desolate asteroid in their system. In gratitude, Dieuvoxyl agreed to share her innate military acumen with them. Leba's mother was not exactly sure that the help was voluntary because most of her life was classified. After serving for many years, Dieuvoxyl petitioned for emancipation. The Tal-Kari high council, the Taw-re, under intense public scrutiny at the time, reluctantly approved her request.

Leba spent hours watching vid demonstrations of Dieuvoxyl's skills, noting when sparring, it was tough to keep an eye on all four of her eyes. Misdirection was her forte, and she seemed always one step ahead of any planned attack. In order to beat her, which was virtually impossible for any one person, a group assault was in order, and even that generally failed or ended with mass casualties.

"I am a student of history. We can benefit from examining past conflicts both large and small." Her fours eyes scanned those assembled. "What you learn here, in this class, should be a reminder no one will be unscathed, be it combatant or bystander." She again paused, one head surveying right, the other left. "I promise you this, if you stay, work hard, practice, and drill until your skills are muscle memory, they will always serve you well." A scowl came to her faces, and she pointed to a muscular woman standing three places to the left of Leba. "Yes, you," she repeated impatiently, "you seem disinterested."

"I'm not much for theory," the young woman said, her eyes rolling as she tilted her head.

"Really?" Dieuvoxyl's voice echoed as both heads answered. Leba dared not let her gaze linger but tried to keep her eyes focused forward. "Well, then," Dieuvoxyl began again, "why don't you show us what you can do."

"More than happy to." She beamed. Leba was unsure of what was going to happen next. It was one thing to want to demonstrate your skills to your instructor, but to disregard her approach seemed insulting. "What do you want me to show you?"

"Let's see," Dieuvoxyl said. "Weapons," the right said. "Or hand-to-hand," the left said. "Or both?" they said in unison.

The young woman, her straight blond hair pulled away from her face, straightened, flexing the muscles slowly in her arms and hands. "Your choice, teach. I'll bow to your preference." Leba was again startled by her smugness.

Dieuvoxyl motioned to the last two recruits in line. "Get some headgear, shin guards, and a pair of focus pads, they're in the locker over there." The neos returned quickly with protective sparring equipment and dropped them at the instructor's feet. "You," Dieuvoxyl motioned to the trailing neo, "put those on."

"Me?" the neo open hand, fingers caged onto his chest.

"Of course," his instructor said. "No one else better." Awkwardly, the neo donned the protective torso pads and, after getting help from his opponent, finally secured the well-padded headgear in place. This thin, frail-looking newbie fumbled with the focus pads until blondie, clearly frustrated with his ineptness, grabbed his hand, shoved it deeply into the mitt, and strapped it into place.

"Go ahead, show me," Dieuvoxyl prompted the blond girl.

"Against him?" She laughed.

"If you beat him," Dieuvoxyl challenged, "then you may go through the rest of these newbies until they are all defeated." She paused. "Then I may deem you worthy enough to challenge us."

One by one, all the novices, including Leba, met the same fate. No matter how hard they tried, how bravely they stood there and took the punishment being doled out. The neos went down and went down hard. How senseless. "Bravo," Dieuvoxyl complimented the blond girl. She, or they, surveyed the haggard and defeated neos.

Leba's head swiveled, noting who had fight left. Dieuvoxyl said coldly, "First lesson, when confronted with a more skilled opponent, blindly taking punishment is stupid." Shock and anger filled eyes of her classmates. "What you should have done is gotten together and attacked as a group."

One of the beaten female neos shouted, "But you said we were to fight one-to-one!" Dieuvoxyl studied her carefully before responding. Leba wanted to ask the same question but thankfully hesitated.

The instructor reached down and offered a hand to the neo, helping her up from the mat. "Second lesson, there are no rules in a fight." She let go of the trainee's hand, and the girl unceremoniously landed back on the mat. "Thank you, Azymie." She nodded to the blond woman. "Excellent demonstration."

The neos looked at one another in dismay. Leba vowed to never let this happen again. She ached all over, frustrated by her and her classmates' utter failure. Leba lived by rules and followed the rules as best she could. Breaking a rule, ignoring an instruction, never entered her mind. This change of tactics was foreign to her, and she would have to rethink her approach to certain situations. She would not be caught off guard and embarrassed in such a way. Leba wasn't sure she was going to fit in. The dichotomy of following strict military rules and never questioning your superior was now in conflict with the wanton abandonment of those same orders during a conflict.

CHAPTER 5

Thanks to her uncle Trent, Leba obtained permission to view the background research the Tal-Kari high council, the Taw-re, used when they decided to pursue this expeditionary mission. Glirase was an enormous gas giant with an elaborate ring system. Obviously uninhabitable, it was nonetheless beautiful to behold. Leba imagined the view from the surface of the planet was even more magnificent. Despite its appeal, what really piqued her interest was Glirase's children. Tucked in and around their mother were a variety of moons. Like children, some were big, and some were small; some were hot, and some were cold; some were light and some were dark, each with its unique characteristics and secrets to explore. The largest habitable moon was Pareq, and it supported a small but significant population. Its burgeoning metropolis benefitted from the resources of its surrounding sisters. Pareq was to be the home for expeditionary mission's base camp. There was an established but small Tal-Kari outpost currently on Pareq, but it couldn't support the upcoming mission. Because a new base would require more acreage and more deployment of personnel, the Tal-Kari decided, as her uncle Trent said, "To go all out." Planned from drawing board sketches was a state-of-the-art facility, geometrically perfect in design; at least that was what the well-compensated architect promised. It would have the latest in stealth technology with negatively reflective surfaces, virtually invisible from overwatch scans. This made the air corp buy-in. The single-soldier housing clinched it for the ground-based commanders. This comprehensive facility would be contemporary, comfortable, and covert. Uncle Trent knew Commander Chalco Atacama, the man tapped to pilot this investment. He was conservative but battle-tested. A fair man who despised politics but nonetheless followed council edicts like a true soldier.

For Pareq's economy, this operation would provide a boost. Locals would be tapped for civilian jobs, construction projects, advisory committees, and the increased base personnel would sample the local offerings, enjoying everything Pareq had to offer. Pareq's infrastructure would gain from the money pumped into updating the moon's transportation systems, communication systems, and cyber networks. In fact, the only downside was the influx of healthy young men and women, with time on their hands and money to spend. The government of Pareq was more than happy to welcome them, well, "Not so much," Uncle Trent laughed. Pareq's governmental senate took a long time to make a decision explaining they needed time to review the past history of other places agreeing to host a Tal-Kari base. After weighing their options, the Pareqi chose to green light the deployment. The entire project to ready Pareq was planned for approximately one lunar year.

The scientific mission specifics involved the exploration of one of Pareq's smaller sister moons, the icy but active Vedax. Visited over its lifespan, Vedax was deemed too hostile to fully colonize. The Tal-Kari's interest was in its system of cryovolcanoes. These active volcanoes spewed not hot lava but a curious mixture of ice and gasses. Although the mission details read like a geoscientist's dream date, Leba surmised, especially after her conversation with Grand Uncle Tosona, the real reasons for exploring Vedax were a mystery to all but the most senior councilors. He implied Trent Crenon wasn't read-in on all the details. A fact Leba confirmed when Uncle Trent initially advised her against going. "Start with something simpler."

Glirase's other unexplored moons were destined for later missions; at least that's what the introductory mission profile stated. Of Pareq's other moons, its orbitary companion, Jareq, its surface stripped and mined, provided minerals for its mate. Jareq didn't have an established population, only a mobile, semipermanent presence, Minecorp. Minecorp was an industrial giant. With facilities scattered across the system, their reputation was to rape a planetary body for its valuable resources and sell them to the highest bidder. Generally, the closer to a planetary body a potential buyer was, the less expensive the project. Inhabited worlds generally avoided contaminating or destroying their natural resources by engaging Minecorp's services. Transcripts of the Pareqi Prime Minister's original objection to allowing the Tal-Kari to establish a significant facility was concern Minecorp would feel threatened. In open dialogue, Pareq's Minecorp liaison, Chief Phinner Brenin, assured them their fears were unfounded. Minecorp welcomed the opportunity to once again interact with the Tal-Kari.

Leba continued reading about Glirase's other children, Wiwas, for instance, was known as the wiggling world. It wobbled as it orbited, almost bouncing off Glirase's magnetosphere. Hfta was pock-marked with craters, suggesting ancient volcanic activity. Leba was fascinated by the wondrous differences experienced by such close proximity planetary bodies. She longed to explore them all each with their own mysteries and secrets. *I have to make the team.*

Her chrono alarm sounded. Time for reflection was over, and tonight's training class was about to begin. She hustled to get ready and flew out the door to the gym. Getting in shape was a chore. Her newly installed training routine was beginning to pay off. Better exercise tolerance, more strength and muscle tone, more mental focus. At least if she didn't make the squad, she would look and feel better.

By the time class was over, Leba's chest hurt. An overachieving university student spent the evening delivering an intense, undialed-down flurry of punches and jabs. Her costochondral joints, holding her upper ribs to her sternum, bore the brunt of the assault. Obviously wanting to impress the instructor, he showed off by beating up whomever his evening's practice partner was. The point of these early classes was to learn technique, but this weasel's point was to see how powerful he could deliver blow after agonizing blow. Not being one to show weakness or pain, Leba took each pounding shot with grit and determination. Only her sweaty hair matted to her head, an occasional wince with certain movements, and her flushed face revealed the extent of the punishment. "Just wait, you little jerk," muttered Leba as she walked out of the dojo. "One day."

A CHANGE IN TACTICS: MAIDEN VOYAGE

Before she could finish plotting how to enact retribution, she arrived at her quarters, entered the unlocking sequence, and went inside. A blinking message light on her info station signaled her over. Although probably imaginary, Leba thought she could detect subtle differences in the signal pattern and tried to determine who left messages from the character of the beacon. Sort of similar to figuring out who was calling by the ring of the sat-phone. *I knew it. Esre sent me the second installment of my comprehensive, kick-butt, sister-killer workout.* Leba marveled at the extensively detailed, expertly typed exercise regimen, education schedule, and energy supplementation now displayed on the screen. Even better, there were handwritten notations, in red no less, scattered throughout the pages. Be they funny or frightening, each comment added richness to the program.

Leba printed out multiple copies of the schedule so she could post a copy, carry a copy, sleep on a copy. "Live, eat, breathe this," Esre wrote in bolded caps. A spasm in her chest muscles sapped her enthusiasm. She was tired, sweaty, and hungry. Shower first, then eat, then sleep, although the order was still in question in her mind. Drink first went to the head of the list as she turned on the shower to get the water other than cold. Her quarters on base were nice but hot water took some time. Twenty ounces later, Leba was in the shower, washing off all the day's grime.

Not feeling much like cooking (besides, what was in the cold box wasn't fancy), dinner was underwhelming: a protein bar, a piece of fruit, and another twenty ounces of water. She would have to restock her quarters soon, but finding the time she needed for basic life scut was tough. Snatching the hard copies off the table, Leba reviewed Esre's workout schedule with amazement. No wonder even after three kids her sister Esre looked great, felt great, and outperformed all her competitors. How did she find time to do all this stuff? Yawning, she plopped down on the couch. Her eyes grew heavy. *I'll close them for a moment.* Awakening in the middle of the night with a crick in her neck and a renewed pain in her chest, Leba wearily got up from the couch and stumbled to her bed. She didn't wake again until morning.

Hand-to-hand self-defense was a skill that seemed to come quickly, but close contact weaponry class proved challenging. So many things to think about, but acting, not thinking, was what was supposed to happen. Almost anything could be used as a weapon if wielded properly. The best makeshift weapon could be used either offensively or defensively. A branch, stick, or old piece of wood made the ideal improvised tool. She wanted to craft her own. Leftover construction materials set aside for removal in the renovated section of the med clinic proved a prime picking site. She tried to ignore the worker who stood in his hard hat and metal-toed boots watching her pick through the rubble. The wood not only needed the proper length but also the correct weight. As she sifted through the debris, she tested the balance of each potential piece. "Can I help you with something, Doc?" Leba looked up at the construction supervisor, who joined his subordinate.

"I'm looking for the perfect…" her voice trailed off as she studied her latest find. "Can I have this?" she questioned him.

"Sure, take whatever you want," he said.

"I know you think this is strange, but I need this." She smiled at him and moved the stick through a series of complicated maneuvers. "I think this will do just fine."

"Let me guess," the helmeted supervisor said, "personal protection device."

"Hey, very good. No wonder you're in charge." She laughed.

After dismissing his coworker, he moved closer to her. "I'll make you a deal," he began. "I'll clean it up for you, sand it down, and get rid of all the splinters if you do me a favor."

"Ask away," she replied.

"My sister's pretty ill, do you think you can interpret some of her tests for me and explain what's going on with her?" He swayed from one foot to another.

"Sure. Is she here on planet?" Leba asked.

"No, unfortunately she lives back on my home world." His forehead wrinkled, and Leba thought he was maybe thinking twice about approaching her.

A CHANGE IN TACTICS: MAIDEN VOYAGE

"Get me the info, and I'd be more than happy to review it all with you, even if you don't fix my stick." Trying not to make too much eye contact and make him feel any more uncomfortable, Leba looked down and brushed the dust off her pants.

"She's seeing the best specialists, but I can't get a straight answer from my family as to what's really going on. They're not medical." He shifted his feet again. "I'm the first to go to university, and they expect I can interpret anything." His eyelids fluttered. "I'm pretty good with schematics for buildings, but not bodies." Putting a hand to his mouth he chewed a cuticle.

"Here's my clinic contact info." Leba handed him her card. "Have her docs send the records to me directly." His eyes locked on hers for a moment, and he smiled. His long lashes made him look boyish, and it was hard for Leba to break away. Putting out his hand, Leba almost grasped it but handed him the rough weapon instead. She could lose herself in his gaze, but now was not the time or place. *Keep it all business, at least for now.*

Training involved using a lot of muscles Leba hadn't used in a long time. Front kicks and side kicks took a lot of balance and core strength. As the weeks passed, Leba began to notice her increasing ability to get the techniques correct and not fall over unbalanced in the process. Her increased respiratory capacity allowed her endurance to improve. The added benefit of sound and restorative sleep made the whole process complete. Feel better, perform better, and look better. It became easier to fend off faux attackers, and Leba decided even if she didn't make the mission, she now possessed valuable life skills. As time progressed, not only did Esre's workout schedule get more intense, but the combat scenarios got tougher with more difficult situations and more skilled attackers. She could fight hand-to-hand with a stick or a knife or defend herself more effectively against those weapons if unarmed.

Unfortunately, one thing kept nagging at her; she inherently felt difficulty wrapping her head around the concept of hurting someone else even if they meant her harm. Toward the final session at the Fighting Academy, she got up the courage to discuss the issue with Dieuvoxyl. "I'm a doctor, and I'm supposed to help people, not harm them." Leba scratched her cheek and then wrung her hands. "Why do I feel the need to help the person who tried to hurt me?" Both heads inclined toward her, four eyes scanning her face. To their credit, Dieuvoxyl seemed to understand her dilemma.

"The theory," they explained, "is to respond to the threat with equal force, disarm your attacker to save yourself, prevent them from regrouping, and coming after you again. If you could help them safely and felt the need to, you could. A sentient being was just that, alive, and despite their misguided motives, they were still a life possibly worth saving. Deadly force should only be a last resort, although war and participation in war often resulted in significant casualties. Each combatant wanted to be victorious, but ultimately only one could win. Multiple historical examples showed collateral damage to be inevitable but not something to be ignored." The one thing Dieuvoxyl stressed was not to let your attacker get a second chance to assault you. Leba knew preventing an assault was her first priority. "Don't get into a situation requiring a fight. Be a hard target. If it occurs, you need to be ready." Dieuvoxyl reiterated, "Attacks don't announce themselves, they're unexpected. You need to be prepared and react from memory, training through repetition. Your actions need to be precise, without mental effort." The heads volleyed tenets back and forth. "The average close-contact fight lasts only a few seconds, and with adrenaline pumping, your mind interferes with your muscles' performance. Thinking should be reserved for before and after an encounter, not during." Professor Othra's stretching routine also helped the body transcend the mind's influence, and Leba was glad she was practicing.

Fighting and sparring sometimes reminded Leba of resuscitating a patient in cardiopulmonary arrest. You learned the proper protocol, studied it, memorized it, and practiced it a million times, but when a life was at stake, you needed to enact it, not think about it. She remembered in medical training the first time she heard the claxon signal a patient in full arrest. Arriving as the only physician covering the house, newly named doctor Leba Brader was expected to take charge, run the code, and resuscitate the patient. All eyes were on her, everyone would react on her commands, and there was no time for hesitation or uncertainty. As time ticked down, every second became one less for the patient. Orders flowed from her mouth, instructing each participant in their role, dismissing those not needed. Assaulted with data, she reacted to all the input with precise and definitive orders. At the end, she was rewarded with a living patient. It felt great. How could she take a life from somebody? Could she really kill if it came down to it? Leba hoped she would never know the answer. She dismissed the idea. This was a routine expeditionary mission, not a war. Satisfied with her analysis, Leba went back to the mat.

Leba wasn't quite sure when she would hear from command about her application to join the expeditionary force, but it had to be soon. JT expected to receive his new orders in the next week or two as to where and when to report for specific mission training. Leba needed enough time to secure her medical practice and transfer care to a locum doctor. She also needed time to get commissioned. One of the stipulations for the mission was her enlistment. Although she worked at a military facility, in order to be on this particular mission, she was required to become part of the service. As a doctor, it was easier for her to transition from civilian to military then the average civilian. In regards to rank, physicians got it right from the start. But what exactly came with that rank she really didn't know. What she did understand was someone who outranked her could make her do whatever they ordered. The military survived on a pseudodictatorial hierarchical system. A tried and true system, it worked, although she wasn't sure how it would work for her. She was not one to disobey orders, be they from her parents, teachers, or employers, but this seemed different. Usually mandates from civilian authorities came with an explanation, and you could question those directives without fear of severe consequences. Orders—no, commands from military superiors were to be carried out without the need for explanation. If they were given, they needed to be followed. There was little wiggle room and insubordination severely punished. The military medical corp was not as regimented and strict as the general corp, but there was still an expected decorum.

    Leba set aside tonight after the gym to review the flora and fauna of cold climates. Her medical academy final project was a tour de force about the effects of cold on human beings, both their bodies as well as their minds. It was so well received, earning her valedictorian honors and a textbook chapter coauthorship. Living things, both animal and plant, needed to be very hardy to survive the intense conditions of the tundra. Leba wasn't sure Vedax could even host natural life but decided if she knew how cold-climate animals could survive and what adaptations they evolved over the millennium, it could one day have relevance to human survival in such conditions. Surprisingly, there was a variety of wildlife calling Vedax home, from small flying polar birds to playful ice monkeys; from herds of snowy white ungulates to their nemesis, packs of ivory wolves; from families of frost foxes to giant glacial bears, who preyed on the frozen lake fish.

The majority of the birds depended on the scarce plant life to nourish themselves and their broods. The plants were hardy too, surviving on periods of minimal light and heat, conserving resources when available, and living off those stores during the long stretches of endless frozen nights.

    Most of the land-based animals sported two coats, an insulating inner layer of fine, soft, tightly packed shorter hairs and a repelling outer layer of dense, durable, multilayered longer hairs. The combination made for an almost impenetrable shield against the elements. Their outer hairs were generally translucent and hollow, allowing whatever sunlight available to be efficiently captured and the heat absorbed and retained by the inner coat. For ever-greater fortification, some of the larger beasts developed thick fatty layers underneath their coats. The bodies of these animals were generally rounded and stout, not necessarily built for speed but for durability. Everything seemed to move slower in the cold in an attempt to conserve energy and heat.

A CHANGE IN TACTICS: MAIDEN VOYAGE

People, on the other hand, were not adapted for the cold. Their extremities extended away from the body, allowing for heat loss. Unlike their animal counterparts, the head was relatively hairless and, if left uncovered, allowed the majority of stored heat to escape unchecked. Despite every effort to design the perfect coverings for cold weather, gear fell miserably short in performance or appearance or comfort or usability. The best garments for cold exposure relied on layering, with perspiration being a major obstacle to peak performance. For short periods, cold and dry was acceptable but not ideal. Cold and wet was deadly. Clothing that wicked away sweat was a must but not always available for every body surface.

Another major issue facing visitors to extremely cold climates was the treacherous terrain. The natural fauna were uniquely designed to handle sheer mountain faces, rocky outcroppings, and sheets of frozen ice. People, on the other hand, didn't adapt well to slippery slopes and nonlevel surfaces. Mountain ungulates could balance on hoofed feet at the top of a rocky pinnacle and not think twice, but man couldn't do the same without a lot of training, experience, and special equipment. Luckily for Leba, her sister, Esre, was an expert mountaineer and taught her the basics of climbing and rappelling.

Then, specifically unique to Vedax, there were the cryovolcanoes, the majestic explosive mountains that rained fires of ice. When they erupted, cryomagma made of water, methane, and ammonia spewed out in a magnificent show, layering the mountainside with a thick coating of icy slush. Leba imagined if there were ice monkeys nearby, they would come out of their hidden caves and dance in amusement at the show. Laughing out loud at the mental picture she painted, her concentration now broken, Leba decided it was an excellent time to take a break and grab a bite of dinner. The next subject she planned to explore was the cryobiology and physiology of cold-climate lichen and fungi. A topic better left for after dinner as it would probably bore her to sleep. Although if trapped on an icy moon, she reckoned, the only meals available might consist predominately of so-called rock-fuzz.

CHAPTER 6

"Hey, Zach, long time no see," Clinic Administrator Sendra Tohl greeted him. Her whole face smiled, but Zach soon found the spotlight shifted to his squad leader. Overseer Company Squad Leader Damond Fiorat was taller than Zach, with close-cropped black hair, expressive brown eyes, and a well-trimmed goatee.

Turning his head almost imperceptibly, Zach waited a moment, watching for his supervisor's reaction, and then proceeded, rather formally, to Sendra's desk. "Good morning, Ms. Tohl." Zach was sure he looked as uncomfortable as he felt. He hoped Fiorat hadn't noticed. Zach continued, "This is Damond Fiorat, my squad leader." Zach watched as Sendra carefully and elegantly got up and came around her desk to shake hands with his boss.

"Pleased to meet you, ma'am," Fiorat said. "Cadet Kixon's description failed to do you justice." Zach could feel the heat come to his face.

"He got your description perfect, though," she flirted, pupils dilated under arched eyebrows. "Zach, why don't you give Dr. Brader a shout, while I give Squad Leader Fiorat a tour of our little slice of heaven." Zach wanted to stay, make sure Fiorat didn't hit on Sendra. But she dismissed him. After all the time they'd shared, she blew him off.

"Go ahead, Kixon, I'll catch up with you in a few minutes," he said, shooing Zach away and returning his attention to Sendra. "I think I'd like to see everything." Fiorat's shoulders were back and his muscular chest out. Zach couldn't compete and lowered his chin to his chest to stare at his feet.

Head down, Zach wound his way through the clinic, taking the familiar stairs down to Dr. Brader's inner sanctum. He took a seat in the farthermost consultation chair and slumped. "Cadet Kixon," Leba said, looking up from her desk, first with a big smile, which faded to lips pressing into a slight grimace. "So good to see you too," she said. "What's up?" Zach rubbed the back of his neck.

"Probably my squad leader," he snarled and then realized where he was and who he was talking to and straightened up, but only a little. Dr. Brader would understand; she always did, and he knew it would be mere moments before he spilled his guts to her. Zach sucked in a breath and met her gaze.

"Let me guess, Sendra's giving him 'the tour.'" Zach shrugged. Her frown softened. This wasn't only about Sendra. "What's bugging you, Zach?" Dr. Brader would poke and prod until he caved. She could drag even the most guarded secrets out of him. He trusted her. "You're not sick, are you?"

Sick and tired of living in Damond Fiorat's shadow. "No." After digging deep down into his pants pocket, Zach stared at the quantum calculator.

"You feeling okay?" Dr. Brader reached for her portable med scanner and thumbed the switch. The unit beeped three times, signaling its warm-up mode.

"Yeah, I guess so," Zach started. "It's just that, well, I wish I could be more like my squad leader." He watched her deactivate the probe and put it aside.

"Equation time, Zach," Dr. Brader prompted. "Give me the equation for what's really bugging you."

He twiddled the stylus between his fingers then tapped it on the display screen. "Well, I guess if I wrote it out, it would probably be something like ZK over DF equals Unknown over ST." He stole a look to check her response.

"I think you'll admit it's a bit more complicated." Dr. Brader's brows drew closer as she tapped her fingers together. Zach nodded in agreement. "I think you need to spend more time reevaluating the represented variables before you find equality."

The slightest noise outside the small office made Zach fidget and take a quick glance at the door. No sign yet of his commander. Fiorat's continued absence was making him crazy. He knew his crush feelings for Sendra Tohl were products of an overactive imagination and wishful thinking, but to see her in action, especially with Damond Fiorat, was seriously disturbing.

"So how's Overseer Company?" Dr. Brader asked, prompting Zach to return his gaze to his calculator. He swallowed hard, his mouth dry.

Rubbing his sweaty palms over his thighs, he slid down in his chair. "Interesting," Zach lied, trying to ignore his urge to race up the stairs and prevent Fiorat from besting him at something else. "Currently we're planning the logistics for the expeditionary mission you're training for." Still hunched over, he tilted his head up to see her.

"I still haven't gotten final word if I made it or not." She twisted her wristwatch. "My application's been in a long time, and I'm getting impatient." Now it was Dr. Brader's turn to be anxious. "Even if I get picked now, I'll have six months more training with the med team." Zach inclined his head, glad the spotlight was off him, if for only a moment. "JT's getting deployed for the mission, he got his orders this morning." She paused and continued, "One more little wrinkle, I have to enlist if I get chosen. In fact, you'll probably outrank me."

Zach laughed. "No way, Doc, you professional types get to skip all the grunt work and go right to officer."

"Like you, I still have to be under a squad leader and abide by his whims and wishes," Leba admitted.

"You don't know the half of it."

Sendra was busy showing Damond all the interesting sights in the clinic. "Let's go to the commissary, I'm sure you're thirsty after such a long trip."

"If you're game, we could grab a bite to eat." He smiled and leaned close. "My treat." Sendra could get used to this, a real man, one not afraid to open his billfold. In the commissary café, the waitress brought over a sampling of their pies. Damond snatched one off the tray, but Sendra begged off ordering dessert. "I need to watch my figure."

Damond grinned. "I'll keep an eye on your figure, and then you can have all the dessert you want." He dug his fork in and brought out a chunk of fruit.

"There's only one sweet thing I want." She giggled, eating off his fork. She agreed with Leba: there was something about a man in a uniform, especially this man. Her sight line went right for his pecs, and boy, what an impressive set. He must spend his entire free time at the gym. That would have to change. His arms were cannoned too. Well, he could spend time at the gym when she was busy. Petite as she was, she imagined sitting comfortably on his broad shoulders. "Uh-oh," she whispered. "Here comes my boss." Damond turned toward the café door and watched Zach and Dr. Brader enter the eatery. As the pair approached, Zach's perturbed look spoke volumes even if he was afraid to. She also picked up Leba's subtle eye roll, and her hand instinctively went for the top few open blouse buttons.

"Dr. Leba Brader," Zach said, his posture rigid, his brow lowered over squinting eyes. "I would like you to meet my squad leader, Damond Fiorat."

Fiorat started to his feet, when Leba stopped him. "No need to get up." Fiorat sat back down and scooted closer to Sendra. "I hope you're putting him to good use."

Sendra looked up at Leba and giggled. "Who, me?" Leba shot her a stare. "I was just showing Damond around."

"I'm very impressed with your operation, ma'am. Sendra, I mean Ms. Tohl says you run a tight ship. Did a fine job with Kixon there too. I didn't have to break him in too much."

Although Sendra enjoyed the jest, she knew Leba really didn't care for cheap shots at Zach or anybody on her team. She was overly maternal when it came to her people. Sendra was her wild child, and Leba stopped trying to rope her in a long time ago. The contrasting styles between the two women made for a complementary pairing. What one didn't know, the other did. That was what scared Sendra and maybe why she was so engrossed in this man she just met. If Leba made the mission, she would be alone for the first time in years. Who would fill the void? A new man certainly would help ease her pain. Maybe that was what Zach needed to be happy as well, a new girl to pine over, someone to not only see things differently but also respect his point of view. Zach needed a wild child, but not her. His jealousy was obvious but healthy. He was still very young. Sendra needed a career military man, someone who could take care of her, someone she could depend on, someone who didn't disappoint her. Sendra's hand rested on Damond's generous arm and felt comfortable there. She would need to convince Leba her first impression of Damond was mistaken, but for now, Sendra wanted to settle down Zach's anger and redirect it. "Mr. Fiorat tells me he's got some questions for you about cold weather climate conditions and the effects of long-term exposure on the human body."

"Yes, ma'am." Fiorat straightened up. Sendra could tell he changed to squad leader mode. He didn't remove her hand, which was definitely a good sign. "I know you're busy, so I can leave a list of questions with Ms. Tohl." He looked over, and his lips curled into a grin. Returning his attention to Leba, he said, "And you can answer them at your leisure."

"I know you're busy too, so why don't we go back to my office for a short chat, then Ms. Tohl can follow up with any further needs you may have."

Sendra looked at Leba, winked, and mouthed the word "Thanks."

"Zach, why don't you fill Ms. Tohl in on what you've been up to." Leba inclined her head toward Fiorat. "If that's all right with your squad leader, and then you can meet up with us in my office, say in half an hour."

Zach looked toward Fiorat for approval. "Sounds good to me," Fiorat said. "Thirty minutes it is." Fiorat got up from the table, offering a hand. "Thank you, Ms. Tohl." He took her hand. "I look forward to working closely with you." Zach's nostrils flared as he watched Dr. Brader escort Fiorat back to her office.

Laterally moving the chair with her foot, Sendra reached up and grabbed Zach's hand, pulling him into the seat vacated by Fiorat. "So," she said, "what's up with you?"

What was up with Zach was a lot of things. "Overseer Company..." His voice trailed off as he turned his head to check for anyone who might be listening. "Let's just say it's not as much fun as when I worked here."

"I told you the first day I met you nothing would be as fun as hanging out with us," she said, nudging him. "No cute girls for you to ogle, huh?" Sendra winked.

"You know I only have eyes for you." Zach batted his eyes. No smart comeback. Ouch. Zach dropped his gaze. "Fiorat's not like Dr. Brader either." Zach held his breath then blew out through pursed lips. "He doesn't care about my opinion. It's his way or no way."

"What did you think it would be when you signed up? That's the military way. Damond, I mean Squad Leader Fiorat is just doing his job. It's his job to think, not yours." Zach bit the inside of his cheek. "You know what I mean." She poked his arm, trying to get his attention.

I wish you didn't like him so much.

"He's trained to be in charge. Shouldering a lot of responsibility to keep you cadets from getting into trouble." She looked deeply into Zach's brown eyes. "I'm sure once he gets to know you, he'll value your opinions too." She brought her hands together to the side of her face and rested her head, tilting just slightly. Her eyes slowly drifted upward and then back to Zach. "He's a rather quick judge of character." She smiled. "He responded quite well to some suggestions I made, and he just met me." *I recognize that look. Do you have to be so obvious?*

Zach scowled. "He would." Zach fiddled with his quantum calculator.

Sendra reached for his hand. "Don't worry, he was a perfect gentleman."

"The Tal-Kari council is acutely aware, Dr. Brader, of your expertise on cold climates and human exposure." Damond Fiorat further explained, "I was tasked to glean whatever knowledge I need from you to plan for the upcoming mission."

Leba watched circumspectly as Fiorat outlined his questions. No wonder Sendra was falling all over herself; Damond Fiorat was an excellent specimen of military manliness. A perfect candidate for recruitment ads—"Join the Tal-Kari, get in awesome shape, ladies will fall at your feet." Trying to avoid dwelling on his attributes, Leba answered each with a concise but complete answer.

"Thank you, ma'am," Fiorat concluded.

"Do you know when the final selections for personnel will be going out?" Leba caught herself wringing her hands. What if she didn't make it? She never failed at anything. How could she face anyone? What excuse would she make, that she wasn't good enough? If she couldn't go on the mission at least she could take satisfaction playing a peripheral part in its execution. That's it. She would say they needed her expertise at home rather than abroad.

"Final decisions for civilian personnel should be announced in the next few days," Fiorat said. "Not too many spots left." Leba dropped her eyes. "But I'll let HQ know we talked and put in a good word for you if you want." He pushed up from the chair, his biceps bulging underneath his shirt.

Leba put out her hand and shook his. "Thanks, that would be much appreciated." Leba rolled back from her desk and got up. "Let me walk you out." The pair headed back toward the clinic.

"We ought to be getting back," Sendra suggested to Zach. He stared at his chrono as the last few minutes ticked off. He really didn't want to leave. He missed this place and the people whom he was so fond of. "Come on," Sendra urged, slipping an arm through his. "Don't want to keep that squad leader of yours waiting, do we?" Tugging him upward, she smiled. Zach understood her agenda all too well.

Sendra always made things more interesting. Now it was Zach's turn. Reluctantly he got up from the table, sighed, blowing out a long breath. "You know he has a wife?"

Sendra's head jerked back, her eyes almost popping out. Red blotches crept up the sides of her neck, and her nostrils flared. "You liar," she spat. She held the pose but not able to contain her amusement, poked him with an outstretched finger and said, "Thought you had me, didn't you?" Zach kept emotionless. Sendra paused, studied his face, her eyes narrowed. "You're not serious, are you?"

Zach caved. "Got you!" Sendra punched him in the arm.

"What did you do now, Cadet?" Fiorat asked as he and Dr. Brader entered the room.

Startled, Zach stiffened to attention. "Nothing, sir."

Before anyone else responded, Dr. Brader stepped in. "Well, Zach, it was great to see you again. Clinic isn't the same since you left." She hooked her thumb toward Fiorat. "Anyway, I think your squad leader needs to get back to base." She turned her attention back to Fiorat. "Thank you for coming by, and please feel free to call if you have any more questions."

Sendra jumped into the conversation. "Here's our contact information, and like Dr. Brader said, feel free to call or stop by anytime." Zach gave her a frown. "You too, Zach, stop by anytime."

CHAPTER 7

The Tal-Kari, like any military organization, didn't like damaged goods on their front line. Or any line for that matter. But Master Priman DeShay Tiner knew it was hard to get rid of grizzled veterans, like himself, whose wealth of knowledge would be wasted if he weren't assigned somewhere. The amount of time and money spent training him, employing him, using him, and rehabilitating him would be recovered if he could help produce new, able-bodied recruits.

He rubbed his left shoulder. It always took the brunt of his early morning workouts. Today, it ached more with the coming of cold weather. The artificial right shoulder performed so much better. For the last few years, when this injury prohibited him from rejoining Defender Company, he'd been assigned to the medical division and stuck training new paramedical recruits in battlefield medicine. Breaking these newbies in and making them conform to Tal-Kari standards and expectations wasn't easy. He first had to train them that his word was gospel, and any deviation would result in significant punishment and retribution.

Day one was always the worst. DeShay Tiner walked into the classroom only to be met by a chorus of nothing. He surveyed the room. There were desks there and people in them, but no greeting, no standing at attention, no nothing. He spied the clock, and as the seconds ticked down to 0800, he shut the door. Today was different; today his classroom was supposed to be filled with the new doctors he needed to train.

Three times he tried to begin but was interrupted by the door opening for stragglers. No respect. At least with the paramilitary people, they already had some taste of discipline in basic and knew the consequences of not following orders. Tiner surveyed the room again. A few pair of eyes focused on him, but the rest stared off into boredom. He could pick out nests of conversations, rustling of papers, and rhythmic tapping. Picking up his portfolio, Tiner tested the weight in his hand and then slammed it on the podium. "First lesson, pay attention." Startling some to attentiveness, Tiner zeroed in on a young man in the second to last row who remained with his back turned. The woman he was focusing on didn't budge either.

Tiner stepped from behind the podium, moved down the row, and stopped at the distracted student's desk. Grabbing the front ends of the desk, Tiner raised it off the ground and dropped it. Then in a very low, deep tone, he said, "Well, boy, I guess you get to go first."

The man swiveled in his seat, his eyes meeting Tiner's glare. "You talking to me?"

Tiner pointed to his ID badge. "Dr. Pratel Jarmin?" The young man nodded. Tiner grabbed his collar and raised him to his feet. Tiner prodded him forward. "Here's how it goes, boys and girls. I ask a question. If you don't get it right, you get to do push-ups, sit-ups, or crunches or whatever I choose." As he let that sink in, Tiner looked over those assembled. This group of supposed professionals was no different than the average recruit. He needed to break them of their arrogance, their know-it-all attitude, their holier-than-thou approach. They had to understand that in the military, things were going to be different. "Second, if I ask a question and you get it right, you get to do push-ups, sit-ups, or crunches or whatever I choose."

"Hey, that's not fair," the blond-haired girl who was the object of Dr. Jarmin's insubordination called out.

Tiner put his arms on his hips and bent forward; slowly the corners of his mouth upturned. "Who said anything about fair? You, Doctor, can drop and give me twenty push-ups." Tiner could hear a gasp or two.

The woman leaned back in her chair. "You can't be serious."

"Serious?" He put an open hand on his chest. "Me, serious?" He inclined his head, opened his eyes wide, and grinned. He started to turn from her and then snapped his head back. This time, his dark-brown eyes narrowed under a furrowed brow. "That'll be thirty. You'd better get started." The room fell eerily silent as he scanned for other dissenters. "I think we understand each other."

The female doctor looked at him. "Yes," Tiner confirmed. "Right there." He pointed to the floor near her seat. She dropped first to her knees and then gingerly placed her outstretched hands on the floor, extended her legs, and began. Tiner rose to his full height, straightened his uniform jacket, and returned to the podium. "You may be doctors, but it's my job to see you not only make it as soldiers but also make it home." He rubbed his chin. "Jarmin, why don't you join her in thirty as well."

Leba sat in the front row, taking copious notes. She liked authority, respected it, and felt discipline was one thing a lot of her colleagues lacked. She appreciated the Master Priman's approach, although as the day wore on, her arms and probably those of her classmates ached from push-ups, legs throbbed from so many squats, and abs burned from endless crunches. "The military is not necessarily fair, but neither is war or conflict or the unknown, and that's what I'm training you for," Tiner lectured. "I need you to be able to work under pressure, mental or physical, and not let exhaustion impair your ability to perform."

Leba thought how straightforward hospital medicine was compared to battlefield medicine. What a pity many of her classmates missed the underlying message—they were worlds apart and required new skill sets and ways of approaching problems. The environment became a crucial determinant in patient outcomes.

Tiner knew his stuff, and it didn't hurt that he could bust out the exercises, daily running circles around his charges. Leba liked Mister Tiner, and as far as she could tell, he seemed to like her too. As the weeks wore on, when he gave extra books to read or advanced skills to master, she could swear he was speaking just to her.

"Dr. Brader, a moment of your time, please," Tiner said as he dismissed the class. Leba turned to watch the rest of the class file out. Had she done something wrong, asked a stupid question? Other students had been asked to stay after class, but it was generally to chastise them. She met his eyes. Tiner seemed more relaxed, his face softened from the gruff veteran with a chip on his shoulder. "Dr. Brader, I understand you're an expert on cold-weather exposure."

"Well, sir"—she furrowed her brow and held the edge of her desk, trying to keep her hands from fidgeting—"I don't know how much of an expert I am, but I have done a lot of studying on the subject."

Tiner moved around his lectern and sat on the edge of the desk next to her. Still holding onto the desk, she inclined her head and looked in his direction. She avoided looking directly into his eyes. He was very handsome, his goatee impeccably manicured, and his skin the color of warm chocolate. Not one hair grew on his bald head. There was strength and power and determination in his look, and that in itself was attractive. She was afraid she would get lost in his gaze. "Do you think you could teach me what you know?"

It was not the question she thought he'd ask, but she really didn't know what to expect. Her head hung down, and her eyes staring at the books on top of her desk. She traced the corner of a book with her finger. "Sure." Leba turned to look at him, this time captivated by his soulful eyes. She stumbled over her words. "It would be an honor, sir."

Immediately she noticed the frown on his face as he straightened up. Had her gaze been too suggestive? She looked down again at her book. "It's after class, so you can drop the 'sir' and call me DeShay." Maybe he knew she thought he was attractive. Maybe this was a come-on after all. Maybe he wanted to secretly meet with her, and tapping her knowledge about the cold was just a ploy. He was too old for her, wasn't he? He must be at least twice her age. But men her age were so childish, and Mr. Tiner was mature and experienced. "And I'd be certainly appreciative of your time."

Leba really wasn't sure what to do next. The corners of her mouth upturned slightly. She didn't want to seem too eager. "Just let me know what's convenient for you, sir." She turned to see his scowl and corrected herself. "I mean, DeShay." That was greeted with a full-toothed smile. She picked up her books, clumsily loaded them into her backpack. She could feel his eyes scrutinizing her every move and quickly exited. She didn't want to linger and say something stupid she'd regret later or have to try and explain. She really needed to stop overthinking everything.

For the next few weeks, for an hour after formal class was over, Leba schooled DeShay, teaching him everything she knew about the cold. It seemed a little uncomfortable at first. She had so much respect for him but was definitely attracted to him. Afraid if their relationship changed, she risked losing a lot. As time passed, he began to feel more like a colleague than a student, and her respect gained an extra layer of friendship. DeShay was a good student; he listened intently to everything she said, but it puzzled her that he never took any notes.

She folded her arms, crossed her chest. "How do you remember what I tell you if you don't write it down?"

DeShay looked up at her, his dark brown eyes staring into hers, his brow furrowed. "With all your note-taking, you didn't remember what I taught you." Startled by his response, Leba tightened her grip on her own arms. "Where are my notes when I'm in a situation?" He slammed his hand down. "They're on my desk." He grabbed her forearms, brought his face close to hers. "I need to acquire information, assimilate it, and act upon it. I remember what I can and what's relevant to me and my situation. I strain out the stuff that's not applicable."

Leba spent a lot of time preparing the information she was teaching him. Did he think he was that smart or that great a student he could understand all this information on the first pass? She wriggled out of his grasp and turned away from him.

He softened his tone, put a hand on her shoulder, and turned her back. "It's not that I don't appreciate what you're teaching me, only 10 percent is useful to me."

Ten percent, that's it. All this work, preparing for countless hours to have him only care about ten stupid percent.

"You don't know which 10 percent, so you teach me 100 percent, and I disregard the 90 percent I don't need."

How dare you take advantage of me like that? How could I ever have liked you or thought you really cared about what I know? "Well, then, I'll keep babbling on, and you filter what you need." Leba hung her head.

"Now don't go getting all pouty on me, girl." DeShay reached and brought up her chin. He shook his head. Despite her annoyance, Leba dutifully continued her dissertation. She tried to shake off the feeling she was somehow less important. She was truly honored that DeShay Tiner, a distinguished veteran, wanted to learn from her. What was she thinking? Esre warned her. Negative thoughts would hamper her ability to adapt. The mental barriers she would face in the military were harder to overcome than the physical ones. Leba must stop worrying what everyone else thought and concentrate on doing her job. DeShay was being truthful with her. He didn't need all the detailed information she presented. Slowly she began to appreciate the simplicity of the situation. DeShay told her, but she didn't listen; the more complexity, the more mistakes. Mistakes got you killed. Keep it simple.

Leba was not looking forward to graduating from DeShay's class as it would mean they would probably never see each other again. Not everyone in her class would be assigned to the same deployment, and after the basic six-week military medical course DeShay taught, they would be assigned to different units based on their upcoming missions. After learning countless important concepts from him, most important of all, she now possessed a better understanding of herself. As an added bonus, she and DeShay were good friends, but all that was about to change.

CHAPTER 8

"I've always liked this place. It's a little out of the way, but since I'm buying, I might as well have a decent meal," Tivon Garnet said. Even in his off-duty black camo fatigues, Defender Company Squad Leader Tiv Garnet possessed the ultimate soldier look, a proud member of the corps. From the perfectly polished black boots to the silver and blue braid on his epaulets, he screamed leader. Loyal, competent, hard-working, determined. Every commander's go-to officer. By the book, like someone else DeShay knew.

"Noticed the majority of folks have the same taste in rides," DeShay looked out the table side window at the array of jet-cycles parked at the entrance.

Tiv held up two fingers, nodded his head, and gave a thumbs-up.

"What, no menus?" Tiner asked. "You must come here a lot." He swiveled his head around, taking in the entire room. There was a healthy amount of smoke from the grill area, and every time a fresh piece of meat impacted it, there was sizzling and crackling as the open fire licked at its prey. The aroma of smoking meat made him salivate. Nothing topped a good steak and cold ale except maybe a warm body to snuggle with afterward. The waitress, an older woman in a grease-stained apron, came to the table and deposited two ales.

Tiv ordered again, signaling with his fingers. "Two steaks, medium rare."

The woman pulled a pad out and made a notation. She reached into her other pocket and pulled out a rag. As she wiped the entire surface, both men lifted their arms off the table. Reaching into her pocket again, she produced two table settings, placing the napkin-rolled utensils down in front of each man. "Be back shortly."

Tiner unrolled the paper blanket and placed his fork and knife on the table. "Classy place, real retro feel." He slowly tapped the butt of the knife. "You'd like her, I think."

"Is that what this is about?" Tiv took a long pull from his ale bottle.

"Not exactly." Tiner tried to keep in touch with the guys from his old unit, but as time passed, it was harder and harder to find common ground. He missed the camaraderie, the missions, the feeling of belonging. He had saved just about each and every one of them at one time or another. This one, though, had been more like a younger brother. Tiv Garnet risked his own life to drag Tiner from harm's way after his shoulder was smashed and his liver lacerated. Tiner wanted to die, not live as damaged goods, but Garnet wouldn't let him. Shortly thereafter, Garnet was promoted the youngest squad leader ever. "I really think you'd like her."

Tiner increased the tapping of his knife until Garnet grabbed his hand. "Stop." He placed the utensil down on the table. "You say that about all the girls you introduce me to." Garnet took up the drumming with his fingers. "I just got rid of the last one you hooked me up with. You know, JT's friend Nilsa, the hot blonde."

"What was wrong with her?" Tiner felt obliged to see to his friend's happiness as an attempt to repay his heroism.

"Where to begin?" Garnet ran his hand through his black hair and scratched at the back. "Way too needy, wanted way too much of my time." He took another pull from the ale bottle. "Not a good breakup."

"Is any ever good?" Tiner thought back to his last breakup with his lover, Emmie Hodd.

"She got really upset. Even your favorite lines—'I'm sure there's someone better for you,' 'It's my fault this isn't working,' 'I just can't seem to meet your expectations,' 'We'd be better off just being friends'—didn't work like they were supposed to."

The corners of Tiner's mouth curled into a broad grin. "I thought I taught you better. You don't use all my greatest lines on the same girl." He picked up his own ale bottle as the waitress slid a sizzling hot steak in front of him. Depositing Garnet's steak in front of him, the woman doled out the greens and potatoes family style. Tiner put the ale bottle to his lips, drained the last bit, and handed it to her. "We'll take two more." The woman took the spent bottles and left.

"Pity you don't have my looks, or girls would be coming at you, and you'd have an endless supply to choose from." Tiner cut through his meat and took a big bite. He knew what an inordinate amount of time Garnet spent on the job. It was hard enough to get together for their monthly dinners. "The way it stands now, I have to usually go searching far and wide to find a girl who would even consider dating a grunt like you."

Not looking up from his plate, Garnet sawed methodically at his steak. "Let me find my own girls for a while. You keep the ones you find for yourself."

Much as Tiner wanted to, he was hopelessly preoccupied with Emmie. Despite their on-again and off-again relationship, he could never seem to erase his feelings for her. His recent encounters with other women had been for nothing more than a night of good times. It wasn't too late for his buddy Tiv, though; he could still find a decent girl to spend his life with. Tiner didn't want Garnet to end up like him, old, broken, and lonely.

"No, my friend, this one is different." Garnet looked up from his plate and met Tiner's eyes. Tiner looked down, poking at the potatoes accompanying his meal. "She's probably too good for you, though." He tried the starch and then another big chunk of steak. He swallowed and looked for the waitress, desperately wishing for another ale. Thinking about Emmie always resulted in increased drinking. Maybe it helped ease the pain. "Besides, I like having her for a friend. After she breaks up with you, she'd probably blame me for introducing the two of you." He settled for the table water, made a face at its metallic taste, and replaced it.

"She's coming now with the ales." Garnet hooked his thumb.

"My girl doesn't know it yet, but I'm being deployed to Pareq with her," Tiner said. *Can't wait to see how she performs under pressure.*

"You didn't tell the new love of my life she has to put up with you longer?"

"No, I wanted it to be a surprise." Tiner gripped his replacement ale and took a needed drink.

"If she's as bright as you say, she probably figured it out by now." Garnet sampled the greens on his plate and then pushed them aside. "Why would some old grunt like you want to learn about the cold unless you were going too?"

"Maybe she thought I was just interested in her, you know." Tiner smiled. Dr. Brader did seem to have a crush on him. He could see it in her eyes and how she blossomed on his approval.

"You"—Garnet pointed with his knife—"you're too old for that stuff." He leaned back in his chair. "You wouldn't know what to do with her anyway." Garnet rocked forward, the front chair legs banging on the floor. He put his elbows on the table and leaned forward, his head resting on his hands. "Sure, I'll meet her, show her what you can't."

"I take it back." Tiner dug deeper into his potatoes. It was time to change the subject. Obviously, Garnet was not ready to be serious. Tiner really thought Leba would complement Tiv. They were both hardworking, dedicated individuals who never took time to enjoy themselves. Pity he wasn't younger. Garnet was wrong, though; Tiner could still hold his own. Just ask Emmie. "When are you guys leaving for Pareq?"

Garnet swallowed his last bite and answered, "Defender Company is shipping out in three weeks as part of the advance team. I suspect you and your med unit will meet us three weeks after that." He poked at the greens again. "We'll have it all ready for you softies."

This time, it was Tiner who leaned back in his chair and folded his arms across his chest. "I told you my group is pretty good. Mevid Anster and Pola Grizzer were picked. You know those guys are top notch. Your buddy JT Hobes, old man Gordie Rensen, and your new girlfriend, Leba Brader, are my docs." He leaned forward, one elbow rested on the table, and he rubbed his chin. "The only issue is…"

Garnet forcibly impaled the steak with his fork, the blood-tinged juices escaping around the tines. "You drew Luth Cathen again."

"I always get stuck with that arrogant little weasel. Not much better than roadkill. How the hell does he get all the plumb assignments?" Tiner knew how people like Cathen got ahead, underhandedly with either bribes or extortion or threats. Cathen knew the right people to manipulate and the ones to avoid.

Garnet stared at the fork standing upright in the center of the plate. "I think he's screwing some councilor's daughter. He certainly doesn't get it on skills like you do."

"What? You mean I don't get it on my looks?" Garnet was right; Tiner did have skills and much more experience than Squad Leader Cathen, and by all rights, it should be him leading the medical squad. But he was damaged, and that didn't play well with the higher-ups. Tiner finished his potatoes and looked at Garnet's untouched ones. "You gonna eat those?" Garnet shoved the side dish toward him, and Tiner dug in. "All I gotta say is, he better leave my girl alone." He peered over the bowl of potatoes he brought up to his face to finish. "I'm saving her for you when you grow up." Garnet stared back at him. "Unless someone better comes along in the meantime."

"Last time I let you finish my dinner," Garnet said, looking at his chrono. Tiner knew it was getting late, and both men needed to be up early the next morning. Unfortunately, there was no time for dessert. Garnet signaled again for the waitress. "The check, please." He stood up from the table, removed his wallet, and handed her the money.

"You still owe me dessert." Tiner smiled as he stood. Garnet nodded. The two men walked out onto the parking lot. Tiner looked out over the assembled vehicles. "Where's your company ride, I thought you were staying on base?"

Garnet moved to where his jet-cycle was parked and picked up his helmet. "I'm staying at my place until we leave."

"That's strange." Both he and Garnet always stayed in base housing right before deployment; it got them in the mood for the mission.

Garnet straddled his ride and started to slowly back out. Tiner followed. "I must be cursed, but lots of strange things have been happening on base, and I think I'm safer sleeping in my own bed."

"Never figured you for the paranoid type." Tiner put a hand on his shoulder. "Oh." Tiner shook his head. "No wonder you didn't want to meet my friend. You got some hottie stashed away and want to spend your last few days—"

Garnet grasped Tiner's arm, his face more serious. "I think I'm being pranked. Not just one and done, this seems to be an escalating parade of inconveniences, annoyances, and downright pains in the—"

Tiner cut him off midsentence. "Who'd you piss off?"

"That's just it." Garnet revved the engine. "I don't know, or I'd string up the bastard."

"A few simple pranks got you all wound up!" he shouted over the roar of the cycle.

Garnet cut the engine, placed both feet back on the ground to balance the bike. "How'd you like to find your duty boots delaced or your uniform pants three sizes too small or your shaver with a dull blade?" He put a gloved hand to the side of his face, moved some of his sideburn to reveal a friction mark.

Tiner pretended to examine the scar on his face, "That all?" and then patted his cheek.

Garnet shook off Tiner's hand. "No, that isn't all." Tiner noticed the veins in his neck begin to bulge.

Wow, someone really is getting to him.

"Try answering incessant comm pages that go nowhere to unavailable, busy, or unknown people." Garnet balled his hand into a fist. "This joker trashed my duty locker and screwed with my gear." Tiner knew how much of a perfectionist his buddy was, and this must really be testing his focus. No one messes with another guy's gear and lives to tell about it. "Wait until I track down this clown. He'll be sorry he messed with me."

Tiner felt for his friend. Pranks were commonplace among bunkmates, but usually they were meant to break up the tension and weren't a slow, systematic torture. Garnet's problem seemed to be more personally directed. Tiner leaned back on his heels. "And that, my friend, is why you need a new girl. Someone to keep you distracted, and somewhere to dissipate all that pent-up emotion."

Garnet relaxed his fist and grabbed the throttle again. "Right about now, I need some peace and quiet." He revved the engine again. "No one to worry about but myself." He leaned the cycle to the side and put his foot on the stirrup. "What I need to do is get focused so I can be ready for this mission."

Tiner put out a hand. "Thanks for dinner. Next one's on me."

Garnet shook his hand. "Great to see you too." Garnet backed the cycle out farther. "See you on Pareq in six weeks." He put down the visor on his helmet.

"That should be enough time for you to decide on our next watering hole." Tiner watched as Garnet peeled out of the parking lot, the wheels screeching on the ground, leaving tire marks. *Old school,* thought Tiner. It was good to feel the road underneath you. It reminded him of the path he had taken. The new hover vehicles took all the excitement out of travel. He figured Garnet would really open the bike up to try and work out some of his frustration. A good long ride with no interruptions, just a few bumps here and there. He thought again of Emmie. Pity there were so many detours and stoppages on their road.

Tiner missed serving side-by-side with Garnet in Defender Company. He watched this young man advance quickly through the ranks, a model soldier, a reluctant hero, and now a premier squad leader and a valuable friend. It was certainly ironic that when they first met, Tiner was dragging an injured Garnet from under a pile of rubble, and when they had parted ways in Defender Company, Garnet was dragging a shattered Tiner to safety. They'd come full circle. Some of Tiner's trainees could take a page from Garnet's book.

Like himself, Tiner knew how truly lonely Garnet was, although would never admit it. Except when having to answer questions about his pro-athlete brother, Kyle, Garnet never discussed his family, and that worried Tiner. Recognizing this, Tiner took Garnet under his wing early on, and the two men became like brothers. Family was an important stabilizing influence in a soldier's life. In fact, for some, their unit mates became the only family that really mattered.

Maybe Garnet was right; maybe he wasn't ready for a new love yet. Leba Brader was different, and Tiner didn't want this relationship to go the way of Garnet's last one or even the last several. There'd be time for this later on when things settled down.

CHAPTER 9

Tiner surveyed the classroom. They were still so green, never having tasted the horrors of combat. He could only teach them so much, hoping some of his lessons sunk in. "Well, well, well, my young charges," Tiner began in a slow drawl. "Seems we've completed our time together, and at least most of you are still standing." Reality was the majority would probably wash out during their second phase of training. They wouldn't be able to form cohesive bonds with their team members or able to take orders without question or able to deal with stressful, uncontrollable situations. "Good luck at your next post, and try to remember at least a few of the things I've taught you." He dismissed the class for the final time.

"Dr. Brader," he beckoned her with a crooked finger. "If I may have a moment." Leba turned to face him. A wide-toothed grin adorned his face as he massaged his bald head and came around the podium to sit on the edge of the table. "I wanted to let you know you won't be able to get rid of me that easily. I plan to haunt you during your next six weeks." Leba tried to contain a smile, but the corners of her mouth upturned and betrayed her delight. Tiner stretched his arms out. "This old dog's been reassigned to your deployment."

Leba leaned forward and whispered, "I kind of figured you might say that." Tiner pulled at his collar. "Otherwise, you wouldn't be so interested in the cold."

Tiner squeezed his chin with his hand and grinned. "He said you'd know. Son of a—"

Leba adjusted her backpack on her shoulder and slightly inclined her head. "Who said I'd know?"

Tiner slapped his thigh and, shaking his head said, "No one. I was just talking to myself." He pushed himself up from the table and put a hand on her shoulder, drawing her slightly in. "Anyway," he dipped his head and in hushed tones continued. "You and I need to talk about the next six weeks. Our squad leader for this mission is a real piece of work." His slid his arm up and across her shoulder. "One Luth Cathen, a righteous, power-hungry mongrel, and you'll need to watch your step."

Frowning, she turned in his grip. "What happened to never question orders?"

"I neglected to tell you Tiner's first amendment to that rule." Leba inclined her head more, her ear positioned in front of his mouth. "If the commander is a jerk, think before you react." He straightened up, shoulders back and chest out. "Follow my lead." He pushed her forward and, with a hand on the top of her head, said, "Keep your head down, or he's likely to get us all killed."

Leba hesitated then nodded in agreement. "You're the boss."

I wish every woman felt that way about me.

Tiner could tell Leba was conflicted about his attitude toward their new squad leader. He knew she would form her own opinions, but it never hurt to give fair warning. She grabbed his hand and pulled him. "Come on, I'll buy you lunch."

After a weekend of moving into the med unit's quarters and readjusting to another list of idiosyncratic preferences from the military hierarchy, Leba was ready to get to the task of specifically preparing for her deployment. Despite DeShay's warnings, she would give Luth Cathen, her new squad leader, a chance. Their unit would employ three docs, each responsible for a rotating shift. Besides herself, there was JT Hobes, whom she already knew from her med clinic, and Gordie Rensen, a career military doctor, whose arrival at the training complex was imminent.

DeShay surprised her by inviting her to dinner to meet his friends and fellow veteran med techs Mevid Anster and Pola Grizzer.

A CHANGE IN TACTICS: MAIDEN VOYAGE

Medvid Anster wore a thick angular mustache, almost brush-like, with a smaller patch beneath his lower lip and a tightly groomed patch on his chin. His slick black hair was pulled back into a tight short tail and fastened with an elastic band. Pola Grizzer's thin mustache got lost over a wide mouth that sported an endless supply of large teeth. His face was flatter and his nose more slender than his partner. Although black and sleek, his thick hair was cut short. The sun servicing their homeworld resulted in their ruddy complexions. They were both smaller than DeShay with shorter and stouter legs but upper bodies and torsos as well developed.

The camaraderie among the three men was evident. The tribal bond between Anster and Grizzer extended to DeShay. Not of their home world, their reverence for the older man was evident. Both were trained medics, their battlefield experience honed during their planet's civil war. After repatriation, DeShay convinced them to join the Tal-Kari and put their skills to use on a more universal level. Despite the fact they served in the medical corps, they ended up on the losing side as members of the rebellion and were treated as outcasts.

Concurring with DeShay's assessment of Luth Cathen, Anster and Grizzer regaled her with stories of his exploits throughout the entire meal. "If he's that bad, why hadn't someone put a grenade in his bunk a long time ago?" Leba asked.

"Rumors and legendary stories, that's where that kinda stuff happens." DeShay's lip curled into a devious smile.

"We never considered doing that. But now that you mentioned it, it doesn't sound like such a bad idea." Anster tapped the side of his head, his ceremonial body art a tour de force down his arm.

"Hey, Tiner, I think she'll fit right in," Grizzer agreed, flashing Leba a wide, toothy smile. The tattoos on his neck also beliefing his warrior clan. Working with them would be fun. Despite being the newbie, she already felt like part of the team. Leba wondered what initiation she'd need to go through to rise above mascot status.

"Roll call," Squad Leader Luth Cathen ordered. Cathen was tall, not exceedingly so, but he stood so straight he gained an inch or two. Remembering what DeShay said about the pole constantly up Cathen's ass, Leba imagined he'd need to stand straight to stay out of pain. Stifling her amusement, she continued working from his head to his toes. DeShay neglected to mention the perfectly coiffed bleached-blond spiked hair or his sharp and intimidating eyes. He also forgot about the well-developed shoulders bearing gold epaulets or the chiseled chest, under his jacket, highlighting rows of military honors. Standard-issued tactical footwear was obviously not appropriate for his tender feet. The upgraded, "see your reflection better than a mirror" permanent shine, "drop a whole month's pay" luxury boots finished his ensemble. No wonder he got what he wanted. Leba hoped he paid his tailor triple for the look.

Cathen began by counting heads. "Thirty-three, thirty-four, thirty-five, thirty…" It felt like lower school all over again. He snarled, his eyes dissecting the masses. "Who's not—" Suddenly, the door to the med unit's classroom flew open.

Cringing in anticipation of the door bang and momentarily closing one eye, Dr. JT Hobes sauntered in. "Sorry I'm late." He put a hand up—"Thirty-six"—and took a seat in the back row.

Typical JT, late as usual. Dr. JT Hobes was Leba's good friend and colleague from the med clinic. Cathen was vid-star material, but JT was boy-next-door, "wish we'd not started out as friends" good-looking. Lighting up a room was his specialty. He was fun but knew when to be serious. No one could question his doctoring skills. Being in his company always made you feel better, and he seemed to bring a smile to everyone's face. He had a way about him, making everyone feel special. Things never changed as mischievousness did not elude him, making Leba wonder how much Hobes and Cathen would butt heads. Turning to face front and noticing the grim expression on Cathen's face, she got her answer.

"That'll be twenty push-ups, soldier," Cathen said, hands on hips.

"Calm down, Luth." With a big smile on his face, JT said, "Just because you're the squad leader doesn't mean you can push me around." Leaning back in his chair, arms splayed wide, his hands interlaced behind his head. "I think I outrank you anyway." There were giggles from some of the nurses and medical assistants seated in the room.

Leaning forward at an almost perfect angle in order to maintain his straight-lined posture and prevent internal injury, Cathen glared at him. "I don't need any screwups in this unit, Hobes."

Looking side to side, smiling at the adoring crowd, JT answered, "Don't see any...sir." JT let his front chair legs hit the floor with a muffled bang. Now sitting up straight, folding his hands on his desk as if he were in grade school, he inclined his head to the side. "Anyway, don't let me interrupt your flow." JT waited for a response as Cathen fumed. "Tell you what, Squad Leader, if it's all right with you, we can take this up after class."

"You better believe we will. Now shut up and pay attention." Cathen shifted his gaze, his eyes locking in on anyone staring at him. Quickly averting her eyes downward to look at her note taker tablet, Leba twiddled her stylus.

"Yes, sir," JT answered. That was JT too, always able to get in the last word. It was hard not to like JT; he was a fun guy. Always happy, always smiling, always in the thick of it. It didn't hurt he was young, handsome, and engaging. Young women flocked to him, but he only yearned for Nilsa. Leba wondered if Cathen knew that was a fact he could exploit. She should warn JT about the possibility, imagining JT wouldn't hold back when it came to Nilsa. Like an animal mating for life, JT would probably do just about anything to protect his status as the dominant male of the pride and the sole owner of the lioness's attention.

Cathen rapped on the podium, startling everyone to attention. "I see here where some of you have never been on an off-planet deployment. Let me set you straight, this will be no picnic. There will be many dangers, many unknowns. It will require hard work and long hours and minimal distractions if you expect to survive."

DeShay stretched his arms over his head and yawned loudly. "You have something to say, Master Priman Tiner?" Cathen tugged hard at his squad leader's jacket. Leba could have sworn she heard DeShay utter a similar sentiment at the beginning of basic.

"No, sir," DeShay said in his most condescending voice.

"Good," retorted Cathen, "then I'll continue." As if choreographed, Anster then Grizzer yawned as well. This stunt, staged over dinner last night, annoyed Cathen. Thank goodness she declined to participate and was glad her new friends didn't begrudge her for it. She knew they were loyal to a fault, their sense of duty and commitment foremost in their daily lives. That didn't mean they were opposed to pranking one another or even their superior officer. Leba wasn't ready to get detention on the first day. Labeling her "newbie," the trio promised her she would join them soon enough. The rest of the morning session went on the same way, with Cathen giving them a long list of things they were required to know prior to the mission.

He, Luth Cathen, personally secured some of the best experts in the field to teach his recruits, his people, all they needed to know to survive on this deployment. Thumbing through the list of guest speakers, Leba was fascinated as to who considered themselves experts in hypothermic exposure, medicine, and warfare. Spending countless hours researching and studying up on the subject, Leba thought she knew who was who. Unfortunately, those names didn't match Cathen's. This frightened her. Could she, a "newbie," contradict an "expert?"

What didn't frighten her was the conditioning and exercise schedule Cathen planned out for them. Compared to Esre's workouts, these were nothing. After four hours of listening to Cathen ramble on, Leba was ready for lunch, even if it was just a protein bar and a caffeinated drink. JT invited her to join him for lunch off base, but she begged off. Leba was sure they wouldn't be back in time, and she didn't want Lord Cathen, as she dubbed him, upset with her on day one. "Suit yourself," JT said. "Don't get so hung up on trying to please Cathen."

DeShay and the other two medics bolted from the classroom as soon as Cathen dismissed them. It was good anyway; Leba didn't want to turn down a lunch offer from those guys either. Only Gordie Rensen remained. "Excuse me, Dr. Rensen," Leba said, walking over to the older man. Gordie looked up at her over his glasses. "I don't think we've met," she said, putting out a hand. "I'm Leba Brader."

Wiping his hand first on his pants then stretched it out to shake hers. "Welcome, nice to meet you." Gordie dug back into his bagged lunch. "I look forward to discussing cold weather medicine with you. DeShay already told me who the real expert is."

"I don't know that I'm an expert, but…" Leba stood in front of his desk.

"If DeShay says you are, then you are," Gordie said. "Here, sit." He pointed to the chair next to him. "Let me let you in on a little secret." After taking the seat, Leba leaned toward him to listen better. Gray hair crept along his temples and made inroads into his formerly black hair. He had a fatherly smell, a hint of standard-issue military aftershave and good old-fashioned soap. "I've been on a lot of these deployments." The snow on his mountain revealed his years of experience, something Leba didn't have. Sure she'd been practicing for some time and had seen at lot of pathology, but there was no substitute for field experience. "I always been impressed with the skills and knowledge of the medics I've worked with. More than some of the doctors I've served with. Tiner, Anster, and Grizzer are the best crew I've had the privilege to serve with."

He continued, "I know you're new and don't want to make waves, but if you disagree with something one of Cathen's experts puts out to us, you need to speak up. If I have your back, you'd better have mine. What I don't know could kill you or one of our troop mates." He waited so Leba could digest what he said and then continued, "It's all in how you disagree." He took a bite of his food then a long drink. "My wife really knows how to make a good sandwich." Staring at the meat-stuffed monster, he finished it in two more bites.

His wife's cooking seemed to agree with him as it settled along his lower abdomen and hips. His obesity kept the wrinkles at bay, and his wide-rimmed glasses hid the bags under his eyes. Seemingly an excellent judge of character, Gordie's assessment of Cathen seemed spot on. This was someone Leba could learn from. The fact he had a life outside of medicine, a wife and children, gave her hope one day she could juggle both as well.

"You don't want to be like Hobes either." He paused. "He gets away with it because he's such an entertaining guy, and Cathen sees him as a rival. Cathen gives him a pass so as not to anger the rest of the flock. My guess is Cathen probably wouldn't give you as much space. Your big advantage over Cathen is he'll underestimate you. Use that knowledge to keep yourself ahead in the fight."

Leba finished her protein bar and sipped her drink. "Thanks, Dr. Rensen."

"You can call me Gordie," he instructed. "Oh, and one other thing. Hobes was wrong." She looked at him quizzically. "In this unit, Cathen does outrank Hobes, and if he chooses to push the point, he could technically make him do push-ups. If Cathen thinks Hobes is insubordinate, he could theoretically get him bounced." She considered his statement. "All I'm saying is, don't push Cathen too far unless you're sure it's worth it."

By the time Leba finished her conversation with Dr. Rensen, there was just enough time to go to the lavatory and get back to her seat. JT actually made it back on time, as did the rest of the class. Cathen again took his place at the podium, rapping to get everyone's undivided attention. The afternoon session was different from the morning one, as Cathen sent them to get fitted for their squad uniforms. The men went one way, and Leba and the rest of the women went another. They were all back in an hour, now in the gymnasium and dressed for workouts. Cathen ran them through the usual calisthenic warm-ups, isotonic and isometric weight work, and finally interval exercises to keep their heart rates up and their muscles confused between slow-twitch and fast-twitch activation.

Cathen promised to mix things up over the coming weeks. Sometimes class work first and strength and conditioning second and other times the reverse. Leba noticed about halfway through the proposed schedule two words: *cold box*. Cathen didn't offer any explanation and glanced over it when he was reviewing the details of their six-week course. Sure DeShay would know, Leba made note to ask him when class was over for the day.

After exercise, still sweaty and dirty, they were required to return to the classroom for Cathen's final thoughts. When someone asked about a shower, he told them they could when they got home. Wasting valuable time waiting for everyone to clean up was pointless. Leba figured on days when working out preceded class, she would use her lunchtime to clean up. She hoped everyone else came up with a similar idea. Although she could imagine DeShay and his buddies not showering just to make Lord Cathen crazy.

"I will see you all back here tomorrow morning, not at the leisurely time of 0800 like today but at 0600." With that parting instruction, Lord Cathen left the room. Leba heard the grumbling among her unit mates. But 0600 was nothing for her. Thinking 0800 was a late start, this morning before class, she did busywork to pass the time.

"Son of a…" Gordie Rensen began as he worked his way from behind his desk. "That's a real pisser. I won't get to see my kids before I have to leave in the morning." Flinging his gear over his shoulder, Gordie strode angrily from the room.

DeShay remained too, chatting with one nurse. This woman's smooth, beautiful skin and large brown eyes could have fit just as well on someone half her age. Usually, DeShay would have acknowledged when Leba approached, but he and the woman seemed lost in their own little world. For a moment, Leba just stood and watched the two interact. There seemed to be a history here, and maybe history to be made. She cleared her throat.

Fumbling for an explanation was not DeShay's style. So he did have a weakness. "Let me introduce you." He smiled wide. Touching the woman's arm, he said, "Emmie, this is Dr. Leba Brader."

"Pleased to meet you, ma'am." Leba extended a hand.

"Emmie." The woman smiled and put out her hand. "Emmie Hodd."

"Emmie is our head nurse for this deployment. One of the best." DeShay beamed.

"Shut up, you old war dog," Nurse Hodd advised DeShay. Leba noticed the glint in his eye but pretended not to notice as Emmie jabbed at him. "I'd better be off to check on my nurses, make sure they all get tucked in." DeShay grinned. "And before you ask, I don't need any help tucking them in." Leba watched as Emmie went from poking his arm to tracing a lazy line down to his wrist. Her tongue gently resting on the underside of her top lip, Emmie mouthed, "Later." DeShay shivered and then sucked in a deep breath.

As his gaze lingered on the exiting nurse, DeShay said, "Did you want to ask me something?"

"Yes. What's 'cold box?'"

"Oh, that," DeShay said, dragging his eyes off the doorway as Emmie passed beyond his vision. Turning toward Leba, he smiled mischievously. "We get locked up in a giant freezer, half-naked, no gear, and have to survive."

"Sounds fun."

"Depends on who you're locked up with," DeShay explained. "Now if I get paired up with Nurse Hodd"—his eyebrows lifted, and his head cocked—"we could generate our own heat." Stopping suddenly, DeShay Tiner was at a loss for words. Leba thought he blushed, but she feigned naivety. "Back on topic," DeShay quickly remarked. "The key to the whole situation is teamwork."

"Our whole group gets locked in together?" Leba asked.

"No," DeShay said. "Different-sized groups go in depending on Cathen's whim. If he really doesn't like you, you either get minimal partner help, added obstacles, or he sends you in already fatigued. If Cathen can't get someone bounced off his team one way, this is the other way."

"So if I were JT, I'd watch my step," Leba reasoned.

"Naw, girl," DeShay corrected. "Cathen likes having Hobes around, gives him someone to compete with, someone to try to humiliate, someone he can show the team he can boss around. If Cathen got Hobes bounced, he couldn't show off as much."

"I thought I left this stuff back in the academy playground." Leba laughed.

"Not even close," DeShay said, shaking his head, then rubbed his hand across the regrowth on the top of his balding head. "In fact, if Cathen saw us talking, he'd ride you for fraternizing with the help."

Leba leaned in and, with hushed tones, asked, "And what does Nurse Hodd think about us fraternizing?"

"I'm hoping it gets her thinking a lot of things." Grinning, he put a hand across Leba's back and squeezed her shoulder. "Then maybe she won't be so inclined to call me an old war dog."

Looking at her chrono, the hour was late, and there was a lot of studying to do. "I guess I'd better be going, big day again tomorrow."

"We're doing dinner again, me, Anster, and Grizzer, want to join us? I'm sure they wouldn't mind," DeShay offered.

"Thanks, but not tonight." She put a hand to his cheek and patted his face. "Don't want to have Nurse Hodd hating me for monopolizing her man. You guys go enjoy yourselves, and I'll see you bright and early tomorrow morning."

Leba left through the same door Nurse Hodd did. Despite what he bragged to Garnet, Leba Brader was not for him. DeShay looked after her but in a different, almost big brotherly way. Sometime during this six-week rotation, he knew she'd get hurt, either her pride or her feelings. He only hoped she'd deal with it and move on. In the past under Cathen's rule, he saw some good people quit.

DeShay recalled an image of a much younger Emmie Hodd. At first, he pushed the thought of reconnecting with her from his mind and then reconsidered. A big smile came to his face as he left the room. Operation Emmie Hodd was a go. He headed out to meet up with his mates and celebrate his revelation.

CHAPTER 10

It was fairly late when Leba got back to her quarters. The mess hall was finishing dinner service, and if she hurried, she could probably still get something. She settled for soup. It was thick and hot, filled with decent-sized chunks of meat and fresh vegetables. The taste surprised her, well seasoned and anything but stale. Base food had a reputation for being average at best, but this was a welcome treat.

New to this facility, Leba didn't know enough people to be social but tried to at least smile or say hi to everyone she met. Sitting by herself at a far table, she remembered her self-defense instructor's words about being alone. Be a hard target. Watch who came and went, know where the exits were, what positions were defensible, and find things that might serve as weapons. Not putting yourself in a vulnerable position was the best way to avoid confrontation. She hated constantly looking over her shoulder. Not that this room was a hotbed of enemy activity or even a place to fear, but good habits, if consistently practiced, were available in times of stress. Even more so after her conversation with Gordie, she was comforted a veteran like DeShay Tiner was at her back. Better still was he adopted her as his pet project, protégé, or little sister. Leba felt sure DeShay would always be there for her.

The next day's curriculum was the opposite of the first day's. Their unit began with exercise and conditioning, concluding with lecture material and a sermon from her squad leader on the merits of teamwork and getting to know one another. To demonstrate his points, Lord Cathen decided instead of having the evening off, they would all report later for a "bonding session." Leba could imagine everyone sitting around a holographic campfire, telling their most intimate secrets. Maybe everyone could bring something for show-and-tell. In keeping with the theme, they could go on a scavenger hunt around the base, each responsible for a different item. She was sure it was not going to be that easy.

When everyone returned for the evening session, Cathen strode in last with a big grin on his face. "Here's how it works, people." His chin jutting out almost as far as his chest. "I give you a task or exercise or question, and for every mistake one of you makes, the whole unit gets punished. So you either help each other out or appoint someone to do the task or suffer the consequences." This brought back memories of Leba's first class with Dieuvoxyl and the beating they all took from Azymie.

Olive skinned with an oval-shaped face and expressive large eyes, Mally Yertha made Luth Cathen stop and take an extended notice. Impeccably braided in thick rows, her hair was deep, dark black. Delicate features complemented her petite frame, although she was not without curves. He was quick to survey the landscape, focusing in on what pleased him the most. And despite the restraint of her endowment behind a tightly cinched bodice, it appeared Cathen found what he liked.

"Are you part of this, Squad Leader?" Her voice lilted with a slightly exotic twang, her words delivered in perfect diction, the product of constant drilling at only the finest of finishing schools.

Pushing his shoulders back and puffing out his chest, Cathen leered at the young nurse. Leba recognized the lean and hungry look, the one she never seemed to get. The one warning you off but too exciting to ignore.

"What she means," JT Hobes quickly interjected, "if we are unable to perform a task, can we ask our esteemed leader to assist us?"

Cathen gazed at Hobes, apparently trying to decide on the appropriate response. What was JT thinking? Going out of his way to antagonize a rival was not his typical style. JT was usually more subtle, more plotting, more devious. Maybe he really didn't want to be assigned to this deployment. His relationship with Nilsa was a bud ready to flourish, and the time away from her would seriously affect its blossoming. After a successful launch, she didn't want to see JT burn up on reentry. With growing uneasiness, Leba watched the interaction. Cathen turned to face the attractive young lady. "If Nurse Yertha needs my help, I would be more than happy to assist." Lowering his eyes to meet hers, he said, "I am, after all, here to set the example for my squad. All she needs to do is ask." Mally Yertha beamed as if her whole being was lit by Cathen's notice. Cathen's grin widened into a sneering smile. Not only did Cathen get the desired response from the lamb, but he roasted Hobes in the process.

Am I the only one who thinks this juvenile display is embarrassing? DeShay's expression of disgust confirmed her suspicions; he too seemed none too impressed with the preening of his male colleagues. By the end of the session, Leba didn't experience any significant "bonding" but did have a better idea of what skills and motivations certain people brought. She also was beginning to decide whom she could count on and whom she could not. Teams were very important to Leba. Doubtful this group could ever function as a real team, Leba knew how they worked and how to lead them. There were parts here that worked and parts that didn't. Although she knew any group could be forged into a cohesive unit, she doubted Cathen could pull it off. DeShay, on the other hand, could have this unit working as one in no time. Unfortunately, Cathen never considered tapping DeShay for his leadership. A good commander would have appointed DeShay as his second and let him carry the burden of aligning the unit to the desired specs.

When she finally reached her quarters, Leba was exhausted. Maybe a shower would wake her up so she could do more reading on cryo-organisms. No, that didn't help. Making a simple dinner, she turned on the vid as she had no desire to concentrate on anything intellectual or associated with this mission. The Wildwings Dologos game was in the final period, and she was satisfied to see grown men run up and down the field in pursuit of the opposition's flag. Pulling her rally cap over her still-wet hair, she promptly fell asleep.

Startled by her alarm going off in the next room, she remembered she was still on the couch. After deactivating the vid screen, she tried to get into her early morning routine, but her couch-sore muscles refused to cooperate. Flipping through the pages of her curriculum binder, lecture first today, good, so no workouts until after lunch. That would give her time to work out the kinks. Fixing a pot of Professor Othra's special tea and adding just enough of the yellow syrup, Leba was able to at least stretch before having to leave. Unfortunately, it didn't leave much time for a decent breakfast. Along with a water bottle and her note taker, she threw in a couple extra protein bars and fastened the closure of her backpack.

Usually the first to arrive, Leba took her seat in the front row and watched DeShay and Emmie Hodd arrive together just before class. They looked comfortable together, more so than casual friends. It was really none of her business, but she was curious and maybe a little jealous as DeShay spent most of his class time partnered with Emmie.

With Cathen reviewing unit protocols, supply and inventory, rotation schedules, and chain of command, morning lecture was relatively banal. He reviewed code designations for the various emergencies they would undoubtedly face. Although she could only remember a few times when some were enacted, Leba was used to this preparedness. Medical codes for cardiac or respiratory arrests were not unusual, but codes for thermonuclear bombardment were generally unheard of. There were codes for every type of radiation exposure, for every conceivable threat, for just about everything. What was true though, even in a cardiopulmonary arrest, your instincts kicked in, and you ran on adrenaline. One of your biggest jobs as code leader was to designate personnel for specific jobs and get the rest to clear from the scene. Your voice boomed above the rest and was the one voice everyone responded to.

Cathen went through the list of those who were the most expendable, starting with the civilians then the paraprofessionals to the professionals to the officers. He really didn't say it that bluntly, but the meaning was clear. Leba was trained to save those that could be saved first. The essence of the triage philosophy. Injured having a chance to survive received top priority. To expend resources on someone with insurmountable injuries was foolhardy, and keeping them comfortable became the objective. She was beginning to despise Cathen's approach despite her best attempts to understand him. Everyone had a different approach, but this was not going to work. DeShay worked with this guy before. How did he do it without hauling off and slugging him?

She couldn't help herself, and it was too late when she noticed her arm was somehow raised in a question. DeShay glanced at her and subtly shook his head no.

"Ms. Brader, I believe," Cathen said smugly. "How would you do it differently?"

Trying to get her confidence up, she said, "Well, sir," she began, "I would set up three teams each headed by a physician, nurse, and medic." Adding quickly, "All under your command, of course, sir." She paused and continued, "That way, each team would be led by people who understand the total picture, who could offer suggestions based on their specific expertise. Decisions would be made by triad, so no one person would have total power." She waited and then finished, "Excluding, of course, you, sir."

"Interesting concept," he mused. "Not applicable in this circumstance." Totally dismissing her thoughts, he didn't even have the courtesy to explain his reasoning. DeShay glared at her. She knew better than to take her argument any further. Disappointed no one chimed in to support her position, when lunchtime came around, Leba didn't linger to chat with anyone but made her way back to her quarters to dress for the afternoon workouts.

"This afternoon, we are going to do things differently." Cathen stared at Leba. She got his meaning loud and clear. She questioned the way he did things, so as punishment, the squad would be doing things *differently*. After the usual cardio work and free weight routine, Cathen decided some "friendly sparring" was in order. He wanted to see what everyone brought to the table. Cathen laid out the ground rules, two minutes of sparring, using any technique, but limiting the effort to 30 percent and above-the-waist targets only.

"Partner up," he advised. As people paired off, Cathen went around and repartnered certain groups. Leba noticed the special attention he gave to Mally Yertha and her pretty young partner, whose name Leba could not remember. He let them go first. They slapped at each other and giggled. Leba saw the disgusted look on Emmie Hodd's face, obviously embarrassed at the juvenile display she witnessed. After class, Emmie Hodd would certainly have words for her two silly charges.

When it was DeShay's turn, Cathen advised his partner, "Go easy on the old guy, his shoulder's pretty busted up." DeShay sneered at him but let it pass. For a guy with a bum shoulder, DeShay more than held his own, although he was breathing a little heavy at the end of the match.

Cathen knew better than to match Hobes with a decent partner. He'd rather see Hobes holding his punches than shining against a stout young orderly. Leba, on the other hand, did get matched with a stout young orderly whom Cathen counseled to go easy on the girl. Duly insulted by Cathen's questioning her skills, Leba was more than ready to take on any opponent.

When the match started, the orderly began tentatively, and Leba was able to quickly penetrate his defenses not with brute force but with agility. Pummeled by strike after strike, the man got sloppier and couldn't maintain his defenses. Leba waited before moving in. After another of his jabs was blocked, the orderly, frustrated with her ability to bypass his protection, kneed her hard. Not 30 percent, not 50 percent, but 100 percent. Gasping as the shock of the blow caught her off guard and sent her backward, reeling in pain, Leba tried to shake it off, but the pain continued. A grossly unfair strike, but it still took agonizing seconds until Cathen came over to officially stop the contest. Maintaining her defensive posture even while on the ground, with Cathen staring down at her, she protested through gritted teeth, "I'm fine."

"You sure you want to continue?" Cathen asked.

Deftly she posted on one arm, slid her leg through to the back, and came up in her fighting stance. "Why not," she retorted. "I'm fine. I just need to relearn anatomy." Arms up protecting her face, she stared at his groin. "Please continue." Dropping one hand instinctively to his groin, the orderly looked at her. Leba could hear DeShay's snicker. The rest of the match proceeded without further incident.

When the sparring rounds finished, Cathen dismissed them without further plans for having them return for the day. Leba was angry and stormed out the door, avoiding DeShay, who would probably want to check on her. "Lesson learned again," she chided herself. "Even if I follow the rules, I have to be ready for those who don't." By the next morning, her anger waned, but the purple mark from the knee did not.

Leba decided it was time for a change in tactics. She was not going to be obnoxious and question everything Cathen said, but a few carefully placed queries might throw him off base. She didn't want to incur his wrath, but if done correctly, she would best him without him knowing it until much later. This worked at first, but Cathen was not as oblivious and self-absorbed as she predicted, and by the third inquiry when his ineptitude at answering her showed, his anger became obvious. "No further interruptions," Cathen snarled. "We have a lot of material to cover, and any burning questions can be taken up after class." Leba wasn't the only one to ask questions but hers were the most exposing of his lack of detailed knowledge.

"Ms. Brader," Cathen called to her after the morning class. He refused to call her doctor, which Leba knew was his subtle way of saying, "I don't care if you're a doctor. As far as I'm concerned, you're a girl just like the others." Leba turned and walked back toward Cathen. "Ms. Brader," he began again, "I understand you are a supposed self-taught expert on some of the subjects we will be covering, but I would appreciate it if you would limit your questions. I hadn't planned to get that detailed on some of the subject matter, and some of the other students can barely keep up with the simple information."

"Yes, sir," she responded but refused to apologize. She was just doing what Gordie Rensen told her to do. Cathen dismissed her, and Leba headed out the classroom door to get ready for the afternoon session.

Grinning ear to ear, JT was waiting for her. "Get your hand slapped?"

"Huh?" Leba replied, startled by his presence.

"Just be careful how bad you make him look," JT cautioned.

"I wasn't trying to make him look bad," she countered. "I was just correcting some information, you know, for the good of the team."

"Whatever," JT continued. "Remember, he can hurt you in a lot of different ways." Leba reflected on his words. "You did get paired with Big Ertle for sparring. By all rights, I should've fought the oaf, not you."

Leba looked at him, her stomach clenching. "Don't you think I can handle some overgrown orderly?"

"You miss my point. Cathen didn't want me to look good sparring with the guy. If he beats up on you, then Cathen proves you're not worthy to watch his or anyone else's back. That's payback for your insinuation that his method for teamwork was not as good as yours."

"But mine is correct, supported by every military," she said, voice raised, her body stiffening. She stepped back from JT and crossed her arms over her chest.

"You're still missing my point," JT said, grabbing her by the shoulders. "Let me make it simple for you."

I hate it when you're condescending.

"You're right, he's wrong, but he's in charge. You'd be smarter if you let him come up with your brilliant ideas." JT smiled at her. "You have to let him think it was his idea. Stroke his ego. That's how I get what I want with him."

Leba listened to his words, and her expression softened. "Thanks, JT."

"Uh-oh, I know that look," he said, shaking his head.

"Don't worry," she said, grinning. "I won't do anything you wouldn't do."

"That's what worries me," he conceded.

By the time they parted, Leba had just enough time to get to her quarters, change, and return for the afternoon session at the gym. She'd been avoiding DeShay, and before class, he pulled her aside. "I know what you're going to tell me," she began. "JT lectured me after class. Guess I really screwed up trying to go head-to-head with Lord Cathen."

"See, now you're one of the accursed grunts like the rest of us." DeShay laughed. "Before the princess tries to dethrone the king, she needs to let her knights know the plan." He looked at her. "If you let us in on your schemes to abuse Cathen in class, we could have your back and deflect some of his anger."

"It was not my intention to make him look bad," she said, insulted again. "I don't think it's good for the team if he gives inaccurate information." She stared at him. "Besides, you know what he said was incorrect, and you didn't correct it. Now what does that say about your dedication to the team?" Leba hadn't meant for her statement to come across the way it did.

"You're absolutely right," he said smugly. "Maybe it doesn't matter anymore. Time I watched over myself rather than worrying about you newbies." He hesitated then continued, "Maybe I am getting too old for this nonsense."

Leba tried desperately to regroup. "I'm sorry, I didn't mean for it to come out that way."

His anger seemed softened by her sincerity. DeShay lowered his voice. "There was a time when I would have been up in his face, but it's a battle I'm tired of fighting. You're right, you know, I should have spoken up, but you were on such a roll, I felt comfortable watching the show." He picked her chin off her chest. "If you were going to ask, and I know you were, I am not mad at you. I'm proud my little newbie has grown up." He laughed softly. Leba stifled a tear, sniffled a little, and returned the smile. "Come on, girl, before Lord Cathen wonders what we're up to." He put an arm around her shoulder, and they walked into classroom outside the gym.

Leba went to her seat, and DeShay headed toward his. Unfortunately, she could hear his entire conversation with Emmie Hodd. "And what, pray tell, is up with you? I know that smirk on your face. Break another heart, handsome."

"You know the only heart broken around here is mine when it comes to you," DeShay said with a mischievous glint in his eye. "But I'm sure you could find a way to mend it." This was a side of DeShay she could do without seeing. Acting like a dog in heat. It made Leba uncomfortable. He shouldn't have to beg for Nurse Hodd's attention. She should be glad he's interested in her at all.

"You sweet talker you." She giggled like a young girl. "You know you're more man than one poor girl can handle."

Stop teasing him. Leba would have to have a talk with her about just how lucky she was.

Before DeShay could embarrass himself further, Cathen thankfully shut the door. "Seats, people, we have a lot to do this afternoon." Cathen settled in at the front of the room. "Before we go into the gym, I want to review the equipment we will need to use in the frigid conditions on Vedax." Picking up a heavy case from the floor, Cathen hefted it onto the front table. After removing each item individually, he gave a thorough description of its specifications and uses. From snow boots to parkas, from thermal undergarments to personal body armor, and from helmets with visors to sophisticated fully tactile gloves, Cathen went on and on.

Why give this lecture before gym class? Leba watched as Cathen repacked all the gear. When they entered the gym and found identical simulation suits waiting for them, Leba knew what was next. They were instructed to don the heavy, bulky replicas. All the exercises today would be done in full gear. Kinda like exercising in a flak jacket. *Been there, done that. Thanks, Esre.* Jogging around the room for warm-ups, looking awkward and uncomfortable, the class made countless circuits. Assuring them he didn't need to repeat the exercise since he had practiced in his simulation suit before they had arrived, Cathen did not join them. Leba found it hard to believe Cathen did any prep work. By the time class was over, Leba was finally getting along with her suit. It was no longer weighing her down and obstructing her movements.

The most fun came practicing complicated surgical maneuvers with her gloves on. These weren't like regular medical gloves; they were bulkier and less dexterous. After a while of practicing, she compensated for the differences and was able to perform fine motor skills without difficulty. Motivating them was the fact Cathen promised, "If you dropped an instrument, you would be doing push-ups or jumping squats or crunches." Negative reinforcement went a long way in some cases. It was hard not to laugh at the clumsiness of some of her unit mates, but she bit her tongue so as not to embarrass anyone. JT was not as concerned. His handsome face and big smile made the victims of his teasing melt. It also didn't hurt he would go over and help the pretty young nurses who were struggling. For a guy who was so into his girlfriend, JT flirted with wanton abandon. This irked Cathen, who told JT if he didn't mind his own business and let Cathen do the assisting, he'd make him live in his gear.

For Leba, the evening was uneventful and allowed her to get time in for both reviewing and relaxing. Cold box was only a week and a half away. Although she was confident in her survival skills in the cold, she was unsure about some of her unit mates.

CHAPTER 11

DeShay Tiner sat across the booth from Emmie Hodd. No longer dressed in fatigues, Emmie was a sight to behold. "I'd almost forgotten how well you dress up." *So far, so good.* DeShay was willing to take one more chance, risk being shot down again, to hopefully reconnect with Emmie. Damn, she was wearing those black stilettos, the ones he couldn't resist, and she still could pull it off. It didn't hurt the little black dress completing her ensemble. She was always the most beautiful woman he knew. His conversation with Tiv Garnet drove the point home. He didn't want to end up dying alone. Emmie blushed almost imperceptibly and sipped from her wineglass. DeShay paused, taking a sip from his ale, and continued in a more somber tone, "Whatever happened with us?" Emmie moved the food around on her plate, pretending not to hear his question. "Hey, I'm serious," he started.

She looked up at him, her brown eyes deep and soulful. "We were young then, and the job, it was always the job." She sounded disappointed. Good, so she had regrets too. The moment was interrupted by the waiter coming to the table and inquiring about the meal.

"Regrets?" he asked after the waiter left.

She smiled. "Of course." She hesitated. "This mission, seeing you again, our time together has stirred up some old feelings I thought I put behind me." DeShay grinned, and she continued, "What about you?"

"You know, baby, I've never felt the same about any other woman the way I feel about you." He let his words linger and gently grasped her hands. "I was thinking maybe we should make another go at it." He squeezed her hands. *Okay, it's out there. Now, it's your turn. Don't disappoint again, baby.*

Emmie Hodd inhaled slowly and exhaled even slower. DeShay knew something of her bad marriage. She once confided to DeShay committed relationships were difficult for her. One of a number of lines she stabbed DeShay with when they split the last time. For whatever reason when she finally found the courage to leave her husband and start her life anew, she returned to the military. DeShay was convinced her marriage was tainted because Emmie could not get over him. They were both young and foolish at the outset, and their previous off-and-on relationship was always so emotionally charged. DeShay wasn't sure Emmie wanted to go there again. A reminder of her once carefree and passionate self. Did she really love DeShay, or did she just love the way he made her feel?

"If we rekindle old fires," DeShay took the lead, "it'll be on your terms, at your pace, two people who enjoy each other's company." Finishing his thought, he said, "No analysis, no rules, and no obligations." In a symbolic gesture, he let his grip go on her hands.

"You're serious, aren't you? You, DeShay Tiner, would let me, Emmie Hodd, control the pace, determine the tempo, and set the mood?" she said, inclining her head.

"Why not?" he said. He needed to keep neutral, not let his face betray his needs. "I've been waiting a long time for the right woman to take me for a ride." He laughed and took a forkful of food and ate. The conversation for the remainder of dinner was less intense, and the light banter made for an easy transition. DeShay paid the bill and helped Emmie from the booth. "I guess I'll see you bright and early tomorrow at class."

Emmie smiled at him, slid her hand into his. "I was planning to make you breakfast before class. If that's all right with you?"

"You're in charge, baby, you lead, and I will gladly follow." The pair walked hand in hand out onto the street and into the night.

Leba watched the rest of the class file into the room. DeShay was wearing the same shirt as yesterday. The way he looked at Nurse Hodd was noticeably different. Leba wished someone would look at her with loving and attentive eyes. As Cathen called the session to order, she tried to put it out of her mind. She was glad her friend DeShay was happy, but what would it mean for their relationship?

"You know the drill, people," Cathen started with roll call. Since there were only as many seats as students, and all were filled appropriately, it was a silly exercise. After so many days together, Cathen still treated them like children. "Now that everyone is accounted for, I have an announcement." All eyes faced forward. Usually, Cathen's announcements involved some sort of added work or punishment or chastisement for improper deportment.

"You've obviously noticed cold box is coming up next week. For those of you who don't already know what it is, it's reality. It's a way for me to determine which of you will ultimately make this team and which won't. Let me explain. Next week, you will each enter the cold box as part of one of four teams. The cold box is a simulation designed to recreate conditions you might encounter on this mission. You and your team will be locked in for four days. Your job is not only to survive but also to complete a number of tasks. At any time, you may signal me, and I will remove you from the simulation. You must understand, however, if you leave prior to the designated end time, you will be terminated from your place on this squad. Also inherent in your removal will be the burden you leave on your teammates who must now pick up the slack."

Mally Yertha raised a perfectly manicured hand. "Will you be part of one of our groups?"

"Much as I'd like to join you"—Cathen looked at her directly, as if his comments were only for her—"somebody needs to be here at the base station, monitoring your progress." Mally shook her head in agreement. The disappointment was evident on her face. "I will announce the teams at the beginning of next week, which should give you enough time to decide on strategies and logistics. I expect each team to appoint a leader, someone who is willing to take responsibility for the success or failure of the mission." There were murmurings and side conversations in the room until Cathen called again for order.

The rest of the week proceeded uneventfully as the class listened more intently at the lectures presented on cold weather survival and practiced more diligently at the exercise drills pertaining to balance, climbing, and rappelling. After coming this far, Leba knew no one wanted to go home, dismissed from the mission. For the first time since they arrived at the unit's training facility, Cathen gave them two days off.

"Must have big weekend plans," JT said after hearing Cathen's news. "No other reason he'd give us off." JT continued, his tone sarcastic, "Probably wants to bed Yertha before she flunks out of the box."

Leba didn't understand. "I thought there was no fraternizing within the squad." DeShay and Emmie aside, they were essentially on the same level, but Cathen was their squad leader, and to be with Nurse Yertha was a much bigger no-no.

JT answered, "See, that's where he's found a loophole. We're not officially a squad until the final day of training. If he's doing her before we're official, then he's skirted by the rules."

"Clever, but very stupid." What was DeShay going to do? He and Emmie were in the same squad, and they both would undoubtedly make the team. Yertha wasn't a guarantee.

"True enough," JT agreed. "His biggest problem is how he explains it to her when he has to kick her off the mission."

"What makes you think she won't make it?" Leba questioned.

"She couldn't get paper to burn if she was given a plasma torch and lighter fluid."

"That's pretty harsh." Leba laughed. "I bet on the right team she'd do okay."

"You can have her," JT offered. "I'd take dumb Ertle and his big broad shoulders over Ms. Ditzy any day."

"You have big plans with Nilsa this weekend?"

"You bet." JT beamed. "Taking her to the Grand Octranian for a getaway weekend. In fact, I promised I'd pick her up in an hour," he said, looking at his chrono and realizing how late it was. "Sorry to run," he apologized. "Got to go." JT sprinted down the hall.

A CHANGE IN TACTICS: MAIDEN VOYAGE

The Grand Octranian was only the most expensive, exclusive, elegant resort on their base planet. Foreign, domestic, even alien dignitaries usually occupied their rooms. It was said a single night there would cost you a month's pay. JT was planning something big, or he wouldn't have dropped that much money. Could he have something more in mind? Something needing the proper setting? Something she'd be hard-pressed to refuse? Would he be asking her? Leba would find out soon enough; JT wasn't one to keep things private too long.

As she made her way to her quarters, Leba's musings turned toward DeShay, and she wondered what he planned for the weekend. Usually controlled, DeShay was all giddy and boyish around his lost love. Holding Emmie's chair as she sat down for class. She made his lunch. They spoke in hushed whispers and giggled. *Giggled*—she never imagined applying that word to DeShay Tiner.

Leba missed not having a love of her own, but duty usually came first, and the boys she met were just that, boys, not men. Not men that could handle her. She wasn't beautiful or particularly stylish or even particularly adventurous. Dedicated and smart and decidedly boring, that was what she was. Her mom told her not to despair; she just hadn't found the right boy yet. She assured her young daughter the man for her did exist, and when she was least expecting it, she would find him, or he would find her. Her mother often reminded Leba about how, in the middle of a hostile kingdom, she met Leba's father. Darian Brader was the guard assigned to her mother, who at the time was a prisoner of the prince of the terroristic Etali Empire. The pair escaped with the help of her grand uncle Baal Tosona. The rest, as they say, is history. Her parents did make history, and a lot of it. Now all Leba had to do was find an evil empire.

CHAPTER 12

His weekend bag in his hand, JT Hobes arrived at Nilsa's door. He took in a big breath and exhaled slowly and, with his puffed cheeks fading, activated the door chime and waited. He couldn't get off base fast enough. Nilsa, on the other hand, beautiful and smart as she was, was a disorganized mess, and when it came to deadlines, she generally blew past them without noticing. Although JT told her he'd pick her up at 1700, he didn't intend to leave until 1800 in order to make their 1900 dinner reservation at the Grand Octranian. Rushing her was a mistake he didn't want to make. This weekend needed to be perfect.

Their relationship, which started as a friendship, changed dramatically after her devastating breakup with his friend Tiv Garnet. Endless brooding about her last great love and how hurt she was thrust her into his waiting arms and forced JT to do something extraordinary. Hoping to capture her full attention and make her forget about her pain, JT planned a weekend at the exclusive Grand Octranian resort. Dropping two months' pay, JT opted for all the bells and whistles, from dinners made personally by a gourmet chef, to an in-room sauna and hot tub, to butlered breakfast in bed. Nothing would be spared for his Nilsa. JT liked the way that sounded, his Nilsa. He searched his whole life for a girl, no woman like her, and now she was almost his. Stories of how other men treated her angered him, and he promised never to let her be hurt again. All his sleepless nights, comforting her, being her crutch, devoting himself to her every need, were finally beginning to pay off. This was his last chance to cement his position with her before his deployment. Everything needed to be perfect.

A CHANGE IN TACTICS: MAIDEN VOYAGE

"You've been crying," JT asked as Nilsa came to the door. She turned away. *Uh-oh, what now?* He went over to her, gently turned her face toward his, and removed a strand of hair from her tearstained face. "What happened?" he said. *This better not be another Garnet sighting.*

"I was just thinking how wonderful you are to put up with me." She sniffled.

For once, JT was surprised by her comments. He was expecting to hear another story about how this reminded her of when... but she was finally thinking of him first. Gathering Nilsa up in his arms, he embraced her. "You know how much I care about you." JT, cocky, carefree JT, couldn't believe how he could be so dependent on what she thought about him, them. This must really be love.

With her head nestled securely to his chest, JT looked past her and noticed the half-filled travel bag open on the table. "Can I help you do something?" he asked.

She picked her head up and smiled. "I'm almost ready. I just need a few more things. Do we have time?"

"Of course," JT reassured her. "Tell me what you need and I'll get it for you." Twenty minutes later, Nilsa finally placed the last item in her valise. "Ready?" JT inquired as he picked up his own bag and headed to grab hers. She nodded yes. JT, both cases in hand, led her toward the door.

"You didn't tell me where we're going." Her lips were crimson red, full and moist, and JT found it hard to break away and answer.

Screw the Grand Octranian, let's stay here. For what he was proposing, he knew she'd need more convincing. He'd have to wait and continue with the plan. "Don't worry, sit back, enjoy the ride." He grinned full-toothed. "I figured this is one of our last weekends together before I get deployed, and I wanted to make it very special."

"You're always so thoughtful," she observed. "That's why I love hanging out with you."

Hanging out. JT was hoping it would be more than that. Struggling through hours of listening how the former men in her life treated her and why they couldn't be more considerate like he was brought him to the brink. If this weekend didn't change things, nothing ever would. "I'm so glad we're friends." She blinked her eyes rapidly, the last straggling teardrops dripping down her face. JT needed more from her. This last breakup from his buddy Tiv Garnet was the toughest to date for her to get over. Their relationship still so fresh in her mind. A wound she found hard to stop picking at. It annoyed the hell out of JT.

JT was a friend of Tiv's younger brother, Kyle. The boys attended lower school and academy together. When Kyle went on to pursue a professional sports career and JT enlisted in the military medical corps, the two childhood friends saw less and less of each other. In the day, older brother Tiv was a fairly decent Dologos player, but he didn't have the ambition Kyle did to pursue it as a full-time career. JT was an all right player, but his destiny was to be a physician, like the three generations of Hobes men before him. JT spent a lot of his time growing up playing Dologos on the Garnet's front lawn, so when JT and Tiv both ended up in the military assigned to the same base, it was only natural for the two men to become better acquainted. JT inherently liked Tiv, but after the way he treated Nilsa, he was beginning to rethink their friendship.

JT was fun. Tiv was stiff and serious and always scowling. Never wanting to get into trouble like Kyle and JT did. Tiv was reserved, disciplined, a rule guy, by the book, unwavering. JT couldn't imagine him being anything other than a good soldier. JT never remembered the older Garnet ever smiling. How could he have fun or make any woman happy? How could Nilsa have fallen for him? Nilsa was smart, sweet, and sexy. Maybe it was Garnet's eyes—the beady ones Kyle made fun of but women seemed to dote over. Nilsa liked them, how they were crystal blue and penetrated to her very soul. Why was he jealous of Tiv? He'd never been before. Tiv was a grunt; he was a doctor. What was Nilsa thinking? She was an environmental bioculturist with her own lab and research assistants.

At Nilsa's request, JT tried to discuss with Tiv what occurred between the two. Engaging Tiv in conversation other than about food or Dologos resulted in an uncomfortable silence. Tiv was an extremely private guy, so much so that his distance seemed almost standoffish. Sure, he had friends, JT guessed, and counted him among them, but even so, Tiv was not one to easily open up about his feelings. To hear Tiv tell it, Nilsa was "nothing special," just another girl. One more failed setup from his blood brother DeShay Tiner. Nilsa's markedly different version kept JT by her side many evenings and nights. Unfortunately, she couldn't get over it. The hit to her self-consciousness was overwhelming.

A single meandering road lazily cut a path through the forested mountains. The air was crisp and the trees beginning to shed their leaves. Intercalated waves of green, punctuated by yellows and oranges, finally gave way to deep reds and purples as the transport climbed. Only halfway in and the slope began to descend, finally emerging from the hills, a manicured carpet of vibrant green lawn welcomed the expectant traveler. Surrounded by stalwart trees to its rear, the lapping sea formed almost a moat at the front of the castle-like hotel. The octagonal-shaped turrets, deeply crenellated, stood vigilant like guardsmen around a central building. The main house also boasted eight sides, each with its own complement of rooks. JT imagined a drawbridge lowered and a portcullis raised as they approached. The Grand Octranian did not disappoint.

Nilsa's eyes were as large as saucers. "I can't believe…" she began, the excitement evident in her voice. "You didn't?" she gushed, flinging her arms around his neck. JT basked in the adulation. Ornamental trees lined the final approach as beacons welcoming them.

After the valet removed their bags from the transport, a grand door slowly opened onto a high-ceilinged foyer. Inlaid gold highlighted the classic architecture, and the marble floor resonated with their footsteps. He led them down a winding and secluded hall and opened the door to their suite. The opulence and extravagance of the room was obvious from the moment they crossed the threshold. Every inch of space flowed naturally into the next, the furniture, the decor, the lighting—all designed for maximal luxury and pampering. JT, his arm around her, felt Nisa tremble in his grasp. At least a hundred times on the way up to their room, she expressed her overwhelming happiness. After this weekend, she would be his forever.

The valet handed JT the room key. "Your reservation for dinner is at 1930 in the Castillion Room." He paused. "You will find fresh towels in the lavatory, and I have the great tub heated to a perfect 104 degrees, if you so choose. There is fresh fruit and candies on the table complements of the concierge. I took the liberty of precooling a bottle of Scintilla. Would you like me to open it for you, sir?" JT looked at Nilsa then back to the bellman and nodded.

Nilsa watched the man effortlessly pop the top from the Scintilla bottle. There was a hint of spiced apple and vanilla. After sampling the intoxicant, JT requested he pour two fluted glasses. JT sensed a slight nutty flavor and then a creamy yeasty endnote as he swallowed. The Scintilla was mildly sweet and slightly fizzy as it went down. Perfect. Rewarding the man with a generous tip, JT sent him from the room. Raising his fluted glass, he toasted, "To us, and the start of something wonderful."

Nilsa gathered up her own glass and took a deep swallow. Her face flushed as it warmed her from head to toe. The intoxicant expressing its desired effect, she momentarily swooned, only to land in JT's embrace. JT took the glass from her hand and placed the two flutes on the table. He gathered her up in his arms again and kissed her. This was going to be a great weekend. She returned his kiss, deep and passionate.

JT and Nilsa got up from their seats in the Grand Octranian's theater. He blotted the tears from her eyes. "I love happy endings," she pined. JT could think of a number of happy endings to this evening. He didn't want to rush things. Knowing Nilsa like he did, his best course was to let her determine the pace, with only subtle suggestions to sway her one way or another. He did need to secure his place in her life but was not quite sure when the right time to ask her was. What if she said no? If he asked her tonight and she said no, the rest of the weekend would be a bust, but if she said yes, then the rest of the weekend would be the best. For once in his life, he was at a loss. What was wrong with him? How could he let someone—

But his thought was interrupted.

"Wouldn't it be great if we could come here every year?" Nilsa offered.

"Kinda like our anniversary place." JT cocked his head.

"Yes, exactly," she finished. "You're so wonderful," she said, placing her arms around his neck and kissing him.

DeShay Tiner arrived at Emmie Hodd's quarters, expecting her to be dressed for dinner. "We have reservations, and you're not even—" he stopped, looked at the mess of papers on the table with Emmie still in fatigues seated in front of them. "What are you doing?"

"Going over the list of candidates for my cold box team," she replied and moved a sheet from the center pile to the stack on the left.

"What are you talking about?" DeShay asked, leaning forward to peer over her shoulder.

"Rumor has it Cathen's going to let us pick our own teams."

"Makes it like recess at lower school." DeShay stepped back to lean against the wall. He cocked his left leg back and folded his arms over his chest. "What makes you think you're going to be a team leader?"

"He told me so," she answered.

"You?" he said, realizing his tone wasn't going to earn him any points.

She turned to look at him. The dart she shot stung hard. "Don't think I can do it?"

"No, that's not what I mean," he retorted, bringing his foot down to the floor. Needing to control his anger, he took a breath and asked, "Who else did Lord Cathen tap for command?"

"Don't know." She softened her gaze. She batted her eyes, and slowly, her mouth curled into an exaggerated smile. "Want to be on my team, sweetheart?"

He looked at her. "Not sure that would be a good idea."

"Don't think I'd make a good leader, do you?" she responded with a tone DeShay recognized all too well.

DeShay needed to backpedal and get himself out of trouble fast if he expected this weekend alone with Emmie not to be a bust. "With my shoulder and all, I might slow you down," he conceded.

Her face softened again, and she got up from her seat and went over to him. Gently stroking his face, she kissed him. "Sometimes it's good to go slow." She smiled, wrapping her arms around him, her big brown eyes gazing deeply into his. "Enough shop talk. I want to hear what you have planned for us this weekend."

Maybe there was hope for this relationship after all. DeShay grinned. "Baby, I can't wait to show you."

Small, smoky, and dimly lit, exactly how he remembered it. The floor was sticky under his feet, the sweet remnants of spilled fruit drinks. A single small votive was the only decoration. One table leg was slightly shorter, rocking the flame with every move. The utensils were dulled and nicked, the glasses with water spots. The plates tattooed with knife marks. This was their place. It was all he could afford at that time, and it was here history was made. The club stood the test of time much better than DeShay or Emmie or their relationship did. For DeShay Tiner, it always reminded him of his youth and a younger Emmie, unbridled and in love. Things were so much simpler here.

DeShay and Emmie were finishing their appetizers when a man stepped to the platform at the front of the room. Emmie looked at DeShay. "You didn't, did you?"

"Do what?" DeShay acted surprised. He slid his seat over so they were side-by-side, facing the stage.

The man at the front introduced a four-person ensemble, who began to play live music. "You," Emmie drew the word out. "You remembered."

"Never could forget our first night together," DeShay reminisced. Countless years ago on an evening very much like this, DeShay took a much younger Emmie Hodd to dinner and a live show. There was something about the soulful music playing that struck a chord and melted her heart. By the end of their date, DeShay and Emmie were an inseparable couple.

Never quite figuring out what caused them to drift apart, DeShay never forgave himself for not trying harder to keep them together. Much younger then, not knowing what commitment was, he didn't realize what he was letting go. His future, his legacy, someone to bear his name. This time he would be wiser and less selfish. Hopefully, she would too.

As the band finished their final encore, DeShay twirled Emmie around the dance floor one last time. "You always were such a good dancer," Emmie said.

"It all hinges on having the perfect partner." He grinned and escorted her back to their table.

"It's getting late."

DeShay looked at his chrono. "You're right, time for us old people to be in bed."

She poked him playfully. "Come on." She grabbed his hand. "I'm interested to see what the old man still has left in his tank." *He shoots, he scores.* DeShay grinned and followed her out.

Mally Yertha was overjoyed. She couldn't stop bragging to her best friend about her private lesson that evening with her squad leader. "He took me to the firing range and helped me with my aim, my stance, my trigger pull." She listened; her friend's remark made her feel warm and tingly all over. "Of course, he was a perfect gentleman, how could you say that?" She started laughing again. "No, I think he wants to meet me later for drinks." She waited. "Not in so many words, but you know he said everyone who's anyone will be at Estando's tonight." She listened and then continued, "No, he's not picking me up, didn't want to give anyone the wrong impression." She paused and then replied, "I know it's late, but I'm a big girl, and I can take care of myself. It is on base, you know." She finished the call and set toward her bedroom to find the perfect outfit for the evening.

When Mally got to Estando's, there was standing room only. The place was packed with military and civilians alike. Large overhead fans circulated and recycled the cloying muggy air. Colored lights flashed on and off, glittering off sequined dresses and decorating the lacquered dance floor. There was standing room only at the bar, and the noise was deafening. No piped-in music, but a five-piece band played hard, backing up a wildly gyrating costumed singer. The vibrations alone shook the entire room. Peering around, Mally took it all in. This was the place to be. But where was Luth? Her head swiveled, searching until she was dizzy. Finally she spotted a hand go up and wave her over. Excusing herself, she pushed through the sea of bodies. Cathen was already seated at a booth, and she sidled in next to him. "You look nice," he said. She felt herself blush and thanked him. Cathen introduced the couple on the opposite side of the booth. "Mally Yertha, I'd like you to meet my buddy Damond Fiorat and his lady."

Fiorat stepped in when Cathen couldn't quite remember her name. "Sendra Tohl."

"Nice to meet you," Sendra said, wrapping an arm through Damond's.

After taking a pull from his ale, Damond smiled at Mally. "Luth here never mentioned how you two met."

Mally blushed again and was going to answer when Luth jumped in. "She's a new member of my team and—"

Before he could finish, Mally continued, "Squad Leader here was kind enough to give me some extra help after class, and since I don't know many people, he thought I could make some new friends here."

"Extra help, that is so considerate." Sendra squeezed Damond's arm. "Luth tells me you're a nurse," Damond began. "Sendra runs the base medical clinic."

Mally smiled. "I'm a relatively new grad, but when this assignment came up, I couldn't ignore it. I think it's so exciting to explore new places."

Sendra squeezed Damond's arm again. "You're getting deployed with Luth here, lucky girl."

"Absolutely. Although I'd rather be going someplace warm and sunny, I think it's much better to spend my first deployment in the hands of such an experienced leader."

Sendra thought she was going to puke. Was this girl for real? In the past, she worked with a lot of young grads, and rarely were they this starstruck. Sendra enjoyed watching them preen, trying to impress their male colleagues or supervisors. Despite all the warnings on day one about who to stay away from, most ignored her advice. They wouldn't listen and ended up paying the price of heartbreak or worse. "I bet I know some of the doctors in your unit." Mally rested her head on propped elbows and listened intently. "There's this doc, you might know him, JT Hobes."

Cathen scowled. "I don't know him well. He seems to get into trouble a lot. Right, Squad Leader?" she looked over at Cathen, who rolled his eyes.

"That's just Hobes's nature, the perpetual joker."

Damond took a pull of ale. "Anyone for ordering dinner? I'm getting hungry." As the waitress brought only two menus, one for each couple, Sendra watched as Cathen moved closer to Mally. Mally didn't seem to mind and snuggled closer to him as well.

Not one for taking a hint, Sendra continued to press Mally for information. "I bet you know my best friend, Leba Brader."

Mally smiled. "Yes, she's really smart."

"I taught her everything she knows." Sendra laughed.

Damond laughed. "Thank goodness you didn't teach her everything you know, or she'd be in more trouble than this Hobes fellow." Staring at her date, Sendra's lips curled into a smile, and Damond leaned over and kissed her.

"Get a room," Cathen growled.

Mally put a hand on his. "I think it's sweet."

"Can we please not talk about work, I came out here to relax," Cathen pleaded.

Sendra was not done but decided to change tactics. "I think I'd like to go to the girls' room before dinner comes." Sendra looked at Mally and nodded. Damond moved out of the booth to let her by.

Mally looked over at Cathen. "I'll be right back." She got up from the booth and joined Sendra.

There was a line for the girls' bathroom, giving Sendra a chance to get more details. "How long have you and Luth been dating?"

"We're not really dating yet." Mally blushed. "That is, I think he likes me." She lowered her head, staring at her shuffling feet.

"Likes you," Sendra said, shocked. "Girlfriend, he's really into you. I can see it in the way he looks at you."

"Really?" Mally's head bobbed up.

I bet he offers to take you home tonight, Sendra thought but didn't say out loud. What she did say was "I bet he asks you out for tomorrow."

Mally smiled. "I hope so."

As they exited the bathroom, Mally placed a hand on Sendra's arm. "Thanks."

"No problem, we girls gotta stick together. Now let's get back to the table, don't want to keep our men waiting."

When the girls were far enough away, Damond began, "Pretty hot number, your little nurse."

"Hadn't noticed," Cathen said and took a long pull from his drink.

"Right," Damond said. "She's really into you, or haven't you noticed?" Cathen didn't respond but took another swallow from his bottle. It hit the table with a hollow sound. Empty. "I have to admit, Luth, you do have a way with the ladies."

"Your little friend's not so bad either." Cathen smirked. "How long have you two…?"

"Few months," Damond began. Before he could pump Cathen for more information, the ladies returned to the table.

"Miss us?"

Damond looked at his chrono. "It's getting late, and my transport leaves early tomorrow."

Sendra leered at him. "Guess you'll have to get some sleep on the flight out." Damond smiled.

"Get a room," Cathen advised again.

"Well, if you insist," Damond said, moving Sendra out of the booth and standing up as well. "See you on Pareq in three weeks, Luth," Damond said, outstretching his hand.

Cathen partially stood and shook Damond's hand. "Three weeks, you better have the place clean and ready."

"I don't know how you put up with this guy," Damond addressed Mally.

"He's not so bad," she said, turning to smile at Luth.

Luth Cathen apologized for not being able to stay. Despite Mally's insistence, he begged off. Cathen knew well the fine line he had to maintain. Crossing it once or twice before, he remembered what it was like to get his hand slapped by internal affairs. This time, he would be smarter. It wasn't that Mally wasn't beautiful, young, or willing, because she was all three. There would be a better time and place to take it to the next level. If he played it right, he could have her and not have any worries. What he did worry about was Fiorat's girlfriend, the one that knew Brader. She could really mess things up for him if word got out that he was seen out with one of his recruits. No, he would bide his time. Besides, the longer he put Mally off, the more she would pursue him. Luth liked being chased. He knew how it felt to be in charge, to manipulate, to lure the prey in and then pounce on his conquest. He didn't want to be like Hobes, pining after some woman, being at her beck and call.

Tiv Garnet was tired. He devoted the entire day getting his company ready to deploy to Pareq. As Defender Company squad leader, the responsibility for personnel and equipment fell to him, and he dedicated every second of the last three weeks making sure everything was set. It didn't help he continued to be victimized by a relentless prankster. Prior to the long deployment, to rest his squad, Tiv gave his people the weekend off to be with their families.

He, unfortunately, needed stay on base to deal with any last-minute logistics. That was okay for Tiv, though. He just wanted quiet. Besides the fact, Defender Company was his family, and the majority of them were on leave. Dinner was another boring mess hall meal. Taking a pull from his ale bottle, he plopped down on the couch. Activating the vid remote, the screen illuminated. He flipped through the sat feed guide until he settled on a very old movie. It was parody on the history of the Tal-Kari. For such a proud and meritorious service of which he was an integral part, the director's ability to blend reality with comedy made this movie one of his favorites. There were scenes where he could recite lines of dialogue from memory, and there were pratfalls and jokes that still made him laugh out loud. Neglecting earlier to notify his parents of his impending departure, it was too late when the movie ended. He figured it could wait until morning. Not that his father would care anyway. He didn't want his mother to worry. Not long after, Tiv made his way to his bedroom, pulled the covers over his head, and fell fast asleep.

CHAPTER 13

Very early the next morning, Leba was already asking her parents about what to expect in the cold box. "When I did my survival test," her mother began, "your grand uncle dropped me in the middle of nowhere and said, 'See you in three days.'"

"That must have been loads of fun."

On the extension, Darian Brader laughed. "You should've seen her all dusty and dirty, scraped up and sunburned."

"But I passed with flying colors, didn't I?"

"You're right. You did the best a girl ever did."

"Seeing as I was the only girl at the time, it would seem so," her mother said. "The smartest advice I can give you is to expect the unexpected. There's always something that goes wrong or doesn't work."

"Your simulation leader also has the option of throwing in a twist or a turn, such as no equipment or faulty equipment you have to troubleshoot. The worst is having to deal with a teammate who's not qualified or one who knows it all. The best thing you can do is stack the deck in your favor."

"What do you mean, Dad?"

"For instance, if you're told you can't take any 'scannable' equipment, hide something you will need that's not scannable. Like that obsidian glass knife you were so fond of as a kid, you know, the one I gave you when we visited Osir twenty years ago."

"The one Mom made me promise to keep locked up so I wouldn't cut myself." She laughed.

"It worked, didn't it, you didn't cut yourself," her mother chimed in.

"That blade is just as sharp as any metal blade but is virtually invisible to most scans. Tuck it away in a pocket and forget it's there until you need it."

"Also remember the point of the drill is survival, so the better prepared you are, the better you'll do. Things have gotten a lot safer since your father and I did our tests. At least you can hit the panic button and be taken out of the simulation."

Leba sounded discouraged. "I guess because we're considered a 'soft' service."

"On the contrary, infantry soldiers and combat pilots expect to encounter dangerous situations and spend most of their careers drilling and preparing for such an occurrence. It's the support services which are expected to rise to the occasion and perform with little or no training. You're out of your element and have to think fast on your feet. You have no time to be wrong, your decisions need to be split-second, or you, your colleagues, or your patients may not make it."

"Well, if you put it that way, Dad, I don't think I'm going to let her go," Reela Savar said.

"I'll be fine, Mom. Don't worry," Leba said and bit at her cuticle.

"I know you will, honey," her mother said.

"We have all the confidence in the world in you, princess, but we're still your parents and will always worry," Dad confirmed.

"Thanks, that means a lot coming from the two of you," Leba said and looked at the drop of blood oozing from her chewed finger. After a little more small talk, the call ended, and Leba set out to search her quarters for the little blue box that held her rock knife.

Leba admired the rock knife's shiny, smooth black surface. She remembered her dad finding it on an outing during one of her family vacations. She begged him to let her keep it. Her uncle Heli said it probably belonged to some ancient tribal warrior, and it could have magical powers. Leba never really believed it did, but it was fun to fantasize and make up pretend stories about its origins. While she tried to figure out where she might hide the knife on her person, Sendra called.

"You'll never guess who I saw last night." Sendra yawned.

A CHANGE IN TACTICS: MAIDEN VOYAGE

Get in late again? "Do you really want me to guess, or do you want to tell me?" Leba knew it bothered Sendra when she tried to guess.

"I want to tell you," Sendra answered.

Leba waited. "Well, go ahead."

"Last night, Damond took me to this club for dinner. You know, Estando's." Sendra sucked in a breath. "We were sitting at a booth in the back when you'll never guess who came in."

"I'm waiting." Leba feigned impatience.

"Your squad leader, Luth Cathen."

"So big deal, I guess a creep like him has to eat somewhere," Leba said annoyed.

"Well, that's not the best part," Sendra paused dramatically. "So good ole Damond invites him over. If Damond wasn't so hot, I would have smacked him for ruining our privacy."

"Lucky you," Leba said. "Let me guess, he stuck you guys with the check."

"No, better than that." She paused again. Leba was growing impatient, but this was how the game was played. These drawn-out conversations were usually her forte, but Sendra's attempt was admirable but unpracticed at best. Leba would be patient even if it drove her nuts. "He was out of uniform."

"So big deal," Leba said disgusted. "Maybe he was trying to pick up some poor unsuspecting woman."

"That's just it. He was expecting a woman to show up. You'll never guess who it was." She was running out of air. "I think it freaked him out when he found out we're best friends. He had to keep it in his pants or risk exposure."

"Okay, I give, who'd he meet?"

"Some little nurse, now what was her name?" Sendra stalled.

"Let me guess, Mally Yertha," Leba proffered. She twirled the knife in her hand then tested its weight.

"You got it, and boy, does she have it bad for him, hanging on his every word. I thought I was going to puke." Leba heard Sendra swallow another breath.

"Not that I really care, but did they leave together?" Grabbing the tip of the knife, Leba aimed it at the wall.

"That's just it. Damond had an early flight, so we left them at the table."

Flipping the knife over, Leba rubbed her thumb on the makeshift pommel. "So I guess JT was right. We're not really a team until the last day of training."

Sendra was confused. "And what does that have to do with anything?"

Leba hadn't realized she repeated JT's comments out loud. "What it means is that Cathen can hook up with her and not be in trouble for it."

"They made such a cute couple." Sendra giggled.

"I hope you and Damond didn't give them any pointers," Leba said.

"Damond was a perfect gentleman," Sendra bemoaned, "unfortunately." Tapping the pommel on the table, Leba waited for Sendra to finish. "By the way, are there any cute guys in your unit?"

Leba hesitated. "I suppose, but I haven't gotten to know anyone too well yet."

"Well, girl, what are you waiting for, you're not getting any younger."

Leba spun the knife on the table, wondering which way it would point. When it stopped, she considered throwing it at the wall again. "Does Damond have an older brother?"

"I'm sorry, I didn't mean to be cold. I'd rather double date with you than Mally Yertha. She's too perky, and Cathen's, well, Cathen. I don't know how Damond puts up with him."

"Enough about Cathen, I get enough about him all week long." Leba threw the knife onto the floor. She really didn't expect it to stick in. It clattered noisily on the ground.

"You're the one who wanted more adventure and left me here," Sendra retorted.

"Hey, if it weren't for Squad Leader Fiorat wanting to talk with me, you'd never met him." Picking it up, Leba shoved it deeply into her boot. She considered it, a perfect fit.

"Point to you," Sendra conceded. "I guess I have a lot to be grateful for." The call ended shortly thereafter as Leba needed to study, and Sendra needed to sleep.

Leba spent the rest of the morning reading and rereading the most important info she accumulated on cold weather survival. What to eat, what to wear, and most importantly, what to avoid. She knew the science but could she demonstrate it practically? She was sure she was better prepared than anyone else in her group would be, but would that be enough? The point of the cold box test was for your whole team to come through it unscathed. She laughed to herself as she imagined Mally Yertha clothed in matching fur hat, boots, and gloves, trying to put on makeup in the frigid tundra. No matter, Lord Cathen would probably give his lady some special exemption where she could bring a giant heater only if she didn't share it with anyone.

Emmie Hodd was flipping hot cakes at the stove when DeShay came up from behind and wrapped his arms around her. He peered over her shoulder and tried to pilfer one of the completed hot cakes from a nearby plate. Emmie slapped his hand with the spatula. "Now wait until they're ready."

"Okay," DeShay said playfully, "but as I recall, last time it was cereal and milk. I see your cooking skills have improved."

He embraced her tightly. "Oooh, get away."

"What, no sugar for me this morning? I thought after last night you'd be—"

"I'd be what?" she asked, "accepting of anything you'd be offering?" He squeezed her tighter. "They're done now," she said as she slid the newly cooked cakes onto the growing stack. She turned to face him. "Now, I have time to give you some sugar, baby." DeShay smiled.

Tiv Garnet spent most of the morning going over equipment in his company's departure bay. Overseer Company deployed earlier on Hydrix shuttle. The base commander and his personal staff would leave tomorrow on Helix shuttle. Squad Leader Garnet and Defender Company were leaving on Lithix shuttle the day after. Check and recheck, test and retest, until everything was perfect. Tiv felt personally responsible for everything associated with his company and the mission, unfortunately leaving little time for anything else.

The series of pranks plaguing him was seriously interfering with his ability to stay focused. He was determined to root out the offender and string him up by the short hairs. As one for attention to details, Tiv was lucky he discovered the latest one before falling prey to it. The pranks to date were generally harmless but rigged for maximum embarrassment. This last one was more devious, significantly raising the bar. While checking his unit's deployment med packs, he noticed his canteen's lid slightly ajar. After borrowing med gloves from DeShay, he approached it cautiously. DeShay watched in amusement as Tiv inspected and then dissected the water bottle. "What are you laughing about?" Tiv questioned DeShay.

"You. You would think that thing was a loaded, pin-out grenade," DeShay observed.

"I told you, man, someone's been messing with my stuff, and it would be just like him to screw with my canteen," Tiv said angrily. He carefully removed the cap, put it up to his nose, noting a faint tin-like odor. "See," he said, shoving the cap toward DeShay. "Smell this."

DeShay leaned over. "You're paranoid."

"Just do it, smart guy, and tell me what you think." Tiv flipped it to him.

"Whatever," DeShay responded, grabbing it out of the air. "Smells medicinal."

"See, that's what I mean. It's probably laced with something that would really screw up my insides." Tiv gathered up all the pieces of the water bottle and dumped them into the waste receptacle and headed toward the supply locker to requisition a new one.

A CHANGE IN TACTICS: MAIDEN VOYAGE

"Aren't you going to give it to forensics so you can ferret out the weasel?" DeShay grinned.

"I really don't have time for this nonsense," Tiv said, pressing his fist against his mouth and tapping.

"Now I'm thinking someone who has access to this stuff needs pretty high clearance," DeShay offered.

"Someone like you." Tiv turned to face him. DeShay frowned. "That's not what I mean, stupid. I know it's not you, but someone like you, someone with your level of access."

"I'm glad you don't think it's me, although I do admire his persistence." DeShay laughed.

"Funny, very funny," Tiv answered. "I'll ask JT, maybe he can give me a list of who'd have high enough clearance."

"So you trust JT but not me, I'm hurt." DeShay put his fists to his eyes and wound his hands.

Tiv threw a nearby empty rucksack at him. Both men laughed. "Hey, thanks for the assist," Tiv said.

"No problem." DeShay straightened up. "I hope this stops after you ship out. We don't need any distractions compromising the mission, especially if your friend is raising the bar."

Tiv nodded in agreement. DeShay reached into the trash can and removed the canteen's lid. "Hey, what are you doing?" Tiv said.

"There's a guy in forensics owes me a favor. May give us a lead to your rat." He patted Tiv on the shoulder. "Keep the faith." DeShay looked closer at the lid. "I think he made a mistake."

"What?" Tiv inquired.

"Follow," DeShay outlined his reasoning, "Depending on the chemical, we may be able to trace its source. It should help narrow the field of likely candidates."

"With my luck, it's probably something anyone could get." Tiv rubbed his temples.

DeShay changed the subject. "Speaking of luck, did I tell you I think I've reconnected with Emmie?"

"The absolute 'love of your life,' 'the sweetest girl you've ever met,' and the 'one who got away,' that Emmie?" Tiv repeated the sentiments he heard DeShay recite a hundred times before.

"Yes, that Emmie." DeShay's posture relaxed, his gaze unfocused, a slight smile creeping onto his face as if he were reliving a past memory. His comm pinged, snapping him back to the present. "In fact, I hope that's her now."

"You go ahead, I've got a lot of work to get done," Tiv encouraged him. Tiv watched DeShay strut out of the bay, listening to the voice on his comm, not saying much but nodding his head. He's hooked. Tiv snickered to himself and went back to checking gear. Despite his doubts, Tiv was glad for DeShay. Unfortunately, trying to rekindle old flames was just that, playing with fire.

CHAPTER 14

The beginning of the week came up quickly as everyone hurried into class to beat the 0600 chime. Cathen still took roll call. Even JT showed on time. No reason for an added penalty before hitting the box. "Well, people, I hope you've all rested because today's the day." Class members looked at one another bewildered. "That's right, it's cold box day."

"But that's not fair," someone blurted out.

"What's not fair?" Cathen snapped. Leba saw his jaw clench as he pinched his lips together. Cathen drew in a long breath and released it in a short burst. "Fights, battles, wars, capture, imprisonment, torture." Folding his arms across his chest, he tucked his chin and stared at the complainer. "I can see it now." He took a stride forward, stopped suddenly, his legs splayed apart to maintain his position. "Wait a minute. Hold on that raid, I have a hair appointment." He perused the room waiting for another remark, but none came. "Children, this is reality. Reality rarely happens on a schedule."

Much as she wanted to despise Cathen, Leba couldn't argue with his logic. Thank goodness she'd been practicing carrying around her rock knife in her boot and left it there. So much for group preparedness. While everyone else seemed to be enjoying an exciting weekend, Leba's nonexistent social life paid off. She logged lots of rest the past few days and was hydrating all weekend in anticipation of the upcoming challenge scheduled for later in the week. The expression on some of her classmates' faces portended a different story. She looked at Mally Yertha, who seemed as stunned as everyone else. Well, at least Cathen did one thing right and kept everyone in the dark.

"So as not to be too harsh"—Cathen grinned and put one hand to his cheek and lazily laid his head on it—"I'll give the class a choice: either I'll pick the four teams or you can choose random lots and take what comes." His eyes roamed the room, searching for a dissenter. "My choices were done with your maximum benefit in mind." Maximum benefit in chance of success or in chance of failure and expulsion from the squad. Leba wasn't quite sure how to take his pronouncement.

For a long moment, no one spoke, and then JT did. "I think I'll take my chances on random picks." He laid his hand over his heart, cocked his head, and smiled. The grin overtook the lower half of his face. "It'll be an awesome adventure to work with any of my esteemed colleagues." There were snickers in the classroom as his sarcasm was acknowledged.

"Suit yourself." Cathen groaned, his mouth downturned. "I assume Hobes speaks for all of you." There was a general consensus in the room. Waving dismissively, Cathen removed four different-colored papers from his binder and tore each into nine pieces. "Oh, before we begin, anyone want to back out?" There was silence in the room. "Great," he stated as he bent over and dumped out the waist can onto the floor. After plopping the vessel onto the desk, he dropped in the small paper lots. "This should do just fine." He gave the bin a shuffle and slammed it back on the table. "Hobes, since you seem to be the spokesman for the group, I'll give you the privilege of drawing first."

JT leaped from his seat, stuck his hand deep into the can, rooted around for effect, and removed a paper slip. He announced, "Yellow."

"Figures you'd be yellow." Cathen smirked. The remaining class members came forward to draw a slip. "Loud and clear," Cathen instructed as each announced their color. When everyone was done, Cathen pointed, "Blues to this corner, yellows to that corner, reds to the far corner, and greens to the remaining corner." As people segregated based on their pick, Cathen went on, "Now pick a leader for your group, and if you can't, I will."

Leba looked at the other greens. Some she knew; some she did not. That is, she knew their names and how they performed in the classroom and in the gym, but she didn't have a grasp on their total package. Not a good start.

Surprisingly, the only men in her green group were a couple of orderlies, Tylor Gref and Joreg Hech. They came as a matched set, both thin and well conditioned, not bursting with muscles and physicality, but able to hold their own. Both men were clean-shaven, above average height and build. Joreg Hech was slightly shorter and more rounded than his partner. His flushed face ended in subtle jowls that seemed to glisten under hot lights. His torso was squatter than his partner's but his legs seemed longer. Despite his best efforts at posture, his shoulders seemed to perennially hunch. The more talkative of the two, his nasolabial folds were deeply creased with all the activity, so when he smiled, they were evident and made your eyes focus on his mouth full of perfectly straight and shiny white teeth. His receding hairline exposed a massive forehead that taking up half of his squared face. Close-set eyes and a broad nose completed his countenance.

Tylor Gref's facial features were more narrow and precise. If not for his dark, bushy eyebrows, he endeavored to keep restrained, his distinctive aquiline nose would garner the prime spot on his face. His lips were thin, and when he smiled, they were almost nonexistent. These two also possessed an unspoken set of cues. The looks they traded spoke volumes, and emotions seemed to turn as fast as they were displayed.

Both men were highly intelligent and well skilled. Their obsessive nature made them excellent teammates if only they would stop bickering. Having one or the other seemed to be a plus, but having both together was probably a recipe for disaster. If they could put aside their picayune differences for only a few moments, Leba was sure they could prove an asset for any leader.

In the midst of going over things in her mind, should she step up and volunteer to lead, Emmie Hodd beat Leba to it. "I'll be team leader." Emmie made her case. "As a head nurse, I have years of leadership experience. This is not my first command." It was hard to disagree with Emmie's logic.

I guess she's a reasonable choice. "Works for me," Leba said. Trust was something Leba struggled with. Although extremely dependable herself, Leba found it difficult to surrender control to others. If DeShay trusted her, Leba should too. The rest of the greens voted Emmie in. The reds chose DeShay, a no-brainer. JT's team, the yellows, chose Margo Lacey, another head nurse.

The blue team, with Grizzer and Anster, told Cathen they would have coleaders. "Suit yourself." Cathen flashed a cold smile. "What I didn't tell you is the leader, be it one or two, is ultimately responsible for their team. That is, if you don't get all your people back, you could be bounced too."

She didn't doubt her own skills, but Leba didn't relish being sent home before the real mission started. And after hearing Cathen's warning, Leba was glad she hadn't jumped at the leadership position. This was all new to her. Thorough preparation had always been the key to her success. There would be other chances to lead. The blue team was at risk of losing both Grizzer and Anster if they failed. Leba couldn't imagine going to Vedax without them. DeShay looked over at Leba, no, over at Emmie. Leba could tell he was concerned. Maybe because the greens lacked a significant male presence. Not that the women couldn't handle the box, it did help to have some strong and tall men to raise a shelter or two.

"I will give you one standard hour to show up at the entry point. Use your time wisely. Call your loved ones and let them know you'll be gone, get some food in you, get your cold weather clothes and gear." Cathen paused, rubbing one hand against the other and then wringing them out into a clasp and continued, "No metallic objects, no electronic gadgets, and no cyber devices unless I issue them." With his index fingers pointing from his clasped hands and shaking them, he said, "We will be checking people. Now get going, you've already used five minutes."

"Son of a," Gordie cursed from the red corner. He was really angry. Probably had something planned with the family and now, with the change of plans, would disappoint his wife or one of his kids. Leba felt sorry for him, but there was nothing she could do. It wasn't like she could cover a shift for him.

There was no time to get back to her quarters, but Leba did want to let her parents know she would be out of touch. A quick sat-phone call was all it would take. Before she left, though, she checked with Emmie Hodd. Leba knew it was very important to establish right from the start she was going to be a team player and would follow Nurse Hodd's lead. Hodd was in deep discussion with Nurse Braids Frence.

Beginning at the apex of Frence's forehead were countless rows of tightly weaved hair radiating down into an intricate pattern. What started as thick matted ropes ended as twists of only a few hairs each. Her forehead was high reminiscent of someone noble born. Her eyes were smoky and dark, offset by glistening white sclera, like ink drops in milk. Her brows were thin and high arched, following the lines of her almond-shaped eyes. The eyelids were colored metallic gold and ended in dark thick lashes. An elongated oval face was punctuated by a narrow flattened nose and well-defined cheekbones. In the gym, she was lithe and agile with cat-like movements despite her height. She was a study in contrasts. Some ways warrior-like and other ways model-like. Either way, her mouth never stopped going.

By her own admission, Braids was the product of a broken home and years of hardship on the mean streets. If not for her Ma Emmie, she'd probably be dead or worse. Emmie Hodd saved her life, and Braids owed her everything. The pair seemed inseparable. Except recently when Emmie seemed occupied more often with DeShay. Emmie and Braids were another pair who seemed to know what each other was thinking and, with only subtle signals, could communicate their wishes. Leba only hoped they remembered there were others on this team not privy to their secret language. She also hoped their close relationship would not compromise either's decision-making process. A leader sometimes made decisions for the good of the team but not so good for the individual. Certain Hodd appreciated her notification and after getting the okay, Leba set off to tell her mom and dad and make final preparations for whatever lay ahead.

Smiling to himself, Cathen finished writing down the members of each team. This was better than planned. Looking up, he saw Mally Yertha's big green eyes staring in his direction, and he quickly turned away, pretending to be looking elsewhere. She was so blessed obvious.

Subtlety usually escaped younger women, but he found their naivety sexy. A nurse graduate still had lots to explore and experience. Giving hands-on guided tours was his specialty. Maintain decorum at least for the short term, that was what he kept telling himself. Although he found it hard to ignore what she kept restrained beneath her blouse. With Mally on the relatively weaker green team, Luth Cathen was sure a majority of his problems would be solved by the end of the week. If Mally failed the cold box, and the now the likelihood was almost certain, then he could see her unobstructed, comfort her in her time of sadness, add her to his list of conquests.

Bouncing self-righteous Emmie Hodd and pissing off DeShay Tiner in the process was an added bonus of the green team's composition. It hadn't slipped past Cathen, Hodd and Tiner were more than colleagues. They had history, but he knew Tiner would ultimately pick the corps when given the choice. The pairing of his other two headstrong head nurses, Lacey and Conte, on the yellow team would keep Hobes at his wits end trying to keep the hair-pulling and bitch-slapping to a minimum. Funnier still was having Otumba and Ertle in that group. Polar opposites in personality and intelligence, Hobes would likely have to keep them apart as well.

"Did you remember to replace your boot laces with the heavy cord?" Darian Brader asked his daughter.

"Yes, Dad," Leba answered.

"And hide your rock knife?"

"Yes, Dad." She touched her boot to confirm her answer.

"Good girl. Now talk to your mom."

"Okay, love you," she said, waiting as her mom picked up. "Hi, Mom."

"Hi, honey," Reela Savar said. Leba could detect apprehension in her mother's voice. "I know you'll do fine. Just keep an eye on the others. When I did it, I was much happier that I went solo."

"I will," Leba said, trying not to sound concerned and bit her cuticle.

"Be careful, and call us as soon as you get done. We love you, honey."

"Me too, Mom. Don't worry, I'll be fine. Gotta go, love you guys." Leba disconnected the call. She would do fine, no worries.

The hour went by quickly, but Leba was able to get everything done she wanted to without much difficulty. She remembered to visit the lavatory before time expired, no reason to start the mission looking for a bathroom. Digging an ice toilet was not an easy task. With all the cold-weather gear, stripping down and being exposed to the elements was not pleasant. A shelter or at least a windbreak would need to be erected first. Frigid winds would bite at uncovered flesh and leave significant damage.

"I think it's better this way," Emmie Hodd told DeShay.

"Don't take anything for granted," DeShay advised.

"You sound like my daddy, and he's been gone a long time," she jabbed.

Stealthing her around a corner, he said, "I bet your daddy never did this." He kissed her.

Breathless, Emmie answered, "No, can't say he ever did."

"Just be careful," DeShay counseled.

"You too," Emmie returned the sentiment.

The last thing DeShay did before joining his team was to grab Leba's arm, pull her into the corner he released Emmie from, and delayed her from last-minute preparations at her leader's prep session. "We don't have much time, so listen closely."

Leba looked at his face. "What did I do wrong this time?" DeShay saw her awkwardly turn away when he made a rather open PDA with her new team leader. "I didn't mean to watch, but it's not like you weren't obvious."

DeShay grabbed her other arm. "Shut up and listen, girl. I don't have much time, and if Emmie catches us…"

"Great." Leba pouted. "You're going to get me in trouble. And it's not like I'm her favorite as it is."

DeShay studied her face, brushed a wayward strand of wavy brown hair out of the way, noticing for the first time how her subtle red highlights peeked out. He refocused and looked deep into her eyes. They were brown with touches of green. He never really looked at her face closely before. Delicate freckles spanned across her nose and topped her cheeks. "You know you have the weirdest eyes?"

She shifted in his grip. Freeing her arms, Leba circled hair around her ears and got it out of her face. "Thanks. Is that what you wanted to tell me?" Her feet turned toward the exit.

He furrowed his brow and felt her shoulders tense and her body turn to follow her feet. He turned her back toward himself. "Never noticed it before." He grabbed an arm again. "Listen, girl, this is important. Emmie can deal with it." Her determined look and intense focus couldn't hide her quiet vulnerability. Her lips were thin, not like Emmie's large and luscious one.

"I may just give you a big wet kiss, piss her off, and land you in a boat load of trouble." Leba snuggled close to him, violating his personal space without written permission.

"Stop it. Be serious. Pretend I'm your older brother for a minute." He held her at arm's length. "Little sister, what I tell you may get you through the next few days in one piece."

Leba stopped. "Okay, I recognize Master Priman DeShay Tiner's serious, "Don't screw around, this is important" face." She poked at him. "You know, the one followed by push-ups, sit-ups, squats, or crunches until you pay attention look."

"Excellent." Out of the corner of his eye, DeShay spotted the searing glare Emmie Hodd was launching in their direction. Leba was turned away, missing the message DeShay heard loud and clear. He felt an obligation to Leba even if it meant angering Emmie. She was his protégé, his responsibility. Making up with Emmie would be worth the price. Placing an arm around Leba's shoulder, DeShay walked her down the hall and out of sight.

DeShay propped himself against the wall of the classroom they were in. Leba took a seat behind the center desk in the front row, sat up straight, and clasped her hands on the desktop. "I'm concerned about your team."

"Should I be taking notes?" Leba jested.

DeShay continued unfettered, "Why aren't you in charge of green team?"

A CHANGE IN TACTICS: MAIDEN VOYAGE

Leba reentered the assembly room to an increasing gathered group. The body language of most of the participants signaled their trepidation, but some, like Clerk 3 Middie Fidelis, seemed to be immune. Her hair, buzzed down to short nubs of shafts, was plagued by bare patches and disarray. With her square face and well-lined forehead, Middie could have passed for a basic drill instructor, her stocky frame able to shoulder even the most difficult obstacles. Her legs were thick and sturdy. But there was something about her eyes. She never quite looked right at you.

Manipulative and deceiving, that was what DeShay told Leba. Middie's expressions usually remained plastered on her face much longer than necessary. Her eyebrows seemed to be at a constant downward angle until the expected emotion needed to be displayed. Middie seemed adaptable and compliant as modeling clay, changing and shaping to suit the situation or to fit the potter's need. And this usually played well with Cathen. In class, Middie often played the martyr, provoking an unsuspecting person into doing something by laying on the guilt. She liked to tell you what you were thinking. She was a master at mind games, and DeShay warned Leba to watch her step.

Yet despite it all, she was one of the best clerks DeShay knew. If you wanted something done or needed something and Middie liked you, it would be yours for the asking. Hyena came to mind, sleek, efficient, part of the pack, but ready to pounce and rip your throat out if necessary to her survival or well-being. At least she found Cathen as distasteful as everyone else did, but she knew who could hurt her and who could really hurt her.

Middie Fidelis surveyed each team and was making odds on the survival chances of each with her other clerk friends. Her own green team, mainly women except for the pale, thin orderly Joreg Hech and his equally pathetic partner, Tylor Gref, sported a lousy chance of returning intact. Not being one to interfere, Middie was unsure of appointing old nurse Hodd as leader of her group. She would've rather seen the young doctor girl, Brader, lead the pack. Middie was stationed at the base for years, watching people come and go, live and die. She was never much for fanfare. Do her job, keep her bosses happy, and stay out of trouble.

Middie didn't want to be part of this group, but someone suggested it would be in her best interest if she did. Someone who promised a substantial improvement in her current status if she applied and qualified for this mission. After the first cyber transfer significantly enhanced her monetary situation, and two subsequent ones followed once each goal was met, Middie Fidelis never questioned their source or desired an explanation. She would know soon enough. Her benefactor would eventually be revealed. They always were. Middie hadn't been asked to do anything illegal, so why not. Why shouldn't she profit, if no one got hurt.

"I would only give you a fifty-fifty chance of coming back in one piece," Middie told Lynol Otumba, a big man with a stern face. Middie knew how to get to him, annoy him, get under his skin enough to throw him off his game.

With a heavily accented voice, Otumba replied, "You have no faith in me, woman. Big Ertle and I could carry our whole yellow team on our backs and never break a sweat."

"Not with those two she-wolves, Lacey and Conte, fighting for Dr. Hobes' attention," Middie observed.

"I will have those women tamed and eating outta my hand by the end of our journey." He roared with laughter.

"Better you than me, my friend." Middie joined in his laughter.

"You, on the other hand, my friend, will have to keep extra tissues on hand to stifle the sobs of your little fillies." He grinned. "The first broken nail and your team is lost."

"Hodd maybe old, but she doesn't roll over for anyone," Middie put forth.

"That's not what the wind says," Otumba whispered.

"And what does the wind say?" Middie asked, annoyed at Otumba's tribalistic reference.

"The wind whispers, she lies with the war dog."

"Who, DeShay Tiner?" Middie scoffed. "He's just stretching his muscles before a big mission."

"That is not what the wind says," Otumba repeated.

"The hell with stupid wind, how much are you putting up?" Middie snapped.

"The wind is nothing to mock, woman," Otumba said sternly but quickly followed up with a significant number.

"I'll match that," Middie stated. "See if Doyal wants a piece of this action."

Armali Doyal stopped paying attention to the others' conversation when his red team leader, DeShay Tiner, called him over to discuss a few mission details. Tiner was such a stickler for protocol, but Middie knew it only applied when he was in charge. Doyal returned to where Fidelis and Otumba were talking. Middie bared her teeth, and Otumba showed an equally toothy smile. "I know that look." Doyal cringed. "How much will it cost me?"

When green team leader, Emmie Hodd, arrived, her first task was to remind everyone to "Do your business now or hold your pee." The sentiment brought a smile to even the most reluctant participants. The other three teams huddled together too, everyone checking one another's gear and making last-minute plans. Their preparations were interrupted by Cathen's entrance. Carrying a bunch of small, fist-sized white rectangular objects, he plopped them onto the table. Picking one up between his thumb and forefinger, he displayed it. "This is your panic button, people." Tossing it in the air, he snatched it back as it was arcing down. "I suspect no one in my unit will have to use it." He closed his hand tightly around the device. "But just in case, if for any reason you need to exit the simulation, enter your last name, and we will have you removed."

One by one each respective team leader came up and received the devices and distributed them. "Now for the fun stuff," Cathen continued, handing each team leader an info-pad with the mission assignment downloaded. "You and your team get five minutes to memorize the mission details."

Emmie Hodd activated the info-pad's vid screen. Scrolling down, she counted thirty lines of text. Leba peered over her shoulder and offered, "You memorize the first two or three, and I'll take the next couple, and so on. That way, we don't have to all remember too much." Emmie seemed annoyed but nodded her agreement. "One thing, though," Leba cautioned. "Read the entire list first to make sure the last line or two doesn't contradict all the rest." Emmie looked bothered at Leba's second suggestion and waited for further explanation. "I one time took a test in lower school with fifty lines of text, but the second line said read all the lines first, and the second to last line said ignore lines three through forty-eight."

Telling Emmie Hodd anything further at this point would only alienate Leba more. DeShay warned her of Emmie's stubbornness and advised her to make Emmie believe the ideas were her own. Let Emmie figure out what you think is the right thing to do. Drop subtle hints. Appear bewildered but give her all the clues to come to the conclusion you want her to. Slowly Leba was beginning to understand why DeShay's relationship with Emmie was so tumultuous. His needs did not necessarily concur with hers, and trying to convince a stubborn woman was like trying to move a mountain.

"It would be just like Cathen to pull something like that." Emmie Hodd snatched the info-pad with both hands, quickly reading through the orders. "Look here," she pointed, and Leba followed Emmie's finger to a line of text. "Son of a," Emmie Hodd cursed. "You were right." Gathering the green team members together, Emmie tasked each to memorize a few lines of text. "I don't care how you do it but remember your part word for word." After taking the first few lines herself, Emmie made sure the others followed in alphabetical order so as not to compromise the integrity of the list's order.

Cathen walked over to the green team, surveying each member. "Uribos, you pulled red, what are you doing here with green?"

"Here's my green ticket, boss," Victos Uribos explained, showing the small slip of paper, clearly colored green.

"Green my ass," Cathen said. "Who'd you switch with?" Cathen ran down his team list. "Where's Kathic?"

"Here, sir, with the reds," the young female orderly answered. Leba overheard Victos's earlier conversation. Explaining to Kathic how she'd do better on DeShay's team, Uribos asked her to switch, citing her chances of survival would increase by a factor of ten on the old war dog's crew. Uribos, on the other hand, wanted to "help out the girls." Leba figured what he really wanted was to be closer to his ex, Riki Sandler.

Uribos's broad shoulders resulted from countless hours of lifting and snatching, clean and jerk. His arms exploded with muscle. Surprising, though, were powerfully built but slender legs, a product of his trim physique and above-average height. Matching his chiseled muscles, a rounded face was masterfully sculptured with a chinstrap angling and strengthening his jaw, giving the impression of stone. A carefully manicured goatee hid his inviting lips and hardened his demeanor. That was it; behind the facial hair was the cherub-like face of a small boy. His only weakness seemed to be his pining over Sandler.

Riki Sandler was classically beautiful with large brown eyes, whose full and lush lashes seemed to beckon you in. Her high cheekbones offset a petite button nose and full, pouty lips, finishing the perfect symmetry of her face. She was muscular but curvy in all the right places. A fact not lost on Victos Uribos. Athletic, limber, and able to get into positions Leba could never dream of without permanent bodily harm, she wasn't strong but didn't need to be because Uribos would fall all over himself to help her with weighty tasks. Different was her thick curly brown hair with ringlets gently framing her face. Despite the military's code for shorter hair, hers still maintained its sexy nature, especially when she shook it out. Even flushed and sweaty from working out, her tousled tresses bounced shiny and playful. And Vic liked to tease her by running his hands through it. Sassy, sexy, and sophisticated. She feigned annoyance, but Leba picked up on the subtle signs of a courtship ritual. Her lips seemed to constantly be forming his name. They seemed the perfect couple, chiseled to fit into each other's arms and form one perfect union, but the tension between the two was palpable, like two animals sizing each other to determine whether they were the compatible pair to continue the herd.

Cathen thought for a moment and then ignored the change. Returning to the front of the room, Cathen announced, "Time's up, people." The info-pads went dark. He collected them up. "Anyone want to back out now?" Not hearing any affirmatives, he pointed to the door behind him. "You will proceed single file and be scanned for the contraband we discussed." One by one, each participant headed through the door.

The blue team went through without a beep, but as the first member of the red team entered, an annoying bleep got louder and faster. "Oh," stammered Vego Cress, "I didn't know you included music players in the restricted category." Cathen pointed to a bin located at the side of the room and pointed. "Will I get it back? I dropped a full week's pay on that."

Cathen looked at him. Bimmy and Kedo stepped out of line and deposited their music players as well. "Tiner!" Cathen shouted to the Master Priman at the end of the red unit. "What's the deal with your squad and not following instructions?"

"Our team follows a different drummer." He snickered and then noticed Cathen's unpleasant stare. "Don't worry, sir, I'll shoot the drummer." A chorus of chuckles and snorts rang from the remaining unit members.

"Don't push me, Tiner," Cathen warned.

"No, sir, wouldn't think of that."

The rest of red team went through without incident. Once the remaining teams cleared the scan, Cathen distributed specially designed chronos. "These are programmed only for time and direction." Cathen escorted the teams to the simulation portals.

Leba watched as the display above certain portals scrolled information. Emmie Hodd pointed at the right-hand doorway lit with a green light. "That must be ours," she announced and moved her unit to the deployment pad.

Each team entered their respective portal. Leba assumed each mission was different but didn't know. A chaotic launch bay and the blare of sirens greeted the green team when they entered the simulation. Stopping in front of them, panting and out of breath, his black hair wet with sweat and his face pained, a young corpsman, possibly a simulatron, ran up to their group. "Come on," he urged. "Your shuttle is ready to depart."

Emmie Hodd stepped forward. "What's wrong, Corpsman?"

Between breaths, he said, "There's been a terrible accident on the mountain, and we need to get you there ASAP."

"Let me see the orders," Emmie asked. He handed her his infopad. "Green med team to depart on Shuttle TKM-772, Pad 9." Emmie Hodd thought for a moment and then asked, "Who had the launch info?"

"I did," Mally Yertha stepped up. "Shuttle TKM-772, Pad 9," she recited.

"All right, folks, that would be our ride." Hodd pointed to the waiting transport. It was a smaller version of a standard medical rescue shuttle, and Leba wondered why. What was missing? Prepare for the unexpected, that was what her parents told her. She logged the info and tasked herself to check at the first opportunity.

"Come on, come on," the corpsman urged.

Emmie Hodd motioned them forward. "Let's go then." The nine members of green med team proceeded forward. Leba felt funny not having her med rucksack slung over her shoulder like in regular dispatches. Something tickled the back of her neck, and she rubbed it. The feeling of impending doom.

It's silly, this is only a simulation.

"Your equipment's already loaded," the corpsman offered before Emmie asked.

The pilot was already running the shuttle through its warm-up sequence as Hodd's team got situated aboard the shuttle. After Emmie made sure everyone was buckled and secured in their seats, she entered the open cockpit to confer with the pilot. The shuttle was so small Leba could hear their entire conversation from her aft seat. Being the first in line to enter the shuttle, she was relegated to the back. No worries, she could keep an eye on everything from here. Situational awareness in action. "Yes, ma'am," the pilot responded to each of her questions. "Now, ma'am, if you don't mind, please return to the passenger compartment so I can get us off this pad. We're on a very tight schedule." Emmie patted his shoulder and ducked her head out of the cockpit only to hear the door shut and lock behind her. As the compartment light illuminated red, signaling imminent takeoff, Emmie took her seat and strapped in.

CHAPTER 15

Launch, this was the part Leba hated the most. Once in flight, she'd be fine, but takeoffs and landings made her stomach do somersaults. Planting her feet firmly on the floor, she braced for takeoff. She tried to keep her shoulders loose and relaxed, but they were tight and hunched forward in a tense yet protective posture. It was bad to be so stiff and rigid because every move of the ship transmitted through her body.

The rumbling of the shuttle's engines permeated the cabin. The vibration under the floor panels numbed her feet. Why did her feet and ankles always have to itch at a time like this? She didn't want to look down, since it stimulated head-swimming nausea. Shutting her eyes tight and gripping the seat arms, she tried to take slow, deep breaths. The recirculated air pumped into the pressurizing cabin. Devoid of natural smells, it too stimulated nausea, and Leba tried inhaling with her mouth and exhaling with her nose. She could feel everyone's eyes monitoring her ritual.

When the engine noises crescendoed, accepting the upcoming g-forces signaling acceleration, the seat restraints locked into position. As the shuttle rocketed forward, everyone was pinned to their seats. Leba refused to look out the viewport and watch the planetary scenery quickly dissolve to clouds then darkness resolve into stars. Through small slits, she stared forward and tried to fix her gaze on a singular point. There was a nagging tingle in the back of her throat, and she didn't want to aggravate it into nausea. Vomiting would dissolve her credibility with her unit mates. After what seemed like forever, the shuttle's interior lights returned to normal, and the ship leveled off. Carefully, Leba peeled her hands from the arm rails.

Thankfully, no one commented on her launch routine as she adjusted positions, her lower back and hips unmolding from the seat back. Swallowing in an attempt to equalize her ear pressure, Leba opened and closed her mouth, hoping a yawn would help. Her head felt hollow like a balloon, and sounds were muffled. If there was small talk between some of her unit mates, she couldn't yet make out the words. Leba waited for her system to equilibrate. Slowly and almost imperceptibly Leba returned tenuously to prelaunch status. Consciously she tried relaxing her back and shoulders. She rocked her feet up and down, trying to stretch tight calf muscles. It was unclear how long the flight would last, but simulation or not, it still produced the same effect on her body. Hopefully, the flight was long enough and smooth enough to lull her into complacency before dealing with landing.

From the back of the shuttle, Leba had a good vantage point to keep quiet and watch how the others interacted. She listened as Tylor Gref and Joreg Hech, longtime partners, discussed mundane household issues. They were arguing about who was supposed to do something about their landscaping problem. By the starboard viewport sat Victos Uribos and then Riki Sandler. Rumor was Uribos and Sandler were involved pretty seriously at one time but now more casually. Leba only caught bits and pieces of their conversation. What she did hear clearly was Uribos giving Hech grief about something and Gref snickering in the background. Sandler playfully hit Uribos and chided him for teasing Hech. Maybe there was still a glimmer of hope for their relationship; if not, Leba was sure neither would have any trouble finding a compatible and willing partner. Pity no one was thinking ahead about the mission except for her. Could she trust these people if her life depended on it?

Farther forward, nursing grad Mally Yertha sat with Middie Fidelis. Fidelis was a seasoned veteran clerk who had self-reportedly "seen it all," with the scars to prove it. Leba imagined Fidelis took pleasure scaring Mally with stories of cold box disaster. Finally to their right were Emmie Hodd and Braids Frence. No one knew Frence's real name, but it didn't matter; everyone called her Braids. Hodd and Braids had history too as Frence credited Hodd with saving her from the streets and getting her into the honorable profession of nursing. Despite the age difference, they acted more like sisters, even if Braids referred to Hodd as Ma.

Nine people who paired up but barely knew the rest were supposed to function as a team. As usual, Leba was the one left out. Being a doctor, seemingly above the rest, somehow better, Leba still wanted to be one of the team. She wanted to be on equal footing without being looked at as different. Sure she was better educated with an advanced degree and got a bigger salary with a higher community standing, but she still wanted to be one of them.

As the shuttle adopted a geosynchronous orbit in preparation for atmospheric descent, Leba slipped back into her landing routine. Intra-atmospheric flight was never as smooth as extraplanetary flight, but the turbulence this shuttle was experiencing was anything but typical. Her knuckles grew white as she clenched the arm rails. Leba could feel her stomach come up into her throat a number of times.

She wasn't the only one holding on tight, though. Emmie Hodd looked back and down the short aisle, trying to comfort everyone, but Leba could read the concern on her face. The crosswinds that zipped through lunar mountains and the ice lightning that occasionally accompanied it could cause turbulence. Intermittent at best. Not this intense. There were stories of how airships could be brought down, plucked out of the sky, never to be seen or heard from again. Leba felt her body stiffen. Not good. She tugged on her harness and cinched it one more notch.

There was a thunderous clap and the shuttle was pelted with ice crystals. Leba peered out the port side window she shared with Tylor Gref. Cryo-volcano eruption, not crosswinds.

"What the hell was that?" Hech shrieked.

Tylor Gref placed a comforting hand on his arm. "Don't worry. It's just a simulation to get you freaked out."

"Are you sure?" Mally said nervously.

"Don't worry, kid," Middie tried to comfort her. "It would be just like Cathen to put on a show to impress you."

"Yeah," Uribos chimed in. "He's that kinda guy."

"Is not," Mally retorted.

A CHANGE IN TACTICS: MAIDEN VOYAGE

Sandler put an arm on Uribos's and whispered loudly, "Are you sure it's just a stunt?"

"Don't tell me you're scared too," Uribos answered sarcastically. He put an arm around her shoulder, kissed her cheek, and said, "Don't worry, I won't let that big, bad ice volcano spew freezing lava balls over our itty-bitty, teeny-tiny cuddle shuttle."

Riki Sandler snapped back, "Let's ask the doc if she's worried." Before Uribos could answer her, there was another thunderous clap, and the shuttle dropped, losing significant altitude. That got everyone's attention.

Emmie Hodd in her most commanding voice advised, "We trained for this, people. Check your harnesses."

Can't tighten them anymore.

"Helmets on, visors down, and make sure you check your seals." In the middle of her recommendations, the lights in the cabin changed to red, and the pilot's voice crackled over the intercom.

"Prepare for emergency landing," the simulated voice said. The noise in the cabin was so loud with panicked voices Leba could barely hear the announcement. She wasn't exactly calm herself, but as adrenaline kicked in, she became more focused and concentrated on getting ready to crash. Depending on what remained of the shuttle's controls would determine landing versus crashing. Either way, it'd be rough and rocky. Feeling the pull and tug of the accelerating gravitational forces, the craft continued to rapidly lose altitude.

With her arms folded across her chest and her head tucked down in crash position, Leba reasoned smashing into a moon full of ice; burning on reentry would not be a prolonged issue. Violent vibrations wracked the shuttle as it hurtled toward the surface. What would a simulated crash feel like? Would traumatic injuries hurt as bad as they seemed or was this the true test for her and she'd have to piece together her unit mates under extreme conditions? As the shuttle's nose impacted with the ground and the craft flipped end over end, Leba's seat restraints snapped sharply, digging into her chest, and knocking the wind out. The shuttle finally came to a halt, and she was thrown back with her seat for a final time.

Leba gasped for breath and opened her eyes. Nauseated from the dizzying tumble but relieved she hadn't puked in her helmet, Leba found herself uncomfortably upside-down. There were grumbles and murmurs and a lot of cursing. Leba stretched out her arm, grabbed the nearest handhold and, with her other hand, manipulated the manual harness release. Feeling the weight of her body pulling downward, she swung free of her chair and slowly lowered herself to what once had been the ceiling of the shuttle. Several others performed the same maneuver, swinging free and landing gently.

As Leba scanned the cabin, she watched Uribos try and free Sandler. The manual release was not working. Leba reached into her boot and pulled out her rock knife. "Need some help?" she offered. Uribos nodded. "You hold her, and I'll cut the straps." Supporting the majority of Sandler's weight on his shoulders, Uribos watched as Leba stood on an overhead light fixture and cut deftly through the restraints. Uribos gently slid Sandler from his shoulders to his arms.

Replacing her knife, Leba climbed down and checked for Sandler's pulse. Strong.

Good. Her pupils were somewhat slow to react. "Probably a mild concussion," Leba diagnosed. Pushing her fingernail into Sandler's elicited a pain response. "She'll be okay," Leba said. "Just keep stimulating her."

"I can do that." Uribos grinned.

"You know what I mean," Leba said, shaking her head.

Uribos gently slid Sandler to the floor. He put his hand under her chinstrap and rubbed the lower half of her face. A groggy Sandler moaned, her words dragged slowly from her mouth. "What happened?" Leba started to crouch down, but Uribos put up a hand.

"Don't worry, Doc, I'll take care of her." He smiled. Leba could see how Riki Sandler could get lost in those eyes. "See what's up with the rest."

Leba nodded and proceeded forward in the cabin. Avoiding the brunt of the impact by sitting in the tail section, she'd lucked out. The simulatronic pilot in the tiny cockpit was probably a pile of chips and circuits.

A CHANGE IN TACTICS: MAIDEN VOYAGE

Middie Fidelis looked funny hanging upside down from her seat, cursing at Mally Yertha to get her free. Leba reached into her boot sheath again, removed the knife, and approached the pair. "Hey, Doc," Middie said rather casually, "do you think you could get me down?"

"Need some help?" Leba watched Braids Frence carefully step over a light fixture and pull up beside her.

"No, I like hanging upside down," Middie said, droplets of sweat beading from her reddened forehead.

Leba flipped the knife in her hand and handed Mally the pommel end. "You cut the straps, and Braids and I will ease her down." Not as deft as Leba, Mally could barely manage to saw through the harness. With Mally's labored strokes, Middie shook violently back and forth. Sliding out from her restraints, Middie unceremoniously landed into Leba's and Braids's waiting arms. After setting Middie down on the floor, Leba outstretched an arm to help her up.

Middie snatched the knife from Mally's hand as she attempted to return it to Leba. "Nice little tool, Doc." Middie rolled it over in her hands. "Snuck it in under Cathen's watch." Running her thumb carefully down the blade, Middie Fidelis puffed out her cheeks and grinned. "I may like you yet."

"Thanks, I think," Leba said, putting out her hand and accepting the knife back.

The sounds of intermittent crackling punctuated the random sparks, which sporadically illuminated the outside of cabin. Steam rose past the viewports as snow melted under the spacecraft.

Tenuously standing on her own, Riki Sandler rubbed her head. "Glad to have you back," Uribos said. Leba watched how Vic Uribos kept one arm around her waist. He would have her back.

"What happened?" she asked, her voice barely a whisper. With a concussion, the muted sound of her own voice in her head was probably still too loud. She must have one killer headache. That's going to make the rest of her journey miserable. The thinner air up here in the mountains wasn't going to help either.

"I can answer that," Tylor Gref said, moving his hand up and then slamming it down. "We crashed." Not helpful.

"That's not what she means, stupid," Joreg Hech corrected.

This team is going to implode before we even get started.

Before the two could resume their bickering, Emmie Hodd stepped back to the assembled group. Her face was smeared with dark marks, maybe blowback from the pilot's cabin. "Pilot's gone, and for now we're stranded." Hands clasped, almost in prayer, she interlocked her fingers and moved them to her chin. "Shuttle can't fly, and I'm not sure how long we can maintain cabin integrity."

"Any good news?" Middie asked, her hands clenched into fists and buried under her armpits.

"Except for Riki's concussion, we seem to all be intact," Uribos reported. "Right, Doc?"

All eyes turned toward Leba, who nodded in agreement.

"What now?" Mally shivered. Leba didn't notice it was particularly cold yet; the trembling was probably more from fear. She knew they would all start to feel the cold soon enough.

All eyes turned toward Emmie, waiting for her to take the lead. Emmie didn't answer right away. Slowly and deliberately Emmie Hodd looked from one person to the next. "First we need to see what we can salvage from the shuttle. Doc, you and Braids go aft and see what you can salvage from our equipment." Hodd leaned against a bulkhead, craning her neck to peer out a window. "Second, we need to figure out where we are. Gref, Hech, see what you can find forward to help us. Third, Uribos, you're with me."

"What about Riki?" Uribos inquired, his concern about leaving her evident.

"Mally, you keep an eye on Riki. Neuro checks every fifteen and report any changes."

"What about me?" Middie Fidelis asked, her arms now splayed, palms up.

"Do what you do best." Emmie feigned a smile. "Keep track of everyone and their progress."

"Got it," Middie agreed.

"What are we doing?" Uribos questioned Emmie.

Her head swiveled to take in the cabin. "We, my friend, are going to see how really screwed we are." So far, Leba was not impressed with Emmie's leadership. She didn't inspire confidence. There was no sense of urgency. Right now, what they lacked was time.

The ambient temperature outside the shuttle was bordering on negative numbers. The frigid wind gusts brought it down even further. It was still midmorning, and as the day progressed, Leba knew the temperature would plunge even further. The shuttle could only protect them so long. When the reserve batteries were exhausted, the interior shuttle temperature would equalize with the exterior, and they would freeze. Given the escaping gases the shuttle was belching out, igniting a fire for warmth anywhere in the vicinity of the shuttle would be suicidal. They needed to abandon it soon, get far enough away in case the reactor core was breached, and set up camp.

Designed only for short-range transport, this type of shuttle was not equipped with escape pods or any significantly redundant systems. Leba thought it was curious they would embark on a rescue mission with such inadequate support, but that seemed to be the point of the cold box, make do with what you have or die trying. Green med team was lucky the aft storage compartment and the back section of the shuttle sustained minimal damage. The impact smashed in the cockpit, and the subsequent rollover left the tail pointing upward. Realizing the contents shifted during impact and would probably spill out, Leba and Braids pried open the storage compartment carefully. Luckily, most of the equipment was secure, and their biggest challenge would be to get the heavy folded travel sled out and righted.

Emmie Hodd asked everyone to reassemble in fifteen minutes. The team reunited on schedule. Middie announced, "Everyone's here." All eyes turned toward Middie. "Hey, don't look at me, I was asked to keep track of all you guys."

"Gref, Hech, any idea where we are?" Emmie questioned.

"Using preloaded data I found on an accessory bridge portal, we were on a northern polar route from an equatorial starting course," Gref said.

"We were airborne approximately three standard hours," Hech chimed in. "Compensating for launch time, I'd say we were about three-quarters of the way to our destination."

"Based on the static topographical map on the auxillary nav board, that would put us at the eastern base of the mountain ridge." Gref crossed his right hand over his chest and grasped his left upper arm.

"Since Victos and I did not see any signs of debris or the objective, we must not have passed our original destination." Emmie was interrupted by Riki Sandler's raised arm.

Riki sat up straighter, shaking Mally's hand off, "My part of the orders said there was a settlement on the western face of the mountain at coordinates 34.7 by 62.8."

"Are you certain?" Gref asked, his brows coming together.

"Why?" Emmie questioned.

Hech answered, "Tylor and I figured we are at 214.7 by 62.8."

"It is a simulation, you know," Middie interrupted.

"Riki's concussion is no simulation," Victos Uribos voiced his opinion.

"Now settle down," Emmie cautioned. "No one said the simulation was necessarily safe, only contrived." Emmie looked at Uribos. "Victos, let's move on, tell everyone what we found."

Victos began, "First, the shuttle landed in packed snow nose first."

"Who didn't know that?" Hech whispered to Gref.

"Shut up and listen," Gref chastised him.

"Second, it looks like the cockpit lost its containment field, and the passenger cabin, although currently isolated, is losing backup power secondary to an external hull breach. We're venting gases, and I'm not sure how long we'll maintain internal atmosphere," Uribos continued.

"Any good news?" Middie inquired, her frustration with the current situation obvious. "I didn't sign on for this."

Emmie took over the report. "For now, the outside ambient temperature is not too bad, and we probably still have a significant amount of daylight left."

"What's not too bad?" Mally asked. Despite grasping both her arms, hugging herself to stay warm, she continued to tremble.

"That's code for you won't freeze to death until later today," Middie offered.

"Enough," Emmie chastised her. "Doc, Braids, how'd you do?"

Leba looked at Braids and nodded to her to begin. "Most of our equipment is salvagable. Our travel sled seems to be intact, and its batteries are fully charged."

"Finally, some encouraging news," Emmie said.

"We have ten survival suits, and most of the med stuff is distributed between a number of large backpacks," Braids continued. Leba saw a slight smile cross Emmie Hodd's face as she encouraged Braids to continue. "In the shuttle's evac locker, we found an ax, a shovel, a small generator, two decent lengths of rappelling cable, some thermal blankets, and three short-range comms. But..." Braids hesitated.

"But what?" Mally said, eyes big and round, her lower lip quivering as she hung on every word.

"Doc." Braids looked at Leba to finish the *but*.

"But we didn't find any rations." Leba waited a moment. She knew her next statement would be met with shock, but maybe it would help pull everyone together in their anger. "It's almost like the rations were removed from the standard survival kits." A common problem required cooperation for a workable solution.

"Are you sure?" Emmie asked, her hand stroking her neck.

"We found the detail list for each pack, and the rations were listed but not there," Leba responded.

"Son of a—" Middie started but was stifled by Emmie.

"So we are stuck in a near-frozen tundra with minimal survival gear, no food, and no significant means of calling for help," Hech recounted.

"You got it, genius," Gref said, and then the bickering started.

"You forgot one thing," Emmie reminded, grasping the front of her chest. "We have each other."

"Great," Gref continued. "We can all sit around a fire, singing camp songs and bonding."

"Hey," Uribos said, cracking his knuckles, "I don't plan to do any bonding with either of you."

"And what do you mean by that?" Hech began. "Scared of showing us your real feelings?"

"I'll show you real feelings," Uribos said, nostrils flaring and arms flexing. He approached Hech with his hands raised.

"Enough," Middie interrupted. "Look here, you big babies." Middie stared between the two. "Sit down, shut up, and let Hodd figure how she's going to lead us outta this mess." Middie's endorsement of Emmie's leadership was suspect at best.

"If I may interrupt," Mally interrupted. Everyone turned toward her. "I think Luth, I mean our squad leader, wants to see if we can work together."

"Really." Someone snickered.

"I think Mally's right." Leba could feel the stares directed at her. She reached into her pocket and pulled out a few protein bars. "I always keep some just in case," she offered. "I'm willing to share."

Emmie smiled. "Anyone else got any little goodies? Now don't hold back."

Victos smiled and then chuckled. "I'll bring the music." He reached into his pocket and produced a small, undetected music player.

Middie removed a flask from her breast pocket. "I've got the good stuff."

Braids laughed. "I've got a holo of Cathen we can watch burn." Everyone laughed, even Mally.

Emmie said, "Not exactly standard, but I think we now have some common ground."

"Yes," Riki said, trying to stand, now without assistance. "We're all rule breakers." Victos Uribos moved to her side and steadied her. Riki produced a small, palm-sized device from her pants pocket.

"That's not what I think it is, is it?" Victos asked. Riki nodded, slightly embarrassed. He kissed her head. "I love you."

"Get a room," Hech advised.

Emmie regrouped everyone. "We need to be leaving soon."

Leba offered, "Based on what you and Victos told us, we probably have at least six more hours of daylight. In that time, we need to find suitable shelter."

"What about food?" Braids asked.

"We can go until morning with what we have," Leba continued. "Our first priority is finding a way to stay out of the subzero temps for long periods of time."

"The doc's right," Hodd agreed. "We can worry about food in the morning."

There was a crunching sound, and a frightened Mally asked, "What was that?"

Emmie looked at Uribos. "The weight of this shuttle and the heat from the escaping gases is melting the snow underneath us."

The tail section moved farther downward as the shuttle shifted again. "We need to get the sled out," Braids said as she twirled a lock of her hair.

Emmie looked over at Riki. "Can you travel?"

Mustering a smile, Riki looked up at Mally and said, "With Mally's help, I think I'll be fine." Mally smiled back at Riki.

Then Emmie Hodd took the lead she was given. "All right then, let's gear up and get out of here." Everyone donned a survival suit, the last one stowed in case of a breach. Leba, Braids, Uribos, and Gref were assigned to free the travel sled and ready it for transport. Hodd instructed the others to gather up the rest of the gear. Hodd took a comm and affixed it to herself. Uribos took another comm before he went out into the snow. Finally, Emmie decided Gref would carry the third.

Uribos manually disengaged the cabin exit door. A sudden burst of frigid air rushed into the passenger compartment. Wind whipped across the threshold, depositing a small dusting of snow onto the floor. "Be careful, it's slippery at the door." Unfortunately, the travel sled was designed to be removed through an outer access panel. Victos was the first to venture out and jumped from the doorway, landing onto the snow. He waved his hand to signal his successful landing. Gref let Leba and Braids go out next. Victos helped each land without incident. "I'm heading to the storage compartment!" Gref shouted and then secured the door.

Leba listened over Victos's comm as Hech helped Gref manually opened the access panel's inner door. The wind whooshed, and Gref yelped as cold flooded the cabin. Making the echo louder, Hodd and her crew already removed the stowed gear, leaving the area barren except for the travel sled.

Gref's comm crackled with Uribos's voice as Victos instructed him how to set up the pulley system they were going to use to get the travel sled to the ground. Leba was impressed with Uribos's engineering skills. The pulley was a smart idea, and the travel sled made it to the ground uneventfully. By the time the ground crew finished powering up the sled, Hodd's team deposited the majority of the supplies on the ground. Leba and Braids loaded the sled, while Uribos and Gref helped the rest out of the shuttle, save for Emmie Hodd.

From outside the viewport, Leba watched Emmie Hodd survey the interior of the upside-down shuttle. Reaching into her shirt, Emmie removed a small necklace, closed her eyes, and mouthed something, then kissed the charm.

"Come on," Gref urged over the comm. Hodd replaced the medal, refastened the front of her survival suit, and dropped to the ground.

Bright sunlight reflected off the snow-covered ground. By now, everyone's visors were down and darkened to prevent snow blindness. Still shaky from her concussion, Riki sat wedged between two large duffels on the sled. Mally sat next to her, keeping a constant vigil. The brightness caused everyone's pupils to constrict, making neuro checks on Riki more difficult. It was decided Mally should ride on the sled too, to keep a closer eye on Riki. This meant some of the gear needed to be carried. Leba didn't mind as the pack she was shouldering partially protected her from the occasional gusts of bone-chilling wind. Victos didn't seem to mind schlepping the extra burden either. Of course, Hech did mind, and he voiced his opinion vehemently until Victos offered to silence him forever if he didn't shut up.

Volunteering to drive the travel sled, Middie sat smiling in the cab. Although rather cramped, she appeared happy not to be in the snow with the rest. Hodd gave her the coordinates they were to follow. She asked Gref to give up his comm to Middie, but he refused. Victos stepped up and handed his to Middie. "That was very nice of you," Leba said to Victos as they walked in front of the slow-moving sled.

"Thanks," he said, his word choppy and curt. Leba could tell he was angry but was trying to be a good soldier. Despite his occasional bravado, Victos was a man Leba felt she could count on. She didn't necessarily feel the same about some of her other teammates. Gref and especially Hech seemed so self-absorbed, as if the world and its events rotated about them. They were at the center of their own solar system with no significant concerns for the others.

Leba liked the way Braids looked after Emmie. Whether Emmie knew it or not, Braids worshipped Emmie and took every opportunity to display her affection. Leba watched the two follow behind the sled, the younger woman locked arm in arm with the older one, helping her navigate through the deep snow. Lagging behind as usual, Gref and Hech brought up the rear.

The group traced a route around the base of the mountain in a westerly direction, and after a grueling two-hour trudge through deep snow drifts, the permafrost ground became palpable under their boots. Victos led the caravan for another half-hour until the entire unit was out of the snow. He jogged back to the travel sled to ask Middie to stop. When Leba returned to the sled, she heard Middie comm Emmie and Gref to let them know why she stopped. It was another half-hour before Gref and Hech reached the group. By this time, there was snow melting in a small pot over a fire.

After the water boiled and cooled, Victos carefully poured some into everyone's canteen. Gref and Hech removed their gloves and stretched their hands over the campfire. Victos helped Riki off the sled, and she lit the smoke hanging from his mouth. He offered her a drag, which she eagerly took. Leba didn't say anything. Smoking would suck away body heat faster, but its calming effect trumped practicality. Carefully removing a smoke from her pocket, Emmie let it hang loosely from her mouth. "How'd you get that lit?" Emmie asked.

"Same way I started the fire," Victos explained as he cupped the lighter's flame and lit Emmie's smoke.

"I know how Vic gets when he's stressed." Riki took the lighter, let her finger drag along his palm. "A good smoke always seems to calm him down." Riki smiled.

Taking a slow and satisfying drag off her smoke, Emmie said, "I know what you mean." Removing the smoke from her mouth, she flicked ashes onto the pure-white snow and watched the small sizzles with each impact.

"Such a dirty habit," Hech said to Gref, who nodded in agreement.

"Shut up and move over," Middie said as she approached the fire. "You keep pissing off Uribos, and he's gonna beat the hell out of you." She laughed. "Or I will."

Reluctantly Hech moved to give Middie some room. "How about you walk for a while and I'll drive the sled?"

"Can't do that," Middie stated, shaking her leg. "Bum ankle and all."

"What bum ankle?" Hech asked.

"The one at the end of my leg, stupid."

"Ignore her," Gref advised.

Leba bent over to look at some moss growing on a nearby rock.

"Whatcha looking at, Doc?" Mally asked as she approached.

Leba turned from her squatted position. "Come down here and look." Mally leaned over but then crouched down beside Dr. Brader to see what she was pointing at. "See these little fuzzy gray cups hiding in between the fissures in the rocks?"

Mally nodded her head. "Uh-huh."

"These are called cup moss. They're actually lichens of the genus Lecanora. These little guys are really cool."

"I know you're really smart, but it looks like fungus to me. Getting excited over some fungus is kinda weird," Mally blurted out.

Ignoring her, Leba corrected, "You're half right. These are lichen, a combination of fungus and algae. That's what makes them so special. The fungus, or mycobiont, and the algae, or phycobiont, live and grow together as a team, helping each other out." Leba gently passed a gloved hand over the lichen carpet. "If I'm right about the type of lichen these are, we may have solved some of our food problem."

Leba noticed the sickening expression on Mally's face. "I'm definitely not eating any dirty fuzz from some stupid rock." Mally got up and sulked away.

You will if you get tired of eating nothing but snow. Turning her attention back to her find, Leba was lucky to spot these little guys. Most times, low-lying patches of Lecanora would be quickly consumed by the larger ungulates. The ungulates living in these snowy regions could see in the ultraviolet range, allowing them to purposely not miss the lichens for the snow. People, who could only see visible light, usually were so overwhelmed by the bright whiteness of the snow that small patches of gray were easily overlooked.

When the wind died down, Leba could hear everything around her. Squatting on her haunches, she paused and placed her palms on the rock in front of her. Taking a knee for better balance, Leba surveyed the majesty of the setting. In the distance, she heard the mountain grumble and belch out steam. She looked up to see a flock of white birds, their wings tipped in brown fly in a V formation. Perfect leadership.

Mally approached the fire where Middie and some of the others gathered to warm their hands. "What's she looking at?" Middie asked Mally.

"Some stupid fungus stuff," Mally said.

"Think we could smoke it?" Middie jested. Gref and Hech laughed, but Mally only sighed. Leba returned her attention to scrapping the gray cup lichen with her rock knife and carefully collecting pieces in a small container. "Hey, Doc!" Middie yelled over. Leba stopped her work and inclined her head toward Middie. "Hey, Doc, think we could smoke that weed?" Leba tried to ignore her, but by this time, Emmie, Braids, Victos, and Riki noted the commotion and were heading toward the fire.

Thankfully, a gust of wind whistled, drowning out the rest of Middie's analysis. Leba closed the container, replaced her rock knife, got up, and headed toward the group. "What's that?" Riki asked.

Leba held up the small container for her and everyone else to see. "Lecanora lichen," she stated proudly. "I think?"

Victos laughed. "You think?" He took a long drag and blew a cloud of gray smoke. Pity to soil such clean air. He took the spent smoke from his mouth, dropped it onto the ground, and crushed it out.

"Don't worry, I'll volunteer to try it first," Leba said as she slowly opened the container and poured it into the small pot dangling over the fire. She scooped up a handful of snow and added it to the container. "Be back in a minute." Leba knelt down over one of the med packs and, after rummaging through it, removed a small ampule. With a pop that broke its seal, she poured the contents into the pot.

"Definitely mad scientist material," Gref whispered to Hech.

"I heard that," Leba shot back. "You'll thank me if this works." Looking for something to stir the brew with, Leba went to the med bag again. Finally, she returned to the now-bubbling pot and gently swirled the contents. She took a whiff. It smelled like freshly turned soil after a rainstorm with a distinct hint of butteriness. "Doesn't smell too bad."

"Too bad?" Mally looked like she was going to throw up.

"Food's food," Middie added. "If the doc doesn't croak after trying it, then I'm in."

After about fifteen minutes of watching the thick gray mush stew, Leba carefully removed the small pot from the fire and plunged the bottom into the snow. A satisfying hiss signaled the temperature drop. The brew cooled quickly. Leba put a small spoon into the mix and raised a dose. "Wish me luck."

Mally turned away. Maybe she imagined Leba would swallow a spoonful and then turn gray, vomit, and die horribly. Blowing over the top of the spoon to cool it further, Leba sipped the liquid. It was slightly bitter, and the little pieces of lichen felt funny on her tongue. "Not too bad," she commented as she dipped her spoon in again.

"No double dipping." Victos laughed. He walked over to Leba.

"Sorry, I wasn't thinking." There was no place to hide her mistake. Leba dropped her eyes down and her spoon arm to her side. A gray drop slid slowly across the back of it and after hanging on for a second made the plunge to the ground. She moved her boot to cover it.

"Just kidding," he said, patting her on the shoulder. "Here, let me try the next spoonful." Leba wiped the spoon with snow and handed it to him. He scooped up a heaping portion and swallowed the mush in one big gulp. There was silence for a moment, and then he moaned, grabbing his stomach and screwing up his face. His lids fluttered, followed by his eyes rolling up into his head, and Victos Uribos dropped into the snow.

Riki rushed over to him. "Vic, are you okay?" He said something imperceptible, and Riki leaned in closer. "What?" she asked, caressing his face. Leba smiled.

"I guess you really do care," Victos said, trying to keep his eyes pinched shut. He opened his eyes and sat up, a big grin on his face.

Riki pushed him back into the snow. Victos fell back, laughing. Red-faced, Riki turned and walked away. Leba helped Victos to his feet. "Not bad, Doc. Not bad at all."

From their perturbed expressions, Gref and Hech were obviously not amused. "I don't think I'm inclined to eat that concoction," Hech said and joined Riki, whose back was to the group, her fists balled up under her armpits.

"Me neither." Mally pouted and went to join Riki.

"I try and avoid gray-colored foods," Gref added.

"Suit yourself," Middie said. "But don't be belly-aching about how hungry you are later." Braids and Emmie already were downing spoonfuls when Middie joined the rest in sampling Leba's brew. "Could probably use some pepper, though." Middie's beefy hand slapped Leba's shoulder.

Nothing's every good enough for you, is it? It's not like I brought a spice rack with me.

Utilizing the same spoon, Gref tried some and retrieved Hech, who reluctantly did as well. "Definitely not doing four days of this stuff," Hech barked. Riki and Mally remained stubborn. Poor Riki. It was bad enough to have a killer headache, but an empty belly made it worse. Vic was obviously not going to patronize her; she'd have to sulk. Mally, on the other hand, was just being childish.

"About time we get going again," Emmie said. "Middie, get the travel sled warmed up and ready to move out." Middie swallowed a gulp from her flask, replaced the screw cap, and carefully secured it underneath her parka before heading for the sled. Emmie Hodd turned toward Leba. "Doc, why don't you collect as much of the fungus stuff as you can, and we'll keep it for later if we don't find anything else."

It's lichen, not fungus. Leba headed back to the rock crevice to scrape off more cup moss.

The exhaust from the engine kicked up a little snow toward the others. "Sorry, guys!" Middie yelled from the sled's cab. She dusted Gref and Hech pretty well. They were pissed, but Middie ignored their curses and turned her attention back to the sled's controls. Gusts of wind whipped through, bringing more frigid air. They needed to find shelter soon. Although their respite was needed, it was too long, and daylight would soon be in short supply.

"I think you should ride at least for now," Emmie told Riki. "Mally, you too, ride with Riki." Both women mounted the sled and wedged between the equipment.

Leba returned to the remaining five. "We better start looking for a place to camp."

"We still have a lot of daylight left," Braids offered. "We could travel a long way before we have to stop for the night."

"Doc's right," Victos said, patting snow off his jacket from where he fell. "Even if we find a good spot, it will take us a while to set up camp." Emmie looked perplexed. Victos continued, "A good place may be as simple as an overhanging rock ledge. We'll still need to construct a shelter for protection."

"In order to maintain our heat when it gets really cold out, we'll have to stay in small groups," Leba advised. "With all of us in one big room, we lose heat a lot faster, especially if our shelter is made from snow."

"I really should've paid more attention to that lecture," Braids bemoaned.

"Unfortunately, it wasn't covered very well," Leba said, picking up her backpack and stuffing the collected lichen in one of the outer pockets. In fact, the "Surviving the Cold" lecture focused more on making sure your cold weather gear fit properly then what to do if you have to spend the night on the trail.

Victos put out the fire and deconstructed the frame they used to suspend the little pot. Emmie put snow in the pot and carefully removed any remaining residue. Once all the gear was loaded, everyone picked up their assigned loads, and Emmie signaled Middie to begin forward. "Victos, you and the doc take point."

Leba and Victos picked up their pace until they were well ahead of the sled. Emmie and Braids walked alongside the sled, while Gref and Hech followed on the other side. Leba noticed the sun high in the sky; it was midday now, and evening would be approaching quickly, and with it, the temperature would drop rapidly. "If we don't find something soon, it's going be a cold night," Victos cautioned.

"I guess we could use the sled as a base and run lines to the ground and cover the top and sides with blankets," Leba suggested.

"Maybe," Victos said. "Or we can build snow huts."

"Snow huts?" Leba questioned.

"When you were a kid, did you ever make a fort in the snow?" Leba nodded. "Snow huts are similar but have a top. The problem is, they have to be small so they won't collapse. That'll mean a lot of work for us to get snow huts made for each of us."

"Maybe we can combine the two approaches," she offered.

After an hour more of travel and no sheltering possibilities, Victos told Leba he should talk with Emmie. The two jogged back to Emmie's position. "We've gotta stop now and start work on shelters for the night." Victos outlined the ideas he and Leba discussed. "So what do you think?" Obviously, Vic hadn't gotten the memo that you needed to let Emmie come up with the plan if you wanted her to agree.

Emmie scratched her cheek. The cold was making her skin itchy. As it got colder, more things would begin to bother not just Emmie but everyone. Emmie was the oldest of the group, and Leba knew this journey would take its toll on her first. She was in good shape, but she was thin and would feel the cold more than the rest. Lighting another smoke while considering Vic's recommendations wasn't helping either. Frustration, desperation, and confusion were real concerns. Emmie commed Middie to stop the sled and asked everyone to gather round. Leba heard the sled power down. Middie popped the sled door but remained in the cockpit.

Wow, Emmie took Vic's suggestions without question. Why couldn't she do that with me?

Hech and Gref joined the others on Emmie's side of the sled. "What now?" Hech asked. He too appeared tired and fed up. Mally and Riki scooted to the side where Emmie was. Middie finally slid down from the cab and joined the rest. When everyone was assembled, Emmie laid out her plan for the proposed shelters.

"You're not serious?" Gref questioned.

"There's no other way," Victos interjected.

"I'm not going to force anyone to sleep in a snow hut, but this is the best plan," Emmie stated. "Right, Vic?"

"I figure we could probably sleep at least four or maybe five in the sled shelter. The rest of us would go solo in a hut." Victos crossed his arms over his chest. Leba kept quiet. The group was probably more willing to disagree with the idea if they knew some of the plan was hers. Challenging Vic Uribos was scary for most. Even Middie seemed to give Vic's suggestions a thorough evaluation before slamming the door.

"Your idea, you get a hut," Gref said.

"Before this gets ugly"—Emmie scratched her chin—"I think Riki should be in the shelter and Mally with her. Someone needs to keep an eye on her." Emmie looked around for an argument, but none came.

"I'll take a hut," Leba volunteered.

"Me too," Braids chimed in.

"Me three," Victos agreed.

"I guess I'll make the fourth," Middie offered.

"No," Emmie said placing a hand on her shoulder. "But I do appreciate the offer." Middie looked at her, not knowing exactly how to react. "I want you to stay up in the sled cab. It's heated, isn't it?"

"Well, yes," Middie replied, turning her head away.

A CHANGE IN TACTICS: MAIDEN VOYAGE

"Would've been nice to know," Hech said, the spittle building up in the corners of his mouth. "No wonder you weren't willing to give it up."

"Shut up and stop your whining." Middie's head snapped around, and she sneered at him. "It takes a lot of work to keep this piece of junk"—she thumbed the sled—"moving through this slushy mess."

"Enough," Emmie demanded. "I'm in charge, and this is how it's going to be. Gref, you and Hech will be with Riki and Mally in the sled shelter. Middie, you stay in the cab, and the rest of us will be in individual huts." She waited through the grumbling and then finished, "This is not easy for any of us, but we'll get through as long as we work together." Middie would do better in a hut, given Emmie's almost cachectic form, but Leba wasn't going to argue. When Emmie's mind was made up, nothing short of divine intervention, or maybe Vic, could change it. Besides, it suggested Emmie was old and frail. A slight to her leadership capabilities.

Over the next few hours, the sun dipped toward the horizon, and four snow huts took shape. The sled shelter's overlapping blankets were secured in place. Finally, as the last bit of sunlight gave way to darkness, Emmie Hodd stood in the middle of the completed shelter and offered a prayer. For once, there was silence in the group as Emmie bowed her head and spoke. At the conclusion, everyone nodded their agreement. Victos made sure Riki and Mally were tucked in. Gref and Hech finally seemed comfortable with their accommodations. Middie climbed back into the sled's cab, reclined the seat back, took a swallow from her flask, and pulled a warm woolen blanket up over her head. Leba watched a gloved hand reach out, fumble for the door latch, and shut it.

Emmie, Braids, Victos, and Leba headed for the four little snow huts. Although they were small, sitting inside was not a problem. Standing, however, was out of the question. Leba didn't mind though; she was tired and wanted to sleep. She wrapped herself in a blanket and reactivated her survival suit's seals. Sleeping in a helmet was no fun but safer given the harsh conditions. Sleep came quickly.

CHAPTER 16

The morning sun reflected brightly off the snow, illuminating the little snow hut. Leba's eyes fluttered open. Forgetting where she was, she tried stretching but was met with a snowy wall. Carefully she got to her knees and ventured out. She grabbed her blanket as she exited. Walking past the other snow huts, trying to keep her crunching footsteps from waking the others, Leba exaggerated her movements, attempting to stretch her stiff, cramped muscles. She guessed the others were still asleep. After folding the blanket and securing it under her arm, Leba heard a scrapping sound. It seemed to be coming from opposite where they traversed the day before. Leba swore she saw something move too. Maybe her eyes weren't adjusted to the intense brightness. Drawn to the disturbance, she crept forward. There it was, big as day, a wooly, long-haired ovibos. Its massive horned head bowed, grazing leisurely. The beast was busy nosing the cold white carpet, trying to get at the hidden plants beneath. Leba stood very still and watched it use its stocky hoofed foreleg to dig into the ground and uncover its prize.

Hearing footsteps, she turned to see Middie creeping up behind her. "Been watching that thing for a while," she said. "I spotted it earlier from the cab. Pretty good sight line up there."

"It's probably more scared of us than we are of it," Leba whispered.

"I was thinking about how many steaks we could carve outta that fellow." Middie laughed. The ovibos, still chewing, raised its head and turned in their direction. "It probably didn't like the steak comment." Middie laughed again.

"Its eyesight is poor at long distances, so I guess it caught a whiff of us," Leba guessed.

"And what a whiff," Middie said, sticking her nose to her armpit. "None of us has showered."

"You just stink naturally," Gref said as he walked up behind them.

"Funny, wise guy," Middie countered. While they bickered, the ovibos sauntered off. "Hey, why didn't you tell me that thing was leaving?" Middie questioned Leba after she turned from Gref.

"Too early in the morning for steaks. Besides, where there's one, there's more. In fact, large mammals often gather near sources of food and water, so I suspect we're in for more encounters with some of the locals."

"What's all the noise?" Victos said, climbing out of his hut, unceremoniously hitting his head on the low doorway.

"Smooth move, lover boy," Gref commented.

Victos rubbed his head. He chose not to sleep in his helmet, and his blanket was still hooded over his head. His face showed a day's growth of beard. He walked over to the assembling group. "Doc here let our steaks get away," Middie said, shoving her hands deep into her pockets and rocking on her heels.

"Huh?" Victos questioned, rubbing his eyes but finding his gloved hands weren't very useful.

"Look, you may like gray fuzzy stuff, Doc, but the rest of us are hungry for some real food," Middie continued. Gref nodded, agreeing with Middie's assessment of the dining situation. As the commotion got louder, Emmie and Braids made it out of their huts.

"Here," Leba said, thrusting her hand in her pocket and removing the protein bars she was carrying. "Take them," she said, shoving them at Middie, forcing her to remove her pocketed hands to avoid dropping the stash. Leba walked away from the group. Tears welled up in her eyes and slowly ran down her cheek. Save for their high salinity, they would have frozen on her face.

Braids caught up to Leba. "Hey, Doc, Ma wants to go over the plan for today before we move out."

Not turning to face her, Leba nodded. "Be there in a minute." Hearing Braids trot off, Leba kicked at the snow, sniffed in a few times, then rejoined the group. *Keep it together. I only have to put up with these people for three more days. Wish DeShay was here.* Leba kept her eyes focused on her feet and waited for the stragglers. Shortly thereafter, Hech, Mally, and Riki emerged from their shelters. Victos greeted Riki at the side of the travel sled.

"Good morning, how's the head?"

"A lot better than yesterday," Riki confessed, and then rubbed the mark on his forehead right beneath the blanket. "How's yours?"

Leba decided to keep quiet and listen, not offer any suggestions. Emmie's plan was stupid. Killing and butchering an adult ovibos was ridiculous, but she would never be able to convince the others, so why try. She could survive without them. Her mom did her test solo; so could she. Leba hated being different. She would have been a much better leader than Emmie Hodd. DeShay told her so. For starters, she was smarter and a better strategist. Emmie Hodd was weak, and the others didn't respect her. Leba wasn't quite sure why she was directing her anger at Emmie. The latest jabs came from elsewhere. Maybe because Leba thought a leader should be respected, and Emmie disappointed her. How could DeShay be so in love with her? An awesome person like DeShay should know better. None of this romance stuff made sense. There was a disconnect. Emmie was too inconsistent and selfish and didn't understand DeShay's needs.

The others, with the possible exception of Victos, were reluctant followers, more concerned with themselves than the team, and that made Leba mad too. Wrong again. Victos was more concerned with how he and Riki were doing than the mission. Braids lived and died by what Ma said, never questioning, just following blindly. Gref and Hech were selfish, Mally was naive, and Middie, well, Middie was mean and spiteful. Now who was being immature and childish? *Get over your hurt feelings, or no one will ever respect you either.* Leba sucked in a big breath and refocused on Emmie's briefing.

Emmie Hodd knelt down and, using her finger, drew a crude layout of their current position, with the crash site behind and the taller mountains to their left. "Straight ahead seems to be some sort of valley, maybe protected to some degree by the mountains on either side." Emmie traced a line through the valley and along the edge of the right sided mountains. "I think it'll be easier going this way. We should be able to make our original destination by nightfall."

Concerned they would be somewhat exposed to the possibilities of hostiles as they traversed the valley out in the open, Leba wanted to comment but held back. The route along the taller mountains was certainly longer but ultimately safer. She needed to tell them or would never forgive herself if something went awry. So she did. As expected, she was met with rebuke and scorn. To her credit, Emmie did say she would consider the suggestion. As she took her assigned position, this time at the rear of the caravan, Leba unhappily acquiesced to the group's decision.

Besides leaving Victos at point, Emmie reassigned the others. While Hech was given the plumb job of driving the travel sled, she made Middie and Gref pair up on the side of the sled and assigned Braids to partner with Leba at the rear. Emmie felt Riki, still recovering from her concussion, should continue to ride on the sled. Mally volunteered her company and promised to monitor her for any signs of worsening. Emmie would join Vic at the front.

"Don't sulk, Doc," Braids said, her cheekbones almost reaching her eyebrows, her smile so wide. "Ma knows what she's doing." Head down and concentrating on keeping pace with the sled, Leba didn't respond. "Be that way," Braids murmured and matched her stride for stride.

Halfway through the morning, when everyone's stomachs were growling in harmony, Victos halted the caravan. Not wanting to make noise, he raised his hand. Unfortunately, he and Emmie were too far in front for hand signals to work. He pointed to a herd of tarandi off in the distance. They were medium-sized ruminants, the male adorned with antlers and the females in a harem close behind. The few young were huddled close by their mothers. "Lunch," he said to Emmie.

Emmie whispered to Victos, "What now?"

"Make your way back to the others and stop the sled," he advised. "But keep them quiet, or these guys will get spooked."

Emmie left his side and went back to tell the others. The herd grazed lazily. Dropping to his belly to watch them, Vic hoped his scent wouldn't alert them. In a few moments, Emmie crawled up next to him. "What do you think?" Victos outlined his plan. "Sounds pretty reasonable, if you can get close enough," she said.

"Unload the sled," Emmie instructed when she returned. "Gref, you and Hech go out to where Victos is, but keep quiet. You two gotta keep an eye on the game." They dispersed, each to their task. There was no way to accomplish it without a lot of noise, but luckily, they were far enough away their sounds drowned in the wind.

When Victos returned, he was still trying to brush the snow from the belly of his jacket. "Good, now I need someone to drive the sled."

"I will." Middie's hand shot up. "Always wanted to drive the getaway car."

Braids chimed in, "I'll ride shotgun."

"Great, then Hodd and I will do the dirty work," Victos stated. He was rooting around in some of the duffels until he found what he wanted. Returning to the sled, he removed the ax and shovel. Leba watched as he used the ax to chop a length of the shovel handle off. After notching both ends, Victos strung his makeshift bow using the suture material from the med kit. "Doc," he said, hand out and looking at Leba, "I'll need your knife."

Reluctantly Leba removed the knife from her boot, flipped it pommel end outward, and handed it to him. It snapped in his glove like a scalpel. Picking up a long thin metal medical retractor, Victos bent the prongs straight to make a tailfin and secured Leba's knife to the other end. Riki knelt down next to him and kissed him.

"What's that for?" he said slyly.

Leba wanted to say, "Get a room. I am standing right here."

"Luck." Riki blushed. Victos was a good shot. There was no luck needed; his skills on the practice range were usually the highest.

Two hours passed as Leba, Mally, and Riki waited for the others to return. Gref and Hech returned first, bickering as usual. Lying on their bellies, watching the spectacle, it must have been hard for them to keep quiet for so long. Rumbling noisily, the travel sled with Middie at the controls grinded back through the snow. Braids's head was visible over the side rail and in the back, helping Victos remove the bloody carcass from the pad. Holding her right wrist, Emmie leaned over the back. The pain evident on her face, Emmie yelled for assistance. Leba and Mally rushed over to find her parka sleeve shredded and smeared with blood. Her wrist was grossly deformed.

"Let me take a look at that." Leba carefully took Emmie's hand in hers and removed the tattered glove. There was blood and mud in the gouge in her wrist, and Leba could feel the crepitus of broken bone in the swollen and now discolored portions. Sitting Emmie down on one of the med duffels, Leba adroitly packed the fractured wrist in snow. "Hand me the black bag over there." She pointed for Mally. Almost losing her footing in a rush to help, Mally brought the snow-covered pack to Leba. "Mally, hold here for me," Leba instructed.

Emmie gritted her teethed when Mally grasped her wrist, the pressure causing Emmie to wince. Leba rummaged through the med bag, removing the supplies and equipment she needed. The snow melted into the wound but left the area somewhat numb. First, Leba irrigated the wound and then, using an ultrasonic device, delivered quick pulses to the affected area, attempting to reduce the surrounding edema further. The decrease in swelling lessened the pain to some degree. Leba wrapped a clean dressing over the wound and fitted Emmie's hand with an inflatable cast. Dialing in the approximate weight-based dose, Leba prepared the antimicrobial injector. When she turned back to answer Emmie, the older woman looked ashen.

"How bad is it?" Emmie asked. Her face was pale and her jaw slack.

"Pretty bad fracture, probably comminuted, but nothing that'll hold you back," Leba answered. Showing Emmie the med-injector, Leba said, "I know it's cold, but I need a spot to give you this." Mally helped Emmie remove her left arm from her jacket. Trying to get her right arm through the sleeve was too awkward and painful. After dispensing the medication, Leba offered, "I'd like to give you something for pain too."

Emmie's answer was silence. Leba explained, "If you want, I'll give you something that won't affect your consciousness or make you sleepy, but it may not be as effective."

"Okay, okay," Emmie gave in. The intensity of the throbbing and pain in her wrist was distracting her already, and it wasn't going to get a whole lot better on its own.

While Leba was tending Emmie's injury, she caught a look across to the sled where Victos and Braids were moving the carcass onto the snow. Dripping blood detailed their trail on the surrounding ground. "Here, use this," Middie said, handing Victos the ax. He took it from her hand and began breaking down the tarandi. It was a young female, given its development was probably in its second year of life. Its front hoot was smeared with blood, Emmie's blood.

Victos temporarily assumed the lead and assigned Gref and Hech to build a fire. Kindling was scarce, but finding material to burn was even more difficult. They were forced to cannibalize some of the supplies from the med packs. Pushing his home-made bow lengthwise through the disemboweled carcass, Victos used it as a spit rod. The eviscerated organs, still warm, lay in the snow, steam escaping in small wisps. The smell of roasting meat covered their increasingly foul odor. Emmie, her hand stabilized in a sling across her chest, made her way over to the fire.

Everyone was scattered around, waiting for the meal to be ready. Riki went over to where Victos was cleaning his bloody gloves in the snow. "How'd Emmie get hurt?"

"After we felled the tarandi, it didn't die right away. I went to finish the kill, and the damn thing kicked Hodd." Victos stood up and finished his thought. "I told her I would take care of it, but she wanted to help. Dammit, I should have told her to back off." He pulled his collar higher up around his neck.

"It's not your fault." Riki leaned in and placed her arms around his neck. "She's a big girl." She hesitated. "And you did warn her." Victos nodded agreement and kissed her gently on the lips. Emmie trembled. She, like Leba, heard the entire conversation.

After wrapping Emmie in the extra survival suit jacket, Leba left to clean up. With the remaining part of the shovel, Leba dug a small hole in the ground under the snow. "Whatcha doing?" Braids inquired.

"Burying the entrails," Leba said, beads of perspiration beginning to form on her forehead. "This stuff will bring out predators if we don't." Leba looked overhead and pointed for Braids to see. A majestic powerful bird soared overhead, its shadow sweeping through the campsite. "Ice hawk. Next'll be an ivory wolf or a pack of them. Then we'll really be in trouble." Leba inhaled deeply, but the cold air burned. "For now, the fire will keep them away, but when it dies down…" Her voice trailed off as she watched the dark smoke rise high into the sky. "That big smoke stack will keep away the animal predators but not the human ones." Braids seemed satisfied with the answer but did not offer a hand in the chore and walked away.

"The doc there says there may be bad guys lurking around," Braids suggested rather loudly to Emmie.

Using her left hand, Emmie shifted the strap looping her neck, the injured wrist heavy in the sling. "I didn't see anything to suggest that. Besides, the mountains keep us pretty well hidden."

Leba shifted her gaze toward the two women and was met with Braids's piercing gaze.

As the shovel dug deeper into the ground, the work was more difficult. The semifrozen undersoil was solid and unyielding as rock, and Leba was beginning to work up a sweat, yet she was determined to finish her task. Finally satisfied with the hole's dimensions, Leba put the shovel down and gathered up the bloodied intestines in her arms. Not wanting their contents to leak out and further contribute the stench of the remains, she gently laid them inside and began to fill the hole. Scattered among the entrails were bits and pieces reflecting the waning sunlight. Curious, Leba picked up some of the larger fragments. They were different than bone with a distinctive fracture pattern. *What had this tarandi eaten?* Then she knew what she recovered. These were the shattered remains of her rock knife, her precious rock knife, the gift from her father. No wonder the tarandi didn't die immediately. Sure-shot Victos's arrow missed its mark, striking instead the animal's hard pelvic girdle, shattering her knife. The blow felled the animal but not killed it. When the tarandi kicked Emmie, it must have been in excruciating pain.

Leba buried not only the animal's remains but also the remains of her rock knife. Carefully she broke a medical ampule over the hole's contents to help speed up the decomposition and finished shoveling back the frozen top soil she removed. Stretching out her cramping thigh and calf muscles, she got up from her crouched position and rubbed snow between her gloves to clean the bloodied guts off.

The sun continued its descent toward the horizon, the pale blue sky melting into darker and darker hues. Victos announced dinner was ready. Leba really didn't have a stomach for roasted tarandi and begged off the meal. The rest took turns filling their plates with roasted meat and feasted as if they'd never eaten before. Leba sat alone on the far side of the travel sled, away from everyone, removing bits of parboiled lichen from the med bag. It was chewy and bitter, but she was sure it would sit better than a heavy meat meal.

Snow crunched, and Leba saw the shadow first before Emmie Hodd was fully visible. "You okay, Doc?" Emmie asked.

"Fine." Leba struggled with the word. She finished chewing and swallowed the last bit of lichen. "Thank you for asking. I needed some quiet time."

Emmie looked down at her. "This arms really throbbing, do you think you could…" Emmie hesitated.

So that's the point of your visit. I should've guessed.

"Sure," Leba said and rummaged through the med bag. She produced two scored pink tablets. "These will help."

Emmie gratefully took the pills, placed them under her tongue, and let them rapidly dissolve. "Thanks," she said and turned to leave. "Gather up your gear and meet us by the fire. We'll be moving out shortly."

Leba acknowledged the order, repacked her gear, and quickly followed behind Emmie. The tarandi bones lay smoking in the fire amid the smoldering ashes. As soon as the remaining flesh burned off, the bones, blackened and charred, met their final resting place. Victos shoveled handfuls of snow onto the pyre until the glowing embers were no more. Victos noticed Leba's return and walked over to meet her. "Sorry about your knife, Doc," he explained. "Not as strong as I thought it would be. It shattered on impact with the tarandi."

My knife was fine. It was your lousy shot that busted it. "I figured as much," Leba said, flipping her hand. "No worries."

Victos smiled. "You really missed a great meal."

Absolutely clueless, but at least you thought I deserved an explanation.

She placed her hand over her upper abdomen. "Stomach," she lied.

"Maybe next time," Victos said then returned to finish his chore of cleaning the fire pit. Leba headed to where some of the others were reloading the sled.

It was now halfway to dusk, and Leba was concerned they continued to make very little progress. Time management sucked. Emmie assured them their destination was not very far now, maybe an hour or two's journey. Leba wasn't so sure, though. How would Emmie know? Even if their destination was close, there was no telling what lay ahead. The team hadn't even touched on any of their ordered objectives, and they were already a day and a half into a purported four-day mission.

Dusk settled in, the sky now thick and graying. Victos returned from his point position, and Emmie halted the caravan. Green med team could barely see their objective. "Big building. Looks deserted," Victos whispered. "Some smoldering debris. Maybe a burned-out transport vehicle or two, but no people. No foragers either," he quickly added.

"What'll we do?" Riki asked.

"I say we check it out," Victos offered, flexing his biceps while he patted snow from his suit.

"Of course you would say that," Hech said.

"I don't know about the rest of you people, but I'm tired and cold, and being inside looks pretty good right about now," Middie stated. Stomping her feet, and then with arms encircling her body, she rotated back and forth on her hips.

"Me too," said Mally. "A hot shower would be awesome." Braids nodded to the suggestion of a hot shower. Two days' worth of grit, grime, and chaffing were quite enough. Wonder if Cathen would arrange it so he could watch her. Cathen was a jerk, but he was supposed to be a professional.

"Sounds like a plan to me," Emmie stated.

Leba chewed the inside of her cheek, trying to keep quiet.

"What, no opinion from the doctor?" Gref chided. "No warnings of impending doom?" Leba sneered at him but remained silent. "If you have something to say, say it," Gref provoked. Leba remained silent, gritting her teeth, screwing up her face, furrowing her brow.

Support came from an unexpected source. "Shut up, Tylor. This time I want to hear what she has to say," Joreg Hech said to his partner. "She's been right about everything else so far, whether you people want to admit it or not."

Then all eyes were on her. "Go ahead, speak up," Hech encouraged. "But do it quickly, before I tell you to shut up too." Everyone laughed except Leba, who was deciding how to say what she wanted to say.

"Don't you think it's strange?" Leba pushed a lock of her hair off her face. "So far, nothing has gone right." She could see each of her words rise on warm breath.

"It's a test," Middie offered. "And Cathen's a jerk. What else is new?" Middie was getting more and more impatient. The effects of constant flasking beginning to show. Mally peered at her. She was going to take serious issue over the Cathen jab. Middie certainly knew how to push people's buttons.

"That's my point," Leba put a fist onto her open palm. "I doubt seriously we are just going to be able to walk down there, find everything to our liking, food, hot showers, comfortable beds, and wait for our pickup." There was silence.

"You know"—Hech nodded—"much as I hate to admit it, I think Doc has a point." He moved close to stand next to her. It was nice to finally have an ally.

"I'm not saying don't go down there. I'm just saying be careful when we do." Leba waited and continued, "What about our orders and the rescue mission? We haven't even come close to anything on the list, except maybe our original travel plans."

"She's right." Emmie tugged her shoulder to try and raise her right hand but withdrew, grimacing, and awkwardly scratched her face with her left hand instead. "Let's take this slow, people. Slow and by the book."

"It'll be dark soon, and we should be able to slip a couple of us in unnoticed," Victos suggested.

"What, and leave the rest of us to freeze out here?" Middie asked, her teeth chattering as she took a pull from her flask. She really needed to back off the stuff. It was not doing her any favors. But Leba dared not broach the subject.

"No," Victos shot back.

"Do you have an idea?" Emmie asked him.

"I think we send part of the team in the sled as if we are arriving for our medical rescue, while the others infiltrate," Victos outlined.

"You're taking a big chance with some of our—" Gref began.

"Even the bad guys usually leave medical people alone," Riki interrupted.

"Especially if the med team consists of all women," Leba added.

"I'm surprised at that sexist remark coming from you, Doc," Middie said.

"She's just being realistic," Emmie confirmed.

"I'm driving then," Middie blurted out.

"I'd have it no other way," Emmie agreed. She gave her comm to Hech.

"You know that'll leave us no way to contact the boys if we give them all the comms," Riki reminded her.

"You'll have to sell that you're alone," Uribos said. "No backup, no support."

"And you better have a plausible story about where your shuttle is," Gref interjected. "And why a bunch of women didn't bring any men along," Gref followed up.

"'Cause we killed 'em for being annoying." Middie sneered a blue-lipped smile punctuated by a murderous glint. "So shut up, like Joreg told you, and be a good little man and get ready for your mission." She watched him turn away. "And don't be late. There may not be any hot water left if you are."

Each of the men grabbed a small backpack and one by one rolled off the back of the travel sled. "Come on." Uribos motioned to the other two. "Let's go." Under the cover of the sled's rumbling engines, as it trudged its way toward the encampment, Uribos, Gref, and Hech slipped into the night.

CHAPTER 17

The front entrance of the main building appeared deserted, no evidence of any recent traffic, either human or machine. Now that was odd. Victos's reconnaissance detailed seeing wreckage. Maybe he was mistaken. Maybe there wasn't anyone left.

As they pulled under the overhanging building entrance, large icicles lined the edge like pickets in a fence. Middie activated the warning flashers. Never one for subtlety, she blooped the siren a few times as well. "What was that for?" Mally asked.

"Might as well let 'em know were here. It's not like this is gonna be a big surprise." The cold was getting to her, and she was becoming more impulsive. Vigorously scratching the shoulder of her jacket, Middie cocked her head. "If anyone is in there, they probably saw us coming."

At first, there was no activity at the entrance. "Think we should knock?" Riki asked.

"I did knock," Middie said. "That's what the siren was for." Middie blooped the siren again.

This time, the door opened. A bright light flashed Middie's face. "Son of a—" Middie cursed but was cut short by the weapon tapping on window. Activating the release, the pane moved down. "Get that outta my face."

A modulated voice spoke. "What is your purpose?" The travel sled now clearly surrounded by a number of lightly armed personnel.

Middie's voice crackled. "If you'd get that thing outta my face, jerk-wad, I'd tell you." Despite the situation and her inebriation, Middie didn't flinch. "We're a medic team, and we were told you had casualties." Maybe Middie was so convinced this was only a simulation and she couldn't really get hurt, she didn't care. Emmie's wrist seemed real enough. Riki's concussion too. Did that even matter? If you were evaluated solely on your performance, Middie already disregarded the manual, stomped on it, and then spit on it for good measure.

"Who sent you?"

"Ask my boss, she's…" Middie began looking across her shoulder and thumbing at Emmie.

Jumping from the travel sled with her hands slightly raised in a nonthreatening pose, she said, "Me, I'm Dr. Leba Brader." Tiner's first rule: if captured, don't give up your leader. Leba needed to diffuse the situation and gather more intel before acting. There were at least eight people, dressed similarly in lightweight white body armor, with small-caliber projectile weapons holstered in waist belts. Some also carried long guns, not typical for a scientific team. Tiner's second rule: never underestimate your opponent. If this was the party sent to greet them, Leba figured there were probably more inside. Victos's plan did not take into account the possibility of overwhelming this many enemy combatants. No matter how tough he was, suicide was not an option. Outmanned was an understatement. "If you don't mind." Leba inclined her head. She needed to keep the demeanor nonthreatening. A little vulnerability would only enhance her position. "If we could come in and explain. We've had a rough trip, and we're pretty busted up." She waited and watched the figure turn from her, another guard stepping up in his place. "He must be communicating with his superior," she whispered to the others.

Her suspicions were confirmed when the man returned and instructed her and her colleagues to follow him into the building. Entering the facility, the women of green med team were staggered by the breadth of activity inside. Despite Victos's initial report that the place appeared deserted, what they found were people everywhere. Walls and shelves were lined with banks of blinking lights and real-time readouts. Stationed along each row, were technician, who jotted notations or toggled switches or tore off data strips for further analysis. The ceiling was portioned, with removable panels. Compressors hummed, and Leba traced intake and output pipes to each station. Thick cables followed a similar path but ended at a large relay at the far corner of the room. There were exit doors radiating from this central hub, each guarded by one of their welcoming party. First to remove her helmet, Emmie clumsily fumbled with her left hand. Instinctively Braids rushed to her aid.

She should have waited and let me go first.

Like Middie, Emmie was too set on her own course, failing to realize the serious lack of information they possessed.

"Good, good," a voice bellowed from behind them. Startled by the sudden greeting, all six women turned almost in unison to see a burly, ruddy-faced man coming toward them. The man was balding, with a high forehead and a receding hairline that ended in a sparsely populated combover. His long overhanging nose almost covered his thin upper lip, which stretched into a broad smile. His exposed teeth were an unnatural white. Well-defined crescents, deeply etched into his cheeks, focused attention on his seemingly permanent grin. He wasn't a large man, but his robust figure exposed the results of little exercise and calorie-laden meals. His steps measured and his gestures deliberate, he walked with authority.

Putting out his arms, palms up in an inviting and comforting gesture, the man said, "I'm Professor Linus Awart, the temporary leader of this research facility, and you would be?" he inquired, looking directly at Emmie Hodd. He seemed to telegraph his every move, leaving no surprises and his meaning never in doubt.

Again Leba stepped forward before Emmie had a chance to answer. "Dr. Leba Brader, Tal-Kari green med team, and my nursing staff."

Awart looked down the line at the cadre of women. "Excellent, we were expecting you." Before he could finish his thought, a young technician thrust an info-pad at him. Awart seemed perturbed by the interruption. "Ladies, if you will excuse me, there's something I need to take care of urgently. Egans, take them to get something hot to drink, and I'll join you momentarily."

"Yes, Professor," the man acknowledged. Despite his quick attention to the order, Egans seemed cocky and self-assured, not a common lackey. His straight eyebrows abruptly curved downward at the far ends of his face. His mop of wavy light-brown hair transitioned quickly into a military-style buzz cut. His eyes were bright blue and almost inviting. He was taller than Awart and stood much straighter. There was something about his stance, the way his legs were splayed, the way his torso projected out, the way he kept his hands strong at his sides. Although he seemed relaxed at the moment as Awart's subordinate, Leba could imagine if the opportunity presented itself, he would strangle the older man, twist his head off without blinking an eye.

"Come with me." Egans motioned to the women. As he led the women into the common room, Awart disappeared through a far doorway. For a supposed subordinate, Egans was better dressed than the other employees. Social breeding not lost on him, though it was curious why he would be in this role as opposed to a high-brow attorney or business executive. Egans seemed out of place. The compensation was either much better, or he enjoyed the power or control Awart gave him over the others. Men like him often exhibited a sadistic streak, and Leba worried about what they were walking into. Leba could feel her heart pounding, and she flexed her fingers. No one else seemed concerned. Too bad.

Egans grabbed the door handle and, acting the perfect gentleman, showed them into the smaller room. He was careful to avoid being trapped between his guests and the door. Definitely mercenary trained. The smell of stale, burned coffee permeated the air. There were a few tables and even more chairs set haphazardly about the room. "Pardon the disarray, but we aren't used to guests. Make yourselves comfortable," Egans advised. "I'll get someone to make new coffee. The professor will rejoin you shortly." Leering, his gaze settled on Mally. Once or twice, he rubbed his hands back and forth while looking her up and down. Mally didn't notice. Maybe she was used to men looking at her like that. Grinning, Egans left the room. Leba heard the almost imperceptible click of a door lock.

Mally started to speak. "I don't like him, he gives me the creeps."
Guess I was wrong.
Emmie shushed her. "Braids." Emmie pointed to her ears and then eyes. Braids surveyed the room.

"What's she doing?" Mally whispered to Middie.

"Shut up, didn't you hear Hodd?" she snapped at Mally. "She's looking for listening devices or a vid feed."

"Shhh," Riki reminded Middie in her attempt to explain to Mally why they needed to be quiet.

"Looks like we're alone," Braids confirmed.

Emmie turned to Leba. "Smooth move introducing yourself as the leader."

"In class, Master Priman Tiner told us never to give up your leader unless you have a full understanding of the situation. We don't know what's going on yet, and you're more effective if they're watching me and not you."

"Point taken." Emmie smiled. Leba wasn't sure whether that was meant for her or was in response to the mention of DeShay's name.

"Ladies," Awart said as he reentered the room, splaying his arm toward the chairs. "Please make yourselves comfortable. We have a lot to discuss."

"Thank you, sir." Leba placed her helmet on the table and added her gloves to bowl. The others followed her lead.

"Sit," Awart encouraged again. The ladies did as they were told. Emmie grunted as she removed her glove from her casted wrist. "Are you injured?" Awart inquired.

Gently placing her wrist on the table as she sat, Emmie said, "It's nothing."

"We understand you have injured. We were sent to help." Leba leaned forward, palms down on the table.

"Shuttle accident on the mountain. No survivors." The statement was emotionless. "Such a pity, we lost a lot of good people." Awart bowed his head and nodded back and forth, repeating, "A lot of good people." His reactions seemed disingenuous, almost rehearsed.

"Is that the wreckage we saw on the way in?" Emmie asked.

Awart paused, inclined his head, and looked from Leba to Emmie. "You are, ma'am?" Leba hoped Emmie could play her subordinate until they could assess the situation. DeShay was right; boy, was she stubborn.

"Emmie Hodd, she's my head nurse, one of the best," Leba answered, glaring at Emmie and lowering her brow, hoping Emmie would take the hint. Leba refocused on Awart, but he seemed intent on staring at the older woman as if he were evaluating her. Something was wrong. Awart was toying with them.

"Yes," he said. "We found it only a day ago and hauled it here for forensic analysis. Until then, I have grounded all our similar vehicles." Curious, they hadn't come across tread patterns. They didn't encounter any significant recent snowfall, and dragging wreckage would have left deep furrows in the permafrost.

"Egans here told me you came on a travel sled. Where's your shuttle?" Awart said, his gaze now shifting to Braids.

"Unfortunately, our shuttle seems to have met with a similar fate as yours," Leba opined. "We lost some good men as well."

Middie snickered. "Well, one good man, the rest were questionable."

Awart slowly turned in Middie's direction. "I don't believe I've had the pleasure."

"My apologies, Professor," Leba said. "I should introduce you to the remaining members of my team." Pointing as she went around the room, Leba named everyone, trying to give as few details as possible.

"Well, ladies, I would be honored if you stay with us for a few days," he offered. The furrows on his cheeks deepened as his smile widened.

"We appreciate the offer, but if you don't need our assistance, we really should be getting back." Leba placed her palms back down on the table, pushed slightly back, and began to get up. "May I please use your communication's array to send a message to our base?"

"Much as I like to honor your request, we have been unable to get a message out," Awart said. When he leveled his finger to make the point, Leba noticed his hands were meaty, his nails well manicured. "The cryo-volcanic activity is interfering with our signals." Leba looked at him curiously, not understanding. Their comms worked fine on the trail.

She didn't say anything but snuck a look at his feet. Tiner's third rule: the feet were the most honest part of the body. Facial reactions could be faked, especially with practice. Eye signs became useless too. If you wanted the truth, ask the feet. Not what he seemed at all. Awart continued, "You will be staying with us until we can get a message out." Raising a finger and flicking it, Awart motioned. "Egans, find some accommodations for our guests."

Acknowledging the order, Egans left his post at the door. The assembled group got to their feet. "Thank you, Professor." Leba put out her hand. His hand was large, the palm warm and sweaty. She didn't like the way he assumed the right to dictate their actions.

Gently slipping a hand onto Mally's arm, Egans guided her toward the exit. The remaining women followed behind. Bringing up the rear, Leba made one more survey of the room. Standing at the center was Awart, his fingers steepled. He glanced her way and nodded, the time for discussion was over.

As they continued toward their destination, there was a commotion at the back of the larger entry room. Leba recognized three figures. They were shackled together, their forward movements awkward and limited by the chains. The tallest of the three, supported by the other two, seemed to be limping. A guard prodded them forward with the barrel of a rifle. Leba moved up to where Egans was and asked, "What's going on?"

"Some locals looking to steal supplies from us. Happens a lot out here. They strip down our equipment for the metals."

What locals? Do you think I'm stupid? This was treacherous mountainous terrain in the shadow of a giant cryo-volcano cone, unsuitable, no downright inhospitable for permanent tenancy. It wasn't like this was a stop on the local shuttle route.

"Looks like they might need medical assistance," Leba said, veering out of line. "We'd be more than happy to check them out for you."

Egans grabbed her arm. "No need. After we get done with them, they tend not to return for seconds." Leba shook him off and returned to her place in line. Egans squeezed Mally's elbow and leaned close. "You needn't worry, pretty lady, I'll make sure they don't bother you." Mally tried to wrench free, but Egans kept hold.

Egans showed them the facilities, apologizing for the scarcity of amenities. Their destination was a temporary barracks with four sets of bunk beds jutting from the side wall. Standard military design, able to be assembled and disassembled at a moment's notice. Mally begged off when he offered to personally meet any needs she might have. He peered out the small row of rectangular windows lining the top of the far wall. "Keep your gear stowed in case we need to evacuate." Turning on his heel, his head snapped around, and he passed between the first set of stacked bunks. "The professor says the volcano is going to erupt soon, and I wouldn't want you buried under a pile of ash." Heading for the door, he stopped, turned around to face the women, his body framed by the doorway. "I'd lock my door if I were you." Smiling at Mally, he said. "Unless you want nighttime visitors." Egans ran his hands down the front of his thighs, another perfect pivot, and strode out the door.

"Disgusting pig." Riki pulled the door shut, rotating the locking bolt into place.

Like that's going to stop him. My guess is he has a key and wouldn't hesitate to use it. Since they only needed three of the four bunk beds, Leba thought about shoving the fourth against the door. They were lightweight, so Leba put her shoulder against the corner of one and pushed it away from the wall. Riki went over to help. The bed staccatoed across the floor until it was positioned in front of the door.

"Braids." Emmie motioned. "Anything?"

"Sweeps clean, Ma," she responded.

All well and good, except this is a simulation, and by definition, someone is watching our every move.

"Great," Hodd replied. "Now we can figure out what to do." She surveyed the others. "Any thoughts?"

"The cryo-volcano didn't interfere with our comms, so I don't think Awart is being totally honest with us," Leba offered.

"Wasn't that Victos, Joreg, and Tylor they were escorting?" Mally asked, her hand rubbing furiously down her own arms.

"What was your first clue, girlfriend, their look or their smell?" Middie took a long swallow from her flask.

"Shut up," Riki said, leaning forward, hands on her hips. "I think Vic is hurt."

"Don't worry." Emmie placed her left arm over Riki's shoulder. "We'll get them back."

"That's right," Middie said, wiping the back of her hand over her mouth. "This is only a simulation, so you don't have to worry too much."

"My headache doesn't feel like a simulation, and I bet Emmie's wrist doesn't feel simulated either," Riki shot back. Emmie withdrew her right arm, tucking it against her body.

"I think our real mission is to figure out what's going on here and get all of us out in one piece," Emmie summarized.

"What's our next move, Ma?" Braids inquired.

"Showering," Middie said as she walked toward the bathroom. "And a decent night's sleep." Everyone looked at her. "Don't worry, the boys will keep till morning. Besides, we're locked in, if you haven't noticed, and I figure the brain trust here doesn't have a plan cooked up yet, so I'm at least going to be comfortable."

It was hard to argue with Middie's logic. They really didn't have a plan yet, so why suffer. In order to keep up appearances, they would have to, at least for the moment, refrain from further inquiries about their comrades. Tiner's fourth rule: evaluate all your options.

As Leba lay on a bottom bunk, staring out the small window opposite her bed, Riki was already lightly snoring in the top bunk. Each time a gust of wind ruffled the overhanging awning, reflected moonlight waxed and waned. Frost crept into the corners of the pane, slowly restricting Leba's view as the temperature continued to fall. At least the guys were inside and not stuck in subzero temperatures. How did they get found so quickly? Leba wondered how much of what they did was captured on vid. Did the situations they encounter change at the whim of a controller, or was everything set in motion at the start to play itself out? How did their shuttle crash, or more curiously, why? At least her thoughts were her own. By the time she fell asleep, the rest were already there.

Leba awoke first, the sunlight peeking through the window and hitting her squarely in the face, the dawn of a new day one surely to be filled with surprise and intrigue. When Leba got out of the bathroom, Riki Sandler stood staring at the exit, arms folded across her chest, and her mind lost in thought. "It'll be all right," Leba said in a quiet voice. "We'll get Victos back and Gref and Hech too."

"How do you know?" Riki asked, her elbows pressed tightly to her sides, her fingers interlaced.

"Because we have to," Leba assured her, placing a firm grip on her shoulder.

Riki was startled by the attempted opening of the door. Slowly the bed grated along the floor as the intruder continued to push forward.

"Sorry to disturb you ladies, but the professor needs to see you," Egans said, his hand still on the door and his head peering into the room. There was a groan from one of the others. "Please don't delay," Egans cautioned.

"I'll go," Leba said, grabbing her jacket and slinging it over her shoulder. "The rest need time to get ready."

"No," Egans said. "He wants to see all of you. Thirty minutes, then I'll fetch you whether you're ready or not." The door slammed shut.

"Son of a…" Middie rolled over and snarled. "Who put in for a wake-up call?"

"Let's go," Emmie said as she gingerly held her wrist. Despite Leba reminding her to keep it elevated, lying flat must have caused it to swell overnight. Now stiff and even more painful, Emmie found it difficult to get up from the bed.

"Come on, Ma," Braids said as she climbed down from the top bunk. "I'll help you." The younger woman put her outstretched arms under Emmie's armpits and raised her to standing. The two disappeared into the bathroom.

"Good." Middie flopped back onto her bunk. "Wake me when it's my turn." Pulling the blanket over her head, she rolled to face the wall.

When Emmie and Braids finished, Mally went in, then Riki.

Staring at the snoring lump on Middie's bunk, Mally gently shoved Riki. "You wake her."

"Hey, you're the one who bonded with her on the shuttle flight. And she was your bunk mate last night." Riki pushed Mally's hand away. "You wake her."

"I'll wake her," Emmie volunteered, pushing past the squabbling women. Grateful, at least this time Emmie acted like a leader, Leba watched, thankful she was spared this chore. And wake Middie Emmie did. She picked up Middie's flask from the floor, sloshed the liquid inside, and threatened to dump it out, if Middie didn't get up.

"Okay, okay," Middie warbled. "I'm going, just give me a minute."

"That's about all you have," Emmie said, looking at her chrono.

Middie finished in the bathroom as Egans returned. "Ladies, if you'll follow me." They went to pick up their gear. "Leave it." He pointed to the table. "You won't need it for where you're going."

Leba replaced her survival suit jacket, the others following her lead. Their med gear was taken away when they first arrived. The professor promised to stow it for them until they were ready to depart.

This corridor was different from the one they traveled last night. Stopping at a nondescript door, Egans paused, waited for everyone to catch up, and then tapped in a series of characters. Her line of sight partially obstructed, Leba couldn't follow the sequence. The door slid open to a smaller room. Behind a rather ornate desk was Awart, fork and knife in hand, busily finishing his breakfast. Not looking up from his plate, he asked, "I presume you slept well?" There were some nods. "Good, good, because we have a lot to discuss." He pointed to the chairs with his knife. "Sit." Leba got the feeling it was an order, not a request.

"Any scraps for us?" Middie asked.

Shut up, Middie. Don't poke the snake.

Finally looking up from his meal, Awart deliberately laid his fork down and then his knife. Pushing himself back from the desk, he looked at each woman individually and then spoke slowly and deliberately. "You weren't particularly forthcoming last night, were you?" No one said anything. Despite the cold outside, the temperature in the room seemed to be rising. With her good hand, Emmie tugged at her collar and settled the hand at the base of her neck.

"Our guests," Awart started again, this time addressing his comments to Egans, "have not been honest with us." Reaching back onto the desk, with two hands he removed a mug and took a long and deliberate sip from his steaming drink. The whistling sound it made as it traversed his mouth was agonizing. He peered over the cup and stared, locking in on Emmie. Something was very wrong. The professor's demeanor was very different this morning. His eyes betrayed him; he was angry, very angry.

"Such a pity, as I had high hopes for our relationship." He put his cup down, his gaze still locked on Emmie. "Emmie Hodd," he deliberated on her name, pronouncing every syllable. "It seems, madam, you are the true leader of this group." Emmie dry swallowed. "And your men." He spread his hands wide apart. "It appears we have your men locked up." He reacquired his knife and tapped its butt on the table. "And after some persuasion…"

"If you hurt them," Riki threatened, coming up out of her chair.

"Sit down." Awart pointed with his knife. Egans forcefully shoved her back down.

Shaking off Egans's grasp, Riki said, "I want to see them, now."

You're not in any position to make demands, Riki. Take some deep breaths. Leba placed a hand on Riki's arm.

"Soon enough," Awart informed her. "First, I need answers to some questions."

Emmie slid forward to the edge of her chair and directly engaged his stare. "I take responsibility for my group. You need to understand, sir, we weren't sure what we were getting into." Straightening up in her chair, Emmie continued, "We'd just survived in a terrifying shuttle accident and were weary from traveling." How much information was Emmie going to give up? Did she have any training in interrogation resistance? Now was a bad time to practice.

"I can understand that," Awart said, tilting his head and raising his eyebrows. His mouth pulled wide. Picking up his fork again, Awart speared a piece of food and popped it into his gaping maw. He chewed slowly and deliberately. Leba wasn't sure what his game was, but the resultant smile didn't seem sincere and quickly turned into a frown. "Unfortunately, I find it necessary to detain you until I have ample opportunity to check your story."

Mally blurted, "But you weren't honest with us either." It was clear the other members of her team forgot the lessons Deshay taught them. Tiner's rule five: don't piss off your captors. Antagonizing the enemy, showing him your weaknesses, wasn't by the book. In fact, it was a good way to get hurt. And the way this meeting was going, they were on a fast track to pain.

Emmie looked at Mally with those smoky brown eyes. "What she means is," Emmie tried to regroup, "you did not tell us about your wounded."

"They're your wounded." He put the fork down with such force the table shuddered. The knife remained in his hand, shaking as he made his point. "Trying to sneak into our secure facility."

"If you hurt them…" Riki couldn't keep quiet.

From the looks of things, they've already hurt them, and you're not making it any better.

"You'll what?" Egans asked, replacing his hand on her shoulder and squeezing hard.

"Ow," she cried out.

"There's no need for that," Emmie stated, staring at Awart.

"Egans," Awart grumbled. "Leave the young woman be. There'll be time for that later if I don't get the answers I want." There was a sadistic tone to his admonition, and Egans obeyed without question. His dog could wait to be fed. Awart surveyed the room, locking eyes with each woman in turn, and then stopped at Leba. My turn. "You, Doctor, if you really are a doctor."

"I am," Leba stated. *But you already know that. In fact, you know everything there is to know about us. What is your game?*

"The tall, lanky one, I believe his name is Gref, mentioned in our conversation, you are an expert in cryo-volcanism."

"I know something about it," Leba answered.

"Come, come now, don't be shy, I need your expertise. You wouldn't want anything to happen to your friends, would you?" Looking up at Egans, who reapplied pressure to Riki's shoulder,

Awart's smug expression was a weak demonstration of power and control.

"Of course not," Leba said, trying to maintain a calm demeanor. She would not be intimidated. During training, DeShay wanted them to consider their responses before speaking. Take a breath, steady your feet, avoid tells, but always be thinking a few steps forward. Microgestures were hard to prevent, but if you could focus on what lay ahead, you may be able to confuse your interrogator. Where was the line of questioning going? What info did you have that they wanted? How bad did they need your intel, and what leverage did you have by resisting? What would be the consequences of your reveal?

"I'm glad we understand each other." He smiled, this time full-toothed. "And you," he said, this time locking his gaze on Braids, "I understand you're an expert too."

All eyes turned to Braids, who sat expressionless. Emmie looked over her shoulder at Braids, seemingly bewildered, not knowing what was coming next. Waiting for his next remarks, Braids shifted uncomfortably in her seat.

Awart leaned back in his plush cushiony chair, folding his hands across his belly and revealed, "I believe your real name is Dierna Bryson, and your family owns Bryson Nanomechanical."

Emmie's eyes widened as she regarded Braids. The Bryson family name was known system wide for their innovations in microtechnology. This woman could be heir to a tremendous fortune. Now things were beginning to make sense. There was an explanation for some of the curious gaps in Leba's knowledge of Braids's history, how an underprivileged girl could get into nursing school, how she possessed an uncanny knowledge of engineering systems, and how she was never tempted by intoxicants or larceny. Emmie's eyes widened, and her jaw dropped, her mouth trying to form words, but none emerged. The girl from the "streets" kept one hell of a secret.

Braids sat there, motionless, as if something horrible was revealed. Emmie looked at her, this time in a loving, comforting way. "It's okay, baby."

"Thanks, Ma," Braids whispered, putting her hand over Emmie's.

"Touching," Awart said, "but we are wasting time. I have big plans for you." He paused. "All of you." Slurping the last of his now-cooled drink, as the breadth of his knowledge sank in, Awart gloated. Pointing to Leba and Braids. "Egans, take these two to Sector 7."

Before he could finish the thought, Emmie stood up defiantly. "They're not going anywhere until we see our comrades."

You've got to be kidding. What does one have to do with the other? He has no reason to submit to your demands. All you are doing is showing him your weakness as a leader.

"So bold, I like that." Awart grinned. "I'll make you a deal."

Can't you see he's toying with you?

"I'm listening," Emmie said, her voice more sedate.

He's got you where he wants you. Hurting and vulnerable. Like the dying tarandi that crushed your wrist, you've lost your focus and are acting without thinking.

"Your two friends here give me everything I need, and I'll see what I can do about arranging a reunion," he chortled. Emmie seemed satisfied with her victory and nodded to Leba and Braids to comply.

Leba got up. Braids grasped Emmie's hand, not wanting to release it. With an encouraging shove from Egans, Braids rose from the table. Emmie pulled her hand free and said, "It's all right." Turning from Braids to Awart, she finished, "The professor and I have an agreement. He promised not to hurt you."

I don't remember that.

Awart's grin spoke volumes; unfortunately, Emmie couldn't read a single line of text.

"You sure you'll be okay, Ma?" Braids said, looking back at Emmie.

Emmie stared back. "Have faith and happiness, child." The code words for resist and escape at all cost. What was Emmie thinking now?

Braids grasped and squeezed Leba's hand. *Like I didn't recognize Emmie's go order. I'm not sure why she picked now.* Middie winked at Emmie, acknowledging her understanding of what was about to go down. *You might as well tell the entire world.* Emmie stared from Mally to Riki. *Let's try to be at least a little subtle.* If they weren't paying attention, the glare sent the message loud and clear. Right now, though, the odds were in their favor. Egans was armed, but if timed right, she and Braids should be able to take him. Certainly Middie, Mally, and Riki could overpower Awart or at least distract him enough that he couldn't alert anyone else. Since they were unable to hear outside noise, the room they were in must be somewhat isolated. Maybe Emmie was counting on that fact. Their biggest obstacle after overpowering these two was locating the men and finding a way out. Hopefully, Emmie already figured out that part of the plan.

As Egans walked to the door, Braids tripped going past a chair. When he leaned over and jerked at her arm, Braids came up swinging. What she didn't expect was the weapon to her head. "Got to have a better move than that," Egans boasted as all eyes turned to him. That gave Leba the opportunity she trained all those painful hours in the gym for. Muscle memory kicked in, and she used Dieuvoxyl's gun defense to perfection. Grabbing Egans' arm, Leba diverted the gun's muzzle and twisted his wrist until the weapon came free. As she continued to apply pressure to the joint, Egans shrieked and fell to his knees. Keeping the gun pointed at him, Leba released her hold and offset to get a better position. Her heart pounding in her chest, Leba so much wanted to fist pump.

"Bravo." Awart applauded. "And Egans, shame on you for letting a girl touch your weapon." Moving to hold his shoulder from behind with her right hand, Leba nudged Egans to his feet and leveled the gun at his head. Awart continued, "And here I thought you man enough to handle a few little girls." Egans's body stiffened under Leba's grasp. Gesturing with his hand, Awart glared at Leba. "Here, here, my dear, put that nasty thing down."

"Listen up, smart man," Middie moved to stand beside Leba. "If the doc here can't blast his head off, I certainly will." Middie wrenched the gun from her hand. "Here, give me that." Whereas Leba was careful not to put her finger on the trigger, Middie's index finger strangled it. "If you don't let us outta here now, I blast him first and you next."

Are you crazy? You're going to get us all killed.

"Such angry words," Awart commented, "when holding an empty weapon."

Leba watched as the energy charge light on the weapon Middie was now wielding slowly changed from green to red. *Uh-oh, boy, are we screwed.* Middie repeatedly pumped the trigger.

"Safety feature, my dear," Awart explained. "Now the two of you go nicely, or I will hurt your friends." He pointed. "The rest of you, sit down, shut up, and behave."

Egans turned and struggled to relieve Middie of the useless weapon. After her continued resistance, Egans poised his hand to strike her. *An empty gun is an empty gun. There'll be other opportunities. I hope. Unless he kills you now.*

"Go ahead, pal, take your best shot, and I'll return it double," she boasted, fists clenched and arms poised on her hips.

Egans ignored her and grasped Braids under her arm. "No more stunts." He moved his hand to her hair. "Or I'll take these, and I promise it won't be pretty." Braids struggled in his grasp.

"Leave her alone," Emmie said, rising to her feet.

"Or you'll what?" Egans snarled at her. "I'll take more than that if you don't sit down and shut up like the professor said." Leba shot Braids a glance and nodded her head. There'd be other chances for escape. Tiner's sixth rule: when no opportunities exist, make your own.

Emmie Hodd slumped in her chair, beaten. "Such a pity," Awart bemoaned as Egans left the room with Braids and Leba. Shoving the remains of his meal into the waste can, Awart picked up his utensils and threw them onto his plate. Mally and Riki, defeat written across their faces, turned toward Emmie for reassurance. Unfortunately, she had none to give. Middie sat fuming in her chair, refusing to look at Emmie. "This is too much to bear." Awart ran the back of his hand across his forehead. He jabbed at a switch on the tabletop console and spoke, "Jekkers."

"Yes, sir," the voice crackled over the comm.

"Jekkers, I need you to come to my office immediately." Awart paused. "Bring one or two of your people."

"Yes, sir," Jekkers acknowledged.

For what seemed like an eternity, no one spoke. Awart studied his desk monitor, while the women sat in silence. Every once in a while, someone would lift their head to catch Emmie's eye, but she stared blankly. Emmie, despite her predicament, was consumed by the professor's revelation regarding Braids. In some ways, Emmie was happy for Braids, but in other ways, she felt betrayed. Braids lied. Braids, whom she'd treated like the daughter she could not have, enjoyed a secret past, one she didn't share. Emmie was deeply hurt.

The door burst open, shattering Emmie's wallowing. Clad in protective armor, side arms at the ready, two men and a woman appeared. "Jekkers," Awart addressed the lead man. Jekkers had a thin, elongated face, with windswept hair that danced on his forehead. Younger than Egans, Emmie swore they could have been brothers, the way he tried to mirror the other man's demeanor. It was difficult to portray a sadistic nature when his show of manliness was hindered by the inability to grow more than a dirty smudge on his upper lip. Rhomboid eyes sat atop a prominent nose that led to a dimpled chin. This too detracted from his attempts at the severely angled brows, squinty-eyed, scary look he was going for. Whereas Egans got the handsome bad boy genes, Jekkers was relegated to compensating with overly developed muscles. His neck was thick, and his arms seemed to struggle under the confinement of his shirt.

"You've brought Faqier and Jihana, excellent choices." Jekkers barely cracked a smile. Faquier had wavy black hair and oily skin, reflecting the probability of a desert home world. His exposed forearms were covered in thick coarse hair. His beard was full and neatly manicured. His pale lips were cracked, likely from exposure to the cold, gusty winds scorching this icy moon. Emmie noticed the way he looked at Jihanna, more as an object than a collaborator.

On the other hand, the woman Jihanna was statuesque and beautiful. Her perfect figure allowed her the uncanny abililty to holster weapons on both hips and not appear fat. Legs made up two-thirds of her body, and she looked like she could hold her own in a fight. This was a Cathen special, the long, flowing dark hair, parted in the middle and cascading down the entire length of her back. Deep-set, piercing blue eyes, with unnaturally thick lashes, danced below sculptured eyebrows. A long narrow nose led to a tapered chin. Dominant was her mouth, the focal point that occupied the majority of her lower face, with moist lips that curled into a sinister but inviting smile. Her hands were delicate, with fingers long and shapely, and nails that could easily gouge an unwanted suitor's eyes out. When he designed her, Cathen surely had an itch that needed scratching.

"Jekkers, would you be kind enough to escort our friends to the detention area." Jekkers nodded. Riki perked up. Maybe she thought she would get to see Victos. As worried as Emmie was about Braids, she imagined Riki was concerned for Vic. The last time they saw any of the men, Victos appeared injured, a bloody swatch of cloth encircling his head. Jekkers motioned for the women to stand. Faqier and Jihana moved into position behind them, weapons drawn.

"No need for those." Awart looked toward Emmie. "I think we have come to an understanding." Emmie nodded her agreement.

"Understand this," Middie said, making an obscene gesture with her hand.

Emmie, using her good hand, put down Middie's outstretched arm. Nostrils flaring and teeth bared, Middie wriggled free of her grasp. "We won't be any trouble," Emmie reassured the professor and was last to follow Jekkers out the door. Maybe she wasn't meant to lead. Looking back before the door shut, she saw Awart leaning forward in his chair, head down over his desk, furiously typing on his keyboard.

A reinforced steel door with Sector 7 emblazoned in red letters greeted Leba and Braids. Egans opened it by retina scan. Large canisters with biohazard warning labels were pushed toward one corner of the room. They continued past rows of heavy-duty containers stacked floor to ceiling. At the far end was another security door, labeled Authorized

Personnel Only. This time, Egans key carded the lock. Leba would need a key card and a weapon if she planned to escape. The security for this place was top of the line, but Tiner's seventh rule stated, find the weak link and break it. Egans was not, but there were others. The door slid open to reveal a long corridor lined with what appeared to be individual offices or labs. Egans stopped at the third door on the left and, with the muzzle of his weapon, nudged Leba forward.

"You get off here, Doc." Egans rotated the top lock and turned the handle. The door opened into a cluttered office. As Leba stepped into the room, a hunched figure looked up from a drawing table, stood, and beckoned her in. This may be the chink in their armor.

"Here, sit here." The wizened older woman pointed to a small stepstool. Declining the offer, she remained standing. Leba heard the faint sound of the outer door locking. "Pay no attention to that, they think that little lock will keep me in."

Who are you? You seem very familiar.

All the regular chairs were covered with books or papers or open containers. Looking around the room, Leba noticed the disarray was not limited to the seats, but papers were also scattered on the desktop and books haphazardly arranged on shelves.

Leba regarded the older woman. She was of medium build and not-so-petite features. Her shoulders were beginning to droop and round as the weight of gravity caught up with her advanced age. Thick gray chaff, wiry and choppy from inattention, sprung from her head. She became androgynous over time, losing her femininity. Her eyebrows were heavy and her eyes lackluster. There was no sheen to her hair. Surprisingly, though, her skin was smooth, seemingly never exposed to the elements. Cooped up in a research lab her whole life, her social skills resembled those of a hermit. But this woman was somehow familiar to Leba. Maybe it was the high-necked sweater or the genderless features? Or maybe it was the dark, thick-lensed glasses hanging from a neck chain.

The woman began to speak. "See here," she said, pushing a paper in front of Leba and pointing to a dot on a graph. "What do you make of that?" Her questions came in short bursts, not waiting for answers. Leba picked up the paper and tried to understand what the woman wanted from her. "Well," the woman said, tapping the drafting table's pyramid-shaped holding rod. "I was told you would know what this means." Leba looked again at the paper; she had seen it before, but where?

Leba looked closer at the paper, noting the labeled axes. The three-dimensional graph displayed output from a cryo-volcano. Leba looked up from the diagram and studied the woman's face. "Professor Lu Roblins. You're Professor Lu Roblins from the Tyvic Consortium at the Wreos Academy."

"Yes, yes, now what do you think that dot means, young lady?" Roblins asked again, this time with more urgency in her voice. "Why would Awart let you in here if you couldn't help?"

Leba felt lightness in her chest as her pulse quickened. She blinked a few times and dry swallowed. "I think the cryo-volcano is coming out of dormancy."

"Yes, yes, very good." Roblins applauded and then handed Leba another graph. "This one, what do you make of this one?"

Leba examined the new graph and then looked up. "This is awesome." Finally pulling up the small stepping stool so she could sit, Leba moved closer to the older woman. There was a musty odor as if she were becoming part of the antiquity. Taking a drawing tool partially hidden underneath more clutter on the table, Leba began making notations. At one time, maybe in her academy days, something changed for Lu Roblins, driving her from the spotlight and into remote corners. Her once enthusiastic and groundbreaking research publications dwindled to a few and then none. As part of her prep work for this mission, Leba reviewed Professor Roblins' body of work. Roblins was quoted, on more than one occasion, that the whole peer review process was a waste of time. No one rivaled her expertise or was competent enough to evaluate her life's work. How dare they even think they could understand what was intuitive to her. She found sharing with outsiders a distraction and relegated herself to anonymity. Yet here she was, plain as day, sharing her brilliance, or insanity, with Leba. "The output from this is much higher than expected. Look here, see the mix of gases? This would be a great source of energy if it could be harnessed."

"My thoughts exactly, my dear," the older woman agreed.

"Is that what this research station is all about?" Leba asked, feeling the trembling electrify her body.

The older woman suddenly became very quiet. Her eyes darted back and forth across the room and whispered, "Too many ears around here. Don't want anyone to know about what we've found. That's why they crashed the shuttle." Leba looked at the woman puzzled. "That's right, they crashed the shuttle," the woman repeated.

"Them, that's who," she reiterated.

"Who?" Leba asked.

"Them, the thugs in body armor. I see things, I know things." Her eyes made another circuit. "Led by that charlatan Awart," Roblins spat. "Pretending to be a professor, he's just an entrepreneur from—" The door opening stopped her midsentence.

"Good morning, Lu," Awart said, tipping his head and exaggerating his steps to avoid knocking over one of her stacked piles.

"Linus," she said, turning only her head, leaving her body facing the table. "I was just showing my young friend here our latest data."

"And, my dear, what do you think of Lu's interpretation?" He fixed his gaze on Leba.

"Professor Roblins is an expert," Leba let the marker roll from her hand and slid the other to cover her calculations.

"I didn't ask you that," he scolded. "What I want to know is what you think." Awart grasped the writing tool before it rolled off. He considered it, placed it back on the table, and scowled.

Roblins looked at Leba, shaking her head. "I think the data is interesting, but more research needs to be done to confirm any of the findings."

"Very well done, my dear." He clapped his hands. *Did he already know this? Was this a test to see if I could figure it out too?* "Why don't you stay here with Professor Roblins a bit longer, while I check on your friends." He turned and left the room as quickly as he came.

Leba wanted to ask him why he was so interested in the cryo-volcano's output. Based on Professor Roblins data, it was only a matter of time before this volcano's neighborhood would be under a river of frozen lava, the atmosphere rank with methane and ammonia.

A CHANGE IN TACTICS: MAIDEN VOYAGE

"Professor Roblins." Leba tapped the older woman when she didn't answer. "Does he know the mountain is unstable?"

"Of course he does," she said, reclamping the prismatic holder to the table. "I told him so." There was anger and regret in her voice. "That's why the others had to die." Roblins scurried around the room, collating papers and shoving mislaid books into shelves. "He said no one had to die, but he was wrong. I fear you and your friends will meet a similar fate."

Leba shuddered, her eyes darting around the room. She could easily overpower Roblins, but what then. She still needed to figure out what was going on here. Leba took a deep breath and asked, "You brought down our shuttle, didn't you?" There was no answer. Leba stared at the dot again and the calculations she made. "We were a test run, weren't we?" Again no answer. When Leba looked up from the graph, there was no sign of the older woman. Leba went to the door, still locked from the outside. So how did she get out? Carefully, she folded up the paper and slid it into her pocket. Leba surveyed the room, trying to figure out how Roblins got out. She cursed herself for not paying attention. Who knew the old lady could move so quickly. Then she saw it, a small patch of floor not mired in a week's worth of dust. Leba went over to the bookcase and pushed. It slid back easily to reveal a dimly lit passageway.

CHAPTER 18

The confinement cell appeared to be a converted lab with the original entrance doors removed and metal bars bolted into a sliding track that could be retracted or deployed as needed. The smell of sweat and other bodily odors permeated the air. Dimly lit by a single miner's lamp hanging from the ceiling outside the cell, it was damp and cold. Smears of blood, mixed with dirt and grime, decorated the walls.

"Oh, Vic." Riki knelt down next to him, examining his blackened eye.

"It's nothing compared to what I gave their buddy," he bragged. He started to get up but momentarily hesitated, his back still hurting from the recent encounter.

Riki extended him a hand only to notice his bloodied and swollen knuckles. "Does it hurt?" she said, gently peeling away the makeshift bandage, brushing his matted hair out of the gash in his forehead. He winced as she pulled the stragglers from the wound.

"No, I'm used to a gun butt to the head." He laughed. "Used to happen in my neighborhood all the time when I was growing up. Takes more to crack my melon than that."

She put an arm around his waist and steadied him on his feet.

"And why aren't the two of you saying anything?" Middie asked. The other two men remained seated on the stone floor. Gref's head was bowed onto his knees.

"They said enough already," Victos spat.

"And if we hadn't, your melon would be more than bruised," Gref shot back.

"Enough!" Emmie shouted, her wrist throbbing more than ever. "I'm really sick and tired of your bickering, so shut up."

"What's she all pissed about?" Victos asked Riki.

"Something about Braids being some fancy heiress," Riki said, caressing his face where his cheek was purplish.

"That's appropriate," he said, gently moving Riki's hand away. "I get my head bashed in, we're in a detention cell, and she's pissed about that."

"In a nutshell," Middie blurted out. "Hodd, I hope you've figured a way out of this, or we are all toast for making this mission."

Mally turned to Middie. "What do you mean?"

"Listen and listen up good." She shook her finger at Mally. "We've been in this stupid cold box for three days of a four-day mission. We've managed to crash our shuttle, get captured, and accomplish nothing. Cathen's probably having a field day looking at our download."

Mally looked surprised. "Don't give me that, sweetheart. Don't you get it?" Middie stared at Mally. "Let me make it clear. If we don't finish our objective, we get bounced."

"And what is our mission?" Emmie asked, sensing Middie was holding back information.

"Well, I guess it doesn't matter much now," Middie said, throwing up her hands. The upcoming revelation seemed to captivate everyone's attention. Gref and Hech finally got up.

Victos interrupted her. "And when were you planning to let the rest of us in on that?"

"I was given explicit instructions not to tell until—" Middie growled back.

"Until what?" Gref shouted. "Until the rest of us were dead?"

"If it was that simple, I would have choked you while you slept." Middie puffed out her chest and moved toe to toe with him.

Hech stepped between the two of them and stood face-to-face with Middie. "Who gave you the instructions?"

Middie pushed him. "Back off."

"Who?" Hech persisted.

"Cathen." She paused. "Yeah, Cathen, it was him."

"I don't believe you," Mally cried. She raised her hands up and approached Middie but lost her nerve. "You blame everything on him. You don't know him like I do."

"And how do you know him?" Gref said, grabbing Middie's forearm, trying to reengage her. With her other hand, Middie shoved Gref's hand off. Feet splayed, she angled toward an unoccupied corner.

Tears were streaming down Mally's face.

"Enough!" Emmie shouted a second time from her corner of the detention cell.

"This is stupid," Victos said, pushing Riki's arm away. "And a waste of time." He looked around the cell. "Where's Braids and the doc?"

Leba made her way forward and stopped at a door. A small rim of light outlined it. The passage she just traversed must have been some sort of access corridor, and she knew eventually she'd have to leave its relative safety if she planned to help the others. Grabbing the handle on the door, she cringed as she pulled it down. No creaking, great. Not the case when the door squeaked on its hinges as she opened it. With only her head poked out, Leba checked left then right then left again. Tiner's eighth rule: always go left. The natural tendency for right-handed people is to go right; no one ever goes left. So that was what she would do, go left and hope for the best.

Hearing commotion directly in front of her, she quickly ducked into a small doorway. It didn't provide much cover, so she flattened herself as best she could and watched an adjacent door swing outward. Harsh voices emanated from inside, along with gasping sobs. Awart emerged red-faced, one hand dabbing his face with a cloth. He was in a hurry, slammed the door, effectively drowning out the exchange, and rushed down the hallway away from her position. There was no way he saw her, or at least she hoped not.

Awart no longer in sight, Leba checked the hallway again and stepped gingerly from her position and proceeded forward, ending at the hinge side of the door. A slap, another slap, then a woman cried out. It almost sounded like Braids, but Leba wasn't sure. As she approached, the cries became whimpers. Louder and sharper voices returned. Maybe two or three distinct voices, it was hard to tell; Leba would need to move in closer to assess the threat. She could feel her heart beginning to pound. She would need to keep her head down so as not to be spotted through the window in the door.

Each step measured and light, Leba made her way nearer to the room and put her ear against the door to listen better. It was thinner than she thought, and she could clearly identify two harsh voices and another sobbing. Resisting the temptation to peek in the window, she slid her hand silently to her boot until she remembered her knife was buried with the tarandi remains. She was still mad at Victos for that. Although the words were barely discernible, their meaning wasn't, as each question that went too long unanswered was followed by a smack. Braids's intermittent sobs continued unabated.

A weapon, I need a weapon.

The offices or labs along this hallway were dark and each handle Leba tried locked. Frustrated, she realized her only option was to return to Roblins's office and look for something she could use. Slipping back through the door she left slightly ajar, Leba surveyed the room until she remembered the glass prism stick the older woman kept on the drafting table. It not only held the paper down but magnified the underlying graph. Wrenching it free from its clamp, Leba was surprised how dense it was for something that looked so fragile. Clear volcanic glass, maybe? Beautiful and crystalline, an incredibly slow- moving liquid that appeared solid but was hard as any rock. It reminded her of the obsidian rock knife.

With the makeshift weapon in hand, Leba returned to the door and listened. It was quieter now, no more shouting and only a faint whimpering. At least now she could make out the words. In order to have even a remote chance of an advantage, she needed to get them to come out. Two voices, a man's and a woman's, were discussing how pathetic their captive was at resisting their persuasion. The window was at eye level and inviting, but she resisted the urge to look. Tiner's ninth rule, and one of her personal favorites: divide and conquer. During training, DeShay presented innumerable examples of how the strategy was effective either on a small or large scale. Based on the conversation, she assumed Braids would not be able to assist her. She would have to tackle each hostile individually. Leba knew the door opened outward and reasoned she could use it as a temporary shield. Taking a step back, she banged her stick into the door.

"What was that?" the woman asked.

"Probably Jekkers returning with the professor," the man said unconcerned.

"There it is again, Faqier."

"Go and check, Jihana," the man said aggravated. "This one will not be any trouble now that she's learned to cooperate." Leba stole a look. Rocking back and forth in the chair, Braids's forehead was nested in her hands, an occasional moan escaping from a split and swollen mouth. "Hurry," he advised. "So you can take this one to clean up." Faqier picked up Braids's head by her hair. "Pity you had to be so stubborn." Leba saw the woman turn toward the door and quickly ducked to the hinge side of the door. *Phew, that was close.* Leba adjusted her right hand up the stick and squeezed it tightly.

Jihana opened the door and peered out. "I don't see anyone." She paused, her hand pulling slightly on the handle. "Faqier, I'll be right back," she said, stepping forward and, as she went into the hallway, released the door to close behind her. The woman turned in the direction where the door shut and saw Leba behind the door. "Where's Egans?" she said, reaching for her weapon. "What are you doing here?"

"Doing this," Leba said, using her left hand to divert the gun muzzle. Her right brought the stick down violently against the woman's outstretched wrist.

Jihana screamed in pain, the weapon dropped from her hand, clattering to the floor. Not satisfied, Leba needed to finish the fight, take Jihana out of the picture permanently. It wouldn't be long before the man, Faqier, realized something was wrong. Offsetting from her original position, Leba thrust her foot into the back of Jihana's knee. Jihana collapsed to the floor, unable to get up. Jihana's wailing must have alerted Faqier, who burst from door. Arrogant and self-assured, Faquier didn't exit the room cautiously. This gave Leba a chance to meet him head-on. Leba could feel her heart beating faster as Faqier closed. With the bottom end of the stick, Leba used a pommel strike to crack Faqier's left clavicle. Unfortunately, the blow only slowed him. Although his left arm hung limply at his side, his right worked well enough. As he tried to connect a blow to Leba's face, she fended it off. His arm was like rock. Her forearm stung where she deflected his shot.

"Ah," he said, brandishing his pointed yellow teeth. "You want to play, do you?"

Ignoring his words, Leba kept an eye on his shoulders, waiting for him to telegraph his next shot. "That your best?" she chided him. His eyes widened, and he hesitated, momentarily losing his focus, allowing Leba to send a kick up his leg and into his groin. Stunned, he reflexively grabbed his crotch and groaned. Leba offset again and smacked his knee hard, sending him reeling to the ground.

"Well done," boomed a familiar voice from down the hall. There stood Awart, flanked by Jekkers and Egans, clapping his meaty hands in appreciation. Leba adjusted her stance to meet the oncoming threat. Breathing hard, she knew she was not ready for a second round with fresh opponents. In order to regroup, Leba needed to make space, so she entered the office and tried dragging the door behind her. A hand reached in until her stick found a new target. With both hands, Leba pulled the door shut and rotated the locking bolt. Taking her stick, she smashed the key card override. Sparks flew from the control panel. The access light turned red and blinked malfunction.

Staring at the door, Leba propped one hand against it and leaned over to catch her breath. Between short gasps, she said to Braids, "We should be safe until they find the proper tools to bypass the door's locking mechanism." Still rocking back and forth in the chair, sobbing, her face swollen and bloodied, Braids looked up blankly. Straightening back up, Leba approached and put an arm on Braids's shoulder. The other woman pulled away. Leaning closer in, Leba said in a more subdued voice, "You're safe now, I've got the door jammed shut." Braids didn't say anything but continued to stare at her.

"I've got to find another way out of here." Leba remembered DeShay's tenth rule, explaining in class most rooms had two ways out, the obvious one and the one you needed. Building codes usually demanded some way to get air circulating in and out of the room, so a window or vent was usually necessary.

I hope this applies to simulated facilities.

Generally, temporary buildings such as these found it easier and cheaper to cut down on wasted space by employing connecting rooms. This room was no exception, and she quickly found the second doorway. Dust was the great equalizer. Behind the large desk, there was a dust-disturbed area beside the bookshelf. "Come on," she urged. "Before they come around to this entrance."

"Too late," a voice shouted as the secondary door burst open to reveal armed guards. This time, they were too many and too well armed. Braids was useless as a backup and was easily overpowered. Maintaining a defensive posture and still holding her stick, Leba raised her hands to waist level as the guards surrounded her. She could make a run for it, aggressively fighting her way out the door, but to what end? With a gun to her head, Braids was in no position to join her.

Awart strode in last, his arms folded across his chest. "You disabled two of my best people." He paused. "And when I'm done with you, I'm sure they would like a word with you."

Egans laughed. "Assuming they ever recover."

Jekkers glared at him and then toward Leba. "And if they don't, I'll speak with you personally."

Leba's orders were to resist and escape at any cost, and that was what she almost did. Not that she would have ever given those orders. Emmie's plan was flawed from the start.

"Put them with the others," Awart ordered.

Jekkers lifted Braids up by the arm and pulled her forward. Leba could hear her whimper as she left the room. Egans looked at Leba and put out his hand. "I'll take your stick." Leba looked at the translucent stick in her hand, wondering how many she could take out before she fell but thought better of it. Tiner's eleventh rule: don't be stupid. Reluctantly she handed it to Egans. He tested the weight of it and then slapped it into his palm. "Nasty, very nasty." He smiled. "I bet I could put this to good use." He rammed the stick in Leba's midsection, prodding her forward. Leba winced but avoided putting her hands on her side.

I need to stay ready. Stay focused. I've taken body shots worse than that before.

Egans apparently respected her resolve because the second nudge was less violent, but the message clear nonetheless. Leba moved forward into the hallway.

"Dr. Brader," Awart called after her. Leba peered over her shoulder. "Be a good girl or it'll go worse for your friends." She glared at him. "I may even let Egans and Jekkers play with some of your little friends." He snorted. "Sometimes, unfortunately, they play too rough." Leba stood steadfast, keeping silent, not displaying any emotion, until Egans jabbed her again in the ribs.

Mally went to the front of the detention cell, trying to peer around the corner. The commotion of the oncoming group piqued her interest. It was certainly more interesting than listening to the others whine and moan about their predicament. Riki was hovering over Victos, smothering him with attention; Middie was mumbling under her breath; Gref and Hech were bickering as usual; and Emmie, poor Emmie, was drowning in self-pity, or at least that was what Mally assumed. "There's someone coming," she announced proudly. She continued, eyes fixed on the hallway. "I think it's Braids, yes, it's Braids, and she looks all beat-up." That got everyone's attention. Emmie quickly got up and joined Mally, trying to glimpse the oncoming traffic.

"Oh my," Emmie said, placing a hand to her mouth at the sight of Braids's swollen and bloodied face. She reached for the locket at her neck and stroked it.

"Back up," the guard said as he opened the door and shoved Braids in. If not for running into Hech, she would have landed on the floor. He steadied her on her feet. Forgetting about her wrist, Emmie ran over to her and wrapped her arms around her. Braids buried her head in Emmie's chest, sobbing uncontrollably. Moments later, Mally, her face almost transcending the bars, announced the second contingent of guards.

"The doc doesn't look any worse for wear," Middie announced.

"Shut up," Gref said as he watched Egans push Leba into the cell at the point of a translucent rod.

"You," Egans said, pointing at Riki with the stick. "And you." This time identifying Mally. "Your turn."

"No, I don't want to go," Mally insisted, gripping the bars so tightly her knuckles whitened.

"I don't remember it being a choice." Egans laughed. "Now come with me." Using the rod, he pointed at Braids. "Or do you want some of what she got?"

Mally looked at Braids, whose face was buried in Emmie's chest, her body shaking. "Come on." Riki grabbed Mally's hand. "We'll be okay." Riki looked to Victos, but he remained still, the veins in his neck bulging.

Tears began to roll from Mally's eyes. "I don't want to go," she said again, wiping her face with one hand, the other still tightly gripped on the bars. With the muzzles of their weapons, Egans's troopers urged Mally and Riki out of the cell.

"Take me," Emmie said, holding onto Braids with her good arm. "I'm the leader, I'm responsible."

"Maybe later," Egans said, placating her. "Right now, these two are all we want." He slammed the cell door shut. The troop moved down the hall, out of sight.

"They gone?" Braids whispered, lifting her head slowly off Emmie's chest.

"Yeah, they're gone," Middie answered, having assumed Mally's perch.

"Here," Braids said, producing a communications device from her pocket. "We'd better move fast, or there's no telling what's in store for Mally and Riki."

Leba was shocked by Braids's quick turnaround.

If you weren't all that hurt, you could've offered some backup.

"What do you mean?" Victos asked.

"They are after something." Braids ran a hand down her dreads. "But Mally and Riki would have nothing to offer them." Emmie didn't understand. "They wanted access to my father's company."

"Did you give it to them?" Gref asked.

"Not exactly," Braids said proudly, wiping blood from the corner of her mouth. She turned toward Leba. "Doc, what did they want from you?"

All eyes turned toward Leba. "They had me look at some data from the cryo-volcano. It was displaying some anomalous readings and wanted to know what it meant." She thought for a moment and then questioned, "Doesn't your father's company specialize in harnessing energy sources using nanotechnology?"

"Yes," Braids said. Leba was slowly beginning to understand what was really going on. "But what that also means is that we are now expendable." Braids spat blood.

"So why do they want Riki and Mally?" Hech asked.

"I'm not going to wait to find out," Victos said, pounding a fist into the wall. "I'm tired of this contrived nonsense. Everything that can go wrong has. It's just too perfect." He looked over at Middie, maybe expecting a sarcastic comment, but none came. Violating her personal space, Victos asked, "You've been too quiet. You know something, don't you?"

She recoiled. "Get outta my face." Everyone stared at Middie. Emmie Hodd should have stepped in to get Victos to back off but didn't. The closer Victos got, the more Middie backed away until she touched wall. Putting her hands up to halt his forward progress, she snapped, "I said get outta my face!" Despite shoving her weight against his chest, Middie was not about to move him. *These people will never make a team.*

Leba walked over and put a hand on his shoulder. "We need to focus on getting out." Not wanting to budge, Victos held his ground and looked at her. "I need you. If we put our heads together, we can get out." Leba didn't bother to look for Emmie's approval; it was time for action. If she expected to complete the mission, she needed to change tactics. Slowly Victos backed away from Middie. Leba hoped she could count on Vic to keep his cool and help her.

"Thanks, Doc," Middie said and took her flask from her pocket and slowly swallowed a sizable gulp.

"What's your idea, Doc?" Victos asked.

"I need you to beat up Middie," Leba started.

"Hey," Middie recoiled, startled.

"I like the plan so far." Victos laughed, staring at Middie and ground his clenched right fist into his left palm.

Victos pummeled Middie with shadow blows as she cried out. Emmie banged on the door to the cell, trying to get the attention of the guard stationed outside. After what seemed like an eternity, a cadre of guards entered the cell to try and break apart Victos and Middie.

"Hey, stop hitting her," one said as he attempted to pull Victos from Middie.

Gref and Hech joined in the fray, pushing the guards into one another as the scene turned into a melee. All the while, there was shouting and arms flailing. The quarters were too close for small-arms fire. The guards, in their bulky gear, found the hand-to-hand confrontation particularly difficult and were easily sent to the floor. One by one, the remaining members of green med team dispatched the guards, relieving them of their consciousness, their gear, and their weapons.

Save for a few welts, bumps, and bruises, everyone came out unscathed. Emmie, who stationed herself as lookout during the fray, pulled the detention cell door almost closed as Leba and Victos, Gref and Hech secured their prisoners. "They'll be out for a while," Leba reported.

"Good." Emmie applauded their combined efforts. "Now," she instructed, "Joreg, you and Middie find us a transport to get outta here." She looked at Victos. "Victos, take Tylor and the doc and go get Mally and Riki. Braids and I are going to call home." She smiled. "Hurry."

Mally and Riki walked down the long hallway flanked by Egans, Jekkers, and their guardsmen. "Don't worry, Mally," Riki said, trying to be brave, "I'm sure they just want to ask us questions."

"We don't know anything, not like Braids, or Dierna, or whatever her name is. And we certainly don't know the stuff Dr. Brader knows," Mally grumbled.

"Maybe this is just a test of how we'd do being interrogated," Riki offered. "You know, part of our simulated experience."

"We're here, ladies," Egans said, opening a door for them. The room was sparsely furnished, a table, a few chairs, and in the center of the table were some bottles of water and a bowl of fruit. After advising them to make themselves comfortable, Egans posted a guard at the door, promising to be back in a few minutes.

"Wow," Mally exhaled, her eyes gazing upward. "I guess you were right not to be worried. I wish I could be as confident as you are."

Riki just nodded and reached for a bottle of water, quietly examining it. She leaned across the table for a piece of fruit, again turning it in her hand. It looked like an Oraconi guavcod. The purple shriveled peel felt fuzzy, and Riki stuck her fingernail into the skin. She sniffed at the zest. It smelled like she remembered, citrusy with a hint of mint. Riki tried to figure out what was up. She hadn't seen one since she visited her nana, on her parents' original home world when she was a little kid. It was hard to remember those lessons from mission training, the ones about sampling foods in captivity, since she spent most of class interested in what Vic was up to. She could kick herself. As Mally reached for a piece of fruit, Riki warned, "I don't think I'd eat anything yet. Let's give it a few minutes to see how this plays out."

Mally nodded her agreement. "How about the water?"

"I'd wait on that too." Seeing the downtrodden look on Mally's face, Riki added, "At least for now." Further explanation would wait as the door opened to reveal Professor Awart.

Taking a seat at the head of the table, while Egans remained standing to his right, Awart drew in a long breath, interlacing his sausage-like fingers together to rest on his paunch. "I assume," he drawled, his eyebrows narrowed. "Please, ladies, have a seat." Riki and Mally took seats on the same side of the table. "As I was saying, I assume you are both wondering why I asked you here."

The conversation was quite cordial between the professor and the two nurses. Awart ate a piece of fruit to demonstrate its nonlethality and washed it down with some water. More comfortable, Mally and Riki joined him. The questions so far were relatively benign, small talk and such, until Riki noticed Egans touch his earwig. He leaned close to Awart and whispered into his ear. A toothed grin spread across his face, and he addressed the women. "Ms. Hodd's word doesn't seem to mean much." Inclining his head, he shook it side to side. "It seems your friends did not keep their part of the bargain, so unfortunately, you'll have to be punished for their disobedience."

Riki and Mally stared at him in disbelief. Egans signaled Jekkers to join them. "What do you want us to do with these two?" As Awart got up from the table, the door slid open with Jekkers's arrival.

"Oh, I don't know," Awart said, throwing a hand up. "Surprise me." With that, he hurried out the door.

Egans smirked at Jekkers. "I like surprises, don't you?"

"We need to get somewhere quiet to use this," Braids stated.

"It seems pretty quiet here, there's no one around. Here, let me shut the door," Emmie said as she went to her left to push the door closed.

"You misunderstand." Braids shook her head. "Somewhere frequency quiet." Emmie stared blankly at her. "There is a lot of noise in this area, noise in a frequency you and I can't hear, but it's interfering with this comm." Braids continued, "Maybe the professor wasn't lying after all. This thing is good short-range, but to get out a long-range signal may be impossible."

"It can never be easy on this mission," Emmie said, rubbing her brow. She was exhausted, and her wrist hurt more than ever. "Nothing is as it seems, everything's a deception, and around every turn is another twisted mess."

"Don't give up yet, Ma," Braids tried to console her.

"Ma," Emmie spat. "Drop the con, you have a mother." Maybe she was more upset than she realized about the professor's revelation. Now it was really beginning to get to her.

Braids eyes widened, and her mouth slackened. She covered her mouth. After a moment, she shot back, her voice shaky. "That's not fair."

"What's not fair, the fact the comm is worthless, or that you've been lying to me?" Emmie's dagger was sheathed in guilt.

"That's not fair," cried Braids, tears welling in her eyes. "Ma, you can't do this to me, not here, not now." The thrust penetrated deeply. Emmie turned her back to Braids and headed toward the door. Twisting the knife in further. "That's not fair," Braids cried out again. "Please, Ma, don't turn your back on me. Let me explain."

"Now's not the time for explanations," Emmie said, her back rigid, arms crossed over her chest. "Now's the time to get outta this room and get somewhere where we can get this stupid thing to work."

"This place is pretty big, so how are we going to find them?" Gref asked as he, Victos, and Leba ran down a hallway. The trio stopped to consider Gref's query.

"I may know." Leba covered the lower half of her face with her hand.

"You seem to know a lot of things," Gref said, pressing his lips into a fine line. "Any little secrets you've been holding out?" He bowed out his arms and drove his fists into his sides.

Leba's hand came away from her mouth in a fist, which she quickly dissolved into a five-finger stretch. Victos scowled at him. "Shut up unless you have any better ideas."

Victos proceeded up the hall until faced with a choice of doorways. "Where to, Doc?"

"We were taken to Sector 7," Leba recalled. "If I remember correctly, it shouldn't be too far from here." Leba opened the right side door slowly and peered out. "Come on," she encouraged them to follow. "I think," Leba hesitated, looking at the signage on the adjacent wall. "Yes, through here." Pointing, she continued in the new corridor, passing a number of closed-door offices flanking both sides of the hallway. "There." She pointed to a door.

"But that says Sector 6." Gref stopped, frustrated.

"Maybe Sector 6 connects to Sector 7," Victos said.

Leba ignored their banter. "Once we get past this door, there may be guards posted."

"I'm in the mood for bashing heads," Victos said, eyeing Gref.

"Funny, very funny." Gref smirked. "Well, it could be worse. I could be stuck with Fidelis instead of the brain and the brawn." Gref peered at one of the weapons they relieved from the detention cell guards, his perennial scowl now replaced by an uncharacteristic smile. Victos's captured weapon was secured in his waistband. There were not enough captured weapons to go around, so Leba opted out of carrying. Feeling more comfortable with a knife or a stick, they never jammed or ran out of energy. Yes, she could shoot and was a fairly good shot, but there were too many variables involved. In a crisis or tough situation, it was always best to go with what you know and what you practiced. She did wish she still had her knife. Even her makeshift stick served her well just a few hours ago. It did bother her Gref was totting the gun around openly and with his finger securely on the trigger. She hoped he wouldn't shoot himself or one of them.

Strangely, when they moved the door slightly open to peer around it, there were no guards in sight, only the door labeled Sector 7 at the end of a long hallway. Shoulders back and chest thrust out, Gref remarked, "Finally, something's going our way, no guards."

The locking bolt chunked as it released, and the far door began to open. The three slid into adjoining doorways. Leba hoped their shadows wouldn't give them away. Mally and Riki emerged first followed by Egans and Jekkers. Mally's face was red and puffy. Riki struggled against Jekkers's grasp on her wrist. "If you don't stop," he scolded Riki, "I may have to hurt you."

"Unless I hurt you first," Riki slapped him square in the face. Jekkers recoiled not so much in pain as in surprise and let go of his grasp on her. Unfortunately, Riki hadn't thought much in advance about what her next move was going to be.

"I'll have fun breaking you." Jekkers reached to strike her back when Victos stepped out from his position.

"I wouldn't do that," Victos declared. Jekkers wheeled around to see Victos standing tall in front of him. "I still owe you from last night." Victos stared at him. As the two men squared off, Egans brought his weapon to bear.

"Gun!" Mally shrieked.

Suddenly and without warning, Egans's head exploded with a single blast from Gref's weapon. Horrified as Egans's limp body fell toward her, Mally stepped back and out of the way. The vomit came uncontrollably up in her mouth and out onto the floor. Victos restrained a stunned and defenseless Jekkers. Leba made her way over to Egans's body, shaking her head, confirming his death. "What did you do?" Victos snapped at Gref.

"Saved your sorry ass, stupid, or couldn't you tell?" Gref retorted.

Leba went through Egans's pockets, found his master keycard, and handed it to Victos. Gref bent down and picked up Egans's weapon and shoved it into his waistband. He pointed his still-smoking weapon against Jekkers's head. "I'm getting tired of all this, so start talking or join your buddy."

Cringing by the door, Mally stood petrified as Leba and Riki moved Egans's body into one of the unlocked offices, while Victos and Gref took Jekkers into another. They shut the door so their interrogation would be private. By diverting her attention, Leba hoped to settle Mally down. Riki watched the proceedings in the other room. There was shouting, and Jekkers was taking a pounding. "Hey, come here, I think they're done," Riki said.

"I don't want to see," Mally cried. "I want to go home."

"You don't have to look," Leba consoled her. "But we do need to get going." Peering in the window, Leba could see Jekkers's limp form, motionless and slumped in a chair. Victos's knuckles were bloodied; sweat glistened off his brow. Gref, on the other hand, showed no signs of having dirtied his hands.

"He didn't tell us much," Victos said as he wiped his hands on the front of his trousers. "That's the problem with simulatrons, they don't feel pain."

"He looked pretty pained to me," Gref disagreed. "Every time you hit him."

Riki looked pale. Maybe she was sickened by Victos's pummeling a helpless man. "Are you just going to leave him there like that?" she asked.

"It's not like he's real," Gref offered.

"How do you know?" Riki's voice trailed off as she stared at Jekkers's smashed face.

"This is stupid." Victos grabbed Riki's hand. She pulled away, avoided looking directly at him. "It's just a simulatron, he's not real. You know I wouldn't do that to a real man." He reached out for Riki's hand, this time more gently. "We need to go." This time she took his hand. He smiled at her, and the corners of her mouth upturned slightly.

Leba handed Victos the comm she removed from Egans throat and the partially charred earwig. "I'm not sure these still work." Leba too was disturbed by Victos's display but didn't say anything. Aggression was often innate and not necessarily a learned behavior. It took a lot to kill someone with your bare hands, especially if they were defenseless. She wondered if Victos's occasionally violent behavior was one of the factors originally separating him and Riki. Leba was beginning to think having the two of them together on the same team was a mistake, the same mistake as having Emmie and Braids together, or Gref and Hech together. Knowing each other's skills was one thing, but knowing each other's hearts was a different matter altogether.

Hech and Middie found a fire evacuation plan fastened to one of the doorways just outside the detention cell. Sometimes rules came in handy. "It looks like if we keep heading towards the back of this place, we'll find their garage." Hech showed on the schematic.

"You lead," Middie encouraged. "I'll watch your back."

And who'll watch you? Hech thought. They arrived at the garage area and found only one guard stationed there. "How do we get rid of him?" Hech whispered.

"Leave that to me," Middie said as she removed her flask. She took a swallow and then sprinkled some on her clothes. Staggering into the hallway, she teetered into a wall. "You think a man could help a lady," she slurred, prompting the guard to rush over. She dropped to the floor, grabbing at the man's jacket on the way down. Unceremoniously, he fell on top of her.

Whatever works. Hech grinned at the sight of Middie flailing underneath the guard. As she struggled, Middie gave Hech a queer look. *Oops, I guess that's my cue.* He placed a gun to the man's head. "I'll take that," he said, relieving the guard of his weapon. "Now, I know you've waited all your life to be on top of Fidelis here, but we have a mission to get back to." The guard untangled himself from Middie and stood up.

"Hands behind you, baby boy, and keep quiet." Middie secured his hands. "You're cute, but not really my type." She patted his head. "Now you sit here and be quiet and you won't get hurt, understand?" The young guard nodded. Middie patted his shirt pockets. The guard looked down as she went into his pants pockets. "Nothing here." She laughed and then hit him in the back of the head, knocking him out.

"Not a good way to end a relationship. No wonder you can't keep a steady man."

Middie glared at him. "You want some of the same, smart ass?"

The pair entered the dark garage. Only a few emergency lights kept them out of total blackness. "Find the lights so I can see what we have to pick from in the showroom." Hech obliged her, and soon the room was fully illuminated. "Not much to choose from. I'm not sure any of these can hold all of us, if they can even get off the ground."

Sirens began blaring, piercing the walls of the complex. "What did you touch?" Middie screamed at Hech over the noise.

"I didn't touch anything!" Hech yelled back.

"This place will be crawling with security in no time. Find the damn door look and keep 'em from coming in."

"Brilliant plan." Hech snickered. "And how do you expect to get the rest of our team in here?"

"You heard Hodd's orders, resist and escape. If only you and I get out, then we've followed orders." She smirked.

What now? Emmie thought to herself as the siren blared. Still visibly upset by Emmie's rejection, Braids did not respond. So far, they were unsuccessful at finding a place without frequency interference. "Come on," Emmie urged Braids as she opened the doorway into the adjoining room. "Bad move!" Emmie yelled as they entered the room.

The room appeared to be set up as a temporary triage or medical area. One harried, cloaked elderly gentleman was tending to a number of bedridden people. There were readouts above each gurney. He turned to engage them. "What are you doing in here? These people are sick. Awart promised he would keep you out."

Emmie wasn't quite sure who the man thought they were. "We need your help," she begged.

"Everyone here needs my help, and if you don't leave, I will need help," he pleaded.

"What is this place?" she said, coming over to examine one of the patient cubicles.

"Don't touch that," the man advised, pushing her arm away and silencing an adjacent bed alarm. "Please leave, I am very busy." He examined the patient in the bed, reached for a nearby syringe, and injected the person.

Briefly assessing each patient, Emmie went from bed to bed. "These people are dying," she stated.

The man scurried between each stretcher, trying to stamp out the small fires as they occurred. "I am barely staying ahead of their dying, and if you don't leave, I will lose the fight."

"Let me help," Emmie said. "I'm a nurse." Pulling back the covers on the closest patient, Emmie gasped at the festering burn wounds. "She must be in terrible pain." The bedside tray was laden with an assortment of instruments. Emmie picked up a syringe. "What's in here?" The man did not answer. Emmie was in no mood for noncompliance. Grabbing him by his lapel, Emmie pulled his face close, locking eyes. "I said, what is in here?"

"Peace," he said in hushed tones. "Peace from the pain." Her grip slackened, and she released him.

Emmie was appalled but understood. Euthanasia was still reserved for animals. People, despite their unrecoverable position, suffered through their terminal illnesses. "What caused these injuries?" she asked. The man did not respond. Grabbing the front of his lab coat again, she yelled, "What caused these injuries?"

"Ask him." The man pointed. Emmie whirled around to see Awart enter the room. This time, he was alone.

"All your questions will be answered in time. Now please come with me." Awart grabbed Emmie's wrist and pulled. Emmie howled in pain, and Awart dropped her hand.

Braids rushed at Awart, knocking him backward. "No!" Emmie screamed as the two grappled on the floor. First a flash and then the hissing discharge of a weapon. "No!" Emmie screamed. Rushing over, she watched Awart's eyes roll up into his head. Holding both hands over the wound in her abdomen, Braids attempted to stand but could only get to her knees and fell back onto the floor. Emmie screamed for the cloaked man to help her. The two dragged Braids to a nearby stretcher. Neither could lift Braids up onto a stretcher. Emmie was too weak, especially with her fractured wrist, and the man too old and frail. "I need help!" Emmie screamed.

The man went over to a nearby cupboard and dumped a number of supplies on the floor. He knelt down beside Braids and began to work. He drew up a liquid into a syringe and prepared to inject her. "No," Emmie said, grasping his hand.

"But it's for the best," the man advised.

"No." Emmie pushed the syringe out of his hand. She grabbed his collar and pulled him forward, flinging him against the wall. Left-handed, Emmie reached into her waistband and, two-handed, leveled her weapon at the man. "Get me a comm or I'll blow your head off." Now panting, her finger trembling on the trigger, Emmie mustered one last word, "Now!"

The man reached under his cloak and handed her a comm. She took it, studied it for a moment as she regained her breath, and asked, "Can you make this thing overhead page throughout the facility?" He looked at her curiously. "I need you to make this thing announce over the entire facility. Now," she repeated, pressing the device into his chest.

The man fiddled with the comm's controls. "Here," he said, thrusting it back to her. "You know you'll bring all of Awart's people here, and they're not going to be happy with what you've done."

"Shut up," she said, pushing him away. "Shut up and keep her alive until I get my people here. They'll know how to save her."

The overhead claxon blared as Leba, Vic, and the rest headed toward Sector 2 and the garage. Leba stopped cold. "Wait, I think I got overhead paged." She pinched her eyes shut. It was hard to hear over the blare of the siren. "I swear I just got overhead paged." The five stopped and concentrated.

"Dr. Brader, code red, Sector 4, stat." The message repeated.

"Sounds like Hodd," Gref scoffed, gesturing with upturned hands.

"Where's Sector 4?" Leba asked.

The far end of the hallway displayed a fire evacuation plan, and Victos went to examine it. "This corridor dumps into Sector 5. Sector 4 is left beyond that." Victos scratched the side of his head. "According to this, Sector 2 is to the right."

Leba squeezed her temples. She couldn't ignore the page. Even if Emmie was forced under duress, Leba couldn't take the chance she was really needed. "Must be pretty serious if Emmie is giving up her position," Riki said.

"Or she's just plain stupid," Vic spat.

"I'll go," Leba said, her feet already pointed toward the exit. "You guys find Middie and Hech."

"Come on," Vic said. "We'd better get moving." He pushed the Sector 5 door and headed through.

CHAPTER 19

"Shut up so I can hear!" Middie shouted at Hech. "What the... what does Hodd think she's doing?"

"Should we see what's wrong?" Hech said.

"Are you nuts, and give up our position too?" Middie yelled. "It's probably a trap. Hodd can't be that stupid." Hech turned away from her and unlatched the door. "Hey! I said—" Middie yelled after him, but Hech didn't look back.

Proceeding out the door and back down the hallway, Hech was drawn to answer the beckon. Something deep inside him burned. Whether for altruistic reasons or a bizarre curiosity, Joreg Hech needed to find out what was up. Maybe because he was medical and lived for the glory, the "Here I come to save the day" accolades, or maybe he was concerned for his partner, Tylor Gref. Would Emmie give up her position if Tylor was injured and needed help? Hech left the security of the hangar bay not knowing which or why. The garage was in Sector 2, and according to the schematics, Sector 4 was close enough, around one or two turns.

Hech burst through the Sector 4 sliding doors and saw Emmie kneeling over Braids. He puffed out a long breath. Thank goodness it wasn't Tylor. An elderly gentleman in a long cloak was attending to her. "Here." Hech knelt and slipped his arms under Braids. "Let me get her up on the gurney."

The opposite side door opened to reveal other members of his green med team. Gref and Uribos pushed past the occupied stretchers. "On three." Hech counted off, and the trio lifted Braids onto the gurney.

Leba rushed to the side of the stretcher. "Status." Hech looked at Emmie. Like the rest, he just arrived, but Hodd saw it go down.

Well? Suck it up and answer the doc's question. Emmie remained seated on the floor. "I got here a few seconds before you," Hech said, his head slightly bowed. Then he watched in amazement as doctor mode kicked in, and Leba Brader began to direct the others.

"Tylor, Joreg, find our med stuff, it must be here somewhere." They looked at the elderly man, who pointed to an upright cabinet at the far end of the room. Gref and Hech snatched their backpacks and returned. "Mally, find me some fluids."

"What kind?" Mally asked.

"Anything, just hurry." Leba tore the bindings as she ripped open Braids shirt. Bloodied hands dropped away. The wound was large, a gaping maw with charred edges. Last time Hech saw a wound like that was in his intern year ride-along when he shadowed a field medic on a remote outpost. Nothing else smelled like burned flesh. And it stayed with you. A hint of nausea bubbled in his stomach, but Hech fought it off.

"What do you need me to do?" Riki asked.

"I need you and Vic to start two large bore IVs," Leba ordered.

Hech held a large cover dressing over the wound to prevent further contamination while everyone else scurried to fulfill Dr. Brader's orders. For a moment, Joreg Hech stared at the young doctor, watching how she engaged the elderly man.

Returning her attention to Braids, Leba gently touched Hech's arm, and he moved the coverlet back. As Leba examined the wound, she felt a warm breath on her neck. The smell of cigar smoke wafted toward her nose. She looked up to see Joreg Hech staring at her again. Feeling a slight nudge on her back, Leba turned to look over her left shoulder. She met the elderly man's peering gaze. Startled, he stumbled backward and shuffled a step or two to regain his balance. Leba reached to grab his arms and steadied him.

"I'm Dr. Brader, sir, and you are?"

The man steadied under her assistance. Now facing her, his eyes disappeared behind thick half-lensed spectacles. The corners of his mouth barely moved when he spoke. "Fragmire, Dr. Rotan

Fragmire." Clearly visible beneath his medical tunic were slumped shoulders topping his stooped posture.

"I'm going to need your help if we're going to save her," Leba said and squeezed his forearms.

His eyebrows rose, and a smile crept onto his face. Fragmire cleared his throat, and she released her grip. "I have some jump grafts stored in the back room and a tray of instruments you might find useful."

"Vic," Leba called, "can you help Dr. Fragmire with his equipment?"

Following a shuffling Fragmire into the next room, Victos shouted back, "Doc, there's a setup back here!"

"Great," she said, framing the doorway. The room's overhead lighting was on directable pulleys. The walls were lined with cabinets brimming with medical equipment. Bolted wall brackets held two gas canisters, which stood like sentries overlooking the scene. Fragmire reached between them and, with some effort, rotated a release valve. Tottering to a console and toggling a switch, Fragmire reincarnated an antiquated anesthesia machine. It protested, coughing and wheezing as it returned to life. Picking up the rubberized facemask, Leba stretched its accordion umbilical cord. She watched the bellows rise with the influx of gases. "Dr. Fragmire, please scrub with me." Leba noticed how he straightened from his drooping posture.

"Of course, of course," he said. "It's about time I was able to save someone around here."

"I'll get the room set up," Victos said. "Tylor, Joreg, bring our stuff in here." Gref and Hech dragged the med bags in.

Now we're acting like a team.

Emmie, although she wanted to help, was having trouble focusing, and Riki told her it would be best to sit this one out. As events unfolded, she watched in slow motion the symphony her team, no, Dr. Brader's team performed. While Mally and Riki prepped Braids for surgery, Leba met Dr. Fragmire by the hand sterilizer, where they both donned protective gear and gloves. Everyone did their assigned job without question. Once they were ready to proceed, Mally was charged with babysitting Emmie, while the boys guarded the door. Slowly Emmie watched the back room door close and waited. What a leader she turned out to be. Her mind was supposed to be focused on the team and their survival, but she couldn't think past Braids. How could she have been so mean and resentful?

"Where's Fidelis?" Gref asked Hech.

"Left her in the garage." Hech smirked. "She's working on securing transport." Hech surprised even himself by not ratting her out. About her ignoring the code red. About abandoning the team when they may have needed her the most. What was the point? Maybe Fidelis was the one with the right idea after all. This attempt to save Braids was at best a futile waste of time. It was about midnight now, and three of their four days were gone in a blur. What Hodd did was put the whole team in jeopardy. The real question was would she have done it for any of them or just her precious Braids? Hech inherently understood why Dr. Brader did what she did. It was her nature to try and beat insurmountable odds, save every last being, an adventure, not a job. The younger nurses too possessed an innate drive to help anyone in need. Hech wondered how Uribos would handle it if they were to be overrun by hostiles while trying to save Braids and his beloved Riki was killed.

Joreg Hech was confused. Why hadn't he heeded Fidelis's advice? Why did he find it necessary to return to assist the others? Did he actually care about these people? Was this the whole point of the mission, to find his inner strength, to overlook his own selfish needs and goals?

"You know, I think they'd do the same for us too," Gref said.

Hech looked up at Gref, who put an arm around his shoulder. Gref handed him a comm. "Uribos wants us to make our way back to Fidelis so when the doc's done, we're ready to move."

"Sure, whatever," Hech agreed.

"Uribos thinks with Awart dead, the rest of these guys are scattered and have more important things to worry about than us," Gref continued.

As Gref and Hech left the med area, Mally quickly secured the door behind them. Walking past the row of vegetative patients, she asked, "What about the rest of these people?"

"I think Dr. Fragmire will do the right thing," Uribos offered. "He told me they were being kept alive as sort of a living experiment." Mally looked at him in disbelief. "He had no choice, there were other lives on the line, or at least that's what he was told."

Emmie remained seated on the floor, huddled in a few blankets, only peripherally listening to the others' conversations. She could not figure out why she was so cold. Did the chill reflect how she treated and rejected Braids when her girl needed her the most? How selfish was she, putting her own needs and feelings ahead of the rest. When the pounding began at the front door, Emmie felt even more guilt. She watched Uribos try and push a heavy cabinet in front of the door.

"Mally, tell Doc to get a move on, we can't hold them forever." Mally leaped up from where she was sitting, trying to comfort Emmie. Emmie unfortunately ignored her attempts at consolation and was beyond frustrated Dr. Brader excluded her from the OR. She wanted to help but was relegated to watching, watching Vic, watching Mally, watching events unfold around her, not being able to participate. Mally was getting her chance to participate, to be a real member of the team, someone people could count on or look to or even notice for something other than her looks or her relationship with their squad leader.

Mally gently knocked on the back room door. Not receiving an answer, she slowly opened the door. "It's okay," Riki said, "we're just about done." Emmie perked up at the rhythmic beeping of the monitor. She vaulted from the floor and trailed as Mally slowly approached. Dr. Fragmire was putting away his equipment, while Dr. Brader was finishing closing the skin with the laser sealer.

"Mally, if you don't mind, could you dress this for me?" Dr. Brader asked.

A wide smile crossed Mally's face. "Of course." She donned gloves and got busy to her task.

"How's Emmie doing?" Riki asked, not seeing her at the doorway.

"Not so good, I think," Mally, head down, focusing on her task, answered.

"I'm fine," Emmie snapped. Folding her arms across her chest, she turned her back on the room.

As information spilled out uncontrollably from Mally, updating everyone on everything, Leba walked over to Dr. Fragmire. "Thought we were going to lose her there for a moment," he recalled.

I guess I made the right choice getting all of you back here. Saved a valuable team member. No need to thank me, though.

"You've done this before, haven't you?" Leba asked as she removed her gloves and activated the foot pedal scrub station water.

"Once or twice." He chuckled as he made room for her and finished rinsing off the cleaning foam and air-dried his hands. "Felt good to be useful again, instead of, oh, never mind, I think I'll revel in this moment." He patted her shoulder. "Thanks for letting me be part of your team." That *your* stung Emmie, and she recoiled. This was her team, not Dr. Brader's.

Leba looked over her shoulder and caught Emmie staring back at her. *It should've never been her team. Vic's maybe, even mine, but never Emmie's.* The stare was uncomfortable, and Leba turned back to Dr. Fragmire.

"Do you know Professor Roblins well?" Leba asked. Waving her hands back and forth, trying to get them to dry.

"Who?" Dr. Fragmire said, his face slack. A blank expression overtook his face.

"Professor Lu Roblins, you know, the scientist from Sector 7," Leba explained again.

"Professor Roblins hasn't been here in over a year," he relayed.

"Then who did I meet?" Leba paused and reached her hand into her pocket only to find the folded piece of paper gone.

"Let us in," Hech commed Middie.

"How do I know it's you and that you're not surrounded by a hundred security people?" Middie asked brusquely.

"Let us in or I'll—" Hech puffed out his chest and banged on the door.

"Or you'll what?" Middie said as she deactivated the door lock and let Gref and Hech in.

"Vic wants you to be ready to leave," Gref told her.

"When he gets here, I'll be ready." She smiled, pointing to an antiquated shuttle idling in warm-up mode.

"What's that?" Gref asked.

"Our ticket outta here, stupid." She sneered at him. "It's the only thing big enough to haul all of us out of here, and even so, that's pushing it."

"You'll have to find room for a stretcher too." Hech looked at her expectantly.

Mally finished the dressing and was met by approval from Dr. Fragmire, who stood admiring her work. She smiled coyly at his comments. "Go ahead," Leba said. "You can bring Emmie in to see her."

"I'll get her," Riki offered. "I want to see how Vic is doing."

Ignoring those assembled, Emmie slowly pushed the door fully open and went over to Braids. Swaddled in bed linens, with only her face exposed, Braids remained unconscious. Brushing one of Dierna's braids out of her face, Emmie leaned down and whispered something into her ear. A tear rolled from Emmie's eye. She leaned in closer and planted a kiss on her forehead. "Sleep, child, I'll always be here for you."

Squad Leader Luth Cathen sat in front of a quad of monitors labeled cold box. Three of four vid feeds were live, and the last was dark.

"I'm letting blue team get some sleep," he mused.

"You're letting them?" the administrative command officer said.

"Yes, I turn down the pressure each time an objective is met," he explained while studying a readout. "See here." he pointed. "Red team is about to finish their triage, and I can let them get some sleep too." They watched DeShay Tiner congratulate his team on a job well done. Entering a string of commands into the console, Cathen deactivated that screen too. "I don't like to watch them sleep, too boring." He spun his chair to face her and rotated side to side.

"What about green team?" she asked, letting out her long raven-colored hair and leaning forward to grab the arms of his chair.

"What about green team?" he retorted, twirling a dangling tress with his finger.

"When are you going to let up the pressure on them?" She pulled back.

"When all my objectives are met." He ran his hands up her arms and tried to draw her back.

"What do you mean when all your objectives have been met?" she snarled at Luth Cathen.

"What part of *my*"—he emphasized the word *my*—"don't you understand?"

"Don't get smart with me." She patted his face, this time her voice gentler, more playful. She leaned in, and their lips met. She whispered, "I can take away your position at any time." She tried sucking his lower lip.

"But you won't." He pushed her away. "I do what you don't have the stomach for." He came up out of his chair and smirked.

"Do what you must, but hurry up," she counseled. "You know how the old man gets when things don't proceed like he feels they should."

"I'm sure you can find a way to appease him." Cathen snickered.

"Just try not and kill anyone else, those simulatrons are expensive," she advised him.

"So are people," he reminded her. "Many are irreplaceable."

She turned to leave the control room. "Don't misunderstand my reluctance to replace you as a sign I approve of your methods."

"I don't expect you to approve just to appreciate." Cathen leaned back in his chair, hands interlaced behind his head, and closed his eyes.

The banging outside the Sector 4 med bay door stopped suddenly. "I guess they got tired and moved on." Riki laughed nervously.

Victos wasn't convinced, though. This was probably the calm before they stormed the door. "Tell the doc we've gotta move now." Riki left his side. Victos looked around, going through some drawers and gathering supplies.

"What are you doing?" Riki came up behind him and rested her chin on his shoulder.

"Preparing a surprise for our friends," he said. "Are they ready to move?"

"Just about," Riki answered. "Dr. Fragmire showed us another hidden exit. He doesn't think Awart's people know about it."

"Don't count on it," Victos advised. "We'd better be ready for some resistance." Riki nodded. "Hold this for me," he instructed. She slid under his outstretched arm and held the little black box against the doorjamb. "This should do it," he announced after securing the device and removed her hands.

"What's this do?" Riki questioned, pointing to the eclectic collection of supplies now attached to the inner doorframe.

"Buys us time," he said and toggled a switch. A little yellow light blinked. "Armed and ready." He grabbed Riki's hand. "Come on." The two entered the backroom. "Time's up, Doc, it's now or never." Victos looked at Leba.

"We're ready," she said, slinging a backpack over her shoulder and handing another to Mally. "We've got what we need for Braids."

"Great," Victos announced.

"Good luck, and thanks," Dr. Fragmire said. "Thanks for giving me a new start."

"I left you the rest of our supplies." Leba pointed to the far corner. "Once we clear atmosphere, we'll notify our base to send more help," she promised.

With Victos at point, Mally and Emmie flanked the stretcher bearing a sedated Braids. Leba and Riki trailed the group. The travel monitor beeped rhythmically, constantly updating Braids's status. Although they argued about the constant monitor noise giving them away, it was ultimately decided not to mute the sounds or silence the alarms.

There was a sizzling sound followed by a burst of electrical discharge. Mally's head swiveled in the direction of disturbance. "What was that?"

"Vic's door alarm and antihostile device," Riki reported. "Vic," Riki called to the front of the stretcher. Halting, he turned to listen. "The door buzzer just went off."

Grinning for only a moment, he made a wide sweep with his arm encouraging the group to hurry. "Sector 2 shouldn't be too far from here."

CHAPTER 20

"Hey, when did the sirens go off?" Hech asked Gref.

"I don't know," Gref replied. "I was busy trying to get the backseats out of this shuttle for the stretcher. I didn't really notice."

"What are you two yammering about?" Middie called from the cockpit.

"The sirens stopped," Hech repeated.

"So?" Middie said. "Maybe they've decided to leave us alone for a change." She knew that probably wasn't true but wasn't about to spend a lot of time trying to figure it out. What she did need to figure out was how to launch the shuttle. Driving travel sleds was nothing compared to an airborne shuttle. Despite the similarities in control panels and readouts, moving in three dimensions was astronomically more challenging than traveling in two dimensions. She was not about to ask the others for help, and toggling switches randomly was eventually going to get her in trouble.

When Victos got to the outside garage door, he signaled Middie, who in turn sent Hech to open the hangar bay. They maneuvered the stretcher through the small door and into the generous open space. "Which one's our ride?" Victos asked until he saw the antiquated shuttle with half the seats lying on the floor.

Middie walked down the shuttle's extended door ramp. "Best I could do on short notice."

"Can you fly this thing?" Victos asked.

"Was hoping one of you could," Middie confessed.

"You don't need to," Leba stated. "It flies itself."

"Think you've been sniffing too much anesthesia, Doc," Middie jested, half-hoping she was actually telling the truth.

"Once you set the nav for your destination, all you do is activate the autopilot, and the shuttle does the rest," Leba said.

"Think you can get this thing to fly?" Victos asked her.

"I know I can get it off the ground and into the atmosphere, the shuttle should be able to do the rest, except..." Leba hesitated.

"There's always an except," Gref lamented.

"I don't think it lands itself," she finished.

"We've got to get Braids outta here," Emmie blurted out. "So we will just have to figure something out when the time comes."

"Like you figured out how to get a signal to base," Mally complained.

"Meek, mild-mannered Mally finally found her manhood." Middie chuckled. Mally blushed. "Hey, Hodd, got any great ideas how you will land this thing?"

Chin trembling, Emmie rubbed her eyes and turned away. She fished into her pants pocket and pulled out the device Cathen gave her. Turning back to the assembled group, both palms up, Emmie showed two recall devices.

Mally put her hand on Emmie's good arm. "I'm sorry, I didn't mean it."

"Yes, you did," Emmie snapped back. She softened her tone. "But you're right." She straightened herself up. "Now for my last order as leader of this group, I am putting Vic in charge. I'm doing something I should have done a while ago." She typed B-R-Y-S-O-N into Braids's device and H-O-D-D into her own device.

"I'm to meet our pickup in Sector 1." Emmie pushed the stretcher to the garage's far exit. She looked back one more time.

"What's done is done." Victos paused. "We, however, are not, and we have a lot more work to do if we plan to get out of here in one piece."

Leba removed her recall signaler from her pocket. "I don't think I'll need this," she said and put it on the floor, then crushed it under her boot.

"Me neither," Hech said, surprising everyone. One by one, three other green team members did the same, except for Mally and Middie. Mally looked down at the device in her hand.

A CHANGE IN TACTICS: MAIDEN VOYAGE

"I won't think any less of you if you hang on to yours," Leba confided. Mally nodded and put it back in her pocket.

"I think I'll hang on to mine too," Middie confessed. "Never know when it might come in handy."

Leba's gesture was one of camaraderie, not necessarily bravery. She wanted to let Victos know she believed he could lead them out of this place.

Gref looked at Hech. "What are you looking at?"

Hech just laughed. "There was a time when—"

"Shut up," Gref snapped. "Keep your stories to yourself."

"Okay, okay," Hech agreed.

"Our biggest problem as I see it," Victos outlined, "is how we get the dome open to get this shuttle launched."

"Easy." Middie smiled. Her eyes grew dark, and her brow furrowed. Her toothed grin spread evilly across her face. No one particularly cared for her look. The same look preceding her last shocking revelation. "We blast it," she said, poking her chest out as far as her chin.

"You're not serious." Gref cringed. "That'll likely bring the whole roof down on us."

"You got a better idea, smart man?" Middie shot her finger at him.

"Maybe she's right." Victos hesitated, grabbing his chin and squinting.

Not a good time to lose your nerve, Vic. Make a decision and stick with it.

Middie nodded her agreement, her face beaming. "Surgical strikes at the locking bolts stationed along the dome's seals would be better." Excellent idea. Now how to execute it? When he was not met with rebuke, he continued, "It'll take some pretty fancy shooting, though."

Keep strong, Vic. Be the leader I know you are. Leba kept quiet. It was Vic's turn to shine. She already demonstrated her worth saving Braids. Leba also met her objective by gathering intel from Professor Roblins. Vic needed to step up and take charge. Prove his worth.

"I'll do it," whispered Mally. When no one responded, the second time, she repeated louder, "I'll do it."

"You've got to be kidding," Middie said in disbelief. "Listen, honey, I know your squad leader boyfriend helped you shoot, but one lesson with his arms around you isn't gonna cut it here."

Mally gathered her courage to face Middie. She walked over to Hech and put out her hand for his weapon. She tested its weight in her hand, checked the settings, and activated the trigger sequence. With the weapon in her right hand, Mally reached into her pocket with her left and removed the recall device. With all her might, she launched the small device into the air as high as she could. Everyone watched as the small object achieved its maximum height and began its descent. Without blinking an eye, she followed the arc it made. She breathed slowly and squeezed the trigger. The weapon discharged, expelling a faint red pulse of energy. On impact, the recall device imploded in a burst of light. So accurate was the shot there was nothing left to hit the ground. Everyone stood in amazement.

Victos wanted to do all the shooting himself, but after Mally's display, how could he not let her help. "Great shot," he complimented her. Mally bowed her head. "All right, everyone in the shuttle. Mally, take out the bolts on the port side, and I'll take out the starboard ones."

"I think she may shoot better than you, Uribos," Middie jested.

"You get in the cockpit and have this junker ready to go once the dome opens," Victos ordered. "Doc, do you think you can get the autopilot set?"

Leba nodded. "What coordinates?"

"Set us for the line we were supposed to come in on," Victos answered.

Riki chimed in, "Along 62.8. That's the line we were on, follow it back."

Victos hesitated then asked, "Before we do this, let's go over the orders we were given."

"What about Emmie and Braids's parts?" Mally asked.

"When we first looked at the orders, there were a lot meant to distract us," Leba offered. "There were only about thirteen relevant lines." Leba recalled, "The destination coordinates were Riki's, the launch pad number was Mally's."

"I have the pickup time," added Hech. He looked at his chrono. "About four hours from now."

"I have the pickup time being six hours from now," Middie corrected.

"I say we go with Hech's," Gref offered and was seconded by Riki.

"You would." Middie snorted. "So don't believe me. You can wait at the pickup, if it's even there."

"What do you mean by that?" Victos asked.

"I believe Hodd's lines instructed which pickup to believe. Isn't that right, Doc?" Middie questioned.

"I believe Middie is correct," Leba remembered. "I'm better at remembering numbers than lines of text." She closed her eyes and tried to picture the words that had been on the screen. "Unfortunately, the orders we were to follow were in a jumbled order."

Victos said, "Let's start with yours. What did yours say?"

"Gather intel on the current research at the facility," Leba recited verbatim.

"What did yours say, Tylor?" Victos asked.

"Avoid disturbing the natives." He hesitated. "Now that could mean just about anything," he quickly added.

"What about you, Vic?" Riki questioned.

"Mine didn't make any sense either," he began. "Stay out of the cold." Leba still had her eyes closed trying to see the words of text. "Well, Doc, does this ring any bells?"

"I think there was a line about determining the cause of the initial accident and rescuing casualties. That must have been Braids's lines." She squeezed her eyes tighter, trying to recall Hodd's lines. "I think Emmie's lines were 'if A happens, do B, and if C happens, do D.'"

"Lotta good that does us," Middie said.

"I remember now," Leba said more confident. "If we leave in our shuttle, we need to be back in six hours, but if we use alternate transport, we need to be there in four hours." She waited and then continued, "I think it has to do with the type of pickup. They will be scanning for our shuttle. This shuttle probably won't be picked up, so they will leave a beacon for us to pick up."

"None of this makes any sense," Victos said frustrated.

"We'd better stop bickering over times," Middie advised. "Or we will miss both pickups."

Vic pulled out a smoke to try and relax. Riki came over to him and lit his smoke. He took a long drag. "You'd better get in the shuttle with the rest," he told her. Riki kissed him on the cheek.

Mally steadied herself on one side of the shuttle, and Victos did the same on the other side. Leba went to the cockpit and set the autopilot. The easiest thing to do was set the coordinates for the farthest pickup point and move the shuttle as fast as possible. She reasoned the earlier pickup point would have to be somewhere along the route. The biggest obstacle they would face was liftoff as the autopilot would not activate until they were in atmosphere. Leba hoped Middie could get it off the ground.

As each energy pulse left Mally and Victos's weapons, Leba heard a faint whoosh followed by a sizzle as the target disintegrated and then a crack as the dome edges moved apart. By firing in tandem, they would avoid stressing the dome too much that it would shear into pieces when each restraint was released. After all the bolts were eliminated, the heavy dome halves fell away from each other. Frigid air filled the garage as Victos and Mally descended from their perches and slid the shuttle's doors closed. Victos headed toward the cockpit, where Middie already began the launch sequence. The autopilot control button blinked yellow, signaling its preset parameters were accepted and awaiting manual activation. Mally settled into the passenger compartment, joining the other four and activated her seat restraints.

Leba knew this had to work. There was no backup plan. They didn't have the luxury of survival suits or even supplies. Save for Middie, they didn't even have their recall devices. Victos slid into the second pilot's chair next to Middie and adjusted his seat harness. Middie pushed the throttle forward, and the craft wearily hovered upward. She continued to slowly give it thrust until it cleared the dome. Victos went to activate the autopilot when Middie stopped him. "Not yet," she cautioned. "We're not high enough yet."

Middie seemed to be stalling. "We need to at least clear the compound's vicinity. Too many variables for the autopilot to handle," she explained. Victos bought her explanation and, for the moment, abandoned his attempt to engage the autopilot. The cockpit chatter abruptly ceased when the cabin door shut.

Leba felt the unevenness of the flight and wondered why Middie still hadn't engaged the autopilot. Maybe she didn't program it properly. No, it was a simple task, and she watched her dad do it a million times. Something wasn't right. That feeling of impending doom, the one she shared with Zach, crept into her consciousness and made her shiver. She needed to do what Gordie told her. If she felt something was wrong, she needed to act on it, for the good of the team. Unbuckling her harness, she headed for the cockpit. Grabbing seat back to seat back, Leba staggered forward.

"What's wrong, Doc?" Hech inquired.

"We should have gone to auto, and we haven't," she answered.

"I'll bet Fidelis is up to something," Gref chimed in.

"Wouldn't surprise me," Hech added.

"I'll be right back," Leba assured her mates in the passenger cabin. She went to the cockpit door and tried to open it. It was unfortunately sealed from the other side. A safety precaution, perhaps, but she still needed to get their attention. The intercom was not functioning, so she resorted to a tried and true method. She banged on the door.

Finally, Victos opened the door and met her in the passenger cabin. "What's up?"

"We should have gone to auto," Leba said.

"Fidelis says it's still too soon. We're not high enough or far enough away from the compound," Victos explained.

Leba looked him straight in the eyes. "She's wrong."

"Are you sure?" Victos questioned.

"Yes," Leba said, clenching her fists. She would stand her ground, the good of the team depended on it, on her. She hoped

Victos believed her too. If he didn't, she didn't like the prospect of trying to get by him to activate it herself.

Victos tucked his head back into the cockpit. "The doc says we need to activate the auto."

"I told you we are too close," Middie snapped. Reaching between the piloting chairs, Victos depressed the button. "It's your funeral," she huffed. Middie continued grumbling under her breath. Under the guidance of the autopilot, the shuttle's trajectory quickly smoothed out. Leba returned to her seat, reengaged her harness, and smiled. She would have no regrets.

The eastern way around the mountain was easier than the way they came. The crosswinds were docile and the atmosphere less turbulent. Leba peered out the window. Usually looking sideways while in flight made her motion sick, but the sight outside the starboard viewport was magnificent. Plumes of white smoke and ice crystals emanated from the craterous top of the cryo-volcano. The setting sun's rays glinted a rainbow of colors off the slow cryoclastic flow. Remembering the graph she examined in Dr. Roblins lab, Leba knew it wouldn't be long now, only a few days or weeks, before the top of the mountain would blast into oblivion, hurling huge ice crystals into the sky. Methane and ammonia would spew fountain-like from the depths below, poisoning the atmosphere. The flora, unable to move, would be covered in any icy sheet, and the fauna would migrate far away in search of new homes. She checked her chrono. The shuttle was making great time and its direction unfaltering as the autopilot kept it on the most direct route. They would reach the rendezvous point ahead of schedule.

Victos wondered what the beacon would look like. With everything that happened so far, he was sure it wouldn't be a big *X* laid out in the snow. It would be more subtle. Right about now, Victos wanted another smoke. He knew he could not light up inside the shuttle; the smoke alone would probably trigger the automatic fire extinguisher protocol and drench both cabins. He drummed his fingers on the console. Choosing who to rely on for information and advice was a difficult job for a leader. "Something worrying you?" Middie asked.

"No," Victos snapped back, unaware he was signaling his concern. "Just looking for a beacon. We should be getting pretty close to the rendezvous point."

CHAPTER 21

An annoying low-pitched hum permeated the shuttle, quickly followed by dimming the interior lights to blackness. Leba slowly drifted to unconsciousness.

When Leba's eyes fluttered open, she was no longer a passenger in the antiquated shuttle but harnessed in back of a more modern shuttle. The designation plate above the cockpit door: TKM-772. The seats in front of her, all eight, were filled exactly the same as when this mission began. There was Emmie and Braids, Mally and Middie, Victos and Riki, and Gref and Hech, all no worse for wear. Had it all been a dream? No, she was sure of that. The overhead comm blasted out departure instructions. "Green med team, please report to the command officer for debriefing." As she released her seat restraints, Leba looked around the shuttle. Everything was as she remembered when they boarded and strapped in, before the devastating crash, before the trek through the tundra, before the deadly encounter at the compound. Reaching down to her boot, she was pleasantly surprised; her obsidian glass knife was still tucked away where she kept it hidden. It was undisturbed, unbroken. Middie, who drained her flask right before takeoff from the compound, found it full again. Victos had a full pack of smokes, and his handsome face was unmarred and unbruised. Emmie's wrist was no longer in the air splint. And Braids, well, Braids was upright, conscious, and fully functional.

What happened, how long was Leba out for? Did everyone experience the same, or was Leba's designed for her? According to her chronometer, four days passed, and she had clear memories of what transpired. She was not achy or sore. There were no discernible bruises, but she remembered everything vividly as if it actually happened.

"Please disembark," the simulated voice repeated over and over as the shuttle doors opened onto a relatively empty room. Ninety-six hours ago, this room was awash with activity, a fully operational shuttle launch bay. Now it was almost deserted. Workers in jumpsuits removed limp figures from the rear compartment. Simulatrons? I wonder if one of them looked and sounded like me. Nine body bags were carried across the hangar and disappeared.

Leba and the rest of green med team were hurried out through an exit at the far end of the room. It took a moment for her gait to smooth out, her legs still a little stiff. Ordered not to speak with one another, each passed through the door and were joined by an intelligence officer and a security guard. Leba recognized this as standard Tal-Kari protocol for an after-visit action. This part of the mission, debriefing, was almost as important as the mission itself. It reminded her of an autopsy, where the mission was dissected and her participation put under a microscope. In fact, it was nicknamed a post-mortem evaluation. At the end, a final diagnosis would be made, incorporating how well you performed, how well your teammates performed, what you could have been done better, and would you be allowed to go on another mission. Mission success or failure would be determined by committee, including your immediate supervisor, the base commander, and a representative of the brain trust who thought up the mission.

Troopers could perform magnificently during an operation but fail miserably when it came to documentation and follow-up. It was bad enough Leba spent a lot of her time in self-evaluation. There always seemed to be someone looking over your shoulder, analyzing and assessing every move. No matter how things turned out, there was always something to explain or answer for. Paramount was the ability to take responsibility for your actions and be able to explain concretely and concisely what transpired. Writing reports seemed to be the downfall of a lot of ambitious people trying to rise in the ranks. Leaders not only needed to be responsible for themselves but also for their charges.

When she was led into the sparsely furnished room, Leba waited to take a seat until instructed to do so. Her parents warned her about this part. She remembered an episode of her favorite serial, Priman Angar and the Tal-Kari cadets, when a mission went horribly wrong, resulting in the untimely death of an alien dignitary. Priman Angar was put on trial by the local constabulary, facing death if found guilty. He was interrogated for hours, almost to the point of exhaustion, but his story never changed. Despite the mental anguish and sleepless fatigue, he never wavered. He followed the rules by the book. Everything he and his cadets did was fully documented. In the courtroom, his young charges sat in a confinement chamber, watching his ordeal. Angar listened to every question, repeated it for clarity, thought about his answer, and responded confidently. Avoiding emotional responses and extraneous data was key.

"Sit, please," the intelligence officer requested. He stood straight and tall, his chest broad and his posture perfect. From his military buzz cut to his impeccably polished shoes, he presented an imposing figure. Leba did as she was told. The security guard took up a position at the door. The chair was anything but comfortable, not cushiony like a couch, but cold and hard. The table in front of her was metal too, without any decoration or design, just four legs and a top. Taking a seat across from her, the intelligence officer placed a folder on the table. No emotion was evident on his face. His body language oozed confidence and authority. Power to determine her fate. Kinda like facing the vice principal in school or the chief inquisitor at a malpractice deposition. Upside down, she could read her name on the folder in front of him, and the word *confidential* emblazoned diagonally across it in red. He slowly opened the folder. "State your name for the record, please."

"Leba Brader." She remembered what her mom told her. Don't give any extra information, only answer what was asked, and in as few words as possible. Be concise but be precise.

"Dr. Leba Brader," the officer corrected. Clasping her hands on the table, she kept her fingers from belying her nervousness.

"Yes, sir," Leba acknowledged his correction then shifted in her seat.

"Dr. Brader, I am Priman Yann Stalus, and I will be conducting this debriefing in regards to your recent mission." He didn't look up from the folder. "I would like to go over the ground rules for this interview." She nodded her head. This time, he did look up and stared at her. Dark eyebrows pointed downward toward the bridge of his nose. His eyes were gray and cold.

What did I ever do to you?

"First rule," he began, "I cannot record nods. You must give all your answers verbally. Do you understand?"

Leba caught herself in a nod and then replied, "Yes, sir."

Stalus glared at her for a moment, seemingly frustrated, and then looked back to the folder. He explained, "I know using paper seems archaic, but I find I am better able to make notations as we go along."

Every mark you make, every note you take is going to drive me nuts, so let's even the odds.

"Might I have a piece of your tablet, sir?" Leba requested. "And something to write with?" *See, two can play this game. Mirroring can help you connect with your subject or put them off their game.*

He looked up again, cocked his head. Leba wasn't sure he would acknowledge her request until he removed a blank sheet from the back of the folder and handed it to her. Reaching into his breast pocket, he removed a writing implement, limply handing it to her.

If it was such a bother, you could have refused.

"Will this do?"

"Thank you, sir," Leba said. The recurring "sir" would get annoying, but it would serve as notice; Leba understood his position, and he would underestimate hers.

"Ready to continue with the rules?" She nodded. Rules are good. Stalus tapped the end of his stylus slowly and deliberately. "Remember, I can't record nods," he chided her.

"Yes, sir." *Got to remember to stop the nods. Don't want to piss him off too much.*

"Rule two: I want facts, not opinions. If I want your opinion, I will ask for it. Understand?"

"Yes, sir."

"Finally." The corners of his mouth turned slightly upward. He paused and waited until he was certain she had his gaze. "See, this isn't very complicated." Grabbing his chin, he finished. "Rule three." Softening his voice, he repeated, "Rule three: if at any time you need a break, water, lavatory, ask." Momentarily turning sideways, he bent down to pick up something. He placed a water bottle on the table in front of her.

"Thank you, sir."

"Now see how easy this is." He put his stylus down, gave her a toothed grin, and quickly picked it up again. "Ready to get started?"

Nice try, but I'm ready.

"Yes, sir."

The questioning was easy at first. A cursory overview of the mission, everyone's role, and how events unfolded. Leba took a drink from her bottle once or twice, watching Stalus's gestures when she did. He was difficult to read. These interrogator types must practice long and hard to make their faces immune to emotion. The sentry too stood unwavering and emotionless. After reviewing the acquisition of the antiquated shuttle and the ride to the rendezvous point, Stalus closed the folder. "This seems like a good place to stop for now." He motioned to the guard. "Why don't you take the doctor down the hall, she may want to make use of the facilities."

"Yes, sir," the guard responded.

So the statue can speak. Not bad. I guess if I don't make the team, I could always volunteer for sentry duty.

As they were leaving the room, Stalus asked, "You hungry?" Leba wasn't quite sure if he was referring to her or to the guard. She hesitated a moment, waiting for the sentry to answer.

"A little," she said, not wanting to give him anything to use as an advantage.

"I'll have something brought in," Stalus informed her.

"Thank you, sir."

As Leba was escorted down the hall, she wondered if similar interviews were being conducted with her teammates or even her entire unit mates. She asked her guard, but he gave her an "I don't know, ma'am" answer, and they continued down the hall. Well, you can't charm everyone. That is, unless you're Sendra Tohl.

Until now, Leba hadn't thought about how the red, blue, or yellow teams did. What were their missions like? Did we all start in the same basic scenario and end up with four different stories? She couldn't wait to tell DeShay how some of the stuff he taught was actually useful. A smile came to her face then rapidly dissolved. How would he react to Emmie's bailing on the mission, putting Braids's safety ahead of the unit's? How did Anster and Grizzer handle being cocaptains? Did two headstrong nurses finally prove too much for JT? She was sure he charmed them both into letting him lead.

Of her team, she was curious what other surprises Mally Yertha kept. She actually liked Gref and Hech, how they bickered but were ultimately each other's strength. Confident Vic and Riki rediscovered their feelings for each other, Leba wondered how long it would last once the mission pressure was off or Riki thought more about Vic's brutal demonstration at the expense of Jekkers's face. Middie was hot and cold, sometimes a team player and sometimes in it for herself. Not engaging the autopilot still bothered Leba. Could Emmie and Braids repair their relationship by understanding each other's motivations and realizing what they meant to each other?

What did she get out of this mission? What strengths did she display, and what weaknesses did she reveal? Would the postmortem uncover anything she missed? Anyway, she failed. Returning to the interview room, there were sandwiches and fruit displayed on the bare metal table.

"Please help yourself," Stalus offered. His demeanor changed. He seemed more relaxed.

What are you up to? Time to be my buddy, maybe? Ply me with food and drink?

"Thank you, sir." Leba looked over the spread, made her choices, and sat back down.

"Please go ahead and eat, we'll continue the questions in a few minutes," Stalus smiled.

This was all part of the process, no, the game. Her father warned her not to let down her guard. Interrogation was a subtle art, and sometimes taking the formality out of the interview was the thing to loosen someone's lips, to give up more than you wanted to, to feel so comfortable you forgot where you were. The officer wanted to be your friend or your enemy or your judge and jury. The only difference between this and real life was you didn't have counsel kicking you under the table, helping you avoid saying the wrong things. You represented yourself. Leba thought about Priman Angar and how he refused food and drink during his trial. He was concerned the sustenance was laced with mind-altering chemicals that could influence what he said or did. Leba was fairly confident Stalus was not being nefarious but being hospitable.

Between bites of sandwich, Stalus made small talk. "What made you want to be a physician?"

Leba always had an answer for that one. "It's a place where I think I can make a difference." She continued, "My dad said I should use my talents to the best of my ability in an occupation where I could be respected and earn enough to support myself without having to rely on anyone else."

"From your record, it appears you excelled in the medical academy. Top of your class, I believe."

She bowed her head and nodded. "I wanted to make my parents proud."

"Did you like having a team composed of nine members? Everyone with a partner but you?"

Whoa, nice segue.

Leba thought carefully before responding. "I was lucky because I got to partner with everyone else at one time or another. I wasn't locked into a previous relationship."

"Didn't that put you at a disadvantage, not knowing who you were working with?"

"I hope by now I'm a pretty good judge of character. My job as a physician requires me to be adaptable to each patient's uniqueness."

Stalus interrupted, "So your teammates were like your patients, and as the partner-less one, you sort of became the leader. The one to settle all the disputes, the so-called tiebreaker."

Slowing herself down, Leba grabbed the water bottle and took a long drink while deciding where this line of questioning was heading. "Not really," she answered. "While I needed to learn about my teammates, they needed to learn about me."

"Come on, Doc. You were far above the rest in class work, well-read, well-informed. You could run circles around these people."

Watch what you say about my teammates. Leba could feel the heat building up inside her.

He stared at her. "Why did you let Emmie Hodd take the helm?"

Feeling her pulse rising, Leba rubbed the back of her neck and remembered her mom warning her about the interrogator trying to provoke her into saying something she wished she hadn't. Inhaling deeply, she answered, "It wasn't only my choice who got to lead this group." She paused. "Especially in her role as head nurse, Emmie Hodd possessed years of leadership experience."

"Are you making excuses for your poor decision? Didn't you check her out ahead of time?"

"First." Leba put up her index finger, her stomach tightening. "Squad Leader Cathen didn't assign teams until right before the mission began."

"Don't tell me you didn't check her out ahead of time, I know you better than that."

Leba bristled at his slip. *How do you know me and how I think? Who did you talk to?*

"If you must know." Her jaw tightened. Through gritted teeth Leba said, "I checked out everyone ahead of time." She paused, trying to regain her composure. "There's only so much information available and only so many people you can talk to."

"I'll ask the question another way then," he continued. "If you had your choice, of all the people in your unit, yourself excluded, who would you have picked as leader."

"That's easy, Master Priman DeShay Tiner," she said, locking eyes with Stalus.

"So are you saying that if DeShay Tiner led green team, things would've played out differently?"

"All I'm saying is that of all the people I have had the honor of serving with, Master Priman Tiner would be my choice for leader. His experience, confidence, and…" She paused, searching for the right word. "And I respect him."

"Ah-ha." Stalus leaned back in his chair. "You respect him, do you?" He opened her folder. "In fact, I believe you are infatuated with him." Tracing his finger along a highlighted paragraph. "It says here you two spent considerable time together outside the allotted classroom time."

Leba was insulted. For Stalus to imply her respect for DeShay came from some carnal impulse was ridiculous. "Those sessions were strictly platonic and served to further my education." *What I feel for DeShay is what a little sister feels for an older brother, or a niece for an uncle.*

Leba straightened in her chair, put her palms down on the table, and leaned forward. "Sir, there are a number of people in my life I consider mentors, people I love for who they are and how they make me a better person. Not because of some childish schoolgirl crush."

"Didn't mean to upset you," Stalus said and, with one finger, scooped up the front flap of the folder and closed it. "I'll change the subject if this one bothers you."

Leba shoved the remains of her lunch aside and took a long swallow from the water bottle. "If you don't mind, sir, I'd like to clean up before we start again." She knew a quick trip to the lavatory would let her boil fall to a simmer and then fizzle out. Stalus had no choice but to oblige her, and when she returned, she'd be ready for round two.

Outside their classroom, DeShay backed Emmie into a corner. She hung her head. "That was my only option. No other choices."

"But, baby, there are always choices." Shaking his head in frustration, he said, "I knew I shouldn't have let you go by yourself. I should've been there with you."

She recoiled in anger. "And what is that supposed to mean? I can take care of myself."

"That's not what I meant, baby," DeShay tried to put his arms around her. She wriggled free. "Come on, Emmie, be reasonable."

"Reasonable," she blurted loud enough for everyone to hear. Lowering her voice, she repeated, "I didn't have a choice."

"There had to be another way," he tried, rubbing her back, but she stiffened at his touch.

Stepping aside to put distance between them, Emmie rationalized, "I made my choice. You have no right to question my decision. How dare you presume to think you could have done a better job or you somehow could have protected me from myself?" She turned her back to him and walked away. DeShay knew Emmie was frustrated. She was tired and hungry and angry. Sympathy from DeShay Tiner, or even advice, was not welcome.

He didn't follow. When she was like this, there was no reasoning with her. She'd come around, she always did, and he'd be there to comfort her. Going after her would only make her angrier. Leaning against the wall, he closed his eyes, folded his arms, and crossed them over his chest. He was tired, dead tired, but he wanted to wait until the rest of his team was debriefed before heading to his quarters. It was what a leader did. It was what Emmie hadn't done. She abandoned her team. DeShay was sure she had a good reason; she had to. Maybe Leba would know. They'd been on the same team. DeShay knew with a little persuasion, Leba would tell him what went down. He'd have to wait, though; Leba was still in interrogation.

Round two for Leba started much the same way as round one did, with Stalus asking routine questions about the people and places she encountered on her mission. The tenor changed when Stalus asked her opinion about the others on her team. He asked her to speculate how they'd performed under pressure. Why did he need her opinion? Leba found this line of questioning peculiar. The facts were recorded, and these evaluations were more suitable for the team leader. "If I may ask, sir." She paused. Trying to choose her words carefully, she asked, "Have you been able to review the transcript of our mission?"

Stalus shifted in his chair, dragging his heel on the floor. Tiny beads of sweat began to pepper his forehead. He snapped back, "The mission was recorded for training purposes, not for my viewing pleasure." Then Leba realized he was being scrutinized for his performance. "Beg your pardon, sir. I thought if you had seen it, I could refer to spots in the recording for me to demonstrate my points."

His demeanor softened. "That would have been an excellent idea, but unfortunately, we don't have access to them." His eyebrows rose ever so slightly, and his lips pursed. "I appreciate your concern, but I think I will be able to do okay without them." Leba heard his feet shifting under the table.

"Let's continue." Stalus changed the subject. "Tell me about your meeting with Professor Roblins."

Leba smiled. "Despite her appearance, she wasn't what I expected."

"What do you mean?" Stalus questioned.

"She looked and sounded like the vids I've seen of Professor Roblins, but she didn't have her essence."

Stalus wrinkled his nose and drummed the fingers of his left hand. "How easy do you think it is to make a perfect replica of the person you are trying to simulate?"

Not what he intended to tell me.

He stretched his shoulders. Leba could see his tension mounting. "Ignoring your assessment of our handiwork, what did you and Professor Roblins discuss?"

Leba didn't answer but drew two perpendicular lines on her paper. She labeled the axes and sketched in the graph. "This," she said, putting the plot in front of him.

"And this is?" he asked studying the graph.

"My guess, the reason she was there." Leba beamed, putting one finger up to rest on the side of her face and resting her chin between the others.

"Explain." Stalus pulled the graph closer, and Leba got up and moved to his side.

"The whole point of this mission was to understand what was happening in the near vicinity of the cryo-volcano. It's about to erupt." Leba leaned onto the table. "That's what this graph is showing. This"—she pointed to the wavering line—"is a plot of the volcano's activity. Seismic readings suggest it's ready to explode. Based on the data Dr. Roblins shared with me, it will be spectacular." She waited, and he turned to face her. His expression changed, and his eyes widened. *Got him.* Leba continued, "When this erupts, the force will be so violent the surrounding area will be uninhabitable for decades. His chin dropped, his mouth falling open. But," she followed up quickly, "if you could somehow harness its power, you could fuel a small moon for a millennium." She contemplated her remark and then corrected herself. "Maybe not a millennium, but certainly for a long time if done right."

"How dangerous is it?" Stalus's eyes narrowed as he lowered his brows.

"I wouldn't want to be at the business end of that. I'd settle for a window seat to watch it, though." She smiled. Now would be a good time to pick his brain and figure out what he knew or didn't know. Time for some razzle-dazzle. *Let's talk cryo-volcano geophysiochemistry.* His eyes were wide with awe as she regaled him with the majesty of the eruption.

"Thanks, Doc," he said, clasping his hands. "I'd be much obliged if you let me occupy an adjoining window seat."

That was her cue. She put a hand on his shoulder and said, "I'd be honored, sir." Making her way back to her side of the table, Leba sighed.

"You can call me, Yann."

She had him. He no longer saw her as a defendant but as a friend. He was less likely to indict her. She did hope her little stunt wouldn't cost him an opportunity to be a prosecutor.

When Leba emerged from the conference room, she saw DeShay leaning against a wall, his eyes heavy. The sound of the door closing startled him. "Hey, girl, how'd it go?"

"Piece of cake."

"Had him eating out of your hand, did you?"

"Something like that. Nice fellow, pity he works for the man." She imitated DeShay's baritone and collapsed into a laugh. Forgetting how beat-up she was, she steadied herself on the wall.

DeShay put an arm around her shoulder. "Come on, girl, let me buy you a drink."

Something was up. She knew DeShay too well to know he really didn't want to buy her a drink; he wanted something. Tired as she was after the long interrogation, it took her a minute to figure out what was up. Emmie, he wanted to know what happened on their mission. "I'm really tired, but thanks anyway," Leba apologized. *Be honest with me and maybe I'll tell you what you want to know.*

"Come on, girl. We need to talk," he prodded.

"Last time I heard that line"—she pouted—"I got dumped." She encircled her face with her hands. "You're not breaking off our relationship, are you?"

He inclined his head, frowning, then inclined the other way, and a smile crept onto his face. "You know damn right well I need to talk to you, so don't be smart."

"Yes, sir," she acknowledged his order. "I'm all yours, but it'll cost you more than a drink. Buy me dinner and I'll tell you everything. Well, almost everything."

He put her in a playful headlock. "Dinner it is."

"This is not the romantic dinner I expected, but Commando burgers and crisps…" She paused.

"Are your favorites and you'd do anything for them," DeShay finished her sentence.

"Well, almost anything." She laughed. DeShay sat wide-eyed as Leba went through the essentials of the mission. "And then she activated the recall device," Leba explained. "I kind of thought everything was stable, and we were about ready to leave."

DeShay shook his head. "That's typical Emmie for you," he said, shaking his head. Taking a long pull from his ale, he rubbed the back of his neck. Leba didn't understand the typical remark and waited for an explanation. "I guess nothing really changes," he lamented.

Leba still wasn't catching on, but maybe she wasn't supposed to. She took a bite of her sandwich, the meaty juices rolling down her face. DeShay looked up at her. "I can't take you anywhere, can I?" He handed her the napkin she was fumbling to get.

"Thanks," Leba said, dabbing her face. "Can I help you figure something out?"

"No, girl, I've got a lot of thinking to do." DeShay got up from the table.

"You're just going to leave me here?" Leba questioned, her mouth full with her latest burger bite.

"I think you can take care of finishing without me," DeShay said as he turned away. Turning back, he handed her some coin. "Dinner's on me."

"Dinner was supposed to be on you," Leba called after him. It was sad to see him lumber out of the café, his shoulders slumped. Defeat did not suit him, and Leba was mad at Emmie for hurting him.

DeShay didn't acknowledge her jest but continued on his way. He needed to sort things out. Maybe thinking wasn't the thing to do; maybe acting was. DeShay headed for Emmie's quarters. Her debriefing was likely over, and he needed to clear the air. Figure out what their next move was. He was being deployed, and she wasn't.

"What do you mean your girl told you everything?" Emmie shouted at him.

DeShay backed into a corner. He shrugged his shoulders and faced her arms out, palms up. "That's not what I mean. I mean she told me about the mission."

"If you wanted to know about the mission, you should have asked me," she reiterated her position, her voice still loud. Emmie tightened her arms across her chest, her face pinched with anger.

DeShay tried approaching her, but she gave him her back. This was a mistake to have this conversation in her quarters, on her turf, with no fallback position. "Come on, baby, you did what you thought you had to do," he said, trying to touch her shoulder but ending up only at mid-arm before she pulled away.

She whirled around like a cyclone, ready for a devastating run. "Don't patronize me, DeShay Tiner. You know good and well you would have handled it differently." She paused, gathering more speed. "You told me not to be the leader. I should have let your little doctor girlfriend be the leader." Her head rocked back and forth, and then she scoffed, "You seem to have so much undying faith in her abilities." Grabbing the locket around her neck, she clutched it tightly and stared at it, refusing to look at him. Maybe there was a picture of the two of them in there; DeShay didn't know. Maybe that was it: Emmie was jealous. But she didn't have to be; he loved her. Leba Brader was like a little sister to him.

With both hands, he grasped her upper arms. "Now that's not fair!" DeShay shouted. She was being childish. When she got this way, there was no reasoning with her.

Raising her head to meet him eye-to-eye, she wriggled from his hold. Emmie had no tears, only fully loaded missiles armed and ready to launch. Target acquired and locked, her arm fully outstretched, with a finger pointing toward the door, she fired, "Get out."

Attempting to bring her close only brought the second volley. "No, I need some time to think."

"Come on, baby, let me help you through this," DeShay offered, his tone more mellow. Cautiously he put a hand out, hoping she'd take it.

She avoided his touch. This time when she spoke, her voice was lower and more somber, "I need some time alone, some time to sort this all out. I'll call you when I'm ready." Walking to her quarters' door, she held it open and stared at it.

DeShay was done; he knew it. When they were younger, this scene played more often than he cared to remember. Making up was always hot and heavy but the emotional ride too tumultuous and eventually became burdensome. After difficult consideration, they opted to go their separate ways. It was a mistake to try and rekindle this romance, especially at this time of their lives. Both were so set in their ways. They were much more like their younger selves than he imagined. Stubborn and unyielding. He did love Emmie, but he knew they could never sustain a long-term relationship. Neither willing to compromise or change the way they saw the world or how they saw each other. Despite how well they knew each other, they still couldn't understand each other. The door closed behind him. The locking bolt clunked into place. Lingering at the entry for just a moment, his back resting against the door, DeShay thought he could hear Emmie sobbing.

CHAPTER 22

When Leba finally arrived at her quarters, made her requisite call home, the only thing she wanted to do was to crawl into bed and go to sleep. Keeping her from the warmth and security of her bed, the flashing light on her info-portal signaling an incoming message. She recognized the ID. *What now? Haven't you tortured us enough? Four days of simulated and contrived torture wasn't enough? Can't he leave us alone for two seconds?*

> **TO:** Cold Box Mission Participants
> **FROM:** Luth Cathen, squad leader
> **RE:** Final Results
>
> **Attention:** There will be a mandatory class tomorrow at 0800 to discuss the results of the cold box exercise. You must attend in full dress uniform. Report to medical classroom 1-7 promptly. There will be no late admittance.

Great. Leba wrinkled her brow. *Can't wait to see what Lord Cathen has in store for us. Probably professionally edited, high-def video from the mission with boosted soundtrack so he can humiliate us in 4D.* Leba wanted to call DeShay to see if he knew what was going to happen but opted not to. DeShay would have bigger issues on his mind. Emmie Hodd was gone, gone from the deployment and probably gone from his life again. Leba didn't ponder long because she was asleep the minute her head hit the pillow.

DeShay really didn't have anyone he could talk to. His drinking buddy, Tiv Garnet, already deployed. Anster and Grizzer were probably getting toasted at their victory party. Why spoil their fun. Although she'd probably be a good listener, he wasn't going talk about this with Leba. There were just some things a guy didn't discuss with his little sister. Despite his fatigue, he paced the floor of his quarters. Punching a bag at the gym hadn't helped, an hour in the steam room hadn't helped, and the stale ale he was drinking was making his head hurt and his stomachache. If he'd half a brain, he would've let Emmie cool down before he confronted her. How stupid to rush and try to comfort her. She was a big girl and really didn't need his pity. And truthfully, that's what it was, pity. Disappointed with her activating her recall device, DeShay understood why Emmie put Braids ahead of the rest of the team but disagreed with her decision. She was going to be bounced from this mission all because she was more concerned about screwing up her relationship with Braids. Didn't she care about him at all? As the evening merged into night and the ale began to catch up with him, he got angrier and angrier. He also got sleepier and sleepier. Barely able to hold his eyes open, DeShay took one final pull from his bottle. Thumping the empty down, his hand still clutching it like he hoped it was Emmie, fatigue overtook him, and he fell asleep at the table the minute his head began to bow. Unfortunately, DeShay's sleep was restless and way too short.

At 0759, everyone sat in med classroom 1-7, waiting, waiting for Squad Leader Luth Cathen to make his grand entrance. Not even JT dared to be late on decision day. The debriefings were done and the data gathered. Only five people activated their recall devices, two from green team and one from each of the other teams. Their fate all but sealed. It would take an act of council or a properly placed bribe to get them a spot on the upcoming deployment. Leba watched each of her unit mates enter the room. As usual, she was there before everyone else. Icy coldness separated DeShay and Emmie. Like two similar poles on a magnet, unseen forces kept them repelled at arm's length. On the other hand, Emmie and Braids were as close as ever, entering the room arm in arm. Leba wanted things to work out for DeShay, but reality intervened where fantasy stopped. Emmie wasn't good enough for him. DeShay needed someone who could appreciate him. JT appeared somber too. His footfalls missing their trademark bounce, he looked like the weight of the world was on his shoulders. But his team did very well, and Leba wondered what was wrong. Two of her favorite men looked as if they lost their best friends. Today was not the day to ask anyone anything. Another two weeks of training remained, but training as a cohesive unit. Everyone who remained earned their spot.

Gref and Hech entered together, and Leba was met with a hearty "Good morning." Getting to know the pair opened her eyes to their skills and camaraderie, and she was glad to count them as friends. Leba felt less an outsider. Maybe Cathen's trial by ice accomplished what it was supposed to. Surviving together either brought you closer or tore you apart. Among her new friends, she counted Vic and Riki, their relationship, too, better for the experience. Leba was starting to appreciate Mally Yertha more. Her hidden talents far overshadowed her naivety. Stepping up when she needed to made all the difference. The jury was still out on Middie. The unit clerk possessed an edge, one of self-preservation and self-aggrandizement, making her a good colleague until she didn't need you anymore. Middie too stepped up on a number of occasions, but Leba still puzzled over her motivations. Some of her decisions were suspect, but overall, she proved an asset to the team. Begrudgingly, Middie paid up her bets, crying foul the whole way. Leba was certain Middie would devise a scheme to get her money back.

Showing off new body art detailing their victory, Anster and Grizzer were merciless, rubbing in their team's first-place finish, beating the war dog's red squad by mere minutes. When DeShay did not respond the way they expected, they backed off and took their seats. As the wall chrono flashed 0800, Luth Cathen strode into the room, the banging door announcing his presence. The gold braid hanging from his epaulet was striking. The medical squad emblem emblazoned over the left breast pocket and the metal studs signifying his rank shone on the Tal-Kari logo at his collar. His black boots were unscuffed and polished to a perfect shine. From head to toe he looked impressive, distinguished, almost handsome in his full dress uniform. Leba peered around to observe Mally, noting her enthusiasm at seeing her boyfriend for the first time in a week. *I wonder if she knows dating within your own squad was strictly prohibited.* Mally earned a spot on the team and deserved to be a member. How would Cathen get around that?

Leba hoped Luth Cathen would not spoil the vision by opening his mouth. He did not disappoint. "Congratulations, my students, or should I say soldiers. You have performed admirably during this test of your courage, bravery, endurance, and ingenuity. Even I was impressed by your efforts." Maybe he did have a heart and a conscience. He didn't belittle those who failed or berate anyone for their actions. The morning was still early, though. He continued, "Your results will be distributed confidentially. If you are confirmed, report at 0900 to med conference room 2-7, directly above us. If you receive a rejection, then you are dismissed, and the Tal-Kari High Command thanks you for your efforts. You may reapply for future deployments. Please remove your belongings from your temporary quarters. There will be a shuttle leaving base at 1100, and you should plan to be on it." One by one he called names and handed out sealed envelopes. Alphabetically, Leba got hers early in the distribution and quickly left the classroom, opting to open her result in the privacy of her quarters. Confident she made it, Leba didn't want to be around Emmie and Braids when they received theirs. It was still hard for them to look at her. Emmie probably blamed her for how DeShay felt about the whole situation.

I told him the truth. You bailed and didn't have to.

Staring out the now-deserted classroom's window, Emmie crushed the paper in her hand. Dark, dense clouds swarmed like locust, blocking the morning sun and coloring the world gray. She knew what the result was going to be. The cold box was only a simulation, and Braids was not going to die. Nobody dies in a drill, well, nobody in a long time, ever since the drills became a simulated experience. The problem was the mental scarring remaining in your consciousness after the experience. The memories were permanent even if the physical events never actually happened. Her break so riveting recalling it made her shudder. She rubbed her wrist, the fracture, or pseudofracture seemed to ache. The ultimate sacrifice was activating not only Braids's recall device but also her own. DeShay shouldn't have pitied her. He made her so angry. He was right, but he didn't have to tell her so.

"Hey," a familiar voice said softly, startling Emmie out of her personal bereavement. Coming to stand next to the older woman, Braids hesitantly put an arm around her shoulder and repeated, "Hey, Ma." Looking outside, she leaned her head in. "Pretty dreary, huh?"

Emmie didn't answer right away but inclined her head toward Braids. Slipping a thin arm around, she brought the younger woman closer. "I guess I screwed up pretty badly, but I did what I thought was best. You understand, don't you?"

"You did exactly what I would have done, Ma," Braids comforted her. "There was no other choice. You did what had to be done for the good of the team—for me. No one better question what you did." Turning her head, her lips now at Emmie's ear, she whispered, "I love you, Ma, and always will. There will be other missions for us, you'll see."

Moving her arm up to Braids's shoulder, Emmie kissed the top of her head. "I'm glad you understand."

"Like I told you last night, our relationship is stronger without secrets."

"Why can't DeShay understand that?" Emmie asked, looking back out the window. There was a faint glow beginning to melt the fog.

Braids left the question unanswered. "Come on, Ma, let's pack up and get out of here. I don't know about you, but I don't feel like hanging around." Emmie nodded her agreement, and the two women left the classroom.

Despite the rain, the departure terminal was bustling. Launch crews scurried like ants, moving equipment and people to their final destinations. Overpowering shuttle emissions, trapped by the heavy air, added to the stifling and sticky feeling. Bodies were plastered against the multipaned observation desk. No one stood on the overhanging balcony.

"I guess I was wrong," Emmie said to Braids. "I thought he would at least see me off."

Braids put a hand on Emmie's. "I'm sure he got tied up."

That was probably not the case. DeShay was older now and more set in his ways. In the past, he was always the one to try and save the relationship, promising her things would be different. This time, things were different. DeShay was different, not the foolish boy she had fallen for so many moons ago. She misjudged his response to her tantrum. Regretting their last conversation, Emmie hoped he would come back one more time, proving his devotion. Through the shuttle window, the training facility shrunk to an imperceptible dot and then vanished. Not this time. It bothered Emmie she might never see him again. Maybe she would call DeShay in a few days.

Purposely arriving after it boarded, DeShay watched as the shuttle carrying Emmie left the tarmac. Staring toward the landing zone, he stood at the far end of the balcony. Rain blew off the overhang, pelting him mercilessly. He didn't want Emmie to know he was there. The shuttle slowly disappeared from view. Rubbing his artificial shoulder, it seemed heavy to him. Tugging on the ends, he wrung out his now soaked shirt and made his way back into the terminal.

In recognition of surviving the cold box, Cathen gave the med unit the weekend off. Pity DeShay wouldn't be able to spend it with Emmie. That relationship was over, over and done, never to be resurrected again. This would've been the last opportunity to blow off steam. The next two weeks, training and preparation, would escalate quickly in anticipation of their departure. He missed her already, the way she moved, the way she smelled, the way she, well, the way she did just about everything. Time to move on.

People shuffled in and out of the busy terminal, while DeShay sat in the observation lounge way too long. Stiff from the awkward position, he stretched his legs. The sky went from gray to almost black, and what started as rain turned into an angry thunderstorm. Making his way to the exit, he opted to walk, following beside the moving walkway. He was alone and would probably die that way. This feeling of pervasive emptiness decorated with self-pity was ugly. This was usually the time he would go and do something stupid, something meaningless, and something he would certainly regret. No matter, it worked for him before and, for an hour or two, would take his mind off Emmie. Emmie, his Emmie, the woman he should spend the rest of his life with. The only woman he ever considered. He needed to rid his mind of those thoughts. Falling harder this time, she hurt him again. When was he ever going to learn? Each crash and burn became worse than the last time. Maybe he was too old for love, real love, and commitment. Why should he confine himself to one woman? He was better off a confirmed bachelor. There were a lot of women in his life, women who would warm his bed but not expect any permanent ties. They knew he was married to his career, but it didn't matter the way it mattered to Emmie.

Emmie's selfishness burned inside him. She never got it. It was always what was best for her, or them, but never what was best for him. He was glad to be finished with her. The ride was nice, but he needed to move on. While he was with Emmie, he avoided his friends, devoting every waking minute to making her happy. He deserved to be happy too. Someone who would put his needs ahead of their own. Tapping out the keystrokes with new vigor, DeShay texted, "Hey, baby, couldn't get you out of my mind."

After the confirmation ceremony, Mally waited to have a moment, a private moment, with her squad leader. She hadn't wanted to be too obvious. Proud of her accomplishments on the cold box mission, she needed, no, wanted to hear it personally from his lips. Vic and Riki got closer, and she wanted that too. Not only to be swept off her feet by Luth but also to experience total Luth immersion. Maybe her acknowledgement letter would have something extra on it, maybe a tiny heart in one corner or anything giving her some hope of a continuing relationship. A commitment, that was what she wanted. And she didn't want to keep it a secret.

Despite her tunnel vision, Luth Cathen didn't seem to notice her waiting outside the classroom for him. After distributing the results, he strode past, not giving her anything as simple as a wink or a glance. Maybe Middie was right; maybe he was using her. Disappointment, no, discouragement. A flurry of emotions raced through her as she followed the back of his head until he rounded the far corner. He didn't even look back. Head down, steps measured, she walked back to her quarters. Fumbling for her keycard and jamming it in the slot, Mally snatched at the door handle. *How dare he use me? How dare he lead me on? How dare he think I wouldn't figure it out?* Determined not to cry, Mally slammed her result envelope onto the side table, knocking a ceramic tray to the floor, shattering as it impacted.

Rising from her knees, her hands carefully cradling the sharp fragments, she noticed a floral smell. Peering upward in the direction of the smell, her eyes found a rather large arrangement. How could she have missed it? Right in the middle of the room, the bouquet's crystalline vase took up most of the tabletop. Despite the varied assortment of flowers, her eyes went right to the nondescript note card attached to a stick implanted into the center. Not wanting to be disappointed when she looked at the card, she forced herself to delicately cup individual flowers and inhale their scent. Mally savored the moment.

"Aren't you going to see who they are from?" a voice said from behind her.

Mally whirled around to see Luth Cathen, still in his dress uniform, arms crossed and staring back at her. "They're beautiful. Thank you so much," she exclaimed as she fingered the card.

"How do you know they are from me?" he teased as she put her arms around his neck and kissed him. "Well, I hope they are from me, or I got someone else's thank you." Grabbing her up in his arms and bringing her close, he kissed her. The card dropped from her hand to the floor. He led her over to the couch, easing her down without missing a beat. They remained there for a while, enjoying each other's company until Luth interrupted, "I think you really should look at the card before this goes any further."

"Don't tempt me like that," Mally teased. "I know they're from you. Aren't they?"

"Look at the card," Cathen advised, nudging her from the couch.

Mally got up from the couch, walked over to where the card had fallen, and bent to pick it up. Feeling his eyes watch her move and hoping to reward his attention, she took her time to accentuate every step. Mally read the card and then reread it, screaming with excitement. "Shh," Cathen put a finger to her lips. "You want the whole compound to hear?"

"The Grand Octranian, you want to take me to the Grand Octranian!" she squealed. "That's the place Dr. Hobes took his girlfriend before the cold box." Judging by the look on Cathen's face, she regretted her reference. She knew how Luth felt about Dr. Hobes, and comparing the two probably wasn't the smartest thing she ever said. "I didn't mean it that way," she apologized.

"No matter." Cathen waved his hand. "If you want to go someplace else, I can certainly cancel the reservation."

Coldness permeated the room. She went over to sit next to him to try and reignite the fire, but he turned from her. "Let me make it up to you. What can I do?"

"I'll think of something," Cathen said.

"Really?" Mally asked. "Are we really going for dinner at the Grand Octranian?"

"Only if you want to go with me."

An impeccably dressed chauffeur held the gull wing door open. Mally and Cathen boarded a private transport. The interior was trimmed in mirrored black panels, the seats in matching black leather. The back of the vehicle was designed to accommodate eight, but Mally snuggled so close the pair took up one seat. Touching a wall panel revealed a well-stocked bar. Removing a smoky bottle, Cathen seemed mesmerized by the tiny effervescent bubbles that traced the contour. "Scintilla, my favorite." Honing down on the label, he noted, "And a fine vintage as well." While deftly holding two fluted glasses in one hand, he filled both.

"You think of everything." Mally beamed as she took a swallow of the fizzing intoxicant.

"You should go easy on that," Cathen warned as he took a mouthful as well. "We may have to stay for more than dinner."

Breakfast at the Grand Octranian was even more delicious than their celebratory dinner, especially after the night she and Luth shared. Mally felt like a new woman.

"I'm not sure how this is going to work once we get back to base." Cathen stroked her hair and grasped her hand.

"What do you mean?" Mally trembled, her voice quavering.

"You know, you, me, our positions back at base camp," Cathen continued as if he hadn't thought of the implications of their encounter. Anticipating his next sentence, Mally wrung her hands, avoiding his gaze. He put a forkful of food in his mouth and chewed slowly, deep in thought. Cathen took a swallow of juice and continued to ponder their situation. Mally's anxiety continued to build.

"Maybe we could keep it a secret," she offered, grasping her own forearms tightly.

"No, I don't think that'd work. People would see how I can't keep my eyes let alone my hands off you." He pushed the food around on his plate. "No, our secret would be common knowledge in no time."

"I didn't mean to get us into so much trouble." She sniffled, the tears barely perceptible.

"Mally, it's as much my fault as yours. I…" He hesitated. "I can't deny the feelings we have for each other." This brought a small smile to her face. "Don't worry, I'll think of something, trust me." Placing a hand on hers, he gave a squeeze and, with the other, reached to stroke her face. "For now, let's just enjoy the rest of our time here."

Returning in the private transport that whisked them away yesterday, Cathen inclined his head. "You're too valuable to waste your time doing busywork." Mally smoothed her skirt, pulling the hemline back over her knees. "I think you're making the right decision."

Mally smiled. "And this way, we can see each other without anyone worrying about it."

"Uh-huh," Cathen mumbled as he went to nuzzle at her neck. Moving up to her face, he kissed her again, his hand making its way down her thigh. Reaching across her lap, he activated the opaque feature in the passenger compartment, signaling the driver he didn't want to be disturbed. Her skirt slowly crept up off her knee.

Mally readjusted her blouse as their destination approached. What a brilliant idea, Luth suggested instead of working in the deployment base clinic, Mally could work with the Pareq base commander's private physician in his personal office. She still got to go on the mission, she still got to be a nurse, and she still could remain as close to Luth as possible without being under his immediate supervision. Simply genius, but that was part of the reason she loved Luth; he was always keeping her best interests at heart.

A sliver of light peeked through the curtains and hit DeShay squarely in the face. Rolling onto his back, the room was otherwise dark, the bed clothes bunched at his waist. As he rolled slightly away from the window toward the other side of the bed, DeShay put a hand out to touch hers, but she was already gone. The regret began to set in. He knew better, but he wanted company, female company, someone who would unselfishly tend to his needs. Someone with whom commitment was not an option. No strings, no ties, no promises. It hadn't taken her long to respond to his text and even shorter for her to join him for dinner and drinks and a private show. Too quickly it was over, and he was beginning to regret the way he chose to relieve his pain.

After a light breakfast and a strong cup of caffeine on his way to the gym, DeShay spent the next half hour hitting the heavy bag. Fearing the surrounding tissues where it was implanted would buckle in the frigid temperatures, DeShay was pleased his artificial shoulder stood up so well to the cold box. After last night's performance, he knew he was still vital and could outperform men half his age. The hell with Emmie. Toweling off sweat, he took a much-needed water break. Reinvigorated, he lay on the bench and began busting out crunches. Finally to work his lower body, he ran on the treadmill until his thighs burned. Toweling dry a final time, he finished the remaining water in his bottle and went to refill it.

"Hey, girl," DeShay greeted Leba as she entered the gym. She walked over to him. "Here for a workout? I'm finishing mine or I'd stay and keep you company."

"Thanks," she said. "I got a late start, was doing some extra reading."

"Just like you, always with a nose in the books. But I guess that's why you're so smart and I'm so handsome." DeShay laughed.

"Pity all men can't be as ripped as you are." Leba's stare lingered at his midsection.

"True that," DeShay agreed. "I know this guy who is almost as buff as I am, and if you remind me, I'll introduce you to him."

"Promises, promises," she retorted. "Go shower, and maybe if you're lucky, I'll buy you lunch."

"You wish," he replied, snapping his sweaty towel at her. She moved out of the way, avoiding a painful welt. "You're learning to anticipate, or maybe you're not as slow as you used to be," he teased.

"Go shower." She pinched her nose. "Before I pass out."

He turned to walk away. "I'm holding you to your lunch offer, girl. Unless it's commissary food, and then you can owe me."

"Commando burgers and crisps with plenty of hots, if your delicate constitution can handle it."

"I'll meet you at your quarters at 1130. Make sure you've showered."

"Count on it," she started. "And I may even use soap."

"About time." Keeping his head covered as he jogged toward the men's locker room, knowing if Leba found a towel, she would launch it at him. When he turned back for a moment, her sweatband was in place, and she was already started on her training circuit.

Meeting her best friend, Sendra Tohl, for lunch at the medical clinic commissary, Leba blew over her tea. "I think you should," Leba nodded and then took a sip.

"It's not such a long trip, and I bet Damond would be surprised," Sendra said.

"The problem would be getting the time off." Leba tapped her spoon.

"I've got a lot of accumulated time."

"But if you take civilian transport, half the trip will be travel back and forth," Leba finished her thought.

"That's where you come in. Can you get me aboard a military transport?"

Leba looked around the room and then back at Sendra. "You talking to me?" She laughed. "I'm almost as low as a neo. I'm lucky they're willing to take me." Leba scratched her head. "I can ask DeShay. I'm sure he knows someone who could help you out."

"Call him." Sendra grabbed her hand and squeezed. "I'd like to meet at least one man who has stolen your heart."

Leba felt herself blush. "We're only friends. By the way"—Leba air quoted—"the love of his life trashed him again. That same stubbornness and selfish attitude got her bounced from the mission too."

Sendra stared intently as Leba detailed the Emmie and DeShay story. Shifting in her chair then grabbing the end of the table, Sendra interrupted, "Are you going to call him or not?"

"Right now?" Leba questioned. The expression on Sendra's face said it all. "Okay, okay," Leba relented. Leba punched in DeShay's comm code, but there was no response. "That's funny, he's usually not offline."

"What do you mean?" Sendra frowned.

"It didn't even give me the pleasantry of leaving a voice message. That's not like DeShay. His comm is turned off."

"He's a guy, he probably left it in the gym."

"I saw him in the gym, and we were supposed to go to lunch, but at the last minute, he begged off."

"So I'm you're second choice." Sendra, with pinched fingers, put the soda straw in her mouth and took a drink.

"I was going to…" Leba fumbled for the right words. "No, you weren't my second choice."

"You don't have to explain. I'm giving you a hard time." She put the glass down. "Promise me you'll call him later."

"Promise. Although I think that you would be better off asking Damond to meet you here. He could probably catch a military transport and get back and forth in no time."

"It's his time I want."

DeShay finally answered her text. He didn't respond to his comm, and he hadn't answered his door, so she texted him. She hated texting; it was so informal, and she found it hard to read emotions from them, but if that was the only way he would answer, she would try. Leba figured if DeShay got a text from her, he would figure it must be important, and he would at least read it and respond to get her off his back.

Rewarded with an info-pad ping, Leba read the text:

> In the midst of a special assignment.
> Sorry about lunch.
> Promise to catch up with you later.
> Thanks for your concern, DT.

Strange. Leba scratched the side of her head. How come she didn't hear about a special assignment and on such short notice? Emmie maybe?

The next two weeks flew by, with preparations being made both at home base for departures and at the Pareq Base for arrivals. Leba spent the last weekend before leaving visiting her parents. Her private quarters were secure, leaving her parents specific written instructions, per her mother's request, on what needed to be done and when. Leba knew for sure when she returned from the mission her home would be cleaner and tidier than how she left it. Nothing would be out of place, and most of her things would be better and more carefully folded, and no dust would be found. Her mother, busy as she was, always kept an immaculate house. Somehow she found time to put her family's well-being ahead of everything else. Leba hoped one day she would be at least half the mother and wife her mom was.

DeShay, spent his last weekend typing a text to Emmie. It was hard to get her out of his mind. Never much for writing, maybe if he put his thoughts to text it would help. A text he never planned to send, but preserved in the Draft bin for all eternity. That part of his life needed to officially end when he left home base. The mission would start without regrets, without baggage, without reservations. Like a reptile molting its old skin, he emerged from behind the keyboard a new man, ready to take on new challenges. Chameleon-like, changing his colors to adapt to a new stimulus.

After meeting Wallen Scoby, the veteran surgeon and personal physician to Chalco Atacama, and being charged with bringing the rest of his things to Pareq, Mally was given the entire week off. Scoby was arrogant and demanding, but she didn't mind. Nothing mattered as long as she and Luth could be together. Scoby's early departure allowed Mally to plan their last weekend at home. Cathen's unit was polished and ready ahead of schedule, so he would be available to enjoy Mally's company uninterrupted. In fact, he told her if he wasn't always so busy, he would spend all his time with her.

Saying good-bye to Nilsa made the weekend emotional and difficult for JT. After their trip to the Grand Octranian, she implored him not to go but to stay and work at the home base. Despite promising her he would visit at every opportunity, she wasn't satisfied. After racking his brain and pulling handfuls of hair out, a solution finally took shape. It would take some doing, calling in a multitude of favors, and owing others big time. But would she go for it? He opted to outline his plan at their final dinner together before his impending departure.

"I made some calls," he began between bites of food. Dropping a bundle at the most exclusive restaurant in town, the candlelight, the tableside chef, would hopefully soften her up. Nilsa, her big brown eyes still moist from tears, listened attentively. "If you're willing, I can arrange for you to come with me." He watched as the corners of her mouth began to curl into a smile.

"What do I have to do?" her eyes widened, and she blinked rapidly.

"You don't have to do anything." He grinned.

"Don't tease me," she pleaded.

He pulled an info-pad from his jacket and dangled it in front of her. Bringing it back, JT said, "All I have to do is push this one button, and like magic, you can come with me."

"Stop teasing," she begged, fingering her necklace and bouncing her toes.

"All right, all right," he said, reaching across the table and holding both her hands. "Here's how it works. I contacted a friend of mine who knows the head of the scientific team. It seems they are in need of a new biocultural expert."

"I'm a biocultural expert," she squealed. He could feel her hands slowly pull away as she looked at him curiously. "What happened to their biocultural expert?"

JT paused for a moment and then continued, "Some last-minute medical issue was uncovered, preventing him from joining the team. Pity, since there was not enough time to recruit a suitable replacement."

"But I haven't trained for the mission," she cried, gripping his hands tighter.

"But you know someone who has, and he's more than willing to vouch for you as the perfect substitute." He put the info-pad back into his pocket, folded his arms across his chest, and leaned back in his chair. There was a long silence until JT asked, "You do want to go with me, don't you?"

"Of course," she started and then stopped. "But he'll be there."

Dammit, Nilsa, why'd you have to ruin a perfectly good plan? JT bristled. "Don't worry, I've got that figured out too." Nilsa didn't ask how, and JT was not in a sharing mood. All he wanted was her undivided attention.

"You think of everything." She beamed, getting up from her seat to hug him. *Well, almost everything.*

That's more like it, JT thought, satisfied he had done the right thing. He embraced her, promising to himself never to let her go. He would make her forget Garnet no matter what it took.

PART 2: PAREQ

Moon Base for Tal-Kari Expeditionary Mission to Vedax

CHAPTER 23

As his shuttle approached the inhabited moon Pareq, Defender Company Squad Leader Tiv Garnet marveled at the massive planet of swirling gasses, looming large in the sky, reflecting light from the nearby yellow star that energized the entire system. Of all of Glirase's moons, Pareq was blessed with the best orbital position, whereas Vedax, the moon in question, lived in shadows. Garnet mapped the route between these moons. He knew how long and what aspect to approach. If needed, Defender Company would leave nothing to chance when lives were at stake.

Arriving at the new temporary Pareq Base over a week ago, Defender Company was almost finished getting their equipment and supplies checked, catalogued, and compartmented into their storage units. Plagued by pranks for weeks, Tiv Garnet was cautiously optimistic. Since he and the other advance units deployed, the mischief mysteriously stopped. Still not knowing who his adversary was, Tiv was glad it was not one of his charges. It would be two more weeks before the scientific, medical, and civilian teams arrived. Multidisciplinary missions were always the most difficult to plan for. Soldiers, real soldiers, lived by a set of well-defined rules. If you didn't get what you wanted, you dealt with it. Chain of command set the tone. But civilians working for the military often were pampered and spoiled and drove Tiv crazy with their demands: demands for equipment, better quarters and food, and always more help. With guys like Master Priman DeShay Tiner doing the prelims for the nonmilitary types, setting them straight and teaching them the realities of a long deployment, Tiv hoped his job this go round would be easier. With a little luck and lack of distraction, maybe Tiv could finally catch a break.

Above all the rest, Defender Company was tasked with search and rescue, extraction and evacuation, dealing with mishaps and malcontents. As such, they ended up, on these scientific expeditionary missions, getting the uninitiated out of their own messes. Tiv thought it strange the large number of personnel expected for this deployment. It was only to explore an icy moon orbiting a gas giant.

Two weeks, two little weeks of peace and quiet before the temporary base would be teeming with people. Tiv and his squad were running ahead of schedule when Overseer Company enlisted them to scout out the local terrain. Over his head in last-minute changes, Squad Leader Damond Fiorat, Overseer's man in charge, couldn't seem to get everything done he needed. Although the construction crews were winding down their main force, it was Overseer's job to go over every millimeter of space and sign off on every project. Late as usual with delivery of the temporary base, the construction unit didn't seem to care if it interfered with Fiorat's timeline.

"Thanks, Garnet." Fiorat shook his hand. "I promise I'll buy your whole squad drinks if you guys help us out."

"For a month," Tiv said and handed him the info-pad detailing Overseer's remaining tasks. "And dinner too," he added.

"Don't push it," Fiorat shot back. "Look, it's not such a bad job getting to know the locals. It's not like my group of nerds and techno-geeks have a shot. Maybe some of your goons will get lucky."

"I don't think my guys will be farming that field anytime soon," Tiv remarked. "We're on a mission, no time for planting seeds on this world."

After tapping a few keys, Fiorat handed Tiv the info-pad. "I also need you guys to set up some surveillance equipment around the area for perimeter watch."

"Anything else, taste the local cuisine, date the mayor's daughter, or take the head cop for drinks?"

"I'll leave that to your discretion." Fiorat smiled. "And by the way, I need your report at the beginning of the week."

Tiv swiped the screen, examined the street grid, expanding and contracting each designated site. "There goes another weekend." Back home on Luac, at the mercy of the prankster, Tiv was reluctant to go out and leave his stuff unprotected. Maybe a tour of the city would be a welcome change.

Tiv returned to his squad's conference room to see which of his unit was up for the detail. As a reward for their efficiency, Tiv gave his unit the weekend off but was sure he could rustle up some takers. Cooped up the past several weeks trying to avoid the prankster, he was going stir crazy; it was about time he got some fresh air.

"As long as you sleep in your own bed, I don't care where you go," Tiv advised the men in the room. About one-quarter of his unit, the majority of which were single men, volunteered to roam around the city, sampling its offerings, and installing the needed security equipment. Tiv continued, "I do suggest you buddy up, though." Priman Brit Belk, one of Tiv's trusted seconds, stroked his circle beard. "Buddy up, not hook up," Tiv reiterated.

Priman Belk usually took it on himself to delegate responsibility. Laughing boisterously, he exclaimed, "You know me too well." Of average height with muscular features, Belk always seemed to be grinning. He could light up a room with a carefully placed self-deprecating remark or off-color joke. Belk's biggest problem was his targeting lock was often distracted by a pretty face or hot body.

The rest of the room filled with laughter. Tiv ignored him. "I'll download data to your info-pads. Split up and decide who's going where so we don't end up stepping on each other."

More often than not, Belk was wingman to his more stoic squad leader. On this jaunt, Tiv gave Brit the command. "Six sectors, fourteen guys." Belk split everyone into teams. "Looks like you're with me," Belk announced to Tiv. "Hope you can keep up," he prodded.

"I'll do my best," Tiv answered, then addressed the remaining members. "Remember, by the book. We don't want to start any problems."

"Do you think they'll let you ride in that?" Tiv asked.

"This?" Brit Belk said, pointing to his patterned and colorful shirt. "I understand this is common wear for the upper class here on Pareq."

"Maybe a decade or two ago." Tiv laughed.

"At least I'll get some attention," Brit said straight-faced.

"The point was not to get attention, genius." *I knew this was a mistake.* Brit, though, was way more social than Tiv was. Brit oozed charisma, and he could charm the pants or skirt off anyone. Tiv knew what usually got him in trouble—not being able to turn it down.

"Maybe some pretty girl will take pity on me and..." Brit rubbed his bald head. The only other thing Brit didn't like about himself was his less than stellar educational record.

"And what? Shoot you and put you out of your misery for such a fashion mistake?"

"You'd like that, wouldn't you. Then you could have her all to yourself."

"I've sworn off girls for now. Too needy, too demanding, too everything." Tiv envied Brit's ability to be everybody's friend. Trust was tough for Tiv, and in his book, it was earned, which is probably why he had only a few close friends.

"Awww." Brit stared at him. "I'll show you how it's done." For whatever reason, women found Brit fascinating. Maybe it was his cockiness combined with bravado. And unlike Tiv, Brit's eventual breakups were always civil. Brit was still friends with the majority of women he'd dated, although Tiv was not sure he could count their parents, boyfriends, or an occasional husband in the mix. "You can't get so involved, my friend. You need to sit back and watch the master."

Tiv ran his hand through his full head of black hair. It was going to be a long day. "If you say so. I'll let you lead, and I'll be your wingman for this excursion." Tiv rubbed his clean-shaven chin. "In fact, any girl we meet, she's all yours."

"Hey, thanks, man."

The pair was heading toward the transport depot when Brit spied a pub. "Let's check it out."

"Your call. You're in charge on this one."

A CHANGE IN TACTICS: MAIDEN VOYAGE

"I have a good feeling about this place," Brit said as he pushed open the heavy door with the name Dugin's etched into the glass. The bar itself was modest, hosting about six cushioned stools. Immediately behind the four taps were two rows of liquor bottles that climbed toward the centerpiece, a large mirror making the room appear bigger. The majority of the furnishings were wood with a few scattered tables randomly set in the dining area. Tiv and Brit opted for the nearest table.

"You guys new in town?" the buxom waitress asked as she set down two menus.

Running thumb and forefinger around his beard, Brit answered, "My friend and I are from the new Tal-Kari base. What's good?" Tiv sat back to watch his buddy in action. Sometimes Tiv wished he were more like Brit; life would be so much easier.

The waitress leaned over Brit's shoulder to show him the menu, but her eyes alighted on Tiv, giving him full view of her assets. "Are you hungry?"

"Very," Brit concentrated on the menu. Any closer and she'd be in his lap. That violation of personal space would annoy Tiv, but Brit seemed to drink it in. He inclined his head to face her, but her eyes were still on Tiv. Brit cleared his throat, and Tiv watched her momentary distraction fade. "Any recommendations?"

"I think you'd like our special. I'll bring two," she said, pulling back from Brit's shoulder and moving more toward the middle of the table.

"Great," Belk said.

"I'll be right back." She retrieved both menus and turned to leave.

Brit watched her saunter away. "Nice girl."

"Hadn't noticed," Tiv said.

"I think she likes me." Brit straightened in his chair and flexed his chest muscles.

"If you say so." Tiv swiveled his head and followed the outline of the bar. He checked his chrono. The menus clearly detailed lunch specials. "Don't you think it's weird that we're the only ones in here?"

"No competition. But then again, I'm in a league of my own when it comes to pretty girls. I'll have to get her name." Brit looked over his shoulder. "What are you looking at?"

"Where do you think that leads?" Tiv asked, spying a door that seemed out of place. He already identified the entrance/exit to the kitchen and the back hall to offices and restrooms. He didn't want to seem paranoid, but in his business, situational awareness kept you safe.

"Right to my heart," Brit answered as the waitress returned to the table. She slid a large meaty burger in front of Brit and lingered when she laid down Tiv's.

"Hope you enjoy it." She licked her lips and brushed his arm as she moved the plate closer to Tiv. "Don't hesitate to call if you need anything, anything at all."

Maybe it's a meeting room. Tiv didn't like not knowing. "Do you host private parties here?" Tiv asked, picking up his fork and moving the slaw over so it wouldn't soak his burger.

"Yes, yes we do." The waitress smiled at him. "Were you interested in our accommodations?"

"Just curious."

"I'd be more than happy to have our manager come talk with you," she offered.

"No, but thanks." Tiv turned back to face his food.

"Sorry about my friend," Belk said softly to her. "He's sworn off women."

"I'm sure we could change his mind." She reached out for Tiv's hand, but he withdrew it. "I have a friend," she turned toward Brit, giving Tiv a view of her tight jeans.

"As pretty as you?" Brit reached up. Tiv thought he might grab her ass, but Brit got elbow instead.

"You're cute. We'll talk later." She put an arm on Belk's shoulder and gave a small squeeze and then walked back toward the kitchen.

"I like this place," Belk said. "I wonder what time she gets off." Silence.

I think she's probably getting off already.

"Come on, Tiv, what harm would it do to see what her friend looks like?" Brit leaned back on his chair and interlaced his hands behind his head. "We could get a real insider's view."

"I remember what happened last time you got an insider's view," Tiv snatched his burger and took way too big of a bite.

"If I remember correctly, she was very pretty, and we got off to a great start."

Forgetting he hadn't swallowed entirely, Tiv nearly choked on Brit's faulty recollection. "Until her husband almost killed you."

"Hey, it wasn't my fault," Brit shot back, stuffing food into his mouth. Tiv glared at him. "Don't look at me like that." Brit screwed up his face. "It wasn't," he insisted. "And if I remember, you didn't find her friend too ugly." Brit pointed his fork at Tiv.

"Let's not go there," Tiv said, shoving a forkful of the dripping slaw into his mouth.

"Listen," Brit garbled, his mouth overfilled with food. He swallowed and picked up the furry green chip from the pile on his plate. He considered it for a minute and crunched down hard on it. Momentarily recoiling from it, he pushed the rest away. "I'm just saying, it might be useful for the mission."

"That's what you always say."

"I'm sure this girl knows all the hot spots. All the places we should keep our guys out of. Besides, I don't think you've had any fun in weeks."

"I told you, I've sworn off girls for now." *It's driving me crazy, though. Maybe I should've taken DeShay up on his latest rec.* "At least until I'm free of the joker who's pranking me."

"Listen, buddy, there's no way it's one of the guys in our unit. Unless it's one of Overseer's guys, I think you're home-free." Tiv considered Brit's assessment. He did have a point. "Besides, you can keep me out of trouble."

Tiv was about to respond when the waitress returned. Brit looked up, smiling. "How's everything?" she asked.

"Better now that you're back," Brit said. Tiv shook his head. Brit could write with authority every section of a women's magazine from what men like, to the latest hot spots, to what's going to soar in the future, to what foods bring out the best for each performance. But sometimes, his pickup lines needed work.

"Ready for dessert?" she asked, this time standing so close to Brit that Tiv was sure he could feel her breathing.

"I think we'd like to come back later for dessert," Brit said.

"Your friend coming back as well?" she asked, the corners of her mouth turning upward into a devilish smile.

"I'm working on him." Brit smiled.

"I get off at ten, if you're interested. Here's my number." She slipped him a small card. "Let me know if I should bring a friend."

Brit grinned as she walked away. "How easy was that?"

"Too easy," Tiv replied as he put money out for the bill. "This one's on me."

"Next meal's mine."

The two men got up from the table and headed toward the exit. Tiv looked back one more time at the door he still couldn't figure out. Brit fingered the card the girl had given him. "I think I'm going to like this place. Dugin's Bar and Grill, my new favorite watering hole." They headed out the door when Brit stopped suddenly.

"What's wrong?" Tiv asked, stopping and turning. Brit held up the card for him to see. The name displayed: Chelli Dugin. "Daughter or wife?"

"Either way, this can't be good."

"Now I'm almost willing to come back here tonight and see which." Tiv placed an arm on Brit's shoulder. "Come on."

Brit stared at the name on the card. "Maybe it's just a coincidence," Brit reasoned.

"Doubt it."

"Must be her father who owns the place?" Brit questioned.

"Dugin's Bar and Grill, and her name is Chelli Dugin," Tiv answered. "If it's not his daughter, then it's his wife."

Brit stared up at the midday sun and pulled a pair of shades from his pocket. Grabbing the frames, he slid them on. "Maybe it'll work anyway."

"How so?" Tiv asked as he stopped at an intersection and waited to cross the street. Brit possessed perpetual optimism, and Tiv was sure he was cooking up some scheme. This was usually the point when Tiv would need to reign him in before things got out of hand.

"Maybe her friend is just as cute as she is. You could keep her busy while I hook—I mean, buddy up with her friend. I think Chelli liked you better anyway."

Tiv's eyebrows crested into a scowl. "Come on." The pair crossed the street. Tiv looked at the street sign and then down at his info-pad. "A little further and we'll be at Fiorat's designated location."

Brit said, "So what do you think?"

"Think about what?"

"You know, about you keeping Chelli busy while I meet her friend." Brit stood watch while Tiv reached above his head and struggled to affix the spy sensor.

"Just about got it." Tiv returned to Brit's side, satisfied with the installation. "What if she's old and ugly?" Tiv asked.

"Pretty girls have pretty friends," Brit announced.

"Guess it doesn't work for guys, does it?" Tiv slapped Brit on the shoulder.

"Funny, very funny. So will you help me out or not?"

"I'll think about it." That was Tiv's problem; he overthought everything. Sometimes, he wished he was more like Brit. Deep down, Tiv knew Brit was insecure, and his jokes were a way to compensate. Tiv was a leader, confident in his abilities and decision-making. Compared with Brit, Tiv took responsibility seriously and thought long and hard about the consequences of his actions. Grooming Brit for command duties took some effort, but the younger man was finally getting it. Well, almost. If he said he had your back, though, you could count on it. "Now, we've got three more of these things to put up." The two looked at the info-pad, trying to figure out the best route to their next destination.

Tiv and Brit finished placing the last of Fiorat's eyes and ears. It was late afternoon, and the air was thick with humidity. Tiv was glad he remembered to keep his wicking undershirt on. Brit, on the other hand, manipulated his shirt buttons and pulled his shirttails out. "Well, what do you think?" Brit asked and finishing taking off his outer shirt.

Tiv stared at the muscle shirt underneath, shook his head, and turned away. "The only thing I'm thinking about is where I can get a cold drink."

"That's not what I'm talking about," Brit said, arms akimbo.

"I'm going to get a drink," Tiv said, pointing to a small convenience store. "You want something?"

Brit handed Tiv some coins. "Drinks are on me."

Tiv pushed the money around in his hand. "You're so incredibly generous. I guess that means we're even now." Tiv returned shortly with two bottles. He handed Brit one, unscrewed the cap on his own, and began to drain the bottle. "What's that grin about?"

"Okay, so it's all set."

"What's all set?" Tiv questioned.

"We're meeting Chelli and her friend at a place called Twardy's on Sixth and Twenty-Ninth at 2300."

"Before this goes any further—" Tiv started to say, but Brit started walking back toward the base. Capping his bottle, Tiv jogged to catch up. "Before this goes any further, I think we need some ground rules."

"Rules? Rules are what get you into trouble, my friend. Without rules, there is no breaking the rules."

"Rules are what keep us out of trouble."

"That's your problem." Brit smirked. "That's why you can't have any fun." Tiv did not like where this was going. "I'm your friend, right?" Brit looked at Tiv. "Don't answer that. But I know what's good for you, and right now, going with me to meet Chelli and her friend tonight is what's best for you." Tiv wasn't following. "Listen, you take things way too seriously, you never go out just to be going out. There always has to be a means to an end. You're too predictable, and you fall into the same trap every time. If she isn't a keeper, big deal, just go and enjoy her company. No strings, no ties, no commitments."

"It isn't that easy," Tiv started to say but didn't finish. Commitments were important to Tiv. They were a stabilizing force in his life. He liked rules because following the rules proved you were honoring your commitments. Maybe it was time for a change in tactics. Maybe he should follow Belk's lead. He would have to think more about it. "But I'll consider it," Tiv finished.

Belk smiled. "I promise you'll thank me in the morning. Now let's get back to base."

It was early evening when Tiv, Belk, and the rest of the scouting parties returned. All their objectives met, Tiv congratulated his team on a job well done. Belk stepped up. "We've decided in appreciation for all your hard work"—Belk watched Tiv closely for his reaction—"That for tonight only, curfew is lifted." Tiv opened his mouth to speak but was met with a stern expression on Belk's face. The others in attendance watched and waited for Tiv's response, but none came. Tiv closed his mouth, folded his arms across his chest, and shook his head. "Without any objections," Belk continued, "dismissed."

The troopers filed noisily out of the room. "Don't say it," Belk advised Tiv. "You told me I'm in charge on this one." Tiv couldn't deny he told Brit he would be his wingman, but he didn't expected it to spill past their earlier excursion. "Wow," Belk commented. "I'm impressed with your restraint, my friend."

"Don't tempt me," Tiv warned.

Dressed conservatively with black trousers, collared long sleeve white dress shirt with a dark-colored sweater, and black boots, Tiv met Belk outside his quarters. "You take fun to an all new level," Belk scanned Tiv up and down. "Do you want these girls to think you are the most boring guy on base?" Belk, on the other hand, with his khaki pants, a three-button, noncollared short-sleeved shirt, and some gold chain around his neck, looked like he just walked out of a cologne ad.

"I didn't want to steal your spotlight," Tiv bowed.

"Hey, thanks, man," Belk said, oblivious to Tiv's sarcasm. Belk checked his chrono. "Right on time." The pair headed for the exit.

I hope you know what you're doing, Tiv thought, not only about meeting these girls, but for lifting the curfew. He was willing to relax but not too much. He adjusted his waistband, surreptitiously checking for his concealed blade, comforted by its presence.

Belk noticed the move. "You're not carrying, are you?"

Tiv glared at him. "Sometimes girls are really turned on by a guy with a decent weapon."

Belk narrowed his eyes as Tiv adjusted his sweater back over the knife. "Really?"

The streets on Pareq were laid out in a grid pattern with even streets going north-south and odd streets crossing east-west, so Squad Leader Tiv Garnet and Priman Brit Belk had no difficulty locating the bar. It was a little after eleven when they entered a crowded Twardy's. Multicolored lights ringed the entrance and opened to a crowded dance floor. Wisps of generated smoke wafted toward the ceiling. Tiv and Brit hugged the perimeter as they made their way to the bar. Compared to Dugin's, this place was loud. The music blared through giant amplifiers. Belk looked across the sea of gyrating people until his gaze alighted on Chelli and her friend stationed at the bar. "See, I told you. Pretty girls have pretty friends."

Chelli slid off her stool when she saw them approach. She was in a short black dress with stiletto heels. "This is my friend Aleece." Her friend sported a dress that barely reached the top of her thighs. Her red boots climbed high up her leg and over her knee.

"Brit," he said as he moved between the two women, almost sitting on Aleece's lap.

"Aleece, why don't you show Brit where our table is." Chelli motioned to her friend as she sidled up to Tiv and put an arm through his. Despite such tight quarters, Tiv kept his hands at his sides, never in his pockets, something a warrior never did. Maybe it had something to do with the need to always be ready. He promised himself not to let her get to him, but she did look pretty hot and certainly was interested in him. He may have to reconsider. Tiv watched as Aleece led Brit ahead. "I wasn't sure you were going to make it."

"Brit's a pretty convincing fellow," Tiv said and then realized how rude that sounded. "And of course, you were so kind to invite us. You look very nice." Tiv took another long look. If he didn't know better, it was almost as if that sexy black dress was painted on.

"Thank you." She moved so close that he could smell the fragrance in her hair despite the overwhelming assault of sweat and heavy-handed cologne emanating from the others of his gender. "Now let's get to the table before they start talking about us." Chelli tugged his arm, pulling on his hand and guiding him to the table. The restaurant section of Twardy's was dimly lit with tall two-person tables. Along the walls, in an even darker section, were booths, lit only by single votives. Aleece was already in near the wall with Brit positioned next to her.

"Glad you decided to join us." Brit laughed. "I ordered ale for you." Without spilling a drop of her bright-orange drink, Chelli slipped into the booth. In fact, she crossed the entire bar that way, and Tiv was impressed. He wondered what other skills she might have. Tiv followed onto the seat next to her and was seriously reconsidering his decision to swear off women even for a short time. The waiter deposited the two ales in front of the men. "I think the ladies need a refill," Brit informed the man.

"Anything else?" The waiter carefully scooped up Aleece's near-empty flute. He waited momentarily, giving Chelli an opportunity to drain her glass.

"I believe we actually came here for dessert." Brit leered at Aleece. "What's good?" he asked, still eyes locked on his date.

"They're famous for their mousse pies," Aleece piped up. "We could share," she said, her tongue moistening her lips.

Brit, with his arm now across the booth over her shoulders, announced, "What the lady wants, the lady gets." He remained studying Aleece's now inviting mouth and asked, "You guys want anything?"

"Not really," Tiv said, turning his head to the side and running his fingers through his hair. He hated being a jerk, and this girl was really into him. One-nighters were not his thing, but it had been a while since he'd been with a woman. Hearing a disappointed moan from Chelli, Tiv corrected, "Well, okay, we'll have what they're having."

"Great." Brit turned from Aleece and held up his fingers. "We'll take two."

"Very good, sir. Your desserts will be up in a minute." The waiter left to fulfill their request.

"So, ladies," Brit began, "Tiv and I were wondering if you like to dance." Tiv glared at Brit. Tiv couldn't dance, didn't want to dance, and had threatened to kill Brit the last time he brought up the subject.

"We love to dance," Aleece exclaimed.

"Come on," Brit said, grabbing her hand and pulling her to her feet as he stepped from the booth. He waited for a moment, fully evaluating the way she filled out her silky red dress, and then looked back to the booth. "You guys going to join us?"

Tiv slowly and deliberately took a long pull from his ale bottle. No, hooking up tonight was not a good idea. They'd just gotten here, and Tiv still didn't have enough intel to go on. The bottle made a thud as he put it down hard on the table. "I figured maybe we would get to know each other a little better first, you know, privately."

"Suit yourself. Don't do anything I wouldn't do." Brit leaned over, his face almost nose to nose with Tiv's. How many drinks Brit already had, Tiv couldn't be sure, but he'd probably blow the legal limit with that breath. At least one of the two of them needed to stay sober and watch their backs.

"That certainly leaves me a lot of options." Tiv leaned back on the booth and extended his arm across the top. Tiv watched as Brit and Aleece left for the dance floor and then felt eyes on him. Chelli seemed to be waiting for him to start. He hated small talk, especially because he really wasn't very good at it. "So," Tiv began, "Dugin's, does your father own it?"

"Uh-huh," she responded. "I've been working there since I was a kid." Tiv sensed that was not the question she was hoping for. "What about you, what's your story?" Chelli asked, working her fingers slowly up his leg.

"Nothing special," Tiv answered, shifting in his seat. "My dad was a soldier, now I'm a soldier. Pretty boring stuff."

"I don't think you're boring at all," Chelli said, moving her hand closer to where his blade was hidden in the front of his trousers.

He had a rule about people not touching his weapon. It made him uncomfortable, vulnerable. "Are you sure you don't want to dance?"

"Never been very good at it. Two left feet and all," Tiv said, moving her hand.

"Come on, they're playing a slow song," she said, grabbing his hand and nudging him from the booth. "I'll show you."

Tiv got up and helped Chelli to her feet. She did look hot in that dress. She gave him a quick peck on the cheek, squeezed his hand, and dragged him to the dance floor. Tiv reluctantly followed her. She deftly cut a path through the other couples' entangled bodies.

Chelli put her arms around his waist. "I'm not going to bite. Unless you want me to," she teased. He awkwardly wrapped his arms across her shoulders. She moved in closer and shifted one of his hands to cup her bottom. "That's better, now follow me." She rocked back and forth, side to side, occasionally nuzzling at his neck and rubbing up against him. Tiv tried not to respond but was unsuccessful. Maybe Brit was right; maybe he should go with the flow, not worry about tomorrow, and just enjoy the moment. The music ended, but Tiv continued to rhythmically follow Chelli's patterned movements even though she was still. "We should head back to the table," she whispered, her hot breath tickling his ear. Tiv raised his eyebrows and blew out a short breath.

Chelli and Aleece excused themselves to the lavatory. "What are you looking at?" Tiv snatched his ale from the table.

"Don't want to admit I'm right, do you?" Brit tapped his fork.

"Shut up," Tiv said, trying to ignore Belk's stares.

"Aleece said their place isn't far from here," Belk offered. "What harm could it do, just to see it?"

"Chelli's nice, but something about this doesn't feel right."

"Are you nuts? That girl is really into you. Why do you keep thinking commitment? Just think of how she makes you feel and go with that." He continued his rhythmic fork tapping.

Tiv grabbed his hand and forced the utensil to silence. "What if her father found out? He'd never let me back in your new favorite place. You do what you want, but I'm sleeping in my own bed tonight."

"So you're going to take her back to the base," Belk jested. Tiv glared at him. "Well, you're going to have to explain it to her."

"Thanks," Tiv said, closing his eyes and resting his head on his hand and massaging his temples. By the time the women returned to the booth, dessert had arrived. *Of course they only brought one fork for the two of us.* Tiv knew that would be awkward. Tiv watched as Aleece offered to feed Belk. Belk eagerly took a forkful, encouraging Tiv to follow suit. Tiv was preparing to put the fork to the pie when Chelli put her finger into it and painted the dripping goo onto his lips. *What the hell.* Eyes staring at Brit, Tiv licked the pie from her finger before it dropped into his lap.

"Now your turn," she said, dipping his finger into the pie and placing it into her mouth. She sucked every last bit off, letting her tongue play with his finger, before she playfully bit him.

"Ow," Tiv said, recoiling his finger and rubbing it with his thumb.

"Here, let me make it up to you," she said, pulling his face close to hers and kissing him.

Tiv was having a tough time thinking how he was going to extricate himself from this sticky situation. He could just imagine Belk's expression and the story he was going to tell once they got back to base. He was trying to keep cool, but Chelli kept turning up the heat.

"You guys want to get a room?" Belk joked.

Tiv snapped back to reality, gently removing Chelli's hand from his thigh. Belk laughed. "You say something?" Tiv asked, knowing full well what Belk said.

Belk was getting ready to answer when Tiv's chrono chimed.

Tiv reached into his pocket and removed the info-pad. He pretended to study the readout. "Bad news, I'm afraid." Tiv sighed. Belk spied him suspiciously. "Seems Brit and I are urgently needed back on base." Tiv motioned Chelli to move from the booth so he could get out. "Ladies, I'm sorry we have to end this way, but maybe we can finish some other time."

Belk slid from his seat against the wall as Aleece exited the booth. "I am so sorry," Belk apologized, sneering at Tiv. "You know the life of a soldier, never a moment's peace."

"Come on," Tiv insisted. "The text was marked urgent."

Chelli stood, her arms crossed over her chest. Tiv gave her a quick peck. "Sorry, love, but duty calls."

Belk's good-bye kiss was longer and more involved, and Tiv pulled him off Aleece. As the two men headed back toward the entrance to the club, Belk kept looking back. "Get over it. This is a long deployment, and tying yourself down so early to one woman only invites trouble. I am officially doing my duty as your wingman to remind you of that."

They walked out of the club and down the street until Brit stopped. "Hey, wait a minute, that was your chrono alarming and not your info-pad."

Tiv smiled. "It was, how'd you put it, for the good of the mission." Brit sulked all the way back to the base. When they were about to part company and retire to their respective quarters, Tiv said, "One day, you'll thank me for getting you out of there."

"Not likely." Brit slumped.

Tiv woke up with a headache. It was way too early to be awake. He'd just fallen asleep, or so it seemed. Last night was a blur, everything happening so fast. He was glad when he turned to roll out of bed, it was his own, and he was alone. He figured Brit would be angry with him, but at this point, he didn't much care. Maybe a hot shower would make him feel better, but he doubted it. His head still hurting as he toweled dry, Tiv dug into his med cabinet for a couple of anti-inflammatory pills. They burned his empty stomach, and he regretted, at least for the moment, taking them. He shaved, dressed, and headed for the mess hall. Early riser that he was, Tiv hoped to find the mess relatively quiet, with only a few staffers on duty. He wanted food, and he wanted quiet. He didn't much care what he ate; he just needed something. His first visit was to the canteen area for a large steaming cup of caffeine. After that went down, his head improved, but his stomach worsened. Maybe just a few slices of toast and hot cereal, although nothing looked particularly good. He deserved it, though. The way he treated Chelli sucked. It wasn't his fault. He explained to Brit he didn't particularly want any company but joined him, for the good of the mission. *Note to self: never double date with Brit.*

When Tiv dated, it was more civilized, no bar hookups with women he barely knew. Although his methods hadn't really worked out stellar for him either. Maybe he was overthinking the whole process. His head hurt again. His eyes burned. The gym was his answer for now, work out his body and let his brain rest for a while. That was what DeShay would do. Tiv wondered how DeShay was doing. He hadn't spoken with him since he left for Pareq. Last they'd talked, DeShay was back with his true love, Emmie. Tiv never met her but recalled DeShay's version of her. DeShay deserved love; maybe Tiv didn't. Maybe there was no right girl for him like there was Emmie for DeShay. Tiv had time to worry about all that later. Right now, he wanted to hit the heavy bag. Anyway, in two weeks, the base would be teeming with all sorts of people, and he would be too busy to worry about dating.

Tiv finished his circuit for the countless time. The heavy bag got boring, so he switched to his weight routine and got through the workout. He hated running, so interval training was a good way to get both cardio and heavy work. At the end of an hour, he cooled down on the exerbike and headed for his second shower of the day.

As Tiv went by his quarters to put on his uniform, he began to wonder about the status of the guys of his unit. With the curfew lifted, he was concerned Defender Company's ready status was other than green. He entered his unit's command office to find Brit Belk waiting for him. "You're up early," Tiv noticed.

"Thanks to you, I got sleep last night," Brit explained.

"Worried about everyone getting in last night?" Tiv swiveled the status monitor and typed a few keystrokes. "See, being in charge carries a lot of responsibility." Tiv squinted at the screen then, missing a smart comeback, eyed Brit, whose feet were shuffling. Upon seeing his glance, Brit bowed his head, averting the inquiry. "Who's not back?" Tiv turned back to the screen and scrolled the list. For a moment, Brit didn't answer. Tiv knew something was up. "Who?" Tiv asked again, hoping Brit would tell him before he figured it out.

"You're not going to like it," Brit said, kicking one boot on the other.

"I'm already not liking it." Tiv stood, towering over his junior officer. He could feel the hairs on the back of his neck bristling. "Who?" he asked again.

"Delan and Wilton and Paque," Brit murmured.

"Paque, he knows better," Tiv said.

"My guess, he's out getting the other two back. Paque only went off-base this morning."

Frustrated at having to pull every detail from Brit, Tiv asked, enunciating every word, "Where are they?"

"You don't really want to know," Brit stalled.

By now, Tiv was ignoring Brit and busy bringing up their coordinates. He activated the newly installed surveillance vid link and typed in a command. Paque and Wilton were in the same location. Tiv switched on the comm and beeped Paque. "Got one, Squad Leader, he's a little wasted but otherwise no worse for wear. Heading for the second one."

"Good job, Talman, I'll send your priman to pick up the second."

"What?" Brit questioned, putting an open hand to his chest. "Why me?"

"Did you recognize the address where Delan is? This will give you a chance to apologize not only for me but for Delan as well." Tiv frowned at him. "I'm also giving you the right as leader to decide on their punishment for not following protocol, even with a lifted curfew."

Brit stared at the address displayed on the monitor. "How do I know that address?" Tiv watched as realization hit him like a bucket of ice water. "That son of a... he stole my girl," Brit blurted out.

Tiv laughed at his friend's red face. "I might have Delan to thank for making the best out of a bad situation. So don't go too hard on him, or Wilton. Try and think about what I would do if I'd been in charge on this one."

"That certainly gives me a lot of options depending on who he hooked up with," Brit grumbled. "I'm taking the new two-seater, if that's okay with you." Not waiting for an answer, he bolted out the door.

While Brit was out retrieving Delan, Tiv headed to Overseer Company's command center. Tiv caught up with Damond Fiorat, who was still complaining about being swamped with data and reports. Handing Damond a memory stick, Tiv reported, "Surveillance links are up and running. Tested them this morning, and they work great. Now I was thinking"—Tiv scratched the side of his head—"I have some guys in my unit who, if you have another simple project for us, would like some more of your generosity."

Overseer Squad Leader Damond Fiorat eyed the ceiling then Tiv. "Well, if you're offering, there is another job I need done, but this one's not as high-profile."

"Let me guess," Tiv said, eyes narrowed and lips pursed, "you need us to muck out some stalls or clean latrines or collect, sort, and dispose of your garbage."

"Something like that." Fiorat smiled, probably for the first time in a week. "I need you to—" Fiorat was interrupted by Tiv's comm.

Tiv put up a finger. "Hold that thought." Stepping away from where Fiorat was sitting, Tiv took the call.

Opening the comm channel, Tiv overhead Paque say, "Did you have to puke in the vehicle?" Wilton groaned. "Couldn't you have leaned out the window? Geez, man, I'll never get this thing clean. If Squad Leader wasn't pissed off enough already, he's really stoked now."

The outer door was wooden and appeared to be of sturdy construction, almost as if it had been specially designed by a protecting father, thinking it would keep bad guys and potential suitors at bay. There was a heavy golden knocker that framed a military-grade peephole. Brit thought it resembled the front end of a sniper rifle site. Quickly calculating where the muzzle might discharge, he moved to the side nearest the knob. It was still early, and everyone inside was probably still sleeping.

A CHANGE IN TACTICS: MAIDEN VOYAGE

Three sharp raps were all it took. Not one but two bolts chugged, and the pins flipped back. The knob turned, and the door slid open. Aleece's robe was short, and Brit could follow her shapely leg from the footed slipper up to the lace panty she was careful not to hide. His eyes widened, and his jaw dropped as he passed the sash and followed the pathway through the soft fleshy mountains that peaked over the matching lace of her bodice. Now he knew what he had missed and what Delan conquered.

Aleece held his gaze. Her moist red lips began to form words. It took him a moment to register what she was actually saying. Delan's voice intruded his vision and invited him to come in. Rather presumptuous, seeing as this was not his place, and he was an interloper. Now Brit knew how Tiv must have felt when he retrieved him not so many years ago. Awkward was an understatement. Anger bubbled to the surface, but Brit found it hard to keep his teeth clenched when Aleece kissed his cheek and blew gently into his ear.

"I knew you'd be back," Aleece said, draping her arms over his shoulders. "You shouldn't have left the way you did." She moved to his lips, sucking on the lower one, lingering for a moment to gauge his response. Grabbing his hand, she said, "Come, I'll get you something to eat."

Brit Belk was tempted, really tempted to take her up on the offer but decided against it. He was sure Tiv was already pissed at him for screwing up the curfew thing, but having two guys AWOL was really bad. Tiv would never come out and say it, but Brit knew he was disappointed. And although his squad leader would likely chalk it up to a learning experience, never to be repeated, Tiv would never humiliate Brit. That was what Brit liked about Tiv's leadership. Everyone not only respected Tiv but also liked him, even if he was by the book. Tiv gave everyone an opportunity to shine, to flex their muscles, to try it their way. Leading by example, he was not an "I told you so" kind of leader. Then again, for his faith and trust, Tiv expected a lot. In fact, at one time, Belk had been a screwup like Delan, young and out of control, but Tiv saw something in him, some potential for greatness. Tiv brokered a deal with him. A deal resulting in Brit's rise through the ranks to the position of authority and respect he now enjoyed. Brit maintained his own style of leadership, though, and strict, by the book just didn't suit him. Tiv gave him rope as long as the job got done with no problems.

Brit tried to foster a similar relationship with the men underneath him, but he was no Tiv. Delan was a particular problem, and Belk so far had been unable to rein him in. Tiv warned him the task might be unobtainable. Not everyone fit into the same mold that Tiv, or even Belk created for their company. Brit was only human, and when Aleece came to the door, scantily clad and unsurprised by his visit, he wondered how much like Delan he really was.

The residence itself was typical, with the living room taking up the majority of the front area. The great room was flanked by a small kitchen. A dining table sat just outside on the carpeted floor. A stark white rail lined stairs that led to a loft and presumably the bedrooms. There was another room beyond the great room, possibly a den, maybe a bathroom or closet. *Maybe another bedroom? Wonder where Delan spent his night? Focus on situational awareness, bonehead, not who Delan screwed. Time for leader mode.*

The walls were decorated with artsy posters; things whose appeal was lost on him. Brit was a simple guy. His only wall decoration was a Dologos schedule and a funky picture of an animated vid superhero rescuing a buxom vixen in distress. Sure it was tacky, but his fantasy relationship with that girl started when he was a teenager, and she stuck with him all these years and hadn't complained once.

"That's my room," Aleece pointed upstairs. "Want to see it?"

Yes, yes I do, but I can't. See, I'm in uniform and much as I'd like to be out of it, I can't. Don't get me wrong, if I could, I'd enjoy seeing your bedroom from every conceivable angle. He looked her up and down again, regretting what he was about to say.

"I'll have to beg off for now," he apologized to Aleece. "Delan," he called.

"Sir," Delan responded from the couch in front of a small table. Chelli was sitting next to him, close enough for them to almost share a single cushion.

"I like this friend better." She smiled, pulling the corners of her robe together.

Delan turned to smile at her. He pointed to the kitchen. "Breakfast, sir, there's enough."

Brit had a choice. He could dress down Delan right then and there or not. He knew what Tiv would do, but what would he do? "Get your gear, we've got to go." Delan excused himself back to the bedroom, hopefully to retrieve the rest of his clothes.

"You're no fun." Aleece crept up from behind, wrapping her hands around his waist and nuzzling at his neck.

"Listen, ladies, I am really sorry for your inconvenience, but we are on a tight leash. Next liberty," he started until Delan entered the room. He was still a little disheveled, but at least all his clothes were back.

"Give me a minute, sir," Delan asked, grabbing Chelli's hand.

"I'll wait outside. If you're not out in two, I'm not responsible for what happens next." Aleece followed Brit to the doorway. He was about to go out the door when he realized she was still attached to him.

"Don't you like me anymore? You seemed to like me well enough last night," she complained.

"I do. I mean I have a job to do, and sometimes my happiness has to come second," Brit explained.

"That's not fair to me, is it." She sniffled. She wrapped her arms over his shoulders again. "Promise me you'll be back next time you're on liberty." She tried kissing him again.

He slowly peeled her arms from around his neck. "I do like you, Aleece. You're very pretty, and we had a good time last evening, but unfortunately, I'm…" He paused, what could he say next that would let her down easy but keep his opportunities open? "Right now, I'm in a lot of hot water with my commander, so leave may be a long time in coming, and I don't want to limit your options."

"You're so sweet," she whispered through tears. "One more kiss, please, so I have something to remember you by," she begged. He obliged her, hoping Delan would take a few more moments in the other room with Chelli.

Brit went out the door, which closed quickly behind him. He wanted to savor the moment for a few seconds, but Delan followed shortly. Delan winked at him. "We're more alike than you want to admit." Brit curled his lip. "She really does like you, you know. That's all she talked about, her soldier."

"Is that all, recruit?" Brit said, sending as much irritation through his eyes as he could. Brit gritted his teeth and cracked his knuckles, first his right then his left hand.

"No, they saw right through Squad Leader, though, all prim and proper and boring." Delan did like to hear himself talk, and he continued, much to Brit's annoyance. "Chelli was much happier with me than him. Finally, I'm better than Garnet at something." He chuckled.

Brit refused to justify his comment. "Our ride's over here." Brit pointed to the brand-new two-seater. Brit got in the driver's seat. "You get to ride shotgun." Delan took his place and strapped in for the short ride back to base. It was quiet for a long while until Belk informed him, "Garnet left it up to me to discipline you for this occurrence, what do you think I should do?" Brit stole that line from Tiv's playbook. He heard it more than once earlier in his career.

"Delan's back," Belk announced, entering Defender Company's command team room. His declaration, however, failed to make an impression, since the room was empty. He activated the display to try and locate Garnet. "Uh-oh." Not Good. Garnet's location was Base Commander Atacama's office. Meeting with the old man before the regularly scheduled afternoon update. Curious, Belk decided to wait. He hopped into Garnet's command chair, adjusted the console and monitors to fit his stature, wondering what it would be like to lead a squad of his own.

Belk knew he was lucky to have scored Tivon Garnet as his squad leader. Sure he was a hard ass, and the first few months under his command, Brit Belk was nose to the floor for more push-ups than he thought possible. Garnet rode him mercilessly. There was nothing he did that was good enough. Belk did appreciate how Garnet got the job done, on time, on budget, and with no indecision. Garnet was the model soldier; Belk wasn't. But he couldn't wash out; Garnet wouldn't let him. Belk stared back at the locator app. Garnet's blinking green dot was still in the old man's office. And although he appreciated his squad leader's personalized attention, if Belk was in charge, he'd make a few changes. He leaned back in the chair, putting his feet up on the desk. Soon, he was fast asleep.

Tiv was not particularly happy when he entered the team room an hour or so later. Dad, as Atacama was informally referred to, gave him an earful in regards to his wayward unit. Tiv opted not to apologize but assured the commander it would never happen again. Seeing his buddy, and second in command, snoring loudly, fast asleep in his chair with his boots up on his desk, did nothing to lighten Tiv's mood. He envied Brit Belk's ability to relax. If he wasn't so pissed off, the sight might have made him laugh. He went to the console, checked that all his troopers were in green status. Thankfully, everyone was accounted for. He was sure Belk would tell him later what went down at Chelli's apartment. Tiv thought about tying Belk's boot laces together, but right now, he didn't have time to give Belk grief. He was expected back in Atacama's office for the daily briefing. Tiv retrieved his status reports and headed out the door. He'd give Belk crap later for having his feet up on the desk.

Afternoon melded into evening, and Tiv was back in his command office. The first few minutes were spent realigning the stuff on his desk. Sometime during Commander's briefing, Belk left. The meeting with Atacama actually went better than expected, with Fiorat crediting Tiv's unit with getting their timeline back on track. That acknowledgement, for Tiv, was better than the drinks Fiorat promised his unit. Priman Denny Tross, Tiv's other second, knocked on the open door. Tiv motioned him in. Tross was the polar opposite of Belk. Married, with children, Tross was a gift for any squad leader. He was dedicated, practical, and his advice thoughtful and sound. Not the risk taker Belk was. Tiv could combine the two men's approaches and usually come up with the perfect plan for any situation. Tross promptly took a seat across from Tiv. "Heard you had an interesting encounter."

"Which?" Tiv questioned. "Lunch with Belk, double dating with Belk, or getting reamed out by Dad for Belk?"

"I missed the reaming out part of the story." Tross yawned. He usually held the fort at night for Defender and obviously had just gotten up.

"That's the part I haven't had the opportunity to share with Brit. He was asleep in my chair with his feet on my desk when I got back from Dad's office the first time."

There were boot steps in the hall, and Tross turned to see Belk coming in the door. "Well, here's the man of the hour," Tross joked. Belk slipped into the seat beside Tross. "You wanted to talk to us?" Tross asked, turning back toward Garnet.

"Yes," Tiv began. "Denny, get the door, if you don't mind."

"Uh-oh." Belk put his hands up in surrender. "I think we're in trouble now."

"We are? You maybe." Tross laughed. "Me, I've been a scout."

Garnet picked up an info-pad from his desk and handed it to Tross. Belk moved his chair closer and peered over his shoulder. "That's what we've got to get done in the next two weeks before everyone else shows up."

"No problem," Tross said. Tross glared at Belk. "What do you think?"

"Doable," Belk confirmed.

Tiv seemed satisfied with their response. "That's what I told Dad." Belk got up to leave when Tiv motioned him back. "Oh, and one more thing." Belk fidgeted in his chair, and his eyes narrowed. "Dad laid down his own curfew on us." Tiv paused and then continued, "We all, including me, have to be tucked in by 2100, no exceptions."

Tross looked at Belk. "Way to go, man."

"Fortunately, we won't need to be going anywhere since we pulled guard duty for the next two weeks."

"Hey, that's Overseer's job," Tross pointed out.

"It was until we screwed up. Dad was kind enough not to share our punishment with our brother company. So as far as everyone else is concerned, we volunteered to help out Overseer. I suspect you two will keep it to yourselves as well." Tiv narrowed his eyes and stared at Belk.

A CHANGE IN TACTICS: MAIDEN VOYAGE

"Sir," Tross responded, joining Garnet's stare at Belk. He whispered, "Last time I let Garnet give you any authority." Tiv snickered as he watched Belk try to wriggle out of the accusation.

"Dismissed," Tiv said. He watched as the two continued bickering, their voices trailing off as they went down the hall. Adding guard duty to their already tight schedule didn't help, but Tiv was confident he and his unit would get the job done without any further missteps.

Two weeks passed without event. Garnet and Defender accomplished all their tasks, and if the information presented at the commander's final premission briefing was accurate, the Tal-Kari Pareqi Base was fully operational.

"The first wave of civvies and softies will be here tomorrow," Belk told Garnet and Tross. "I hope they're ready to behave. I hate having to drag their butts out of trouble."

Tiv laughed. "You've certainly had enough practice being on the other end of that."

"Look, man, I've been in every night by 2100," Belk retorted.

"Unless you count—" Tross started but was stifled by Belk's glare.

"I don't want to know." Tiv scrolled through his info-pad. "I'm proud of you guys. Excellent work." Tiv closed the info-pad, pushed away from his desk, leaned back in his chair, and interlaced his hands behind his head. This was the calm before the storm.

"How about a drink to celebrate?" Belk asked.

"Sounds good to me," Tross agreed.

CHAPTER 24

Leba sat on the floor amidst neat piles of stuff, clothes, shoes, toiletries all destined to be squeezed into one standard-issue duffel and join her adventure. Maybe if she vacuum-packed, everything would fit. Organizing her life into piles left no countertop or seat cushion or floor space available for anything else. But what was essential? Surveying the assembly, everything did. DeShay told her it only took him ten minutes to pack. Clean socks, shorts, a few uniforms, and the boots on his feet, what else was there? All the toiletries came standard and prepackaged. Men had it so much easier. Despite the same initial starting points, they all ended up wonderfully different. Women seemed to need an inordinate amount of stuff, and all to try and achieve the same look. Despite lessons, a look Leba could never seem to replicate.

Loud banging at the door forced her from the floor and the protective fortress of columns she arranged. Leba glanced at the wall calendar, the one with the giant red circle identifying launch day. She didn't have anything scribbled for this evening. It was nearly 1900, and this was supposed to be her quiet time, the "What the hell am I getting myself into" reflection time. Recognizing DeShay's shout, a smile blossomed on her face, and she deftly negotiated the castle keeps to activate the door release.

"What is all this stuff?" DeShay asked as he snaked his way to the table, shoved aside a few of the stacks, and plopped down a large grease-stained satchel of food in the middle of the table.

"Hey, watch it." Leba caught one stack as it leaned toward the floor. "It took me a long time to get all this straight." Anster and

Grizzer, following in DeShay's footpath, made it safely past the piles as well.

"What part of essential don't you understand, girl?" DeShay said as he handed both men a pile off the table. Leba quickly moved to intercept and scooped up her stuff, replacing them on the floor of her kitchen. "Cathen is never going to let you take 90 percent of this stuff." He surveyed the nearest pile and began to lift up an item. "What is this anyway?"

She slapped his hand away. "Something essential."

"As I see it, eating is essential, sleeping is essential, and—"

Leba put her hands over her ears. "I don't want to know."

"Cathen's got his hands full with little Ms. Yertha." Grizzer picked up a textbook off a nearby floor pile and tested its weight in his hand. "This would make one hell of a weapon." Leba outstretched a hand, and Grizzer looked at her, then at the text, then back at her. He tossed it to her. It was heavy, and she needed two hands to secure it before it crashed and started the dominos falling. "My bad."

"Yeah," Anster chimed in. "He didn't even notice you got us all assigned to your shift." He patted her on the arm. "Of course, he'll never notice your three bags full."

"Three?" DeShay rubbed the lower end of his face. "More like one hundred and three."

"Stop it," Leba said, gathering up a few more piles before her friends caused further destruction.

How Tiner and his friends got anything done, Leba couldn't figure out. Dinners out, sporting events, vids, cards were the norm every day. They played as hard as they worked. Now as their adopted mascot, she was expected to join in. Leba never really had much of a social life. Work monopolized the majority of her time, and when she finished her shift, showered, ate, reviewed her correspondences, caught up on the news, it was time for bed if she expected to function in the morning. Weekends were never exciting and mainly involved catching up on the life scut, laundry, food shopping, cleaning she couldn't get done during the week. The addition of at least an hour of training or self-defense class every night carved out a significant chunk of her time but was a necessity that needed consistency.

The tabletop fortress now leveled, DeShay ripped the meal bag open and set out four enormously calorie-laden burgers and a mountain of crisps. Using his foot, he slid a carpet pile away and looked for a chair. By this time, Anster and Grizzer were sitting on the piles covering their chairs. Arms crossed, Leba frowned at him. Looking up with a full-toothed grin, it was hard to resist DeShay's engaging smile and handsome good looks. DeShay offered, "If you take a little break from your project here and eat with us, when we're done, the boys and I will pack for you." Both Anster and Grizzer pulled back their shirtsleeves and brandished their cannons. Their biceps were huge and each adorned with intricate illustrations representative of important events in their lives. In their culture, the more artwork you had, the greater your accomplishments.

"Thanks, I think." Leba found it hard to ignore DeShay's charm. As the oldest of three children, she liked being the little sister for a change.

"Knew you would forget about dinner." DeShay pushed a burger toward her. "And it always helps to have company to get the yipes out before a first deployment." He took a big bite of his sandwich then napkined his face. "You were smart to get us all assigned to your shift."

"That way, we can set things up our way before anyone else has a chance to screw it up," Anster added.

Grizzer, with a mouth full of food, continued, "I think we got a good set of nurses too."

"When I got the terrific trio, I'm not sure I need anyone else." Leba opened her burger to see the works. *Won't be good for my flight tomorrow.* She replaced the bun. *Tough call. I do want to be one of them. Can't wimp out now.*

"Watch what you say, Doc, you know how moody nurses can be," Grizzer advised.

"I was just kidding," Leba apologized. She forgot about Emmie, but DeShay hadn't. Setting his burger down, he brushed off his hands, got up, and headed for the kitchen. His head disappeared when reached into the cold box.

"He's just having a hard time," Grizzer continued. "Don't pay him any attention. He's still pissed about Hodd."

"I heard that," DeShay echoed from inside the fridge. "Don't you have anything to drink besides water?"

"Shut up, Tiner, and leave the girl alone," Anster chided him. It was hard for Leba to understand DeShay's continued pining over Emmie. Couldn't he see how selfish she'd been? DeShay deserved better.

"What, now the three of you are ganging up on me?" DeShay, his arms laden with four water bottles, returned to the dining area.

"I believe they call this an intervention," Leba started.

"I'm fine," DeShay explained. "It's done and over, and I've moved on. You people need to get over it." Three sets of eyes stared at him. "What?" he blurted out and dropped the drinks onto the table.

"We are just concerned about you," Leba said softly, putting a hand on his arm. "We're your friends, and we love you."

"I'm not sure I'm willing to go that far." Grizzer laughed. "Tiner, you really aren't my type. But I feel for you, my friend, really, I do," he said, his fists to his eyes, winding dramatically.

DeShay balled up his greasy napkin and launched it at Grizzer's head.

"Enough already," Anster pleaded. "If you tell us you're okay, then you're okay, and we'll back off."

"I'm okay," DeShay shot back. "But thanks."

"Then we won't discuss it anymore," Anster promised. Everyone shook their head. Leba wasn't sure about it. Keeping his feelings about Emmie bottled up wasn't healthy. She never realized how vulnerable he was. But what could she do? Thereafter, nothing was said, but the sounds of chewing and drinking permeated the room.

For a long while after DeShay, Anster, and Grizzer left, Leba was still unable to get to sleep. She tried reading, watching part of the Dologos game, listening to a local Pareqi broadcast, but nothing was helping. She was so anxious about starting this new phase in her life, this expeditionary mission with all its unknowns. Despite its attractions, starting something new was very stressful, especially for a control-oriented person like Leba. After the initial apprehension, there was a phase of excitement, which slowly eroded into tediousness, and finally boredom. This time, things would be different, and Leba promised herself she would try new things, maybe take a few risks. She chewed the corner of her lower lip.

This was her choice to leave her comfort zone and venture to parts unknown. Maybe she would meet someone new, someone handsome, someone exciting. Already making new friends was important, but she wanted more; she wanted a real relationship. She tried to imagine the scenario, how they'd meet, what her mystery lover might look like, but that never worked. Sendra and her new boyfriend, Damond, were in the early stages of their relationship. What fun. They planned secret dates, tried to surprise each other, did cute little things to show their affection for each other. Since Damond came into her life, Sendra was always smiling. Nothing, not even the clinic director's visits, bothered her anymore. Jealous of how comfortable Sendra was with men, Leba was always awkward with guys she found attractive. They seemed to like her well enough as a friend, but to expect anything further, well, that was different. Like DeShay. *I bet he never thought anything about me other than being his pet project.*

Leba Brader was the one everyone came to to discuss their relationships. Even her guy friends would ask her for advice on how to deal with their girlfriends. Maybe DeShay was right; maybe she did have a hard time accepting her feminine side. She liked being rough and tumble, felt uncomfortable in a frilly dress, and avoided makeup like the plague. She wished she was more like Sendra, who could turn on sex appeal like turning on a light. Men were attracted to Sendra for different reasons than they were attracted to her. *There must be a man out there who will like me for who I am.* Was that the real reason she was embarking on this mission? How stupid was she to give up safety and security? Tossing and turning, Leba finally drifted off to sleep.

Red circle day. The military hangar bay was a constant chaos of activity that seemed perfectly choreographed. Technicians negotiated pressurized fuel lines with ease, cables crisscrossed the floors and ceilings. Extremely territorial and constantly moving, intensely focused on their mission at hand, ground crews scurried around, their headsets reminding Leba of the rounded ears of the mouse-like Sorex. The ancient volcanoes that once blasted smoke and ash onto this barren moon-world left fertile soil, and the quiescent caldera was carpeted with a lush green forest. And unlike their animal brethren, these natives in their fluorescent jackets were busy directing traffic, keeping both travelers and transports from colliding.

A giant vid board displayed arrivals and departures. Heavily armed security troopers stood sentry, reminding everyone trouble would not be tolerated. Credentials and orders were checked, retinas scanned, palms digitally printed, everything needed to be exact. Fuels and lubricants combined, making thick emissions and exhaust fumes choke the air. Travelers moved single file along a designated route. Noises of incoming and outgoing flights dopplered, while idling vehicles whirred or roared as they waited.

Without special permission, visitors were relegated to the overhead observation gallery, a multipaned transparent enclosure covering the near wall. Banks of light blinked a rainbow of colors, reflecting off many of the ship's surfaces. Now and again, a warning beacon would blare, and an intensely bright strobe would spotlight the vehicle next to take or leave the stage.

As they approached, Leba shivered, noting the designation emblazoned on the side of their shuttle: TKM-77. Similar in configuration to the simulation shuttle except larger, this ride could hold their entire unit. Hoping its fate would be different, Leba felt a nagging sensation. That feeling of impending doom tickled the back of her neck. Reaching behind, she grabbed DeShay's hand and squeezed.

He cocked his head. "What was that for?"

She smiled. "Just couldn't help myself." Momentarily searching his face, she pumped his hand again. "Thanks for getting me this far."

"Stop it, you're embarrassing me." He grinned. "And people are going to talk." Placing his other hand on top of hers. "Aw, hell, let 'em talk." He pulled her in, enveloping her in a big hug. Leaning in, he put his mouth to her ear and whispered, "I wouldn't have it any other way. Even if you can't dress right."

She pushed him away. "There's no serious with you, is there?"

"Nope, and just wait, by the time this deployment is over, you're going to be just as relaxed as I am." His teasing was merciless, but she knew he was still smarting from his breakup with Emmie Hodd, and any show of real emotion would probably have him sulking or worse. For now, she would put up with his mockery, be a friend, and when he was ready to talk, she'd be there.

"Girl, do you clean up well or what?" DeShay's gaze started at her newly polished black tactical boots. "You remembered to change the laces, although pink would have probably done your love life better."

She slapped him. "Stop looking at me."

"See, you've gotta learn to handle the attention and adulation better. Like I do." He waved at some fellow travelers. "Ladies." Moving closer, he tugged at her shirt, pulling it partway out from her trousers.

"Hey, what are you doing?" She slapped his hand again. "Leave me alone."

"Trying to loosen you up some." Smoothing the front placard of his own shirt, DeShay demonstrated. "See how it covers the top half of my belt, much less stiff. You have to give folks the impression you're other than an ice princess."

Rising on tiptoes, she tilted her head, wiggled her hips, and pranced forward a few steps. "This better?" From her new vantage point, the few inches gave her height enough to look past DeShay and see JT making his dramatic farewell to Nilsa. JT's ride was leaving well before mission specialist Nilsa's, and he seemed quite pleased she saw fit to get up early and see him off before they deployed on separate shuttles. JT told Leba his last-minute arrangement for Nilsa to accompany him on the mission cost him a few well-earned favors but was well worth the effort. Despite the fact her quarters would be on opposite side of the base, he was confident they could spend a lot of time together.

A CHANGE IN TACTICS: MAIDEN VOYAGE

To the far side and certainly to what he believed was out of range, Luth Cathen made a similar display. Mally Yertha was pinned up against a wall, and Cathen was attempting mouth-to-mouth resuscitation. Unable to maintain her lofty stride, Leba plopped back onto the soles of her feet.

"You know, in a dress, you might be passable." DeShay tousled her hair. "We should get this cut shorter too."

Leba scratched the side of her head. "Not only are you my fashionista but now my beautician." *Well, two can play this game, Mr. DeShay Tiner. If JT can do it and Luth can too, well, so can I.* She puckered her lips and planted a big noisy kiss on the side of his face.

"Oops, I guess that means you'll have to stay since that was a good-bye kiss." She winked at him then ran for the boarding ramp.

Leba hated long shuttle trips. There was no other way to get to the new base on Pareq. The military transport she was on was fast but not fast enough for her liking. She watched the clouds hovering over Luac get thinner and thinner as the shuttle left the troposphere for the blackness of space. She checked her seat restraints for the millionth time until DeShay grabbed her hand. "Stop that, you're embarrassing me, girl."

"Sorry, I don't like long flights."

"I don't get it," he mused. "You must be adopted or something. Your parents are two of the most decorated pilots the Tal-Kari ever produced, and their eldest daughter is scared of flying."

"I'm not scared," Leba said, rubbing her nose. "It's just that my stomach does flip-flops and..." She paused. "Never mind," she stroked the sides of her neck and rubbed her nose again. "Pay attention to yourself and leave me alone." She shut eyes, folded her arms across her chest, and leaned back in her chair.

"Did you know this newly configured base has single-soldier housing? That means, and I know this is a foreign concept for you civilian types, you don't have to bunk with a roommate. Although I was kinda hoping that we'd be roomies. That way, my life would be so much easier 'cause you could keep all our stuff tidy and organized in one hundred and three stacks. There'd be dinner on the table every night, and all my stuff would be spit-shined and polished."

DeShay leaned over and, with one finger, poked her nearest shoulder. Leba purposely didn't acknowledge him. "Guess she's done." Leba heard his seat recline. "Might as well get some shut-eye. This promises to be a long and boring flight." Adjusting to get comfortable, DeShay knocked into her a few times.

Anster and Grizzer sat in the row behind, playing cards and making a lot of noise. "Hey." DeShay pushed his head into the opening between the seats. "Keep it down. Some of us are trying to sleep."

That was the last thing Leba heard until DeShay poked her. Eyes still closed, Leba rolled to face him and, adjusting to the new position, tried to sleep on her side, but he poked her harder the second time. "What gives?"

"Getting ready to land in a few minutes. We're on final approach," DeShay said.

Leba's eyes snapped open, and she stiffened in her seat. "But that's the worst part. Couldn't let me sleep through the worse part?"

"And let you miss all the fun? Girl, you know me better than that." DeShay grinned. "Now get the seat back upright and check your straps. It's time to secure for landing." Leba did as she was told. She shut her eyes tight and grabbed the seat rails so firmly her fingers turned white. There were a number of shuttles waiting both ahead of and behind the medical shuttle, so it circled the landing area three or four times before it was authorized to make its final approach. The banking turns did not help Leba's constitution.

DeShay elbowed her. "Watch." He turned her head to make her look out the viewport. "From the upper atmosphere, our new base is virtually undetectable. No footprint or electromagnetic signature."

Through squinted eyes, Leba peered out, but there was no void where the base was supposed to be, only a continuation of the surrounding landscape. "Great, it looks like a grove of trees." As their shuttle approached, the Tal-Kari base slowly took shape. Her Uncle Trent showed her the artist's rendition of this state-of-the-art facility when she was making her decision about going. When viewed with the naked eye, a twelve-pointed tiered star fortress spiraling in a counterclockwise direction came into view. There were negatively reflective surfaces invisible from altitude. It was covered in absorbent negative index metamaterials that further cloaked its presence. This base was one of the attractions she was looking forward to on this mission.

"The central core is topped by the only planar surface, reserved for the newly minted jetcopters to arrive and depart." DeShay read from the mission brochure. "A feat of architectural genius."

"It's a dodecagrammic antiprism," Leba quoted from memory. It was extraordinary to look at, but after staring out sideways for so long, by the time they touched down, Leba was grateful she'd forgone the in-flight meal. The burger from last night was already doing a number on her.

Cathen's voice boomed over the passenger compartment intercom. "Grab your gear and meet me at Incom Three." One of the conditions the government of Pareq required before agreeing to the Tal-Kari base was all new arrivals be processed and thoroughly vetted. Everyone needed to be imaged, examined, and approved before being issued an official alien identification card and allowed to roam the countryside.

When all the med personnel completed the intake process, Cathen instructed them to pick up their gear at the other end of the terminal. After intense Pareqi scrutiny, forty identical duffels sat idly on a revolving carousel. "There's yours." DeShay pointed to a duffel. Earlier, he showed her how to mark her bag so it would stand out from the rest. "See, the one with the pretty pink ribbon."

"No, that's yours." Leba laughed. "Mine's over there with the blue string."

DeShay pulled the bag with the pink marker off the turnstile and unfastened the closure. Anster came over to where DeShay was kneeling by his bag. "Pink, it goes nicely with the color of your face right about now."

DeShay ignored him, hoisted the bag over his shoulder, and stood up. "Unlike you, I'm comfortable with my feminine side," he said, staring at Leba.

"And what's that supposed to mean?" she asked, slinging her own bag over her shoulder.

"Leave the girl alone," Vic Uribos leaped to her defense.

The two men squared off with Leba stuck in the middle. "It's okay, Vic, he's just teasing, but thanks." Vic backed down and put out a hand.

DeShay shook his hand and acknowledged, "I'm glad my girl here made some friends from her time in the cold box."

"It's all good," Vic replied and rejoined Riki at the carousel, who was still waiting her bag's arrival.

Once their personal gear was stowed in their assigned quarters, Cathen made the medical unit unload their supply shuttle. Their task over the next few days was to set up the mini hospital and decide how their duty shifts would look. Cathen wanted them to form three shifts. Two shifts would share a complete day cycle, with one group working the morning and the other working the evening. The third shift would be off. No one need work more than four days or four nights in a row. To Leba, this felt like she was back in medical training. The clinic she worked operated during the day with a light on-call schedule. There were calls, but true emergencies were few and far between. On a fully deployed mission, with shifts of soldiers and civilians working day and night, anything could happen at any time.

The med squad was also responsible for updating Pareq's health services as part of the SHARE program. Cathen constantly reminded everyone if this state-of-the-art medical center performed well, it would become the standard for other off-world deployments. "So don't screw it up, people." Despite the resources the Tal-Kari offered to a host, there was still a hefty price to pay. For opening the base on Pareq, her father told her the bottom-line price couldn't fit on one page. Leba thought it funny that Pareq gained so much more than the Tal-Kari did but seemed to feel they got the short end of the arrangement. No matter, she loved to teach and signed up right away to do some SHARE programs for the local schools. She couldn't wait to share her knowledge of health and nutrition with the children of Pareq.

"Where are you going?" Priman Brit Belk asked Delan as the junior man headed toward the transportation depot.

"Want to check out the new arrivals with me?" Delan asked. "Or are you too involved with Aleece to care?" Belk stared at him. "Don't think I don't know you sneak out to hook up with her."

Delan was just pulling his chain. Belk was very careful to cover his tracks and not be out after 2100 curfew. "I've got things to do. I don't have time to be screwing around. You should be doing something useful, like realigning the transflux acclimator on the travel sled."

"I've got time, and besides, Garnet doesn't need it fixed until 1600. It's only 1200 now."

"That's because he knows it'll take you that long to fix it," Belk retorted. Delan brushed him off and started to walk away. "And stay out of my private business." Delan missed the last part of Belk's warning and continued walking away. "Son of a," Belk cursed. How'd he know? Belk realized if Delan was seeing Chelli, and Aleece told Chelli about their late-night hookups, and Garnet was going to kill him if he ever found out. Losing his squad leader's trust was something he didn't ever want to do. No girl was that important, at least this girl wasn't, to lose everything he achieved. Belk went back to his quarters and typed out a text. Hesitating for only a moment, he depressed the send key.

"It's all good so far," Belk reported to Garnet. "No shuttle incidents, and everyone seems to be finding their designated areas without trouble."

"It's not going to get interesting for a few more hours. Once everyone's checked in and is allowed to roam free, then the fun starts." Tiv checked his chrono. "Dad's supposed to have a meeting with all the squad leaders in two, so you and Tross are going to need to be here, monitoring the situation."

"Don't worry," Brit Belk assured his squad leader, "my calendar's free for the next few months at least."

Tiv looked away from him, staring into the distance. "You and Aleece break it off?"

Belk thought for a moment, searching for the right words. "Too much of a drain on my resources." *Now I know how you feel. With all your responsibilities, it can't be easy to keep a relationship healthy.*

Belk knew Garnet had assigned him as the base's point person for the Pareqi chief diplomat, Ambassador Wiljon Sohut, as a veiled punishment for the curfew incident. Garnet explained the experience would be important for Belk if he expected to move higher in rank. The higher you rose in the military, the more politics crept in and colored the situation. Belk possessed no stomach for diplomacy; he was a point-and-shoot kind of guy rather than a "Let's see how we can work this out" kind of guy. That's why he fit in so well with Defender Company. By the time they got their orders, time for talk was over, and problems needed urgent solutions.

The SHARE program was another way the Tal-Kari promised to reimburse the Pareqi for their hospitality. As the liaison, Belk got stuck having to arrange school visits from some of their soldiers. At first, Belk thought it might do Delan some good to have him speak to the kids, but then changed his mind. Belk imagined Delan painting some gory picture of death and destruction. The public relations nightmare would not soon be forgotten. When Belk was approached by the Pareqi liaison, he begged off and offered his squad leader's services without hesitation. Tiv, on the other hand, with two nephews he adored, would be the perfect representative. He knew how to deal with kids, taking the young boys camping and actually enjoying it. Besides, Belk knew Garnet could never say no when kids were involved. All he needed was the right moment to break it to his squad leader, and now wasn't it.

CHAPTER 25

While his unit was working hard, Cathen was enjoying life. Quite pleased with his last-minute brainstorm, Mally Yertha, no longer assigned to his command, was free to be his open consort. Having arranged for her to be part of Atacama's private entourage also gave him unprecedented access to the commander's private doings. Always needing to be one step ahead, information and contacts were key. It didn't hurt his newest contact was young, pretty, fairly naive, and lived for his every whim.

Running a medical outpost was certainly less stressful than trying to keep a bunch of grunts in order. These people under his leadership were intelligent professionals who were good at what they did and were scared of making him angry. When Base Commander Chalco Atacama visited, inspecting his unit, Cathen received his highest praise. In fact, Atacama invited him personally to join a select few for drinks at a private welcoming session. Atacama was pleased to find out one of his personal staffers, Mally Yertha, would be accompanying Cathen for the diplomatic meet and greet.

Cathen arrived in his dress uniform with Mally on his sleeve. He was not announced but just ushered in with the rest. The select few turned out to be all the current on-base squad leaders. When the Pareqi liaison took the podium, Cathen downed a shot of thick orange liquor. Ambassador Wiljon Sohut was dressed in formal Pareqi garments, a floor-length tunic with a traditional long sword sheathed at his sashed waist. Slightly behind and to his left was an exquisite woman, dressed in shimmering gold. The diaphanous cloth highlighted her delicate features, leaving no mystery as to why she was his consort. The man's voice was deep but pleasant and melodic with a subtle reverberation. He recounted Pareq's long and glorious history, their triumphs and achievements, and their hopes for the future. Sohut spoke of the beginning of a long friendship between the people of Pareq and the Tal-Kari. By the time the ambassador finished his dissertation, Cathen finished his second shot and was searching for a third. *What a waste of time.* Finding the right bottle, Cathen poured a double shot and swallowed it in one gulp.

Commander Atacama tugged at his multidecorated uniform jacket, smoothed his moustache with thumb and forefinger, then stepped to the platform. "I want to begin by thanking the Pareqi government and its citizenry for their most generous hospitality. This is the start of a unique partnership, setting the standard for many years to come." He looked to the ambassador and began to applaud, his meaty hands clapping loudly. Those assembled picked up the rhythmic ovation. Ambassador Sohut, his lips pursed, nodded. When the ovation tapered off, Atacama invited, "Everyone, please enjoy the rest of the evening."

Despite Cathen's attempts to persuade Mally to leave the party early, she begged him to stay, citing Atacama's insistence she personally see to it everyone, including herself, had a good time. "How would it look if we left now?" she asked. Cathen didn't answer but leered at her. The intoxicant made him too tired to argue. Besides, keeping up appearances in front of the base commander could only bolster his career opportunities. "I promise if you stay, I'll make it up to you later." Mally smiled at him, running her tongue under her top lip.

"Promise," Cathen slurred and stroked her shoulder.

"Promise," she reiterated, mouthing a kiss. "Now eat some food before you get sick." She pointed him in the direction of the buffet.

"Hey, Luth, when did you and your softies arrive?" Striker Company squad leader Tem Myaronitz greeted him with a slap to the back. Cathen ignored him and proceeded to shovel stuff onto a plate as he walked down the length of the table. "Hey, Luth, I'm talking to you." Cathen was not in the mood for any ribbing from Tem and whirled around to meet him face-to-face. "Geez, man, you could start a fire with that breath." Tem Myaronitz was at least a head taller than Cathen, and his chest certainly bore more ribbons and medals. The bigger man's bushy eyebrows met in the center as he stared at Cathen.

Eyeing the woman on Myaronitz's arm, Cathen asked, "What's your problem, Tem, you and your goons got nothing better to do than hook up with the help?"

Myaronitz slammed his drink down, the contents sloshing onto the buffet. "You're lucky I'm a gentleman, Cathen, or I'd deck you right here and now."

"You and what army? The sorry bunch of lowlifes you call a squad?"

Turning to face his date, Tem said, "Excuse me for a moment. This officer and I have something to discuss. Why don't you get us a table." The woman nodded curtly and walked away. "That was uncalled for, you stupid son of a..." Tem turned back to Cathen but paused when he saw the commander coming over toward them.

"Gentleman, this is Ambassador Sohut." Atacama was such a blowhard, trying to impress this backward diplomat. "Wiljon, I would like you to meet two of our finest squad leaders, Tem Myaronitz of Striker Company and Luth Cathen of our Medical Company."

Sohut steepled his fingers and brought them to his mouth. After an uncomfortable pause, he said, "Gentlemen, I hope my staff will have a chance to meet with you and your people personally for an exchange of ideas and technologies." Sohut dropped his hands to his sides, resting the right on the pommel of the ceremonial weapon. He regarded each man separately and then looked past them.

Trying to reengage his attention, Cathen spoke up first. "It is an honor to meet you, sir. My unit has been already assigned to participate in the SHARE program, and we expect it to be a great success."

"Yes, yes," Sohut acknowledged, waving his left hand in the air.

Spotting another of his senior staffers, Atacama put out a hand to lead the ambassador away, and the two older men exited the buffet, allowing Cathen and Myaronitz to pick up their conversation where it left off. Myaronitz grabbed his upper arm and squeezed. "This isn't over, Cathen."

"Looks like your local found you a table, better not keep her waiting." Cathen pointed and wriggled free as he accepted Mally's arm in its place.

"Hi." Mally beamed. "You must be Striker Squad Leader Myaronitz. I've heard so much about you."

Myaronitz inclined his head and smiled. "I haven't had the pleasure, ma'am." He looked her up and down. Putting out his hand, he gently took hers.

"Mally Yertha," she introduced herself when Cathen didn't. "I'm assigned to Dr. Scoby, Commander Atacama's personal physician."

Cathen gritted his teeth. He hated how Mally was pleasant to everyone. *You'll never have the pleasure, Tem.* Cathen put an arm over Mally's shoulder, bringing her close. *Stick with the locals, pal.* Tem continued to ogle Mally. "Hey, Nitz, I think your friend is getting impatient. Maybe you ought to join her. Don't want good money to go to waste." Cathen moved his head in the direction of the seating area, hoping Myaronitz would take the hint.

"Okay, okay," he said, staring at Cathen. In something just above a whisper, he leaned toward Mally. "If you ever get tired of him, look me up. I know how he can be. Especially when he's in one of his moods."

That made Mally giggle. "Don't be silly, Luth is always wonderful."

"Your loss, sweetheart," he said in parting and headed away from the couple.

"Don't be mad," Mally looked up at him, leaned in, and imprinted her hand on his chest. "He was just teasing."

"Can we go now?" Cathen implored her.

"Only if you make it up to me later." She smiled and ran her index finger along his face.

Explorer Company squad leader Antog Hirousey stood by as the chief Tal-Kari scientist was explaining in excruciating detail the purpose of the expeditionary mission. Atacama was bored as well but was politically savvy enough not to show it the way Hirousey was. "Should we put Antog out of his misery?" Belk asked Garnet. Belk was one of the only junior officers invited to the welcoming party, and that was only because he was assigned to Sohut for the beginning of the mission.

"I'll go get Antog, but you'll have to take his place," Garnet said.

"I've changed my mind." Belk put a hand to his forehead and shaded his eyes. "Let Antog suffer through it. It's the current story of my life. All that scientific jargon gives me a headache."

"Everything gives you a headache unless it's in a dress," Garnet observed. Pulling out an info-pad, he typed some text. "Come on, I have an idea."

"What are you doing?" Belk said, looking over his shoulder.

"Helping your career." Garnet handed the info-pad to Belk. "Give this to Dad."

"You're kidding, aren't you?" Belk questioned. Garnet crossed his arm over his chest and motioned with a hand for Belk to join Atacama's party. "This better not backfire," Belk warned.

Garnet watched as Belk tapped Atacama on his shoulder. The older man turned and accepted the info-pad. After tapping the screen, Atacama bowed his head to the ambassador and strode briskly to where Garnet was standing. "Priman Belk and I thought it was high time Defender Company came to your rescue, sir." Garnet exchanged the info-pad in Atacama's hand for a cuvette filled with ebony liquid.

Holding the drink between his thumb and forefinger, Atacama considered the shot. After he threw back, his face screwed up momentarily followed by boisterous laughter, then just as quickly resumed his diplomatic decorum. "Brilliant, Garnet, just brilliant." He slapped the younger man on the back. "And you too, Belk, excellent timing." Atacama held up the glass, eyeing the bottle Garnet poured from. "Good year," he said, accepting the refill. "I get so tired of those windbags touting the merits of this and that. Give me a good firefight any day." His voice trailed off, and he took another mouthful. "Well, boys, unfortunately I can't stay here all day. Duty calls." He handed the cuvette to Belk and turned to retake the ambassador's side. Stopping and pivoting, he returned his gaze toward his junior officers. "Garnet, why don't you and Belk take the rest of the party off and go check out something that needs checking."

"Yes, sir," Garnet and Belk said in unison, saluting their commanding officer and then leaving the room.

"How did you know Dad wanted you to give him a break?" Belk asked.

"If you hang around Dad long enough, you'd see when he gets bored, he starts to scuff one boot on the next. It drives him crazy because he's a stickler for perfectly polished boots. Once he screws up his shine he gets annoyed and then takes it out on whomever is giving report. That was why he likes us to give concise and compact briefings." Garnet waited for a moment and then continued, "So when you report to Dad about your time with Sohut, make it short and sweet, or you'll be sorry."

"Thanks for the tip, man," Belk said as the two men continued down the hallway.

Unable to escape unnoticed, Cathen was back at the bar, talking with Hirousey as Mally attended to the commander. He watched Garnet and Belk leave the room and wondered what the info-pad said. "Antog, any idea what's going on here?" Once the Pareq Base was up and running, the scientific outpost on Vedax needed to be completed, staffed, and maintained, and there were way too many people deployed.

Explorer Company and its squad leader, Antog Hirousey, were charged with the logistics pertaining to the Vedax deployment's scientific operations. Cathen hoped he could glean new insight by tapping Hirousey. "As far as I'm concerned, this is a glorified baby-sitting mission. I like it better we get charged with first contact missions, colonizing new moons or planets." Cathen poured Hirousey two fingers of Red Devil and ignited the drink. "The worse part of this deployment is the cold." Hirousey blew out the flames and waved off Cathen's offer of ice for his drink. "Give me a desert, hot and sandy, over a frigid ball of ice any day."

"I thought our chief scientist would never shut up," Cathen said as he fixed himself another orange bomb.

"I am impressed with how much Sohut knows about Vedax's geophysiochemistry. Usually a diplomat takes a more hands-off approach." Hirousey took a mouthful of his drink, swallowed, and winced as it went down. "His questions were on point and probing. The ambassador seems to know more about Vedax and its resource potential than our chief scientist does."

Hirousey, a veteran of many expeditionary ventures, should have been read in on why the Tal-Kari deployed such a major force to study such an unassuming ice moon. But he too seemed to be in the dark. Why did the Tal-Kari high council tell Cathen to run such a specific and contrived cold box scenario? Slowly, a thought was beginning to coalesce in Cathen's mind and he was going to ask a question when a buxom server brought over a tray of finger foods. Cathen stabbed a chunk of green gelaphus meat, dipped it in the accompanying mustard sauce, and popped it into his mouth. Not bad for catered food. He hadn't realized how hungry he was. He stabbed two or three more pieces of meat, slathered them with sauce, and forgot his question.

"Place got a lot more crowded since all the civvies moved in," Brit Belk commented as they passed a number of people on the way to Defender Company's team room.

"I'm hungry, want to grab some dinner?" Tiv Garnet asked, his stomach beginning to rumble.

"Commissary food?" Brit frowned. "No." A big grin materialized on Brit's face. "How about we go to this new restaurant I know about, it's only—"

"No, not tonight," Tiv started. "I was going to grab something at the mess and then watch the Dologos game."

"Your brother playing?" Brit asked.

"Yeah. I know it's only preseason, but I want to see how they look. Kyle says they should be pretty decent this season."

"You got ale?" Brit asked.

"Always."

"Tell you what, you ice two ales, and I'll go grab some Commando burgers and meet you in the team room in half an hour."

When Brit entered the team rec room, the Dologos game was already underway. Slowly sipping from a bottle, Tiv was positioned front and center. Brit reached into the bag and handed him a burger. "Thanks," Tiv said and moved over so Brit could also pull up a chair. For a moment, Brit stood there, looking at the screen. "It's better if you move away from the front of the monitor," Tiv said, trying to peer around his friend. Brit picked up his ale from the table, opened it, and took a long drink, almost finishing it in one swallow. "Hey, go easy on that," Tiv cautioned. "What's up with you anyway?"

"I was thinking." Brit ran his hand back and forth over his bald head.

"That can't be good." Tiv dropped his eyebrows but still tried to keep an eye on the game. "Whoa," Tiv exclaimed, watching the Dologos ball sail over the goal. "Kyle was lucky it didn't connect. He looks slower, gained some weight in the off season." Brit didn't respond. Tiv turned toward him as he continued to stand, obstructing part of the monitor. "What's bugging you?" Brit was silent, his eyes hollow as he rubbed the heel of his hand against his chest. Tiv deactivated the monitor and stared directly at Brit. "Something's bugging you, and if you don't spill it, I'll order you back to the party."

Brit polished off his ale and pulled up a chair, flipping it backward so he could straddle it. Putting his duty cap back on, the brim facing away, Brit rested his chin on his hands. "I screwed up big time, didn't I?"

"Listen, we all make mistakes that in retrospect seem like colossal screwups. You're no different than the rest of us." Brit stared at his feet. "Sometimes we need to make mistakes so we can grow." Tiv stopped for a moment. "Now I sound like the chaplain who counseled me after my first squad leader went down. His mistake cost him his life but, in the long run, made me better for it." Tiv waited for Brit to respond. Nothing. No joke, no smart-ass comment, only deafening silence. This was serious. Brit was never at a loss for words. Never. Part of the problem was Tiv not being exactly sure what Brit was referring to in regards to his screwup. Could it be the curfew, or the way Delan was turning out, or something else. Tiv didn't know and wasn't about to press any further.

"I texted Aleece I couldn't see her anymore," Brit moaned, his ankles suddenly locking behind the chair legs.

"Is that what this is about?" Tiv snorted. "I thought you wrecked the new two-seater or lost some guys to enemy fire." Tiv reactivated the vid monitor. "And I'm the one who gets too involved." Tiv picked up his ale. "And you gave me grief?"

"But this girl is different."

"That's what you say every time this happens," Tiv remembered. "I think you had it right when you came in. Go get another ale, shut up, and watch the game. It's already two-nothing."

Brit went to the fridge, popped the cap on the bottle, and took a long drink. "I'm hungry." He opened the bag, retrieved his sandwich, and dug in.

"Feel better now?" Tiv asked, and took a bite of his burger.

With his mouth full of food, Brit said, "Much." After the trailing team scored a goal, Brit asked, "What did you think of the girl with Cathen?"

That was a quick recovery. All ready onto a different lady. "Pretty, but way too clingy. Did you see the way she fawned all over Luth?"

"I here she's a nurse," Belk offered, waiting for Tiv's response. "I also hear she was originally part of Cathen's unit, but he got her transferred to Dad's private entourage just so he could keep seeing her."

"How do you hear all this?" Tiv asked, not really caring. "You must not be busy enough, you know everyone's dirty laundry." Brit possessed an uncanny knack for being the source for all things rumor, gossip, or scandal. Which was why Tiv anointed him Defender Company's chief intel officer.

"I hear things, especially now that I'm attached to the Pareqi liaison. By the way, the woman with him was pretty hot too."

"Is that all you think about? How about some relevant intel?"

"Pretty much." Brit laughed.

The score was now five to one and Tiv, frustrated with the poor play of his brother's team, deactivated the vid monitor.

"Hey, why'd you turn it off?"

Tiv didn't answer him but got up, cleaned his garbage off the table, and replaced his duty cap on his head and headed toward the door. "Bed, and that's probably where you ought to be heading too." Tiv reached for the door then turned to Brit. "You know, what's always worked for me is to tell the girl you've reconsidered and you want to try and work things out. I'm sure you can find a way to convince her to take you back." Tiv smirked. "Or you can tell her you were drunk, that works too."

CHAPTER 26

Over the next several weeks, everyone at the Pareq Base was getting settled in. Details were being attended to, and routines were established. The med clinic duty rotations were streamlined, and busywork assignments were rampant, with manuals being written and rewritten, inspections conducted, and procedures reviewed. *Boring, boring, and boring.* Scientists and mission specialists shuttled back and forth between Pareq and Vedax. Equipment would be set up, break down, get fixed, and finally replaced. The cold played havoc not only on supplies but also the people involved as well. The other morning, while Leba treated two Explorer cadets for frostbite, she couldn't help overhearing Luth Cathen's conversation with Explorer Company's squad leader, Antog Hirousey. Cathen was probing for some information, but she couldn't tell what he was getting at. Explorer was helping Striker Company establish a more expansive scientific outpost on Vedax than the one originally envisioned by Tal-Kari ruling council. From the way Cathen was talking, he didn't particularly care for Striker's squad leader, Tem Myaronitz, and was trying to get Hirousey to answer his questions instead.

Most of what the medical clinic saw from Vedax was exposure injuries. What they saw from Pareq was entirely different. Healthy young adults working long shifts, cooped up most of the day, ran wild at night. Like academy students on summer vacation. She was sure they tested the limits of their commanders' patience as they got into all kinds of trouble. Leba laughed at some of the situations young soldiers found themselves in, especially on a planet where partying seemed to be the national pastime.

"You're being polite, girl," DeShay told her. "These kids may have needs, but fulfilling them off base is a dangerous practice."

"What do you expect to happen when you put this many single people on a moon with such gorgeous natives?" Middie chimed in from her perch at the front intake area.

"What do you know of mingling, woman?" DeShay snapped.

"Shut up, you old war dog. Hodd was right to leave you for greener pastures." She snickered.

Before DeShay could respond, Leba put a hand on his arm. "Leave it." He looked at her frustrated and then toward Middie. "We'll continue this discussion later. Now mind to your business, woman."

"Glad you are able to keep your hound on a leash, Doc," Middie said, returning to her work. DeShay growled through bared teeth.

"Right away, sir." Leba jumped at Cathen's order to show him the logbooks. Every day Cathen would come by the med clinic and evaluate a different part of the daily progress logs. He was always looking for something to ding them on. Today was no different, except he was accompanied by Wallen Scoby, the base commander's private physician. Scoby was taller than Cathen and stood even more erect. At least twice Cathen's age, he showed only a small amount of gray at his temples. Retiring from military service a few years before his wife passed, he landed the plush job of physician attaché after her death. He probably hadn't operated in years. Distinguished was the perfect word to describe him. It was fun to watch Cathen squirm. Finally someone more arrogant than their own little weasel. Cathen prattled on about the state-of-the-art clinic, which could be mobilized if needed or perform even the most delicate of surgeries on a moment's notice. He regaled Scoby with anecdotes of past triumphs, never once acknowledging the little people staffing the place. The way Cathen told it, he could do everything, including raising the dead, with his fancy hospital. Despite Cathen's best attempts, Scoby seemed unimpressed. Leba was sure she and her colleagues would hear about it later in their change-of-shift briefing, how they needed to do better because the chief didn't think them adequate.

Leba ran a tight ship, and her crew did everything by the book, maybe not Cathen's book, but even so, he found it hard to find legitimate fault with anything they did. Let him pick on JT's crew or Gordie's crew, if he could. But don't mess with hers. One thing Leba didn't do was make Cathen look bad. At least not intentionally. No matter how he acted, showing him up served no purpose. Unfortunately, the sheer efficiency and performance statistics for her team's work made Cathen boil. With nothing to criticize, Lord Cathen would occasionally make things up to pick on. Today was no exception. He found a missing log entry. It really wasn't her fault; the data was supposed to be collected the shift before. She filled in most of the missing entries, but there wasn't enough time to cover for her fellow's discrepancy this early in the shift. She refused to make up a statistic. Sometimes it would take the better part of the morning to track down all the delinquent information. Cathen didn't like excuses, and so Leba didn't make any. She took his reprimand stoically and promised not to let it happen again.

"Why didn't you tell him it was the night shift's screwup?" DeShay asked.

"She's scared of taking Cathen head-on," Middie observed.

Leba took a deep breath. "I told him it was Middie's mistake," she said straight-faced.

DeShay pointed a wagging finger at her. "I bet Fidelis is up for detention after school in Headmaster Cathen's office."

"Shut up." Middie snorted and shot her hand up in an offensive gesture.

DeShay turned toward Leba. "Another big day at hospital boring."

"It's our last shift before we switch to nights, and that's when all the fun begins," Leba corrected him. "I live for the excitement of spending twelve hours sobering up soldiers, dealing with problems day shift ignored, and making excuses for people who don't want to go to work in the morning."

DeShay agreed. "Sums it up pretty well."

Leba took most of her meals at the commissary. She wasn't one for venturing out alone at night. Despite being offered by some of the nurses to go out for drinks, Leba begged off. Bars weren't her thing, and drinking intoxicants never held any appeal. At least three to four nights a week, she tried to get to one of the base's gym rooms for a workout. That worked when you were on day shift, but when pulling night shifts, your day was so upside-down it was impossible to keep a routine. It was more important to sleep as much as you could during the day. Unfortunately, the rest of the world was awake and endeavored to do everything they could to bother you while you slept, comm calls, texts, info-alert, sirens, whatever. Worse than night shift was the transition between working days and working nights. Once you finished days, you didn't have to return to work until the evening, and if you went right to bed after you finished days, you would be ready to go for days, not nights. It was crucial to stay up later the first night off and sleep later into the next few days to get your cycle right. Her last day shift ended up being super busy, and Leba found it difficult to stay awake once she finished dinner. DeShay told her he was meeting a friend for dinner later in the evening or he would have hung out with her. She thought about all the things she could do to stay up but succumbed to an early sleep.

Squad Leader Tiv Garnet and Defender Company seemed to spend more time retrieving wayward soldiers than shoring up the base's defenses. "I still don't get why we have so many people deployed out here," Garnet said, cupping his elbow in one hand while tapping his lips with the other.

"Ask Dad. I'm sure he knows," Belk said, picking at his fingernail.

"Hey, Dad, just curious. What's the other part of this deployment, you know the one you're not telling us about. I know its top secret, but come on, have a drink and we'll talk," Garnet improvised.

"And your point?" Belk said.

"If Dad wanted us to know, he would tell us." Garnet clasped his hands on the tabletop and leaned forward. "It's our job to figure it out without asking."

"So how do we figure it out? You can't even figure out who's pranking you." Belk went back to digging at his finger. Garnet furrowed his brow. "Yep, I know it's started up again, that's why you hang out in here all the time." Belk lifted his head up and stared past Garnet. "It's the only place secure enough to keep the joker out."

Garnet thumped his fist. Rising from his chair, he came around the desk and headed for the door. "The only good thing about it is I narrowed the search down to the two thousand or so people stationed on this base."

"Bravo." Belk clapped slowly.

"One can only hope he decides tormenting me is not enough and starts to go after my friends," Garnet said, slapping Belk across the back.

Belk ignored Garnet's last comment. "Wait." He slid into the seat at the team room's info-portal keyboard and began to type. "I've got an idea," Belk said.

"That would be a first," Garnet shot back, waiting at the doorway.

"No, seriously," Belk explained.

A voice came over the console. "Zable here."

"Zable. Belk here. Can you meet Garnet and me in the squad room? We have a project that requires your expertise."

Tiv put an open hand on his chest and mouthed, "We?"

"Right away, sir," Zable responded.

"Sums it up pretty well," Zable told Garnet and Belk. "If you want me to sneak around the classified files, I'm going to need someone else's access to cover my tracks. Not only someone with high enough access the intrusion would appear part of an everyday routine but also someone who wouldn't get in too much trouble if a pattern is detected." Zable paused and then added, "Unless you want them to get in trouble."

Belk thought for a moment before responding but never got a chance. Holding up his hand, Garnet warned, "Don't even think about it." Garnet waited for Belk's comeback, but none came. "How long?" he asked Zable.

"Few hours, unless the stuff's encrypted higher than my pay grade." Zable rocked back on his heels.

"That's a given." Belk chuckled.

"Well, I guess I can rout it through a buddy of mine back home, but it's gonna cost you." Zable shrugged.

"How much?" Belk asked.

"A lot," Zable answered, planting his fingertips wide apart on the table.

"I have a sister," Belk offered. "Cute too."

"You are such a pig," Tross said, entering the room.

"Doesn't anyone knock anymore?" Belk asked.

"I asked Denny to meet us here," Garnet confessed. "I find it easier to make decisions when I compare and contrast the opinions of my seconds."

Tross noted, "Yeah, Brit, Garnet needs someone who considers the consequences of his actions."

"Funny, very funny," Belk said.

"About your sister." Zable grinned.

"Stop with the sister," Garnet cautioned. "I'm not trading Belk's sister to keep some decrypter friend of yours satisfied."

"Not for him, for me." Zable smirked. "I was thinking if she's hot, I'd do the job and her myself."

"You pig, that's my sister we're talking about." Belk snorted.

That evening, Tiv Garnet met his buddy DeShay Tiner for dinner. "I heard Dugin's was the place to go," DeShay noted as he and Tiv approached the small diner.

"This place is not too bad, food's pretty good and the service fast," Tiv remarked.

"Sounds like an overwhelmingly positive recommendation." DeShay pressed his lips together in a grimace.

The two men entered the restaurant and took a seat at a nearby table. The settings and menus were already placed. Shortly thereafter, an elderly woman, her hair drawn back into a tight bun and secured with a black net, approached the table. Her white apron was old and fraying, her rounded face pink with exertion, and her eyes drooping with age. Her voice was gravely but cheerful. "What'll you have, boys?"

"Any specials today, Gran?" Tiv asked.

Her front teeth worn to nubs, she smiled. "The same." She thumbed toward the kitchen. "Except Petrok got in some fresh fish."

"We'll have two steaks and your usual sides," Tiv said, closing the menu.

"Order will be up in a few minutes. I'll bring you some ale," she replied and walked away from the table.

"Take it you're a regular here." DeShay laughed. The waitress tottered back and placed two brown bottles on the table. She left, leaving DeShay and Tiv to open their own drinks. Once the caps were off the bottles, DeShay put up his bottleneck. Tiv clanked his on DeShay's. "So catch me up on what's going on," DeShay said and then took a long pull of ale.

"Nothing much." Tiv studied the bottle for a moment, trying to avoid eye contact. "Heard about you and Emmie." Tiv knew it was a sore subject but better to get it out of the way now.

"Yep." DeShay's bottle thudded on the table. "The past has a way of repeating itself." DeShay finally caught Tiv's gaze. "Heard your prankster's followed you all the way out here."

"Son of an Etali witch," Tiv spat. "I finally filtered all my comm calls through central to get the incessant paging to stop."

Pointing his bottleneck at Tiv, DeShay said, "Someone's really got it in for you, man."

"Did you get any info from your forensic guy?" Tiv asked.

"No, the stuff was too commonly available to trace its origin." DeShay surveyed the other restaurant patrons. "But now at least you have it narrowed down to someone deployed on this mission with us."

"Speaking of large deployments, any idea why we need so many companies on an expeditionary mission?"

"I was thinking the same thing, but no one seems to know anything. At least, no one's talking."

"I had this idea about how to figure it out, but it may involve some undercover work." Tiv leaned forward and lowered his voice.

"Count me in, you know I love this cloak-and-dagger stuff." DeShay beamed. Before the conversation could proceed, the aproned woman returned with their steaks. She placed them carefully on the table along with two new ale bottles.

"Enjoy your meal," she said and left for the kitchen.

DeShay poked at his steak with his fork, hot juice escaped from the prong marks. "This place may not look like much, but they do know how to make a decent steak," Tiv said.

"So what happened at Dugin's?" DeShay said, cutting a piece of steak with his knife.

Taking his time, Tiv finished chewing, swallowed, and answered, "Long story."

With as few specifics as possible, Tiv retold the sordid tale. "I agree. For now, I've sworn off women too." DeShay started but then corrected himself. "I've sworn off relationships, not women."

Both men shared a hearty laugh as the waitress returned. "Let me take those," she offered, gathering up their dirty plates. "I'll bring dessert."

"They make the best pies." DeShay smiled. The women returned with two large triangles of pie exploding with fruit. With the side of his fork, Tiv carved off a piece and ate.

After unroofing the pie with his knife and examining it closely, DeShay replaced the top crust. As he ate a forkful, his eyes widened, and a smile crept up, overtaking his entire face. "I may have to swear off women forever if there's pie like this every night." DeShay gobbled down the rest in two enormous bites.

"Getting back to our discussion of what's going on here on Pareq that requires so many of us, I need a favor." Tiv's fork remained empty.

"Name it, especially if you're going to let me finish your pie." DeShay reached over to grab Tiv's plate.

"Go ahead, I'm stuffed anyway," he said, holding his stomach and pushing the half-eaten pie toward DeShay.

Tiv explained, "I need to borrow someone's access codes."

"Trust me," DeShay laughed. "I know just the one."

When Tiv returned to his company's barracks, he headed for the command room to check in with the duty officer. It was just before 2100. Not that he didn't trust his unit, but he confirmed everyone's status anyway and then headed for his own rack. Since the pranks started up again, he was careful to vary his routine. Tiv left specific instructions with the duty officer to log in and log out any visitors whether authorized or unauthorized. So far this worked, and tonight he was too tired to put up with any interruptions. Dinner with DeShay was a satisfying change from being cooped up on base.

After hearing DeShay's recounting of the disastrous turn of events with Emmie, Tiv was glad for the moment he was not in a relationship. He didn't miss having to worry about how someone else felt or having someone track his every movement or the constant interrogations about this and that. Terminating his relationship, if one could call it that, with Nilsa was the right thing to do. He was glad she found new love with JT. JT seemed to finally get the girl he obsessed over, pined for, dreamed about, and fought so hard to impress. Tiv did miss company, though, the smell of freshly washed hair, the softness of a woman's touch, the nervous excitement of the chase. Chelli was hot, but she was too willing, too easy, there was no challenge. She could certainly push the right buttons, but the fun was finding the right buttons and the route you took to get there. Tiv almost envied Brit, how he could drift from port to port, finding companionship and comfort around any and all turns. Not this sailor, though. Then Tiv remembered how stable and satisfied Denny Tross was, married to his academy sweetheart. Always knowing he had the same place and same person to come back to.

Lying in his rack, the room dark, the window facing the western sky, Tiv could barely see the faint outline of Glirase. The enormous gas giant giving life to this solar system slowly faded from his view as dark low-lying clouds gathered in anticipation of the upcoming storm. It was still dark when Tiv awoke the next morning. Clouds, gray and dark, consumed the sunrise, as rain pelted the moon. Tiv got up, showered and shaved, and dressed. Looking again out the window, he hoped it wouldn't rain all day. Rain always delayed everything.

Tiv was right and ended up working late for it. Shuttles were delayed, the incessant thunderstorms seriously hampered ground transports. Evaluating the day's stats and trying to reconcile the numbers with the actual data proved taxing. The door hissed and slid open. Zable entered the team command office. "Any success?" Tiv asked, repeatedly tapping his stylus on the monitor screen.

"No," Zable responded.

"That's it. No. Not even a ray of hope?" Tiv returned his gaze back to his work, disappointed.

"It's not like I didn't try," Zable whined. "There's some pretty sophisticated encryption involved, not to mention the dead ends are endless."

"So you're saying you're giving up?" Tiv, still staring at the accounting discrepancy, tapped louder. Zable was quiet. Tiv offered, "You know Belk has twin sisters."

"Hey, that's not fair. If I'd known that, I would've tried harder," Zable retorted.

"Would this help?" Garnet asked, handing Zable an info-pad displaying a long string of numbers.

A big smile came to Zable's face. "Where'd you get this, and how much did it cost you?"

"Don't ask," Garnet replied. "More importantly, will it help?"

"It might," Zable thought out loud. "It just might."

Luth Cathen sat on the couch with Mally Yertha snuggled beside him. He played with her hair as she nuzzled at his neck. "How was your day?" he asked, not really caring, but he knew that some attention to her needs would pay dividends for his needs later.

"Busy, very busy," she said, straightening up. "Dr. Scoby didn't need me, so Commander Atacama asked me to run errands all over the place."

"I'm sorry," Cathen said, moving her face upward and kissing her gently. There were way too many people deployed for this to be a simple expeditionary mission. It bugged him that he was in the dark. Myaronitz and Hirousey knew, Cathen was sure, but they weren't talking.

"Where did he send you?" Cathen asked, stroking her hair and face.

Mally, in between kisses, detailed her stops throughout the day. So far, Cathen couldn't detect a pattern, but he would; he was sure of that. But as he continued kissing Mally and she melted into his embrace, he decided to leave that line of questioning unanswered as more basic urges consumed him.

CHAPTER 27

"Whatcha looking at?" JT said, sneaking up behind Middie.

Middie quickly exited the screen she was pouring over. "Nothing," she snapped.

"Nothing seems very important," JT probed further. "Looks like you were—" But Middie shooed him away.

"There's a patient waiting for you, Dr. Hobes in cubicle two," Middie changed the subject. "He's complaining of ankle pain." She handed him the chart. "Yes, the triage nurse has already seen him. And before you ask, I did put your favorite drink in the mug on your desk."

He leaned over and gave her a hug. "Thanks, love, you're the best. Wish all the girls put my needs ahead of theirs."

"Not all women are as special as I am," she said, turning to grab him.

"Missed me," he said, slipping past her hand.

"Not for lack of trying," Middie grumbled under her breath. When Dr. Hobes was out of the immediate area, Middie relaunched the program she was scanning. The money was there, like the man said it would be. Both deposits were on time and accurate. She could get used to this relationship. Of course, it did require some efforts on her part, but the rewards far exceeded her risks. The man implied that there would be more opportunities for her but to be patient until he contacted her again.

Middie didn't mind the night shift, and hanging out with Dr. Hobes was an added bonus. He even let her call him JT. She had a mind to have a talk with his girlfriend and tell her she should be grateful to have such a great guy and stop running him ragged. Given the chance, Middie would show JT a good time and make sure all his needs were met.

"Middie," Dr. Hobes returned to her station, chart in hand, and ankle-casted cadet in tow. "Can you give Cadet Jengal a slip for his c.o.? He'll need to stay off his ankle for at least two weeks. Also, please give him an appointment back here in a week."

"Right on it, Doc." Middie smiled as JT walked over to get his mug. "That Dr. Hobes, one of the good ones," she confessed to the cadet. "You were lucky he was available to see you." The cadet nodded his understanding, accepted the work slip, and the appointment reminder. "Let me get an orderly to take you back to your barracks."

"I expected you to show up a little later," JT said to Dr. Gordie Rensen, handing him the logbook. Middie swiveled a little so she could catch their conversation.

"I'm not you, Hobes," Rensen said sarcastically.

"Your loss, pal," JT jested. "You probably wouldn't fit in my uniform anyway. I think your wife feeds you too well, my friend."

Ignoring the last remark, Rensen asked, "Anything pending?"

JT detailed the patients left from the night shift, an older Pareqi woman with chest pain waiting for a final set of cardiac enzymes, a teenage Pareqi boy with asthma finishing a breathing treatment, and a striped feline getting antibacterial therapy for a foreign body injury to her forepaw. "You treated someone's pet?" Rensen said, pulling his glasses down and looking over the rims.

"Our orders were to keep relations with the Pareqi people healthy," JT reminded him.

"Let me guess, its owner had a healthy set of—" Rensen was interrupted by JT's shushing.

"She's sleeping." JT walked over to the curtained area where the feline was curled up in a ball in the arms of a little girl. JT whispered, "Now, honestly, Gordie, how could I refuse." JT pulled the curtain closed, isolating the cubicle. "One thing, though, I'd get them out of here as soon as the med is done or Cathen will have your head."

"My head?" Rensen's objection fell on deaf ears as JT waved him off and left the hospital. Middie stared until Rensen's scowl persuaded her otherwise.

When Leba returned to night shift, Gordie was glad to be rid of JT. Every handoff from JT to Gordie brought an unwelcome surprise. "Hobes drives me crazy with all his antics," Gordie groaned. "When you sign out, everything is neat and tidy, not a royal mess. It takes me at least an hour or two to untangle his twisted tales."

Leba laughed, knowing she faced similar issues with how both JT and Gordie left the place. "No worries," she promised. "By the time you get back, everything will be right and ready to go." Dr. Rensen detailed the remaining patients and left for the evening.

"It might be Rensen and Hobes are the two most disorganized people on the planet," Leba complained as DeShay walked into the patient care area. "It would serve them right if I shuffled everything around so in the morning they wouldn't be able to find their own," Leba continued until DeShay interrupted.

"Come on, girl," DeShay gestured. "We need to meet an incoming transport from center city."

Leba grabbed her gear as the charge nurse came over to join them. "I'll watch the house," she said, handing Leba the portable med chest. "You go with Tiner. I assigned Beffet and Olike, they'll join you in a minute." Beffet and Olike were two very skilled nurses, and Leba was grateful to have them as part of her team. The three women hurriedly followed DeShay to the hangar bay to meet the med transport. Anster and Grizzer currently posted to the first responder unit, triaged at the scene, scooped up the patients and were already en route back.

At the hangar bay, the controller gave Leba the comm so she could communicate with her field medics. There was crackling over the comm for a moment, and then Anster's voice boomed through. "Two males. The first has a stab wound to the flank. Vitals are holding, and we've got fluids running wide. The second, an older guy, is combative but restrained, probably blunt-force trauma, I'm thinking depressed skull fracture." Anster's heavy breathing punctuated his report. Squeaks and thuds radiated inside the emergency vehicle's patient bay, echoing loudly through the comm. "Grizz is piloting as quickly as he can, but obstacles from the busy street festival is like flying through an asteroid field." Leba didn't know whether they were military, civilian, or Pareqi, but it didn't much matter.

"ETA?" she asked.

"Hey, Grizz, how long?" Leba heard a muffled voice and then Anster repeated, "Probably ten."

Once the immediate medical issues were resolved, Leba was sure the Pareq constabulary would want details. Cathen drilled it into everyone, "Our guys get a crack at the casualties first, no matter what it took." After she finished the en route consult, she picked up the intra-comm to let him know.

Once the two victims were settled into the hospital, stabilized and treatment in progress, Leba took a long time documenting their injuries and subsequent therapy. Anster's assessment was, as usual, right on pointe, making her job much easier. The Pareqi with the displaced skull fracture needed to be transported to a higher level of care. A hospital at the edge of center city with a neurosurgeon available accepted the patient. Tiner volunteered to staff the flight. He didn't want to leave anything to chance; plus it would give him an opportunity to see the only state-of-the-art hospital on Pareq. It was always good to know what the competition could bring to the party. The Tal-Kari soldier with the edged-weapon injury was stitched up and ready for the brig, pending military escort.

When morning came and the Pareqi constable arrived to interview and detain the soldier, Leba apologized, explaining the nature of his injury dictated his immediate disposition. Even pleading his case to Cathen didn't allow the detective access to the man. A drug deal gone bad. Leba hoped she left drug-related crimes behind at the medical clinic, but she was wrong. Sometimes the addiction was so great unreliable sources were tapped, resulting in disaster. She wasn't sure what the trooper faced, but she imagined it wasn't good.

"How did the med guys get to him before we did?" Belk questioned Garnet.

"Some Pareqi local called it in as a medical emergency, and the command center sent Cathen's guys. No matter, the doctor got our guy patched up, gave us the heads-up, and Tross's team scooped him up and out."

"I see Cathen finally caught on this is a team effort," Belk suggested.

"I'd venture it was Tiner who commed us," Garnet said. "Or at least told his doc to."

"Nice having one of us on the inside," Belk commented. "Amidst all those softies."

There was a ping at the door. "Come in." DeShay Tiner stood at the threshold. Getting up to greet him, Defender's squad leader put out a hand. "Thanks for the heads-up."

"I taught her well," DeShay explained.

"Who?" Belk questioned.

"My girl." DeShay grinned. "Her first call was to you guys. I was so proud."

"What girl?" Belk asked again.

"The one I'm saving for Garnet." DeShay peered at his friend. "If he ever decides to start bothering with women again."

"Is she pretty?" Belk asked.

Garnet ignored Belk and addressed DeShay, "I told you my abstinence was only a temporary condition. A guy can only go so long, except Brit, and that would be maybe two days, a week at most without getting some." Belk pounded his chest.

"Glad to hear it. I'll keep that in mind next time I see her. We, however, have bigger things to discuss." DeShay let the door slid shut. "The IT guys have been snooping around at the med clinic. You're going to have to ask your guy to back off using the access code I gave you."

"Brit, get Zable on the horn," Garnet requested. "Tell him to find another way in." Belk went over to the comm board and punched up Zable's frequency code. "I may have to give him Belk's sister after all if I want any information."

DeShay laughed. "Did you use the twin line?"

"Hey, I trained under the master, didn't I?" Garnet laughed. "Brit, tell Zable he can have both your sisters if he finds another way in." Brit snarled at him.

"Anyway, our soldier with the slash wounds came up positive for bliss on his tox screen," DeShay said, handing Garnet a memory stick.

"Not good. How'd they get that stuff way out here?" Belk scratched his head.

"Good question," Garnet said, his lips tightening. He reached up and rubbed his eyes. *Dammit, something else to worry about.*

Leba was tired. She signed out to Gordie over two hours ago and really wanted to get something to eat and then get some sleep before the next shift. But Luth Cathen was pissed and told her to wait in his office until he was done. Shortly after she finished charting and Lord Cathen finally appeared, an investigator from Overseer showed up. She already waited through the Pareqi investigator's questions, and now Cathen was going to make her wait through the Overseer officer's inquiry as well.

"There's been unusual and unauthorized traffic linked to your access Id," the officer began. In his haste for privacy, Cathen hustled the man to a small alcove nearby, not realizing Leba could hear the entire conversation. "Any thoughts as to why?"

"Good question," Cathen agreed. Not what she needed right now. Lord Cathen was already angry, and this was only going to make his tirade worse. "But as you can see by my badge log-ins, I was off-site at the time without access to an info-terminal and a score of witnesses."

The Overseer officer couldn't deny the facts. Leba knew there was no way, at least last night, Cathen tried to access the restricted files. "Did you give your code to anyone else?"

"Now why would I do that?" Cathen answered, upturning his nose, clenching his fists, and shoving them under his armpits.

"Okay, okay," the officer said. "Even so, we are going to issue you a new profile and put a back trace on the old."

"Let me know when you get the little rat. I'll have a confinement cell with his name on it all ready to go."

"Let us handle the situation, sir," the officer cautioned. "Be careful with this new code."

Cathen watched him walk away. His face was blotchy, nostrils flaring, the veins in his neck cord-like and pulsing. Not too good for the conversation he was about to have with Leba. Cathen walked back to where Leba was stewing in his office. This time, he remembered and shut the door.

"Your first call should have been to me." Cathen stared at her, his fist pounding on the desk. There were tiny bits of spittle in the corners of his mouth. She shuddered, snapping her eyes shut every time he pummeled the desktop.

"Your orders were to call our guys, so I did," Leba said, trying to keep her voice low so he'd have to stop screaming to hear her. "Besides, I tried your comm ... it was offline."

"My comm is never offline," he bellowed and slammed his fist down again.

"I asked the clerk to try, and he couldn't raise you either." Leba sat uncomfortably, her arms across her chest, trying not to tremble.

"Nevertheless," Cathen started again, but it was hard to argue with her.

He knows his comm was off, and he knows it's against regulations. He'll never admit it. But it bugs him I know.

"Don't let it happen again!" he shouted at her. "Next time, have someone bang on my door."

No, sir, you can bet the next time there'll be no place you can hide. Leba stood. "Yes, sir."

Cathen waved his hand at her. "Dismissed."

He should be glad I notified Defender Company so quickly. That way, he won't have to explain not advising the Pareqi authorities first, he can blame it on me.

"Missed you at breakfast," DeShay said. "Saved you a seat."

Leba put her sweatband over her forehead and straightened her ponytail. "Cathen gave me a raft of crap for not calling him first." With a gloved fist, Leba struck the heavy bag so hard it swayed backward.

DeShay, similarly attired in workout clothes, steadied himself against the bag she was striking, holding it fast. "Don't worry, girl, you did the right thing," he consoled her.

"That's just it." She puffed out the words between jabs and crosses. "I did call him," she said and then took a breath to strike again. "But his comm was offline." She hit the bag again.

"Offline? He's not supposed to go offline. None of us are, especially on a deployment." DeShay too went offline the other day, but Leba chose not to bring it up.

"That's what he told me, but I know he went offline. Even the clerk couldn't raise his comm." She continued striking the bag harder and harder.

"Calm down, girl, or you'll break your hand," DeShay advised. Leba kept pummeling the bag. "Listen, you did the right thing. Defender was really appreciative."

By this time, Leba stopped listening to DeShay and was concentrating on putting a hole in the bag with her fists. "Enough already," DeShay warned, pushing away the bag. Offsetting her position to reengage the bag, she almost hit him with her next strike. "Enough!" DeShay shouted to break her concentration. "Enough," he repeated, this time quieter. "Now take off those gloves and run a circuit with me."

"I hate running," Leba snarled. "I'd much rather hit something."

"Run a lap or ten with me, then I'll spot you for some lifting, deal?"

"If I must," Leba conceded. "But you'd better make it worth my while."

DeShay grinned. "I may have an idea in that regard."

"Huh?" Leba eyed him and brushed a loose strand of hair from her face.

"I'll tell you later," DeShay said as he raced ahead.

Night shift the next few days for Leba and her crew were relatively uneventful. No more crime victims, only a handful of chest pains, sprained ankles, head colds, bellyaches, and a holdover from the day shift, a curious urticarial rash that defied diagnosis but was responding to anti-inflammatories. Despite the undertones left from their first night shift's casualties, there was no further evidence of bliss use. Leba was looking forward to two days off before the next day's shift cycle. When she handed the reins to JT at the last sunrise, he was late. Later than usual, that is. Leba loved JT's excuses for being late. There were only so many times his alarm chrono didn't function. She even offered to give him a wake-up call, but he told her it wasn't necessary. That was the last time he used the broken chrono excuse. Subsequent mornings brought better and more creative excuses. Her favorite to date was where the laundry hadn't pressed his uniform so he had to do it himself. Problem was he came to work in scrubs, and no one pressed their scrubs.

The next few months saw more of the same tedious routine. Leba became frustrated with the same complaints and ailments. Granted, every once in a while a scientist or soldier from the Vedax base camp would be airlifted to their clinic with cold exposure, frostbite, gastroenteritis from eating something bad, or an upper respiratory illness from venturing out in the rain and cold without proper gear. What Leba longed for were their tales of the beauty and majesty of the Vedax moon they were studying.

Tiv Garnet was unable to crack the mystery of why both Explorer and Striker Companies were deployed in such numbers to the Vedax moon. His company was busy retrieving wayward soldiers from town and helping rotate troopers back and forth between Pareq and Vedax.

"Please, something else," Garnet begged Belk. "I'm tired of hearing what you and Aleece did or where you went or how many times you—" Garnet was cut off by Zable entering the room.

"I finally did it," Zable announced.

"Look," Belk said to Garnet, "our little boy finally got laid."

"Shut up," Zable demanded. "Besides, I lost my virginity with your sisters, both of them at the same time."

"You are one sick dude," Belk informed him.

"Stop it," Garnet said, rocking back on his heels.

Zable sneered at Belk, who stared back at him. "I think I finally found a way in."

"Told you he got laid." Belk laughed.

Garnet ignored Belk's vulgar comment and encouraged Zable to continue. "What's that mean?"

For the next ten minutes, Zable regaled them with his foray into computer hell, ending with how he got past the first of five layers of security. "Let's see," Belk said, "it took you six or so duty cycles to get through level one, there are four more levels, probably more complex than level one, giving you the benefit of the doubt, I figure sometime next year you'll be in. By that time, who'll care?"

Zable crossed his arms over his chest. "You want to try, pal?"

"You got a sister?" Belk asked.

Garnet put an arm out to halt Zable's approach. Zable tried staring Belk down instead. "Easy, I think that's Belk's way of saying 'Good job!'"

CHAPTER 28

DeShay still not over Emmie needed a diversion, and this scavenger hunt was just the ticket. He came close on more than one occasion to sending his text-mail draft to her. It was way too soon to pour his heart out to her. Something always came to his mind, a remembrance or a feeling, halting his finger dead in its track. Supporting Leba in her contest with JT, getting his favorite little sister to loosen up and enjoy life more, would hopefully get him out of his depression.

Leba stood, arms crossed with DeShay by her side, and listened as JT explained the rules. Gordie looked bored, probably thinking this was another of Hobes's schemes to get out of doing something. "Ah," JT said with a smile. "You want to know what the prize is, do you?" He rubbed his chin and then clasped his hands in front and said, "It has to be something big, something meaningful, something worth all the hard effort we are about to expend." He paused for effect. "I've got it. The losing teams will work the winning team's shifts for an entire duty cycle."

"Big deal," Gordie said frustrated. "We do that for you anyway, you slacker." DeShay snickered at the truth in that statement. "If we counted the times you showed up late for a shift and Leba and I covered for you, it would probably add up to two duty cycles."

"Okay, something else then," JT retorted. DeShay inherently liked Doc Hobes; he was an inventive guy, but the theatrics got old.

JT challenged the other two med crews to a scavenger hunt. He chose items either particularly difficult to find and acquire or ones, if you were caught with, would result in severe penalty. Some were just downright devilish, like obtaining Lord Cathen's favorite writing tool, the one he incessantly spun between his finger and thumb like a baton twirler. DeShay found it difficult to convince Leba to participate at first, but when he appealed to some of the other members of her shift, who were more than eager to play, especially with the enormity of the prize for winning, she found it impossible to decline. The true challenge was determining if JT already acquired a majority of the needed items and would present them surreptitiously, much to the dismay of the other participants. With Vic and Riki on JT's team, Leba assured DeShay they would at least try and keep the game fair. Doc Rensen told DeShay he really wanted the extra time off so he could get back home and see his family.

Leba did, however, object to some of the items on the list that required protective gear to obtain. It maddened DeShay when she put her foot down, declaring any radioactive item off-limits. Gordie too thought it a little much to take items deemed essential for the function of the base, like the satellite antenna. Both Leba and Gordie felt some of the stuff JT selected was a diversion so once they were disallowed and struck from the game, other items would be readily accepted. There was also another rule they agreed on. Once you obtained an item and verified its authenticity with a member from another team, the item could be returned. Oftentimes returning the item was more of a challenge than obtaining it.

"I'm not sure of this," Leba explained to DeShay. "I'm really not comfortable with stealing."

DeShay laughed. "It's not stealing when you return it. Let's just say it's borrowing."

"What are you going to do if you get caught?" Leba asked.

"Blame you." He paused to enjoy the expression on her face. "You're our leader, aren't you?"

"I've got a great idea," Leba said. "For this mission, I'll be your wingman." She put her hands on her hips, waiting for his reply. "In fact, if we win, you can have my share of the pot."

"Suit yourself," DeShay chided her. He wondered how long it would take her to beg off this unconventional challenge.

"What do you mean it's missing?" Belk stood, watching Garnet rummage through the materials on the desk. Pushing past him,

Garnet emptied all the waste bins in the room and pulled all the books off the shelves. "Do you think it was the prankster?"

Garnet didn't answer him but continued tearing apart the room. "I'll have his," Garnet mumbled. "Stay here," he ordered Belk. "I'm going to check my quarters." Garnet left the room, slamming the door in the process.

Tiv tossed his rack to no avail. It was nowhere to be found. DeShay met Tiv in the hallway on his way back to the team room. "What's up, man?" DeShay asked.

"Not now," Tiv cautioned and continued angrily down the hall.

DeShay knew when to back off. He did, however, look down at the scavenger hunt list, spying the reason for Tiv's fury. One of the listed items belonged to Defender Company. Now the rules, according to JT, required no disclosure of the game to anyone outside the hunt. DeShay chuckled. "Don't worry, my friend, I'm sure it'll be back by sunset."

That evening, DeShay found his friend Tiv working out in the gym. "Can I join you?" DeShay asked.

Tiv looked up from the heavy bag, his brow laden with sweat. "About this morning." DeShay waved him off.

"I'm sure it was important, it's all good." DeShay touched fists with him.

"You up for some sparring?" Tiv inquired.

"Always. Just let me get some headgear and my gloves," DeShay said, reaching into his gym bag.

Tiv, still gloved, fumbled to open the clasp on his bag. He removed his headgear and fitted it in place. Both men moved to a matted corner of the gym. Tiv put his mouth guard in as DeShay came forward. "Ready," Tiv mumbled, the guard making his speech sound garbled.

"Bring it on," DeShay warbled out. The two men set about trading jabs and crosses. For an older man, DeShay still could move pretty well, but Tiv was taller and stronger. By the end of the contest, both were tired. Tiv unstrapped each glove, dropping them one by one into his bag. He wrestled out of his headgear and walked over to rinse out his mouth guard.

DeShay followed behind. "Nasty things, but they keep my smile for the ladies." DeShay laughed. "Wanna grab dinner?" DeShay inquired.

"Can't," Tiv said. "Pulled guard duty."

"You, but you're a squad leader," DeShay reminded him.

"I wouldn't ask anyone to do something I wouldn't do," Tiv said. "In fact, I remember someone telling me the same a long time ago."

"I hate it when people throw my words back at me. I wasn't serious, you know."

"Bull." Tiv snorted and wrapped an arm around the older man's shoulder, placing him in a loose headlock.

DeShay easily slipped out. "You need a shower, man."

After showering himself, DeShay met Tiv in the dressing area. "Next time for dinner," Tiv suggested, closing his locker. "Gotta go."

DeShay nodded and finished toweling his head dry. The workout was good but exhausting. Not as young as he used to be. He tried to get the gym often, but his natural joints were beginning to betray him. He'd given Tiv a good go but knew he'd pay the price once the adrenaline high left. Stretching out stiffness became a regular part of his morning routine. DeShay wanted to feel young again. No, he wanted to be young again. Digging his hand into the gym bag, he fumbled with the info-pad. He squinted at the contact list then tapped out a text. He knew what would make him feel young; it always did.

"Good job," JT applauded Middie's obtaining their team's first item. "How'd you get that?"

"Don't ask," Middie warned. "You don't want to know." She laughed evilly. "Just say I owe big time."

"Go find one of Rensen's team and get it authenticated," JT advised. "And by all means, put it back."

"Are you kidding?" Middie said. "This is a keeper." She trotted off in the direction of the departing shift.

JT smiled. He was tired of being the one always in trouble. Now he had devised a way to rope everyone else in too. Even Ms. Goody-Goody and Old Man Gruff were exposed. He hoped no one would rat him out if caught with the goods. His biggest challenge was keeping the game off Cathen's radar.

Certain items at the top of the list were easy to obtain, but the ones toward the bottom, well, that was a different story. Middie spent the majority of her efforts on those elusive items. Being showered with praise from her shift mates, especially Dr. Hobes, was almost as good as the bundles of joy delivered to her account. No, not really, but it would do for now. Lately her benefactor was quiet, but she hoped it would change soon. The game rules were in Middie's favor since once she logged in a difficult-to-obtain item, heightened security would make it almost impossible for another team to duplicate the effort. Determined to win, enticed by the promise of a bigger share of the reward commensurate with the risk she undertook, Middie volunteered for the tougher finds.

By engaging the services of one or two others outside of the game with promises of ample compensation for their help, Middie bent the rules. "Here's the transflux acclimator, brand-new, fresh out of the box," the Defender Company corpsman told her. She despised meeting in Defender's section, but Delan refused to come to her, and besides, she didn't want any of her competitors to get wind of this. Unlike the medical clinic, she didn't know all the blind spots down here.

"How come it looks like it has grease on it?" Middie asked.

"It's new enough," he said. "Listen, you asked me for it, and here it is. Now I need it back before tomorrow or the price will be double."

Smug bastard, I'm giving you a great deal. It's a win-win for you. "Don't worry, it'll be back," Middie assured him. Delan fingered the voucher. "It's all there, just like I said, with a little extra to keep your mouth shut." Middie rubbed her head and tried to wave him off. She needed to be in and out of here, not screwing around explaining everything to this guy.

Not taking the hint, Delan continued, "What I don't understand is why you only need it for a few hours."

Every noise a potential threat, she kept her eyes darting back and forth. Last thing she needed was for one of his squad to come around the corner. "You let me worry about that," Middie said, rocking side to side. "You sure your company's travel sled wouldn't be needed?"

"You let me worry about that." Delan smirked.

The next morning came and went, but no Middie Fidelis. *Okay, I guess she owes me double,* Delan thought. Later that day, the med clerk texted him the object was ready for pickup, as was his second payment. Delan, pleased with the tidy sum he was about to come into, walked into Defender Company's team room. Priman Denny Tross was watching the monitor closely. "What's up?" Delan asked.

"Travel sled malfunctioned big time," Tross reported. "Garnet and Belk were supposed to take the Pareqi ambassador on a jaunt when the sled flipped."

I swore the ambassador's trip was scheduled for next week. "Anyone hurt?" Delan asked.

"No," Tross said. "Garnet was able to right it with a roll, but the liaison lost his lunch in the process."

Delan snickered. "Bet it takes a week to get the puke out."

Tross said, "Put it this way, I wouldn't want to be anywhere near the vehicle garage when Garnet gets it back. He off-loaded Belk and the Pareqi at the scene. They're on their way to the med clinic now, but Garnet stayed in the rig to keep it upright while they hauled it back."

When his squad leader had asked him to repair it, Delan found it easier to put in a new one rather than fix the old one. Lucky for Delan he hadn't taken the transflux acclimator out and given it to Fidelis, leaving the sled inoperable. He replaced the new one with the old one he was to have fixed. If questioned, Delan could say the old one malfunctioned again. A plausible story since the new one worked fine until he switched it out. He won all around, double payment from Fidelis, no evidence of his switch, and his favorite squad leader got puked on. Delan suppressed a smile. It was about time he was the one that came out smelling good.

Supporting the ambassador under his arm, Priman Brit Belk entered the med clinic. Unfortunately, no one came over to help. The pair approached the empty reception desk, and Belk watched Dr. JT Hobes in full scrub attire, with his surgical mask pulled down to his chin, talk to a stocky woman in a short med tunic.

"I don't know how you do it." Hobes smiled, planting a kiss on a middle-aged woman who stood in front of the back door to the reception area. Belk waited a moment then loudly cleared his throat.

"For you, Doc, I'd—" she reached for him but was cut off when Hobes pointed toward Belk. As the woman's head swiveled to face Belk, an angry stare locked on. Hobes disappeared from the doorway as the burly woman snapped, "Take a seat."

"This is Ambassador Wiljon Sohut. He was just involved in a vehicular accident and needs medical attention right away."

"Have a seat." The clerk pointed to the chair in front of her desk.

"But he's sick," Belk insisted.

"I can see that, but there are rules, and he needs to take a seat." She gestured to the chair again.

Belk helped the slumping ambassador take a seat. The man was green and shaky. The woman, whose badge identified her as Middie Fidelis, Clerk 3, Medical Company, seemed to take her good sweet time asking an inordinate number of questions.

I wish she'd hurry up, I think he might hurl again.

Finally, Fidelis said, "Follow me." Grabbing him under the arms, Belk helped the ambassador up. "Not you." She stared at Belk. "Him," she reiterated and pointed at Sohut. "You, trooper, have a seat, read something, stay out of my way."

Challenging Fidelis was not something Brit Belk relished doing in front of the Pareqi ambassador. Protocol dictated he handle her later. Right now, keeping Sohut happy, or at the very least comfortable, was his main concern. He'd get Garnet to talk with Cathen later, squad leader to squad leader. The clerk grabbed the man's arm, jerked him from Belk's grasp, and led him over to the nursing triage area. "Orderly, transport," she bellowed. A tall thin man burst forth from an adjacent cubicle with a hover chair and joined her. He helped the liaison sit. She patted Sohut on the shoulder. "The triage nurse will be with you in a moment."

The orderly escorted the ambassador to a cubicle at the far end of the reception area. Belk slumped in a chair, feeling totally inadequate. He was glad, however, he got this assignment rather than piloting the travel sled during its tow.

"That guy was a real piece of work," Middie observed when JT emerged from the treatment area.

JT laughed. "I guess we know now why a transflux acclimator is so important." Middie was silent. "Bet they ground all the travel sleds until they figure out what happened."

"Don't worry, Doc." Middie grinned. "Everything is back where it's supposed to be. Wiped clean and ready for service."

"That's why I love you, Middie, you always come through for the team," he said, placing both hands on her shoulders.

"No problem, Doc." She beamed.

"Would you like to return to your suite?" Belk questioned the Pareqi ambassador as they left the med clinic.

"No," Sohut said, the acid in his voice magnified by his reverberation. "Please return me to my personal residence in Center City." He wriggled free of Belk's arm. "I've quite enough of you Tal-Kari today." Belk wasn't surprised by the admonishment. "That vile creature," Sohut grumbled under his breath as he straightened and smoothed the rumpled cloth of his soiled day tunic. "The council will hear about this." Belk knew better than to say anything and commed the hangar bay to arrange for the fastest ride possible to take the liaison back to his home. "No," Sohut said brusquely, "I will arrange my own transportation, thank you."

The Pareqi land shuttle met Belk and Sohut at the front of the base complex. With curt formality, Sohut dismissed Belk and entered the vehicle. The hatch slid shut quickly. Raindrops that at first fell lightly now pelted Belk's face. He stood and looked up at the gray clouds looming overhead. Today started out wrong, and he was sure it wasn't going to get any better.

Garnet was mad but didn't have time to explore his feelings as piloting a travel sled on the end of a towline without a functioning transflux acclimator took all his concentration. The smell of vomit permeated the cabin, and each inhale was as vile as the next. What the hell did these people eat for breakfast? No more babysitting with Belk. If he ever got back to base, he would, well, he really wasn't sure what he was going to do, but he was certain he would figure something out. His mind raced with all the things he needed to do to understand and rectify this situation, as well as all the duties and responsibilities he was missing because of it. A steaming hot shower and a lot of ale kept popping into his mind.

Belk joined Garnet in Base Commander Atacama's outer office. Neither had time to clean up before being summoned by Dad. "At least I don't smell as bad as you do," Belk said as they entered the commander's office.

Garnet fumed. "I take full responsibility," he told Atacama.

The commander ordered, "Figure it out and never let it happen again." Atacama slammed a fist on his desk. "I expect better from you, Garnet. Your equipment better be in perfect operational order." The older man took in a breath and blew out, "There will not be a next time, understand, Squad Leader?" Second reprimand in as many weeks. This deployment was not starting well for Garnet. Both transgressions were beyond his control, but he took full responsibility for both. Atacama must think he was a total screwup.

"Understood, sir," Garnet said, his jaw tight and teeth gritted. Garnet was a model soldier and a damn good leader. Right now, he felt like neither.

"It wasn't your fault, crap happens," Belk offered as the two men left the office and continued down the hall.

My fault? I'm thinking you're the one who should have manned up. The travel sled checked out fully operational only a day ago, and for it to fail so badly…

The burning question looming in Garnet's mind was what actually caused the malfunction. The last person to touch the transflux acclimator was Delan. And if it was Delan's fault, he'd make Belk deal with his failure. Garnet planned to spend the rest of the day, evening, night going over the sled piece by piece until he determined what caused the accident.

"No problem, Doc," DeShay said to Leba. He never called her Doc. "I told you if you didn't want to be part of this, you didn't have to."

Leba was furious at the risks some of the people on her shift were taking to obtain the items from their list. "You don't understand," she insisted.

"No," DeShay snapped. "You don't understand." As she sat finishing a chart, he stood, put his arms on the table, and leaned forward to meet her face-to-face. "This is good for morale. You can opt out if you want, but don't tell me what I can or cannot do."

Startled by his aggressive comments, Leba got up from her desk. Sometimes he could be so unreasonable, and she wasn't in the mood to fight with him. "All I'm saying is that after the shuttle accident today—"

"Who says it was because of the game?" DeShay countered.

"Do what you want," she shot back, "but I'm telling JT I'm out."

DeShay blew out a breath. "Sometimes you can be so stubborn."

"Me?" she said as he stormed from the room. Leba felt the heat bubbling up to the top of her head and buried her face in her hands.

"Stubborn girl," DeShay spat as he met Grizzer in the hallway.

"What's up?" Grizzer questioned, cradling an item in his arms.

"She can be so rigid sometimes." DeShay stared at what Grizzer was carrying.

"Was about to let our leader know what I scored."

"Not with her, she's out. I'm in charge now." DeShay took the object from him. Grizzer looked at him. "Don't ask."

Needing to authenticate Grizzer's find, DeShay found Dr. Gordie Rensen in the med clinic break room. The smell of sewage burned his nostrils.

"You really need a shower," Rensen said to Big Ertle. "What did you have to do to get that thing?"

The ripe orderly was covered in head to toe with mud and dirt. "I climbed down the drainage shaft near the port latrine."

"Why?" Rensen looked at him from head to toe. "Why didn't you just grab one from the scrap pile out back?"

"Oh," said Ertle embarrassed. "I didn't think of that."

"Tiner, can you verify this before it's missed?" Rensen pointed to the object Ertle was cradling.

"Sure." DeShay grinned.

"And once you get it back in place, take a shower." Big Ertle nodded his head in agreement and left the room.

"I hope he gets the order right." Tiner laughed.

"You'd better have some good news," Garnet said as Zable entered the command room.

"Yes, sir, I do," Zable confirmed. "I'm through level two."

"Thank goodness, something going right for a change," Garnet said.

"It's not all good, though," Zable lamented.

"Of course not." Garnet shook his head. "Story of my life. Well, let me have it."

Before Zable could report, Belk burst into the room. "Hey, guys." Belk wrinkled his nose. "You didn't shower yet?" he asked Garnet.

"This is my new cologne, Puke d'Pareq," Tiv said. "It's designed so you'll say what you've got to say and then leave me alone."

Trying to hold his breath and speak at the same time, Zable reported, "In that vein, I got through level two, but level three needs an override code I don't have."

Belk glanced over Zable's shoulder at the info-pad and typed in a series of characters. The words *access granted* appeared on the screen. "Don't ask," he cautioned.

"Great!" Zable exclaimed. "If you don't mind, I'll be leaving to finish my task." Rubbing his nose, Zable left the room in a hurry.

"You smell like vomit and are covered in vehicle exhaust." Belk frowned.

"Oh, that," Garnet remarked. "I figured out what happened to the travel sled. The brand-new transflux acclimator malfunctioned." There was a long pause. "I want you to find the old one, the one Delan supposedly fixed. And find out how the brand-new one ended up in the sled." Belk stared at his feet. "I'm heading for a hot shower and a tall ale."

Garnet couldn't figure out why water wouldn't come out of the faucet in an adequate or heated flow. The last thing he needed was a cold shower. Unfortunately, though, that was what he ended up getting. The plan was to start in the gym facilities so his place wouldn't stink. At least the gym's locker room was industrially disinfected daily. He would have to shower again in his own quarters.

When he finally got home, he stood in the stall for an inordinate amount of time, letting the hot water pelt his skin. No matter how hard he tried, it was difficult to wash away the day's events. Unlike DeShay, he didn't have a woman on speed dial, summonable on a moment's notice. He would have to settle for iced ale and blasting bad guys on a virtual reality game. Sitting in his gym shorts while he waited for his uniform to be returned from the cleaning service, Tiv activated the game console, the vid screen bursting to life with the battle scenario. Before donning the VR helmet, he took a pull off the long-necked ale bottle. After adjusting the visor's sensors, Tiv selected a weapon from the case and launched the game. Being somewhat of a student of history, Tiv chose to participate in an ancient arena battle, pitting man versus alien beast in a fight to the death. This time armed only with a single-edged weapon. No armor, no shield, no mechanical devices. Dressed simply in cut-offs with bare chest and bare feet, he pushed through the gated entrance. The arena bleachers were tiered, filled with screaming fans who wanted to see him mauled and clawed to death.

The despot ruler who commanded the arena sat enthroned, a large goblet in his hand. He rose, and the arena fell silent. Even the beast struggling against the confinements of its stall seemed to acknowledge his authority and quieted while the man spoke. Tiv didn't particularly care for this part of the simulation. All he wanted was to engage the beast. No fanfare, no speeches, just raw aggression.

"Today's test of our combatant will decide his innocence or guilt," the bearded dictator began. "It will be a fight to the death." The crowd roared. "Any last requests?" he asked Tiv. Tiv waved him off. He was tired of talking; that was what usually got him into trouble. He turned to face the beast. "So be it then." The ruler waved his robed arm. "Release the beast." That line always made Tiv laugh a little and, although he vowed to reprogram the king's speech, never gotten around to it. The snorting animal burst into the walled arena. Froth bubbled from its tusked mouth. Six powerful legs pounded the dirt, making the ground quake under Tiv's feet.

Tiv approached the beast, trying to avoid its sweeping tail. One good swipe and his legs would be useless. He knew all the weak spots on the beast; the challenge was getting close enough to reach one. Tiv knew from previous encounters, movement was the key to defeating this beast. The randomly picked opponent was one of the fiercest the game offered and one of his favorite to fight. The gnatha beast was twice his size, with muscular extremities that could generate a bone-shattering wallop with little or no effort. After conquering the standard-issue beast, Tiv downloaded a spiked tail to enhance the challenge. He'd been knocked from his feet more than once when fighting the new and improved version. A few sessions ago, he upgraded its rudimentary brain. This augmented simulation proved even more formidable than he imagined, and to date, he only survived but never beaten it. The timer on the game stopped his certain death on more than one occasion.

Each time he fought the beast, it was programmed to compensate for his previously used tactics. This time, Tiv would have to change his approach if he planned on besting it. He started to the right like he always did, circling around the beast. It watched him move, snorting and stomping, waiting for Tiv to charge. This time, he didn't rush it. He danced with the beast, confusing its programming by moving back to the left before launching his weapon at it.

A CHANGE IN TACTICS: MAIDEN VOYAGE

The beast was caught off guard as the knife penetrated the fleshy part of its leg. Tiv followed up with a kick to where he thought the beast's knee was. He connected solidly, and the beast howled as its foreleg buckled.

Nice move, soldier. Tiv congratulated himself. The crowd roared with anticipation of his next move.

A courtier whispered to the king, "Foolish as he is now without a weapon."

"He has become the weapon," the king said as he watched Tiv use his outstretched hand to deliver an eye strike to the beast's bowed head. The beast roared again, its head flailing back and forth, its mouth groping for the blade Tiv put in its leg. The beast's rasp-like tongue finally wrapped around the knife, pulled it from its leg, and flung it across the arena floor. The king flicked a finger, and a wrangler let loose another beast into the arena.

Tiv spun around, stunned to see a second beast charging toward him. With only a moment to react, Tiv dove headlong toward the blinded beast. Suddenly, everything went black. "What the?" he spat angrily. Had he died? No, definitely not. His room resolved into view. Tiv wrestled the game helmet off and flung it on the couch. Activating his blinking comm, Tiv grumbled, "Garnet here."

Interruptions were the bane of his existence. Being a squad leader meant he was on call continuously, never any away time. He rarely took vacation because coming back was worse. Now with the prankster back, most interruptions these days were not legit, making his decision to pass on shore leave even more aggravating. There was silence on the sender's end of the comm call, no voice, no message, only static. Getting back into the game was not a realistic option. The mood was broken, and his aggression focused elsewhere. If he didn't find the prankster soon, he would have to change tactics and take a more offensive approach.

CHAPTER 29

Weeks melted into months as things settled down on the Pareqi base. The scientific expeditionary mission was going better than expected, or at least that was what the head scientist reported via sat-link. They were making great strides in understanding the geophysiochemistry of Vedax. Beautiful images of its surface were transmitted for all to behold. JT's crew won the scavenger hunt, much to the chagrin of DeShay, who finished a close second and swore JT must have cheated. DeShay was slowly letting the memory of Emmie Hodd be less intrusive on his everyday consciousness. Luth Cathen was starting to get bored with Mally Yertha and found excuses not to spend time with her. Unfortunately, this made him more insufferable.

"Find him another girl to release his—" Grizzer began.

"Who do you not like that much?" Anster asked.

"How about Middie?" DeShay laughed. "Now that would be a sight."

"She's so up JT's tailpipe you'd have to remove her with mega-forceps." Grizzer laughed.

"Maybe we pay someone to take him for a ride and leave him in the woods," Anster offered.

"Never been one for leaving loose ends," DeShay bemoaned.

Squad Leader Tiv Garnet was buried under a lot of loose ends. The unorthodox deployment numbers bothered him, as did the true reason for the Vedax exploration. Zable was close to cracking the code, but as Belk predicted, each higher level took longer to unravel. Belk, tired of Aleece and her need to see him regularly, volunteered for extra duty shifts. Belk also shared with Garnet he almost but not quite figured out what happened to the travel sled. He reasoned there must have been more than one transflux acclimator, one old and one new, but he wasn't sure how or when they were swapped in and out or by whom. Garnet didn't know who his tormentor was, and the plague of pranks escalated. Tross and some of the other married people were allowed to take short trips home to visit their families. Finally, Tiv Garnet missed having a woman in his life. Someone soft, someone who smelled nice, someone who could make him forget everything else, if only for a few hours.

"Remember that dinner you owe me," Tiv told DeShay.

"Sure," DeShay said. "I know just the place. Swing by the med clinic at 1930, and we'll leave from there."

"Okay, 1930, I'll be there," Tiv said.

"I have a lecture for a Pareqi women's group tonight or I'd join you," Leba apologized to DeShay.

"I want you to meet my friend," DeShay tried to persuade her. "He's about a head taller than you, maybe six two. Black hair, blue eyes, clean-shaven, straight as an arrow. You know, everything you like in a guy."

"Now how would you know that?" Leba asked. A faint blush pinked her jawline.

"There's a lot about you I know." He nodded his head. "Did my homework, talked to people." Her blush blossomed, and her chin fell to her chest.

With an outstretched hand, he lifted her chin. Her eyes remained down, and a sad smile finished her face. She shook off his touch. "Next time, I promise." She sniffled then patted his arm. "I barely have enough time to finish this shift and meet the transport." Her eyes met his. "But thanks for thinking of me."

Tiv arrived at the med clinic at exactly 1925. "You are prompt," DeShay said.

"And you never are." Tiv laughed.

"Let me change out of these scrubs, and I'll be right with you." DeShay scuttled away.

"Nice place you got here!" Tiv shouted after him.

"Shhh," the clerk scolded him. "This is a hospital and we have sick people."

An older man stepped from behind a curtained cubicle and offered a hand to Tiv. "Gordie Rensen, I'm the late-shift doctor tonight. Can I help you, son?"

"No, but thanks. I'm waiting for DeShay." Tiv put out his hand. "Tivon Garnet, Defender Company."

"You and Tiner served together," Gordie recognized. "Tiner speaks highly of you."

"Don't pay him no mind," DeShay said, slapping Dr. Rensen on the back.

"I was telling the squad leader here he could teach you a thing or two about discipline and decorum." Gordie laughed.

DeShay laughed. "Him, discipline, I taught him everything he knows. Decorum, that's another thing. Never could get him to dress right. That's why he has so many problems with the ladies."

Gordie rolled his eyes. "I give you credit for putting up with him. Luckily, I don't have to put up with all his antics like his shift doc does."

"Hey, my girl loves me, and you know it. All the ladies love me, 'cause—" he recited.

"Yeah, yeah." Tiv mocked, "Because you're so handsome, we all know the line."

"Have a quiet dinner." Gordie put a finger to his lips. "I've got work to do." And then he left to attend to an incoming patient.

"Where is your girl?" Tiv asked. "The one I've heard so much about."

"She's out doing one of those SHARE programs or she would have joined us."

"Uh-huh," Tiv said skeptically. "She's probably twice my age and has three eyes under one large furry eyebrow."

DeShay bristled. "See if I let you meet her." The two men headed toward the door. "I promise you'll like her when you meet her." DeShay winked.

A CHANGE IN TACTICS: MAIDEN VOYAGE

The Pareqi transit shuttle let the two men off at the Center City Metro station. The trees lining Main Street already shed most of their leaves in anticipation of the season change. The air was crisp and smelled of snow. DeShay pulled up the collar of his jacket. "Never much liked the cold."

"So why'd you pick a mission to an ice moon for your comeback performance?"

"I had my reasons." DeShay picked up the pace. He pointed to a retro overhanging awning. "That's it." He rubbed his hands together for warmth. "I know it doesn't look like much, but they have great music here." DeShay pulled the heavy door open. Tiv ducked under the hanging door sign and entered behind him.

Tiv surveyed the room. The lights were dimmed and the music slow and soulful. "Listen, Tiner, I like you, but I'm not one for this romantic stuff, especially with you."

"Shut up and sit down. This place has great food, great service, and great sights." DeShay cautioned, "But if you touch, you've got to pay."

"Classy place," Tiv commented, plastering his arms to his sides to avoid any accidental contact. Both men took seats at an inconspicuous table toward the left of the stage. Strategically from here, they could see the kitchen, the restrooms, and who entered and left the building. Situational awareness, never a moment's peace. Always on guard. Not everyone appreciated the Tal-Kari and their role as an intra-galactic police force. The men ordered, and the server brought their appetizers quickly. "So," DeShay drew out the word. "What do you need to talk with me about?" Tiv was silent for a moment. "Don't get all quiet on me, I know that look. Come on, what's up?"

Tiv hesitated before speaking. "I needed a night away from the farm. The animals were driving me crazy."

"Tough place to keep all the livestock accounted for," DeShay observed. "Too many distractions, huh?" he said, turning to observe one of the women at the bar flirting with him. She was younger than he was and dressed provocatively in a short crimson-colored satiny dress exposing her dark, slender, shapely leg, which ended in a matching stiletto. She dangled one shoe off the tip of her toes then bent over to replace it.

"You're just like Belk." Tiv cleared his throat.

"And you're not enough like Belk," DeShay observed, his focus still on the lady at the bar. "Loosen up."

Tiv bristled at his remark. "Down boy, heel," he commanded the old war dog.

"I'm just looking. Don't have enough coin to pay for that," he retorted and turned back to Tiv.

The server removed the appetizer plates and gave each man his entrée. Both dug in quickly as if neither had eaten in a week but then slowed. Tiv finished chewing and was about to ask a question but stopped and thought better of it and forked another piece of meat. DeShay possessed an uncanny knack for being able to see right through him, and Tiv knew it. Tiner would eventually be able to wean it out of him, get him to spill his guts. Tiv often wished he had an older brother. DeShay initially assumed the role when Tiv met him years ago, but since his injury, they saw less and less of each other. They still met for dinner now and again, but it wasn't like old times. Having grown up a lot since their first meeting, Tiv wasn't green anymore, and he found himself acting as big brother to some of the guys in his unit.

"Come on. Tell me what's bugging you," DeShay said. "If it takes too long, I'm going to ask red to come over and seduce it out of you."

"Be serious," Tiv implored him. "She'd have better luck with a…" He hesitated.

DeShay started, "So it's that serious, huh?"

Reluctantly Tiv detailed his current predicament. "You usually have solutions for just about everything. I was hoping you could fix my problems."

"That won't get you anywhere, listening to an old war dog like me," DeShay humbled himself. "As long as I have known you, you have always been able to figure out your own problems, never needed my advice before, except maybe how to dress and how to…" laughed DeShay.

"That's just it." Tiv inhaled deeply. "I'm usually able to take counsel from you or Tross or even Belk and put it all together and figure out what to do. This time, something's different." He tapped his hand on the table. "This time, I can't put my finger on it."

"As I see it"—DeShay rubbed his head—"you have two serious problems preventing you from doing your job the way you want to." DeShay elaborated, "The first is the constant annoyance from the prankster. Avoiding his traps is taxing your patience. You're out of your routine, rattled, and bothered. The second, well, the second is the lack of a lady." Tiv buried his nose into his food and continued to eat. "You know it's true. You're getting older, and you're afraid you'll end up like me, alone."

"When did you get all philosophical?" Tiv said annoyed. He didn't want to admit it, but DeShay was on target. He hated not being in control.

DeShay dug back into his food, and there was silence for a long time at the table. He finished the last bit of gravy on his plate and sighed.

Tiv waited, but DeShay remained quiet. He even stopped flirting with red. Finally, DeShay spoke, "You know, once, I was where you are now. I was career military, a great job, plenty of good friends, but alone. Emmie and I parted ways. I didn't need her, I didn't need anyone, that is, anyone steady. I had time for settling down. I knew one day I'd have a wife, kids of my own, a house in the country, and a big fat pension to live off of. But I was wrong..." His voice trailed off. "I was wrong. I waited too long. Life was passing by, and I was coasting through. Until..." He paused again, rubbing his artificial shoulder. "Until this happened and brought me crashing back to reality."

Tiv never realized how truly regretful DeShay was about his life. Tiv always respected DeShay's choices, his career path, and his love for life. He was wrong, though. DeShay was melancholy, regretful, unhappy. Beneath the fun-loving exterior was a broken man, never truly recovered from his devastating accident. He put on a good show, but beneath the surface was a deep, pervasive sorrow. "I'm sorry," Tiv said.

"I don't need pity," DeShay snapped at him. "Don't repeat my mistakes." DeShay got up abruptly from the table. "I'll be back." He headed toward the lavatory.

Tiv sat stunned at DeShay's revelation. He was truly unhappy, and Tiv felt badly for him, not pity, but sorrow. Tiv didn't realized how much DeShay's recent breakup with Emmie stirred up old emotions and pains.

By the time DeShay returned to the table, the entrée dishes were bussed, and fresh ales replaced the spent ones. Straightening his collar, DeShay winked at red. She waved a few fingers at him but remained at the bar. "Nice, very nice," he said as he finished taking a swallow from his ale.

Tiv didn't say anything. He really didn't know what to say. The man he admired for so long was as human as he was, flawed, imperfect, and confused. "So I was thinking that it's about time I meet this girl of yours, you know, the doctor friend of yours."

DeShay smiled. "I think she'd like that. Let me talk to her and see when she's available."

Leba arrived early as usual for her presentation. The auditorium was still quiet save for the tech trying to get the projector working. A gentleman garbed in traditional Pareqi robes came up and introduced himself as the spiritual leader of the congregation. The program Leba was about to deliver was specially requested by a member of the sisterhood. The clergyman informed her the ambassador's own consort would be in attendance, and she should be honored. Leba humbled at the remark, expressing her sincere appreciation for their most gracious invitation.

Leba's presentation to the hundred or so Pareqi women was well received. The question-and-answer session went on longer than expected, and the postprogram inquires continued until the clergyman announced it was time for Dr. Brader to leave. He promised to have her back in short order.

"I don't know when she's available again," the clergyman said to the female moderator as they escorted Leba to a waiting transport. Leba knew better than to answer. She didn't want to embarrass her host.

"You don't understand," the woman told him. "A very important benefactor requested she do a similar presentation for her organization. She demands immediate attention if we expect her to match her original contribution."

"I'll see what I can do," the clergyman assured her. "I'll have to speak with the liaison's office. They coordinate the SHARE program."

"Excellent," the woman said, clasping her hands to her chest. "I'll let her know."

As she rode back to base, Leba was still bothered by some of the questions. The inquiries were definitely off topic. The ambassador's consort asked about her expertise in cold-weather physiology. Out of courtesy to the Pareqi diplomat, Leba answered the question. When another woman, elegantly dressed with flowing red hair beneath a head scarf, asked about the extent of the Tal-Kari base deployment, the moderator quickly stifled the query and reiterated to the audience to save those questions for a different venue. The second unidentified woman left swiftly after her question was rebuked.

The next morning's shift began as usual, with Leba arriving earlier than everyone else and relieving Dr. Rensen as soon as sign out was complete. The night shift quiet, Gordie was able to catch up on charting, leaving Leba time to review the day's tasks at a leisurely pace. Unfortunately for Leba and her crew, the day started out exceptionally busy. A street festival the night before on the eastern side of town resulted in many attendees up all night with vomiting and diarrhea. Food poisoning was rampant in not only the locals but also in the deployed personnel who visited the fair.

Besides the gastrointestinal ailments, there were also a number of postbrawl participants as intoxicating beverages flowed like water from the booths. Leba notified the Pareqi public health authorities of the mini-epidemic and spent half the morning and late into the afternoon rehydrating very sick patients in between suturing lacerations, splinting injured limbs, and sobering up drunks. When the shift was finally over, most of her crew hadn't eaten or sat down the entire day.

Earlier, at the start of the shift, DeShay wanted to talk to her but never got the chance. "Nice job, girl," he complimented. "We did good work today." Leba nodded, exhausted and spent. "Come, I'll buy you a drink," he offered.

"No, thank you." Leba sighed. "I need a shower and lots of sleep. Tomorrow," she said, her eyes heavy. "We'll talk tomorrow."

DeShay too was tired, more than he realized. "Tomorrow it is," he said, more chipper than he should have.

"You need some sleep too," she advised.

"I need to wind down, have an ale, my bed will be there waiting," he joked.

"Okay." She yawned and walked from the clinic.

DeShay was proud of how well she matured under his tutelage. But she deserved better than this dreadfully boring clinic, a waste of her skills and talents. Dangerous as it was, she would do great in the field. Before leaving for the commissary, DeShay sent an info-text:

> Rough day. Busy clinic.
> No time to talk.
> Will get back to you with an answer. DT

Garnet felt a soft buzz from his info-pad and removed the portable comm from his pocket. He scanned the info-text and typed in a response.

> DT, No worries.
> Think I can hold out another day.
> Ha! Ha! Tiv

Garnet sent the message and tucked the comm away and returned to the data he was analyzing. Overseer Company picked up strange interference from the communications array on Vedax, and Squad Leader Damond Fiorat asked Tiv to see what he made of it.

"You up for dinner?" Belk questioned as he walked into the room.

"What do you make of this?" Tiv asked, rotating the monitor around for Belk to see.

"Looks like static," Belk observed.

"When's the last time you've seen patterned static?" Tiv asked, pointing to the recurring oscillating waveform partially hidden by overlying voice traffic.

Zable walked into the room. His eyes widened as he stared at the display. "It takes me countless weeks to get through level five, and you have it on the monitor."

Tiv and Belk looked up at him in unison. "What are you babbling about, cyber boy?" Belk inquired.

"That same pattern, it's what level five was hiding." Zable pulled up a chair. "Let me explain." He pushed his way to stand in front of the monitor. "About two standard years ago, one of our listening posts picked up a signal similar to that. At first, the scientists thought it was a rotating pulsar or neutron star deep in space."

Garnet furrowed his brow. "I know where this is going."

Zable continued, "On closer inspection, there was no spectral pattern marking the presence of a previously undetected natural celestial body." He took the stylus and drew on a blank screen. "This is us on Pareq." He pointed to a small circle. "This is Glirase." He pointed to the larger circle. "This is Vedax." He motioned to a smaller circle in an elliptical orbit. He then drew semicircular arcing waves emanating from Vedax and bouncing between the bodies on the screen. "My guess is level six details what intel we have gathered so far and what Operation Surf is all about."

"Cute, waves, Operation Surf," Belk said, shoulder back, chin high, proud he made the connection.

"You think it's some sort of weapon?" Tiv asked Zable.

"That's just it. I don't think the brain trust knows what it is, but I bet that's what they're here to find out."

"Why don't we just ask?" Belk said.

"Ask who?" Zable shot back.

"The Pareqi," Belk offered.

"And what makes you think they'd know?" Zable queried.

"If there was something going on in my backyard, I am either responsible for it or know who is."

"And you're just going to knock on the Pareqi ambassador's door and ask him?"

"Yep," Belk agreed.

"Think Dad knows?" Zable asked Garnet, who was looking at the sound wave in a new light.

"Can't imagine he doesn't," Garnet responded. "Think you can get through level six?"

Zable frowned. "That's what I came to tell you. Level six is not on any terminal on this base. Not even Dad's." He waited. "In fact, since I first started looking, someone has wiped it out of the root memory."

"They must have seen your intrusion," Belk jabbed.

"Not likely. I don't mark my trail like you do." He laughed.

"Now, what's that mean?" Belk bristled.

"Now, what's that mean?" JT said to Nilsa.

"It's just that." Her eyes filled with tears. "I wish we could spend more time together."

JT sighed in relief. For a moment, he thought she was going to say they needed to take some time apart. But the exact opposite was true; she wanted more of his time. She hated being alone, especially in this place, with all the memories. Earlier in the day, she caught sight of Tiv Garnet in her sector. They exchanged pleasantries and small talk, but it bothered her nonetheless.

"I heard he's being pranked. Well, good for him. He deserves everything he gets," she said angrily. "If I knew who his tormentor was, I'd give him a big fat kiss." She paused for a moment as emotion began to overtake her. "I'm sorry I ever came here." She sniffled.

A CHANGE IN TACTICS: MAIDEN VOYAGE

So I guess hanging out with me just isn't good enough for you. She began to sob uncontrollably, until JT put an arm around her shoulder. Slowly she composed herself and corrected, "I'm glad we're here together, but I wish we could really be together, you know, all the time."

JT really didn't know what to think. He believed Nilsa was over his friend Tiv, but he was wrong. Just the sight of him made her regress. Maybe it was wrong to have brought her here. Could Nilsa be obsessed? No, he assured himself. She was perfect. Perfect for him, the girl he dreamed of but always out of his reach. Until now. Now she was his. What else would he have to do for her to forget Garnet?

"Anyone up for dinner?" Belk asked those assembled in the room.

"I've got a few more things to do," Tiv begged off the invitation.

"Me too," Zable said. "Especially since I've completed the task you charged me with, it's time you paid up." Belk looked at him curiously. Tiv smiled because he knew what was coming next. "That's right, Belk, I need the contact information for your sister unless you want to do the introductions."

"You can't be serious?" Belk said at the sight of Zable's outstretched hand. "Tiv, he can't be serious, can he?" Tiv remained quiet. "Come on," Belk urged. "You didn't really think I would let you date or even meet my sister, did you?"

Zable stood firm, crossing his arms across his chest.

"You better come up with something else, hotshot, because I think he's serious," Tiv added.

Belk backpedaled. "Come on, man, she's my baby sister, and you're..."

"I'm what?" Zable asked.

"I'd stop there before you really step into it," Tiv cautioned.

"You're a guy," Belk said.

"Brilliant, and what gave you your first clue?" Zable puffed out his chest, splayed his legs, and crossed his arms over his chest.

369

"Enough," Tiv demanded. He turned his attention to Zable. "Z, I'll put you in for a field promotion. Comes with a pay raise and a stripe if you're interested."

"Thanks," he said. "Better than Belk's sister."

"Hey, that's not fair," Belk reacted. Garnet and Zable began to laugh and watched as a red blush crept up Belk's face. "You guys." Belk turned to leave, finally realizing he'd been played.

Zable added, "I still want to meet your sister, Belk, despite Garnet's promise of a better life at a higher rank."

"Shut up," Belk snapped. "Join me for dinner and I'll tell you all about her, especially since you'll never meet her."

"Why not? I can always dream." Zable chuckled. The two men left the team room with Garnet comparing Zable's drawing and the signal on the monitor. After a few minutes and rubbing his eyes for the fourth time, Tiv deactivated the screen. Today was a relatively quiet day, not too many rescues or recoveries; more importantly, the prankster seemingly took the past week off.

Tiv got up and headed toward the door when an idea struck him. He reactivated the team room's info-portal and situated himself in front of the keyboard to type in his inquiry.

> Tal-Kari Personnel Database
> Enter Location:
> **Pareq**
> Pareq Deployment files located. Please enter name:

Tiv scratched his head for a moment and then typed again.

> Search by Technical Specification/Company
> Enter Technical Specification/Company:
> **Medical Company**
> Medical Company, Pareq unit, files located.
> Please enter job description:
> **Physician**

A CHANGE IN TACTICS: MAIDEN VOYAGE

The cursor blinked for a moment or two and then displayed:

There are 4 entries that match your search criteria. Would you like to see them displayed?

Yes
Retrieving data...

1. Leba Brader
2. JT Hobes
3. Gordon Rensen
4. Wallen Scoby

Please enter the number of the entry you wish to see displayed.

Tiv hesitated for a moment, wondering if what he was doing was a good thing. He should trust DeShay, but he was never one to leave anything to chance. With his index finger, he pushed the 1 character key.

1
Retrieving data...
Personnel file: Dr. Leba Brader

Tiv scanned the display. This friend of DeShay's was not what he expected. DeShay only told him about the person, not her background or history. Tiv scrolled through her dossier and was impressed not only with her education but also with her accomplishments. What was DeShay thinking? Why would a girl like this want a grunt like him? Tiv brought up her picture and looked at her eyes, which seemed to stare back at him. He deactivated the screen. The face on the screen slowly faded away, but the image seemed to linger in his mind. Maybe it was time for a change. DeShay never steered him wrong, well, not often, so what the heck, he'd at least meet her. If she wasn't what he expected or even if she was, he'd find out.

Tiv walked to the door for the second time, extinguished the lights in the room, and headed down the corridor. He couldn't get the image from the screen out of his mind until the corpsman at the guard desk interrupted his contemplation. "Night, Squad Leader," the young cadet saluted.

"Night," Tiv saluted back.

"Night," DeShay said to the sentry posted outside the med unit's sleeping quarters.

"Night, sir," the cadet returned the sentiment. DeShay was mad at himself for not speaking with Leba about Tiv. No matter, he would have time tomorrow. Right now, he wanted to sleep, but before he did, he reviewed the letter waiting in the draft bin. Emmie, sweet Emmie, if she only knew how much he really cared. Tomorrow, thought DeShay sleepily, tomorrow was a new day, and maybe he would feel differently. He decided then and there things would be different when he woke in the morning. He would stop reminiscing about the past and move on to the future. Satisfied with his decision to change tactics, he left the letter unsent. Sleep came unusually quickly for DeShay, and he slept the best he had in a long time.

CHAPTER 30

Violently shaking his bedside alarm chrono, DeShay slept later than expected. Its malfunction would cost him extra duty unless Leba covered for him. He knew she would; she always had his back. Hustling to get himself together to make it to work on time, he slurped down a cup of prebrewed coffee. The bitterness stung his throat, but the caffeine rush was augmented, and that was what he needed to get his juices flowing.

"Good morning," Leba said cheerily. Despite his lateness and her need to cover for him, she wasn't angry, only concerned. Why couldn't Emmie be like that? "I was worried you weren't going to make it." She tossed him his med jacket but didn't probe his lateness any further.

She deserved an explanation, though, because she didn't ask. DeShay rubbed his chin, the stubble scratchy under his fingers. "Overslept."

"No worries. I kinda like the roguish look." She smirked. "You're just lucky Lord Cathen's been mysteriously late too. You guys double date or what?" He frowned at her. "Something's up, but I don't know what."

DeShay scratched his head and felt the beginnings of rough growth there too. "Night shift say anything?"

"No, but there's been a lot of activity at the hangar bay. I keep hearing departure flights."

"Don't worry, we'll find out soon enough." DeShay patted her shoulder. "This place has more gossips than a bunch of old ladies at a retirement home." Leba's mouth fell open. He raised a finger. "And don't go asking me how I know." She laughed. Figuring he could sneak in his morning routine while away, DeShay offered, "I'll check our travel gear."

"Already done," she said.

"Smart girl, I wish everyone listened like you do." Shrugging off the need to spit, shine, and polish, he turned to retrieve the daily log. For a moment, he wondered what it would be like if she were his lady. Naw, he knew it wouldn't work. It wasn't that she was too young or not pretty enough; it was something else. It was the way she made him feel. Not all hot and bothered like Emmie, but loved and cared for. He didn't want to spoil it with some relationship based on mutual loneliness they'd both regret.

She caught him staring and then looked down at the front of her shirt. "What, did I miss a button or something?"

"Before I forget again, there's someone I'd like you to meet." She stared back at him. "Buddy of mine, squad leader, I've been telling him about you, and he'd like to meet you."

"Sounds interesting." She put a finger to the side of her face and tilted her head. "If he's anything like you, I'd love to meet him." She smiled. "Especially if he's sporting the bad boy look you've got going this morning."

"I wish he were more like me." DeShay raised an eyebrow and rubbed his chin again. "No, he's always regulation just like you. I've been working to fix him for years." He paused and then corrected himself. "It's not that he's broken, but he's a little on the stiff side." She looked at him again, another odd expression. "You know what I mean." He laughed. "He's by the book, like someone else I know."

Hands firmly planted on her hips, her brow furrowed. "And what's wrong with that?" she asked.

"That's why I think you two would be perfect together," DeShay concluded.

"You do, do you? Well, I guess I'll have to see for myself." Moving closer to him, she gave him a small peck on the cheek. She whispered, "Thanks for thinking of me. I'm sure he's very nice."

DeShay gestured with open palms. "Sometimes I have to do things for the good of the team."

Leba pushed him away. "The team, you're doing this for the good of the team?" She stood back, arms crossed over her chest. "See if I cover for you next time."

"See if I cover for you next time," Tross said to Belk as they entered Defender Company's ready room. Both men were geared up for the upcoming shuttle flight. Garnet's early morning rally call to assemble Defender Company left Belk scrambling. "Where were you anyway?" Tross whispered to Belk.

"Shh," Belk said, "I'll explain it to you later."

His jaw tight, the tension in his shoulders evident, Squad Leader Garnet approached his unit. The men and women of Defender Company stood at attention. Organized by rank, Tross and Belk were in the first row to the left, facing their squad leader. Belk hoped Garnet wouldn't notice he was still wearing his duty shirt from the night before. Cold-weather gear covered Garnet's uniform. His balaclava was bunched at his neck, and his side arm cinched over a heavy white long-waist jacket. With his helmet nestled under his arm, Garnet briefed them. "As you know, we have been monitoring transmissions from our Vedax units. Early this morning, communications were lost. Overseer Company was able to reestablish the connection only a short time ago." The small lines near his eyes now more prominent, his mouth pursed, Garnet's face darkened. "What we know is a significant incursion from an unidentified source attacked our people. This attack was unprovoked. Moon-side ground units report heavy barrages from an unknown weapon and have taken multiple casualties." Belk knew this wasn't good. The damage must be colossal for Garnet to be this tight. "Striker Company called up its reserve troops to reinforce the forward position, and we are charged with rescue and retrieval. Get on cold-weather gear. Our shuttles are warmed and idling in hangar bay six, plan to debark in fifteen minutes."

The assembled dispersed as Garnet called for Tross and Belk. "Denny, Brit, we will be in for some hellacious conditions. Surface temperatures are freezing and, with the wind picking up, subzero.

Don't take any chances. Get our people in and out. No heroics." Both nodded their approval. They turned to leave when Garnet added, "We'll also be supporting Cathen's Med Company."

"We're going to be a glorified taxi service." Belk kicked his boot on the floor. Tross glanced sideways and frowned. Belk could hear Denny Tross in his head yelling, "Shut up, stupid."

"Whatever it takes, guys, we have our orders, and I want all our people back," Garnet reminded them. "Now get going or you'll miss your flight."

"Yes, sir," Belk and Tross said in unison.

"Doc," the clerk summoned Leba to his console, "I can't locate Cathen, so Overseer wants you in HQ right away."

"Let them know I'm on my way," she said. *This can't be good.* She sprinted toward the door then looked back over her shoulder, trying to remember if she left anyone unattended.

DeShay waved. "Go on, I'll watch the fort."

Leba could feel her heart pounding as she headed down the hallway to the command hub. Would she be up for command? No worries, she had DeShay. During medical training, Leba learned asking for assistance and advice was not a sign of weakness but made you a better leader.

Dodging people scurrying back and forth, Leba picked up speed and raced down the corridor. She turned into the next hallway and was met by strobing red lights. The door at the end labeled *Section One: Operations*. Whipping her TK identi-card from her lab coat, she touched it to the card reader. *Access granted: Leba Brader* flashed on the screen. She heard the locking bolts whirr, and the heavily fortified door slid open. Outside the secure command station, she identified herself, and the security cadet checked the roster and let her pass.

"It's bad, really bad!" Leba heard shouting over the scanner.

An officer, short with a mop of black hair, looking like he'd pulled an all-nighter, came over to her. He adjusted his headset, pulled the mic away from his mouth, and said, "Priman Gwittrel, communications officer. Dr. Brader?"

"Leba Brader," she acknowledged. "What's going on?" The nerve center of her base was a mass of blinking lights and busy people. She looked at the multiview vid screen; some showed the hangar bays and the departing flights, some were static filled, others showed smoking wreckage, and one in the lower corner showed the inside of some Pareqi office building. Gwittrel angled her away from the displays and handed her a decoded message:

Antog Hirousey, Explorer Company to Pareq Base Operations:
Multiple casualties, send med, evac, we need covering fire.

Leba noticed the time stamp. "This was sent hours ago."

"There was an interruption in our communications." Gwittrel's eyes darted around. He pointed to a graphic on the nearby screen. Listed were the Pareqi Tal-Kari units and their status. Her eyes alighted on the reds, greens, or yellows following each name. Her Medical Company's designator was blinking yellow. "Defender Company just left for Vedax to join Striker's reinforcements. They need you guys up there too."

"Did you let Squad Leader Cathen know?" she asked. Leba's mind raced, trying to process the data and come up with a plan.

"Couldn't raise him on the comm, but we'll keep trying," Gwittrel explained. *Comm off again? Never go offline, huh?* She filed that away and refocused on the situation.

Fingering the message as she reread it. "Wait, covering fire? I thought this was a scientific mission?"

"Get going, Doc. Grab your gear, get your people mobilized, and report to Portal Five. You're shuttle is on the pad, waiting.

By the time Leba got back to the clinic to rally her troops, Luth Cathen was front and center, lecturing. "People, we have a situation." Always a flair for the dramatic, Cathen paused after every couple of words. Chomping at the bit, Leba was ready to sprint to her locker and don her gear, but with Cathen in charge, she would have to wait. "Glad you could join us, Brader," he noticed.

Don't push me or I'll tell everyone your comm was off again.

DeShay looked over his shoulder and mouthed, "What's up?"

Leba mouthed, "Later." DeShay turned back. Standing there, listening to Cathen ramble on, Leba felt a prickling at the back of her neck, and her hand instinctively went to it, and she squeezed. Cathen was no leader. And with this emergency, she hoped he wouldn't get them all killed with his antics.

When Leba led, she led by example. First teaching her charges what they needed to know and then demonstrating how it was done. See one, do one, teach one. If she did her job right, her charges would do it right and then be able to teach others. It worked in school, on the playing field, and in the med clinic. Luth Cathen, her squad leader for this mission, hadn't demonstrated anything. Sure, he knew how to talk a good game. He was entertaining, putting it when training began. "You're a bunch of scientists, not real soldiers. You're soft." Bragging how if they didn't listen to him, he'd be bringing them home in body bags. What she learned about fieldwork, she learned from DeShay and his buddies.

DeShay taught Leba a lot in their time together. Impressed with her uncanny ability to size up people after only brief encounter with them, DeShay told her to rely on her own instincts. Never one to question authority outright, Leba was puzzled. How could command put Cathen in charge if he didn't know what he was doing? DeShay repeatedly told her, "Girl, you need to trust yourself and your decisions. If you expect me to follow your lead, you need to stand up and take charge." Leba didn't understand how a team could survive if the members did not trust or respect their leader.

Leba remembered DeShay telling her how he ended up in the medical corps. Old-school military, enlisted career soldier, DeShay was thrust into the role of medic after his shoulder was shattered during the Etalian war. While recuperating in the base hospital, he saw his military career coming swiftly to an end. His c.o. said as much on a visit after his shoulder joint replacement. DeShay loved being a soldier, defending the damsels and defeating the demons. It was all he knew how to do. He was good at it too, until the unfortunate day when his green commanding officer sent him out on a suicide recon mission. In his youth, he thought he was invincible, so volunteering to prove his squad leader wrong was a great opportunity to move up the ladder. Leba thought DeShay reminded her of her uncle Heli. Although she was sure Uncle Heli still considered himself indestructible, she knew DeShay did not. He was only a man, a very brave man, who turned a tragic life event into a positive. After recovering from his liver laceration and shoulder injury, DeShay transferred to the medical corps.

When Cathen finished talking, Leba raced to her duty station locker and removed her rucksack. She slipped off her shoes and jacket, stripping down to her insulated form-fitting undershirt and leggings. She pulled on her thermal tactical trousers, cinching the gear belt at her waist. After tucking in her insulated long-sleeve scrub top, she slid her arms into the snowy-white long-waist cold-weather jacket. Leba slipped her head and neck into the protective balaclava and laced up her ice boots. She reviewed each seal, making sure they were in place without any breaks. Grabbing helmet and gloves, she slung the rucksack over her shoulder and slammed her locker shut. About to run to the hangar bay, she hesitated, reopened her locker, snatched her rock knife, shoved it deep down into her boot, and ran down the hall.

The overheard claxon repeated, "Code gray, this is no drill! Report to your code gray duty stations." Code gray, a level nine disaster. The only thing missing was nuclear contamination to make it a level ten, code gray prime. Things had gone so well, medically boring but relatively incident-free, so much so she thought she could get used to this deployment stuff. More time to explore the other things life offered. Hang out and learn more stuff from DeShay. Experience the adventure of a new place and new people with the best tour guide she could think of. Leba imagined as she entered the hangar bay her opinion was about to change.

Portal Five was a flurry of activity. Ground crews were charging fuel cells, supply techs were wheeling cargo sleds full of equipment to each waiting shuttle, and pilots were making final inspections of their birds. DeShay lumbered in and joined her. His jaw was tight, the veins in his neck pulsing. "In all my years," he said, his baritone voice rough, laden with remorse, "I've only seen two code grays. I hoped to never see one again."

"Isn't this what we trained for, day in and day out?" she questioned.

"War is different, you expect casualties. You take some, they take some. It's expected. Don't get me wrong, not that you want anyone killed or maimed, it's that you expect it. This unexpected stuff rips your guts out." This was a side of DeShay she hadn't seen before. Leba was ready to jump in, but DeShay seemed different. Not in fight mode like she expected. He was restrained and concerned. Where was the self-assurance, the coolness? The "Let's spring into action and kick some enemy butt" DeShay. The save-the-day attitude?

"Going down fighting, that's what it means to be a trooper, a soldier. But an unprovoked attack on civilians... this sounds like a slaughter. War ain't pretty but this..." He trailed off as their squad leader entered. Leba and DeShay were joined by the rest of their medical shift team as well as their support unit. When Cathen pointed to their shuttle, she gasped at the active response unit designation. This TKM-77 was identical to the small cold box shuttle. This was not going to be good.

Overseer Company took up a command position at the Pareq Base to orchestrate the evacuation operation. Base Commander Chalco Atacama sat in his command chair perched above the lower tier where Squad Leader Damond Fiorat and his staff worked earnestly to coordinate the outgoing flights. Fiorat received sketchy telemetry from both Myaronitz and Hirousey. Both squads had taken multiple casualties. Scrambled from the base earlier, Myaronitz's Striker reserves were providing cover fire to allow the remaining survivors from Striker Company to escape. Hirousey's Explorer Company was charged with gathering up the scientific personnel and getting them out of harm's way. Explorer's reserves would help staff the evac shuttles. Defender Company was rocketing moonward to provide recovery and retrieval and back up Cathen's medical team. Given the projected casualty numbers, Overseer requested two of the three med shifts go to the moon, but Cathen argued that was putting more softies in harm's way, and he could do it with only one shift. The first med team would triage and stabilize the injured for transport, and the other med team would await incoming shuttles. The third med team would be available for rotation if needed. Fiorat was not happy but acquiesced when Cathen agreed to go and personally supervise the operation. Fiorat glanced over his shoulder and spied Atacama drumming his fingers on the console. He'd never seen him so rattled.

Once the med shuttle was loaded with personnel and equipment, Launch Control signaled the pilot he was cleared for takeoff. "Med team is airborne," Fiorat informed Atacama.

"Anything from Striker or Explorer?" Atacama, stroking his moustache, questioned.

"They've both gone dark," Fiorat reported.

Leaning forward, elbows propped up on the rail, his hands clenched, Atacama, forehead wrinkled with deepening furrows, looked down at Fiorat. "Can you get the base camp punched up?"

"We're working on setting up a relay now, sir." Fiorat waited when Cadet Zach Kixon handed him a message. Scanning its contents, he reported, "Chief Science Officer reports all his remaining people are ready for pickup."

"How many people did he have in the field?" Atacama asked, shifting in his seat, dabbing at the beads of sweat forming on his forehead.

"Reports are sketchy, sir. It appears at least half his complement were at forward positions when they were attacked." Fiorat scratched the hair behind his left ear, under his headset. "What I don't understand is why they didn't see it coming."

"There'll be time for speculation later," Atacama grumbled. "Why don't we have a vid feed yet?" he snapped.

Fiorat checked his console. "Striker Two Flight will be in range for visual in five, four, three, two, one." There was silence for a moment until the comm crackled.

"Pareq Base, this is Striker Two Flight Leader, forward position demolished. I repeat no survivors at forward position one. No hostiles, but—" the transmission abruptly terminated.

The monitor where Striker Flight Two's cam was broadcasting was now nothing but static. "What happened?" Fiorat yelled over the commotion.

"We've lost Flight Two, we've lost Flight Two!" screamed a voice.

"Who is this?" Fiorat demanded.

"Cadet Pragen, sir. Something hit Flight Two, and he went down. We are taking evasive action. Nothing was on my monitor, sir. I swear."

Atacama walked the few stairs down to the lower level, toggled a switch on Fiorat's console, opening the comm for outgoing transmission. "Cadet, this is Commander Atacama, do you have eyes on the hostiles."

"No, sir," the cadet answered, his voice quavering. It was obvious to Fiorat the young flyer was in shock seeing his flight leader drop from the sky. Maybe hearing his base commander's grandfatherly confidence would strengthen his resolve. "No, sir," he repeated, this time his voice stronger.

"Cadet, get the rest of your flight regrouped and lay covering fire in a reverse trajectory from what hit Flight Two, understood?" Atacama advised.

"Yes, sir," the cadet acknowledged. On his sensor board, Fiorat watched the sortie adjust their headings to carry out their assignment.

"Punch up Striker's last known position and plot a presumed launch point for the hostiles," Atacama ordered one of Fiorat's men. The cadet ran to a terminal and began his calculations. "How far is Defender out?"

"Not very, they should be entering atmosphere in just under thirty minutes. The med team shouldn't be very long behind, maybe sixty minutes after."

"Still nothing from Explorer One yet?" Atacama asked. "Wish we had more eyes on the ground."

"Explorer Two is working to get the relay up now. Whatever the hostiles are using, it's really screwing up our communications," Fiorat said.

Minutes seemed liked hours to the people in the HQ at the Pareq Base. "I should have been on one of the shuttles to Vedax." Fiorat felt the same way. There was nothing like being there himself, not from behind a desk. He could only imagine how tough this was for a seasoned war vet like Atacama, whose experience was invaluable in situations like this, to sit here and watch events unfold.

A CHANGE IN TACTICS: MAIDEN VOYAGE

"What the hell happened?" Belk asked as Defender Company's number two shuttle penetrated the cloud cover and could at last see the moon's surface. After being updated on Striker Flight Two Leader's demise, Defender was instructed to approach from a different aspect. The communications relay was almost fully operational as trailing shuttles followed them in. There were smoking craters where buildings and equipment had been. There was no sign of the forward position except for the temporary embankments erected to try and forestall an invasion. Defender Company's shuttles circled around to the fallback position and landed in sequence.

"Defender is on the surface, sir," Kixon informed his commander. "We should have eyes and ears momentarily."

"To my console as well, cadet," Atacama said as he returned to the higher tier and sat on the edge of his chair.

The static on the screen slowly resolved into a room scattered with desks and info-terminals, abandoned workstations, and chaos. "Talman Paque, Defender Company, over."

"Overseer here, we are receiving your feed, go ahead," Fiorat requested.

"We are setting up a triage area. Med Company should be touching down shortly. Once the perimeter is secure, we will dispatch recon and recovery sorties. Garnet is trying to raise Hirousey and Myaronitz now. Unfortunately, something is jamming our ground communications, but we're working on it."

The chief science officer interrupted the briefing, his face taking up most of the view screen. "I've never seen anything like it." Professor Muruq explained in a hurried voice, sweat beading on his forehead. He was a short, stout man, his lab jacket rumpled and soiled. "All of a sudden we were hit with some type of wave." He paused. "No time to prepare. We couldn't raise Striker or Explorer.

You need to get my people out of here now. Many of us are injured." Hands flailing. "You need to off-lift us now."

"Atacama, here. Professor, do you know the nature of what we're up against?" There was a low rumble. The room shook, and debris rained down from the ceiling.

"Get us out of here!" Muruq screamed.

Further discussion with Muruq was futile, and Atacama's attempts to reassure him fell short. "Muruq, the evac shuttles are on the ground now. Please get your people ready." Muruq's face shrunk on the screen, allowing Atacama to see Talman Paque. "Paque, can you tell how many we've lost?"

"Not yet, sir. We're trying to get a count of who's where, there's a lot of confusion up here," he confided. A cacophony of noises behind Paque caught his attention, and he turned to see what caused the interruption. "One moment, sir." The men and women in command stared at a wall until Paque returned. "Sir, the med company is here, and I'm needed. I'll report back shortly."

"Tell Garnet I want an update every thirty," Atacama ordered.

"Yes, sir," Talman Paque acknowledged and broke off the communication.

Leba and her team set up a temporary triage area in what was the previous squad's staging area. Her team covered the work desks with thermal blankets and laid out their trauma equipment. Work cubicles became med bays, bookshelves supply closets. His snow parka decorated with his rank insignia, a side arm strapped to his waist, Luth Cathen strode in and pointed. "Tiner, Anster, Grizzer with me." Leba looked at him, waiting for her name to be called. "Not you, Doc, we get to have all the fun and bring you bits and pieces."

What a callous jerk. Leba was abhorred at his references to injured soldiers and almost said something but for DeShay giving her a glare. As Cathen led them out the door, DeShay shot back, "Be ready, girl, this is a scoop-and-run operation, and we'll be coming in hot and fast."

A CHANGE IN TACTICS: MAIDEN VOYAGE

Leba gave him a thumbs-up signal as he dashed to catch up with the rest. She thought and then shouted after him, "Keep 'em cold!" Although hypothermia was nothing to joke about, significantly lowering their body temp would buy the casualties a little more time. Stasis fields were only good for smaller injuries. With hypothermia and the intense cold of this planet, all bodily functions would slow down. Not only necessary processes would become sluggish but also the effects of their wounds would be retarded, giving her more time to stabilize them and ready them for transport. *You have to be warm to be dead.*

As DeShay and the other medics brought in litters with injured troopers, Leba kept repeating to herself, this was supposed to be a scientific expedition. Leba never saw such bizarre injuries before: no thermal burns but frozen burns, weird shrapnel injuries with clean entry sites, no dark powdery residue stipling the wounds, and cold blast trauma as if you ran smack into a glacier. The weaponry was strange, leaving very little collateral damage. The injuries were so devastating that the casualty count mounted quickly. Killing was effective and efficient, clearing the battle theater in the blink of an eye. *Battle*, she turned the word over in her mind a dozen times. *This was supposed to be a scientific expedition.*

DeShay placed a young trooper on the near table. Leba asked, "What's he got?"

"Never seen anything like it before," responded DeShay. "Looks like a stab wound, but there's no blood flow."

Gloved, Leba placed a finger into the wound track and quickly removed her finger, shaking it, and muttering a curse. "Wow, is that cold! My guess is that whatever weapons they're using must have some type of insta-freeze compound in its tip that sears the track."

DeShay responded, "Makes sense they'd develop a weapon like that."

"How so?" she questioned as she treated the trooper's wound.

"Blood loss out here would attract wildlife, and as we've seen, some of the native fauna is pretty ferocious."

"You might even say cold-blooded," she quipped, trying to break the tension in the room. "Where are you going?" she questioned DeShay as he turned to leave.

"Got to get back to the line, few more guys to bring in."

"How bad is it?" Leba questioned.

"It's strange," DeShay began. "Lots of guys down, but very clean, very antiseptic. Something hit these guys hard and fast and then was gone. We're trying to account for everyone."

"Be careful," she called after him and was met with a broad grin and a wink.

Moving to the next in line, Leba saw the trooper on the stretcher in second cubicle was gasping and short of breath. The Talman found it difficult to talk, so she didn't ask his name. His shirt placard said Revil. Every inspiration pained him, and he splinted his right chest with his left arm. Audible gurgling produced foamy bubbles that crept from beneath his hand. Valiantly trying to cover the sucking hole in his chest, Revil's lips were becoming bluer as the cyanosis associated with his decreasing oxygen tension persisted. Leba quickly pushed him flat on to the gurney, snatched a small scalpel from the bedside stand, palpated the first two ribs, and shoved it into his chest just below the second. Panicked, Revil watched in horror as she pushed a small caliber tube into the cavity and attached a flutter valve. Instantly his tortuous suffocation abated, and he could feel his breath returning. Now each rise and fall of his chest was rewarded with oxygen. Leba squirted gel adhesive around the tube and then into the chest wound. "That'll do for now. You can get a permanent fix back at base. Now move on so I can take care of some really hurt people."

Revil smiled. "Thanks, Doc. Owe you one."

"Don't let it happen again and we're even," she replied softly, patting him on the arm and motioning for an orderly.

The casualties kept coming. Striker and Explorer Companies were decimated. Reports coming into the makeshift triage center were horrifying. At least half their Vedax deployed contingent were down, and a third more were wounded. Leba and her squad could barely evaluate one trooper before two others were ready to take his place. Concussion injuries were common, as were blunt and penetrating trauma. Shattered lives of such brave young soldiers lay between life, death, and permanent limbo. Defender Company was deployed to assist them to try and prevent further loss. They were hustling to get everyone off the forward position, out of the fallback position, onto the evac shuttles. Although her medical company occupied a specially classified unit status, Leba felt a certain kinship to the regular issue soldiers. Right now she felt like she was fighting alongside of them, stabilizing the wounded enough to get them off moon.

Despite the warnings about tourniquets, the controversies over insta-clot, she utilized all her skills and training to keep them alive. There was only so much she could do. Definitive therapy was out of the question. Her focus needed to be stopping hemorrhage, stabilizing penetrating trauma, plugging the holes, keeping them breathing. Make the ones who weren't going to live comfortable. Decide who was salvageable and who was not. But to what end, what would be their fate? Would these people ever be the same? Who or what did this to them? No time for academic inquiries. Scoop and run, treat 'em and street 'em, as DeShay was fond of reminding her. She was careful to lower the temperature on all the med sleds, trying to buy time for her patients. Her supplies of hemasyn, anti-infectives, pressors were running low, and there were still more coming. Cathen, that arrogant jerk, was wrong. They did need a second medical unit to help. Inundated by overwhelming numbers of casualties, Leba smelled the icy coldness of the death around her, the pain and suffering indescribable. She needed to focus, not give way to emotions. Be immune from feeling and do her job.

"What's she got?" she questioned Pola Grizzer as the medic delivered another injured trooper.

"Concussion, I think, maybe skull fracture," Grizzer surmised. "I noticed some serosanguinous fluid oozing from her ear."

Leba looked carefully at the matted hair of the wounded soldier, feeling the clear sticky substance draining from the woman's ear. "CSF leak, good pickup, Griz, must have a temporal bone fracture. I'll take it from here." Leba smiled, patting him on the back. After placing a sterile absorbent plug in the trooper's ear to prevent contamination, Leba felt behind the woman's cheekbone and upward to the crown of her head. The crepitus of bony fragments with gentle palpation confirmed her suspicions. She carefully raised the head section of the med sled to try and prevent further loss of spinal fluid. The trooper remained unconscious, her face pale and lifeless. Long blond hair no longer neatly arranged in a bun was matted and sticky over the skull fracture. Leba splinted her head and neck and signaled for her to be removed to the departure pad.

Leba was so impressed with the efficiency of DeShay, Anster, and Grizzer. The diagnostic skills of her medics rivaled the best of her colleagues. Back and forth, in and out, they scurried, trying to recover as many as they could. Where was Cathen? Of course, on the comm, as always, or giving orders and directions. Avoiding getting his hands dirty. Leba was a hands-on leader, never one to wait in the wings, never one to let someone do something she herself wouldn't do. She would never understand the military. How could they put Cathen in charge, and how could people follow his example if he never demonstrated one? She watched from a distance Defender Company's squad leader do his job. He was right in the thick of things, moving equipment, transporting bodies, giving orders, leading by example, getting dirty, and his troopers respected him for it. She could see how efficient and professional they performed.

After he was injured and ended up in the medical corp, DeShay was previously assigned to Defender Company as their travel medic until that position was deemed excessive. Budget cuts made the role temporary and only for specific situations. Troopers were deemed capable of providing basic life support to their comrades, and the need for a tagalong eliminated. DeShay was relegated to teach troopers to stabilize their buddies until a higher level of care was available. More recently, he was teaching battlefield medicine to newly minted military doctors. Bored with teaching, he asked to be transferred to Leba's unit under Cathen's command for this special deployment. DeShay often commented on how Cathen would have probably been eliminated by his own charges if he ran a "real" company. In some ways, Leba was insulted DeShay felt their company was not real. That somehow their unit was soft. She never considered herself particularly soft. She was anxious to prove DeShay wrong.

"When this is over, girl," DeShay often joked, "I'll get you assigned to a legit unit, if you've got what it takes."

"You're on!" she shot back on more than one occasion.

"I know a certain squad leader that's willing to break in a girl like you." He laughed. "He's been known to break a few hearts too."

Leba looked at him, laughing. "Bring him on."

"I just might," mused DeShay.

Leba liked DeShay a lot and was smart enough to learn from his exemplary example. Rough exterior but all heart, he taught her about tactical medicine. Not the stuff you read in textbooks but the real stuff. There's that word, *real*, again. People were dying; that was more than real enough for her.

By the time she looked at her chrono, she was amazed at how much they accomplished and in such little time. Time was certainly not something they had a lot of. Given the unknown threat, getting off Vedax with as many survivors as possible was top priority, and according to her count, almost everyone who was involved had been accounted for.

Garnet and his squad found more and more casualties the farther forward they went. Tiner, Anster, and Grizzer tagged along to help with the survivors, but less and less were being located as the perimeter grew. Garnet halted his troops behind an embankment as they waited for Striker's reserves to make a strafing run. DeShay rubbed his good shoulder. "One good thing about my artificial shoulder is that it doesn't know from cold."

"It is cold out here." Garnet adjusted his balaclava and looked at his info-pad for a moment, wiping the condensation from the screen. Frustrated, he called, "Zunel, give me the map, we're going old school." A green-scaled cadet reached into his pack and removed a drawn map. Garnet spun the cadet around, avoiding his accentuated spinous processes to use his back as a desktop. He signaled

Tross and Belk to join him. "This is where we are now." He pointed at the map. "And this is Explorer's last known position." He moved his gloved finger a few clicks forward. "From base intel, Striker was supposed to be here." He pointed to another location.

"But we didn't find any sign of them," Belk said.

"That leads me to believe they probably didn't want anyone to know where they were." Garnet thought for a moment. "Zable."

Zable popped up. "Sir."

"If you had to guess where the signal came from, you know, the repeating static wave signal."

Zable pushed past Tross and Belk to reach the map. "Here." He tapped on the map. "Right here."

"Then I bet that's where we'll find them, or what's left of them," Garnet reasoned. "Paque, send an encrypted message to Dad updating him. Tell him we're going to get Striker out from their operational location." He paused. "Give him the coordinates, Zunel."

Paque moved back from the group to send a tight beamed message back to Pareq via the relay. Garnet assigned the rest of his squad their tasks. "Denny, take your people and approach from the right. Brit, take your guys and approach from the left. I'll take my team and go right up the gut."

"What do you want us to do?" Tiner asked. Garnet pulled him aside. "I want you and your guys back at the LZ, and make sure this gets to Dad." He handed him the info-pad with their data.

DeShay refused to take the recording device. "You're not thinking of coming back, are you?"

Garnet looked squarely at him. "I don't know what we are going to find, but this data is critical."

Tiner grabbed his arm. "Your squad leader did this to you. You're trying to prove you can do this better than he did."

Garnet assured him. "I know what I'm doing. I'm getting what's left of Striker out of there. You'd do it for me if I were missing, wouldn't you? In fact, I'd guess you'd do it for any of our people."

Tiner looked at him, up and down. "Son of a gun, you did turn out right, didn't you?" He laughed. "Mom and I gave you everything and look how proud we are of our little boy all grown up."

Garnet took off his glove and offered an outstretched hand. Tiner removed his glove and grasped Garnet's hand and brought him close. They embraced. "Don't take any chances."

"You either," Garnet said. "No stops. Get back to base and have a cold ale waiting for me."

"Count on it," DeShay confirmed. "We're sitting this one out guys," Tiner informed the other medics as Anster and Grizzer joined him. Garnet assigned Cadet Raix and Neo-cadet Methor to accompany the medics and made sure his friend boarded Defender's extra travel sled for the ride back to the LZ.

"I don't think we have any other choice," Garnet informed Dad of his decision to proceed. By the book. He would follow protocol. Garnet wasn't looking for glory, just a go-ahead.

"I'll have Striker's remaining flights provide cover. They should be coming around for another pass any minute now. Fiorat!" Atacama shouted. "Time to the next strafing run?"

"Defender should see them overhead, just about now," Fiorat answered.

Garnet looked up to see the sortie breaking cloud cover and speeding ahead. "Got 'em."

"Then you are good to go, Defender, good luck and happy hunting, Atacama out."

Garnet and his squad moved out as three waves swarming quickly over the embankment and down into the area of Striker's last holdfast. What they found was not what they expected.

CHAPTER 31

Tiner, Anster, and Grizzer were approximately halfway into their journey when the travel sled cadet picked up a transmission. "What is it?" DeShay asked.

"A signal sir, on Explorer's frequency." Cadet Raix looked toward him, sitting in the copilot's chair. Dark skinned, with long eyelashes and full red lips, her green eyes sparkled with her discovery.

"Show me," Tiner requested.

"I was scanning across the frequencies when I picked up this," she said with nervous excitement in her voice.

"Good job, girl." DeShay placed a hand on her shoulder and leaned over to look at the nav grid. The faint scent of a floral perfume wafted toward him, and he momentarily closed his eyes and drank her in.

"Thank you, sir," she responded. "It's coming from about thirty clicks starboard of where we are." Raix showed him the relative positions on the nav grid.

"Let's check it out," Tiner suggested. *Garnet sure knows how to pick 'em.*

"But my squad leader told me to take you guys back." She licked her bottom lip, keeping her eyes glued to the sled's readouts.

Tiner looked toward Anster and Grizzer. "You guys up for a little adventure?" Both nodded in agreement. "Listen, Cadet…" He paused.

"Raix, sir, Cadet Jemey Raix," she finished his sentence and turned her head, locking eyes with him.

"Cadet Jemey Raix," he began again. "My guess is that signal is from Explorer Company's forward unit. They are probably in need of some assistance, and we should check it out."

"But Garnet told me to take you back." She tapped her foot on the floor.

"If we go to base first, by the time we get back, they may all be dead. You wouldn't want that, would you?" Tiner knew how to persuade her. "I'm sure your squad leader would understand. He and I go back a long ways."

"If you think we should, Master Priman, sir?" she conceded. "I guess it would be okay, sir." Raix's foot tapping increased.

"Call me DeShay." Her lips parted. "I think we should," he said, patting her again on the shoulder. "I don't think we have any other choice."

Cadet Jemey Raix maneuvered the travel sled in the direction of the signal and headed out. Tiner heard boots clattering behind him and peered over his shoulder to see Neocadet Methor carefully making his way up to the pilot's seat. *Let's see how she handles this.* "Raix, what's up?" he asked, his voice not fully mature. "We changed course." DeShay folded his arms to watch her poise.

In an authoritative manor, Raix answered, "We picked up a signal from Explorer, and we're going to check it out."

Methor challenged, "We have our orders. Squad leader said no stops."

"You're not paid to think," she snapped back. "This is my call, Neo. Now sit back down and strap in. We're in for rough terrain." Methor hung his head, kicked his boot on the cabin floor, and returned to his seat. When he was out of earshot, Raix blew out a short breath and then glanced at DeShay. She was only one rank level ahead of the boy but still did a good job of exerting her authority. DeShay gave her an approving nod and was met by a tentative smile. He recognized the look. He still had a way with the ladies.

DeShay put a hand on her shoulder. "Nice job, Cadet. When we get back, I'm sure your squad leader will give you a medal for your heroics."

Her lips parted, eyes wide, her whole face smiled. "Thank you, sir."

"There, over there!" Grizzer shouted from his seat. "I see something, someone."

Raix turned the sled forty-five degrees farther to the right and headed toward the figure. As they approached, a person waving his arms furiously rushed toward them. Using both feet, Raix punched the brake pedals, stopping the sled abruptly. The whole transport rocked back and forth. Opening her viewport, the man's shouts were swallowed up by the frigid wind.

"He's one of us!" Raix shouted. "A cadet, I think."

DeShay opened the travel sled's doorway and put up his hands. He shivered as the cold blasted his face. "Slow down, son, and tell me what's going on."

Out of breath, bent over with hands on his thighs, the young cadet gulped in air. Slowly he settled down and stood up and saluted.

"Cadet Dakad Botofole, sir. Explorer Company."

"Okay, Botofole, where's Hirousey?"

"Hurt, sir, badly." He sucked in more air. "I'm not sure he's going to make it. We lost Melpan, and Priman Warres took a lot of shrapnel."

"Who's in charge?"

"Priman Henjin, he's the one who sent me to meet you and warn you about—" he started until a barrage of ice shards began to pelt the travel sled.

"Take cover, and get the sled stealthed," DeShay ordered Raix. "Anster, Grizzer, with me," he called. Returning his attention to Botofole, DeShay said, "Take me to your priman."

After the sled went to stealth mode, the ice barrage ceased. The two Defender troopers joined Tiner and his group as Botofole led them to a makeshift holdout. "Priman, sir." Botofole caught the attention of his commanding officer. "They're from Defender Company."

"Thank goodness you found us," a haggard Henjin exclaimed. "We haven't been able to get a consistent signal out."

"Cadet Raix picked up your signal, that's why we're here," DeShay explained. Raix smiled broadly.

"What's your situation?" Raix asked.

See what a little taste of leadership does for a girl.

"We've lost over half our group, and we're pinned down. Warres took a lot of shrapnel, and I don't think he's going to make it. Hirousey's hurt bad, in and out of consciousness. Lasif over there took a blast to the leg. It's splinted, but I'm not sure how well he can travel. Pragen, Wod, and Quoxy are nicked up but can still fight."

DeShay looked at the faces of the young cadets, pained with the loss of their comrades and the terror of their predicament. "We're here to get you home, all of you."

"Thank you, sir," Henjin said, unable to smile but appreciative nonetheless.

"Raix, you and Methor get the sled and get back here ASAP. And keep her in stealth mode."

"Sir," Raix and Methor said, and both raced out the encampment.

"Henjin, gather up your people. The sled will be here in a moment, and we'll have to carry the injured on board."

Grizzer looked at DeShay. "We'll have to strip her down."

"We've done it before. Take Anster and make it happen."

The travel sled was not forthcoming as expected, and DeShay was getting anxious. "What's taking them so long?" Henjin asked.

Before DeShay could make up an explanation, the travel sled screeched to a halt. "Check it out," DeShay ordered Anster.

Stumbling into the room, with red and swollen hands covering his face, Methor screamed, "My eyes."

Anster was the first to reach him. "What happened?" He gently peeled the young man's hands from his face. "Where's Raix?" Anster asked. DeShay listened to the exchange.

"Something hit us, and Raix went down," Methor cried. "I tried to drag her, but she was deadweight."

"Where is she?" Anster asked again.

"I got her in the sled, she's breathing but won't wake up," Methor said.

"You did good, kid." Anster put an arm on his shoulder. "Probably saved her life. Now let me take a look at those hands."

DeShay nodded to Grizzer, who joined Anster at the entry. The master priman could hear the concern in his buddy's voice.

"Raix is down, the neo probably saved her life, but his hands are frozen, and his eyes took a pretty good blast from the explosion."

Grizzer replied, "I'll take the kid, start getting the sled stripped. Tiner doesn't think we have much time before we start taking incoming fire."

Once Methor was settled with the other walking wounded, Tiner and Grizzer returned to find half the travel sled's seats outside on the frozen ground.

"Hey, Anster!" Grizzer yelled.

"Raix is stabilized. She's secured in the back." Anster popped his head out of the canopy. "You going to stand there, or you going to help?"

Leaving Anster and Grizzer to finish deconstructing the sled, Tiner returned to the shelter. "You're going to help," DeShay informed the trio of remaining cadets. "Pragen, right?" DeShay asked, and the red-furred cadet nodded. "Pragen, you and Quoxy, take Warres. "Wod, help Lasif." DeShay looked to Botofole. "Botofole, help my guys finish getting the sled ready to travel." Henjin looked at DeShay and shook his head. DeShay glared back at him. "Everyone goes."

"What about Hirousey?" Henjin asked.

DeShay looked back to see Anster at the doorway. "Got the hover stretcher, thought it might come in handy."

DeShay gave him a thumbs-up. "Get the others loaded, and send Grizz back to help me with Hirousey."

"Sir," Anster mocked the others salutations.

"Henjin," DeShay requested. "I need you to pilot the sled."

"On it," Henjin said.

Bet he's relieved to give up some responsibility.

As Henjin walked out to join the others at the sled, Anster came back in. "DeShay, we can't fit everyone in, especially with the stretcher." He paused. "Besides, I don't think Warres has a shot."

"I'm not leaving him," DeShay snapped back.

"I'm not saying that," Anster backed off. "All I'm saying is that we'll have to make two runs." He looked at DeShay. "I'll stay with Warres. You get the others out. Don't be late picking us up."

"I'll stay," Tiner informed him. "It was my decision to veer off course. I'll stay." *Besides, Garnet is going to kill me for getting his kids hurt.*

Grizzer came back to the encampment. "Come on, we've got to go."

"Get the other hover stretcher off. We need to get Hirousey out of here first," Tiner ordered.

With the delay, the passengers were getting antsy. Henjin returned, as did Botofole. "We figured there was a problem," Henjin said. "Botofole and I will wait with Warres while you get the others back."

Tiner rebuked his offer. "I'm staying with Warres, and that's final."

"We don't have time for this," Anster informed them. "They're going to pick up on our heat signature soon, and then all bets are off."

"Priman Henjin," Tiner said, his voice calm and steady, "you need to go with them, report what you know. If Botofole wants to stay with me and Warres, then okay, but the rest of you need to leave now."

Once the arrangements were settled on, the travel sled uncloaked and left for the staging area. "Do you think he's gonna make it?" Botofole asked Tiner.

Tiner shook his head. "The best we can do is keep him comfortable and keep our heads down." Botofole looked at him warily. "It won't take the hostiles long to zero in on our position."

"I'm having trouble zeroing in on their position," Fiorat told Atacama. "If the telemetry from Defender is accurate, they've picked up three survivors from Striker Company."

"Three," Atacama whispered, the breath taken from him. He repeated, "Three."

"Defender should be reaching the departure area soon. Also, there's something else." Fiorat paused, not knowing how Atacama would react to his next statement. "There are a few stragglers from Explorer waiting for pickup." Fiorat explained as Atacama sat with a blank expression on his face.

Atacama rose from his chair and in a calm but stern manner said, "Give the order to evacuate now." Fiorat looked at him stunned. "You heard me, Squad Leader, launch the shuttles. I want everyone out of there, now. The longer they remain on the moon, the more vulnerable our people are, and I'm not losing anyone else."

Garnet's ground transports arrived at the LZ with the three Striker survivors. His people quickly escorted them over to an evac shuttle and got them situated.

"What now?" Tross asked as Belk came rushing over.

"Raix is down, and Methor is badly hurt."

"What happened?" Tross questioned.

"They detoured to pick up some Explorers," Belk relayed.

"Raix did what?" Garnet roared. "I told her to comm us for any deviation." He quieted his voice after his initial outrage passed. "Are they going to be okay?"

"Doc stabilized Raix and sent her with the seriously injured to the relay ship. Methor's on his way to Pareq with the others." Belk paused. "There is one other thing." Garnet was likely to blow a head gasket with what he had to tell him. "Anster and Grizzer went back for Tiner. They didn't have enough room on the travel sled, so he and a cadet stayed with a dying Explorer guy."

Tross spoke first. "So let's go get him."

Belk said, "They're supposedly on their way back now. Besides"—he started handing an info-pad to Garnet—"Dad ordered everyone off this rock now."

Garnet studied the message. "Overseer picked up increased hostile activity approaching our position, and we don't have enough resources to repel another barrage." He sighed and then ordered, "We'll leave last. Denny, get those other shuttles airborne now. Brit, get our guys to the last fallback before we leave. I'll update Dad. Plan to be on your shuttle within the hour."

One by one, Leba listened as the evac shuttles left the moon's icy surface. Distant explosions were documented first by flashes of light and then by resounding booms. They were edging closer. The unknown hostiles were approaching the remaining Tal-Kari contingent. The sickest patients were being transported to a relay ship that would whisk them back to Luac for level-six trauma care. They would be held in cold stasis, keeping their tenuous lives frozen in time until life-saving procedures could be accomplished. The less sick, or walking wounded, were transported back to the Pareq hospital, where the other med team was waiting. The trip was much shorter, and their injuries were less severe. The battered members of the scientific teams were on different shuttles, slowly making their way back to Pareq. Last to leave were the rescue shuttles. With the most of the casualties triaged, Leba sent the majority of her nurses home with the transport shuttles to keep the patients monitored and stable for their journeys. She waited for Anster, Grizzer, and Tiner to return from their final run.

Leba's back was to the triage area's entryway when she heard heavy footfalls approaching. "I'll be right there," she said, drying her hands at the hypersonic washing station.

"Doc," Mevid Anster's voice quavered, "it's really bad. We did the best we could." Leba put the towel down, grabbed a pair of exam gloves to evaluate the next patient. "Doc," he repeated, this time with more urgency. She heard him approach. "Leba," Anster said softer as he lightly touched her shoulder. He never called her Leba. She whirled around. Anster extended his arms, gripping both her shoulders. "Wait."

"What..." She tried to read his face, his eyes were swollen and red, his thin lips pursed tightly. Over his shoulder, she saw Pola Grizzer bent over the wounded trooper lying on the hover stretcher. Her stomach clenched, the sickening feeling tightening her throat.

"Where's DeShay?" Leba's head swiveled back and forth, searching. She pushed past Anster and ran to the gurney. DeShay's grossly misshapen body was prostrate. The high-pitched hum of the stasis field was evident. *He can't be dead. No, please no.*

"My G-d, what happened?" She caressed DeShay's battered face, feeling its coldness, despite the beads of sweat glistening on his head.

"Girl." He coughed, his chest heaving as he gasped for air.

"Don't talk," she said, snatching a respiratory support mask from a nearby shelf and fitting it on him. "I'm in charge this time. Let me see how bad it is." She reached for the blanket, feeling the tingling vibration on her skin as her hand penetrated the perimeter of the containment field. Something was terribly wrong. He had no leg outlines—just an amorphous mass. Grizzer looked at her, his eyes wet with tears, and shook his head. "No," she said forcefully. "I can save him. He doesn't have to die. Let me do my job."

"Girl," DeShay said sharply and grabbed her arm so tightly she couldn't remove the cover. Barely able to hear his voice through the mask, Leba bent down to put her ear next to his mouth. She gently pulled the mask off to one side. "Girl, there's not much you can do for me. They're coming, and you all need to leave." Lifting the sheet, she peered underneath. The lower half of DeShay's body was crushed, fused and frozen beyond recognition. Only the stasis field was keeping him from melting away. Everything tingled as she racked her brain, searching for a way to stop his death.

"Let me help you!" she insisted. "Please don't die. I need you. This is not fair, you can't die."

"What did I teach you? Sometimes it's best not to." His voice was gravelly, and Leba found it hard to hear over the evacuation signal. Heaving a labored breath, DeShay growled, "Let me go. I won't live like this."

Squad leader Cathen burst into the room, shouting, "We're out of here, now! Anster, Grizzer, Brader, move it!" So focused on DeShay when she looked up and surveyed the room, she hadn't realized Cathen already evac'd their makeshift hospital. It was all but empty save for their abandoned equipment strewn haphazardly in the rush to bug out. Anster and Grizzer turned toward DeShay, each gripped one of his hands, nodded, and Leba could see the unspoken words between them.

Arm pointing at the exit, Cathen ordered again. "Go." Stunned, Leba watched as both Anster and Grizzer hustled out of the treatment area. They obeyed Cathen's command without question, but Leba couldn't move. "Brader, time to go. That's an order!" Cathen shouted.

"I'm not leaving him," she said, grabbing his hand. "He's not dying alone."

"Then give him a shot, put him down, and come on!" Jaw clenched, Cathen's eyes darted between her and DeShay.

"Do what he says, girl." DeShay sucked in a breath. "Leba." He grasped for her arm, his grip beginning to fail. "For once, he's right."

"Okay, okay." She motioned to Cathen. "I'll meet you there. I..." she hesitated. "I have to get the stuff." *Screw you, you heartless bastard.*

Arms akimbo, with his thumbs pointing back and legs splayed wide, Cathen leaned so close that she could feel his breath on her neck. He enunciated slowly, each word biting like the Vedax wind. "If you're not there when our shuttle leaves, you're on your own."

"Understood, Squad Leader." She refused to look up at him, trying to focus only on DeShay. She inclined her head as Cathen strode from the treatment area.

Face paler, DeShay tightened his jaw. "You're not gonna leave, are you?"

"Don't ask me silly questions," she responded, trying to hold back the tears. Leba knew the stasis field would only forestall the inevitable. Without aggressive treatment, DeShay didn't have much more time. "You wouldn't leave me, would you?" She mustered a tentative grin. "No, don't answer that."

He whispered something inaudible. She leaned down close, her ear near his swollen blue lips so she could hear him. His hand slipped down her arm. She grabbed it and squeezed tightly. *I'll never let you go. This can't be. Please be an awful dream. A stupid simulation. Don't die. I need you.* So many thoughts tumbling through her mind. So many things he'd probably consider weak if she spoke them out loud.

"I don't have much time." He wriggled his hand free. Struggling at the collar of his shirt, DeShay tugged the chain around his neck. Leba helped him slip it over his head. Dangling the medallion, he stared at it with bloodshot eyes. His gaze rose to meet hers and he said, "There's something I need you to do for me."

She sniffled, unable to hold back the tears. "Name it." Leba trembled as he handed her the medal.

Suddenly, a thunderous clap violently shook the makeshift hospital. It wasn't designed to take incoming fire. Pieces of the temporary ceiling rained down, and Leba tried to shield DeShay with her body.

"Leave, girl. Before it's too late." Shaking the dirt away as she got off him, Leba brushed powdery debris from his forehead and pulled over an empty box.

"I plan to sit here by your side." Leba flipped the container over, sat on it, and bowed her head to put her face next to his. "I'm not leaving you. You won't die alone." Leba licked her lips. She still needed to ask him so many questions, to tell him so many things. "I love you." Sobbing now, she continued, "You want to know why?"

Turning to face her, the corners of his mouth curved slightly upward, his breathing more labored. DeShay nodded. "I know," he sputtered, "because..."

Oxygen starved, breath short and shallow, he couldn't finish the sentence, so she finished it for him, "It's because you're so handsome and all the ladies love you." A big smile crossed his face... and then slowly faded. His eyes glazed over and stared vacantly as DeShay exhaled his final breath. Leba touched her hand to his face, feeling the stubble of his chin. She kissed his forehead. There was no breath to caress her face. She checked each pupil—nothing, not even a slight twitch. Passing her hand over his face, she closed his eyes. There were no more tears to come out; she was numb. Regarding his face, she was glad her last memory would be of the way he was so peaceful in death.

Extending the blanket to cover his head, Leba activated his death sequence module and turned her face away. She did what she had to do. But she couldn't bear to see his form melt away. A faint beep of the warning signal, then a small hissing noise, and then he was dust. His life cycle complete. Carefully removing the cover, she gently swept his remains into a small vial. Leba closed the top and tenderly placed it in her jacket pocket. She rested her hand on it. *I'm sorry.*

Exhausted, she collapsed back onto the container. Gulping in a large breath, she opened her palm to look at the medallion then clutched it tightly, bringing her hand to her lips and cried. The floor rumbled. Another bang shook the building, peppering her with more debris. Ozone stung her nostrils. Cathen's parting words—*You're on your own*—finally bored into her consciousness. She snatched her rucksack off the floor, secured its straps, and ran out the back of the building.

Leba needed to be strong. Prove DeShay was right about her mettle. Make him proud. "Who cares if Cathen's already gone," she muttered as she made her way to the departure area. There was still one shuttle left. It's side emblazoned Defender One.

"Doc, over here!" a helmeted trooper, hanging onto the boarding ramp door, shouted over the engine noise. "We saved a spot for you." He bent down and gave her an arm up.

"Thanks," she responded out of breath. After she was settled, her seat restraints in place and tight, her body stiff with shock, she noticed the trooper standing to her side. He put out his hand.

"I'll take that from you." His deep voice resonated past his comm mic.

She knew what this squad leader wanted. But it was hard to let DeShay go. Reluctantly she reached into her pocket and removed the burial tube.

"What you did for him, Doc…" He hesitated, the words catching in his throat. "We'll never forget." Taking DeShay's remains, he took her hand, together they clasped around the tube, and he looked straight into her now tearing eyes. "I mean it, Doc. I'll never forget what you did."

The rest of the shuttle flight back to base camp was silent save for the occasional beeps, grinds, and other machine noises from the shuttle. Human noises were limited to coughing, sniffling, and sighing. These troops took devastating losses today and didn't really understand why. Besides Leba's medical squad and their support troops, there were five other squads. In all, ten medical people, now nine, and one hundred ninety-five regular military expeditionary troops. Now, only two-thirds were returning. Of those remaining troops, at least one-half were injured. What a mess. This was supposed to be a scientific expedition, but it wasn't, and Leba wanted to know why. Maybe her new friends of Defender Company, here with her on this shuttle, could shed some light. Leba waited her turn as the shuttle landed at base camp and people debarked. As each surviving member of Defender Company, DeShay's old unit, passed her seat, they gave her a pat on the shoulder.

Finally, when it was her turn to debark, a newly familiar voice said, "Let me help you with that." Defender Company Squad Leader seemed roughly her age and was tall and stalwart. His dark hair laid in wisps around his forehead and ears. It was tousled ever so slightly now that his helmet was in his hand. Except for where his right was interrupted by a scar, he had full, strong eyebrows. Boy-like lashes highlighted his smoldering metallic blue eyes. "I'll take that for you, Doc"

The first time she interacted with him on this flight, she hadn't paid attention except to his voice. This time, she noticed the rest. His strong, angled jaw was stubbled with the beginnings of a dark beard. His thin upper lip topped a fuller, pouty lower lip that rested over the subtle dimple indenting his chin. Not sure what she was searching for, Leba continued to study his face. His nose bore a hint of a previous break, but she kept returning to his penetrating eyes. "I've got it, thank you," Leba squeaked a response. Clearing her throat, she added, "But thanks anyway."

"We're having a memorial for DeShay tonight in the starboard observation deck. We'd be honored if you join us, ma'am."

"I don't know," she sniffled. "I think I'm probably in a lot of trouble with my squad leader for disobeying his orders, and I'll probably be on restriction for the next year or out of a job."

"You let us know, and we'll bring the memorial to you," he countered and then continued, "By the way, Cathen's a, now how did DeShay put it, an arrogant little weasel."

They shared a laugh, and Leba bowed her head. "Thanks." She disembarked the shuttle and headed over to where her squad was regrouping.

The Vedax outpost was only a horrible memory. The base med unit couldn't know how she felt, what she experienced, what her team went through. She felt sick inside, drained and empty. Stretchered patients were already in medical shuttles heading back to the orbiting relay ship. The walking wounded transported to the base medical clinic for a higher level of care. She could only do so much with the resources she had. Leba and her medical squad triaged, stabilized, and readied for transport more than sixty people. Unfortunately, many others were unsalvageable, dead on arrival, and her team's job was recognition, retrieval, and reduction to dust. How awful. She couldn't save them all, no matter how much she wanted to. Leba needed to try and remember how many they did help. Only to face long rehab stays if they didn't die from posttrauma complications. The last thing she needed right now was Luth Cathen. Yet there he was, military stiff and uptight, striding toward her. She knew what was coming. She disobeyed his direct order, staying with DeShay in his final moments, not making her squad's departing shuttle, and having to hitch a ride with Defender Company. She didn't care. Wow, that was different for her, not caring what trouble she might be in, disobeying her superior officer, not being a team player.

Here she sat, alone, in her cabin, confined and restricted, like a young child punished for breaking a fancy family heirloom. Leba felt very small. After arriving at the base camp, Leba went through decontamination procedures, showered, put on a fresh uniform, and was summarily dressed down by her squad leader, Luth Cathen. It was bad enough to be repeatedly screamed at, reprimanded for her insubordination, failure to act like a real trooper, letting emotion get in the way, but to be sent to her room. Now, that was uncalled for. Lord Cathen specifically forbade her from any outside activities other than her assigned duty shifts for at least one duty cycle. Even her parents never punished her for that long. She was a good kid and maybe spent a few hours, at the very most, in her room, and it was usually self-imposed.

As a kid, she could usually figure out when she had done something wrong, and even though her parents accepted her apology, she still felt a short self-imposed personal exile would be in order. She would lie across her bed and read or line up her dolls for a game of make-believe or look out her skylight and try and imagine all the wonderful things the universe beheld. She liked watching the distant stars twinkling on and off, trying to guess the next to flicker. Usually she would fall asleep only to awaken for a meal or one of her parents gently rapping on the door to see if she was all right. But she was an adult now, a fully trained, highly skilled doctor with more commendations and awards than Cathen could ever hope to garner, and he had just sent her to her room for misbehaving.

The starboard observation deck lounge was loud with the sound of glasses being raised in recognition, the sound of raucous laughter at the retelling of a favorite story, the sound of surviving soldiers glad to be alive. This was a celebration of DeShay Tiner's life and the lives he touched. Sure, a lot of good men and women died today, but none touched so many others as DeShay Tiner. Anster and Grizzer were the first to offer a toast in his name. Leba wasn't there, though. Cathen specifically banned her from the celebration. She didn't particularly care, though; she never quite understood funeral wakes. Why honor people when they were dead. Treat them with honor during life. Although she was intrigued by the possibility of spending more time with Defender Company's squad leader, and no, she hadn't gotten his full name yet. She didn't want to have DeShay's death and life rehashed in a thousand ways. What she did, she told herself, was what really mattered, no matter what Cathen or anyone else thought. Wow, that was different for her too, not caring what anyone else thought. That was always a difficult thing for her, worrying about what other people thought about her, her actions, or her decisions. Her teachers, instructors, mentors liked her because she tried to do it their way, follow their instructions, be the perfect example of their tutelage. This time was different. She was beginning to change, and it felt uncomfortable but a little exhilarating. Emotionally, she was drained, and lying across her bed, she was only able to watch a few minutes of the simulcast from the starboard lounge before she fell asleep.

Startled by a rapping at the door, it took Leba a minute to reorient. Her room was dimly lit; the automatic timer changed the daylights to night-lights. The simulcast feed from the memorial was dark, and there was only blackness on the screen. Sort of deep and pervasive, like the emptiness she felt without DeShay. More knocking. She rubbed her eyes, looked at the digital time display, and shouted, "Hang on, I'll be right there." Her uniform jacket hung on her shoulders, Leba approached her door. More awake and thinking more clearly, she questioned, "Who is it?"

"Defender Company, ma'am. We told you that if you couldn't make it, we would bring the party to you."

"It's kinda late, and I'm beat, maybe another time!" she shouted through the door. What was she thinking, she was on restriction? When a whole company of men comes to your door... she trailed off. *I'm not Sendra.* The banging continued. "Okay, okay," she said, cinching up her jacket. She ran a hand through her hair, not that it did any good, and tucked in her shirt, remembering to pull a little up like DeShay taught her. Her eyes welled up, and she wiped them with the back of her hand. She activated the door entry access. There was a line of Defender Company troopers gathered at her entryway. "You know, I could get in a lot of trouble for this." She bladed her body as people pushed past and into her front room. "I guess you"—the small room filled quickly—"all can fit in here."

"Don't worry about Cathen, ma'am," one of the cadets confirmed, "Squad Leader arranged for him to be gone for at least an hour."

"You sure?" she said, realizing she was committing her second act of disobedience in less than one day.

"Sure enough, ma'am," the cadet explained. "When Squad Leader says he's taken care of something, you can count on it."

Leba was curious as to where the Defender Company squad leader was. She didn't want to seem too anxious by asking. After the last trooper entered, she peered down the hall, left then right, then left again. Sniffling, she lingered at the door, looked at the crowd, then back to the door across the hall. Nothing. She sighed, tucked her head, and turned to host the crowd. A hand jutted across the shrinking threshold, preventing the door from sliding shut. "Sorry to barge in on you, Doc, but a promise is a promise." His body was now keeping the door open. She looked up at him. His blue eyes flickered. Entering the room, he made his way through the assembled. Like a ship cutting through waves, his charges parted to let him pass. Leba followed in his wake. Without the bulky parka, his athletic build was apparent. He strode with confidence. When she caught up, slightly touching his arm, trying to avoid another, he inclined his head to her. "DeShay Tiner taught me everything I know about being a soldier. Saved my ass a number of times too." He pointed to the couch. The seated cadets jumped up, allowing their squad leader and honored hostess to sit. He angled toward her. "In fact, over the years, he's pulled a number of us out of harm's way."

Leba spent the better part of the next hour talking with Defender Company's squad leader. She didn't say a whole lot but listened to the admiration this man felt for DeShay. After the third time he called her Doc, she stopped him. "You can call me Leba."

"But Ma'am?" he replied.

"I'm not one for formalities." She shifted her feet toward his. "It's just Leba. Not 'Doc' or 'Ma'am' or any other title, just Leba."

Although initially startled, his eyes narrowed, and the corners of his mouth upturned slightly. He reached for the clasps on his uniform jacket and popped the first two open. "Okay by me, and if I may be so bold"—he put out his hand—"Tivon H. Garnet, but you can call me Tiv, everyone else does." Leba took his hand. The palm was a little rough, and the back of his hand nicked up. This was a man not afraid of work. A man who led by example.

"Tiv, I like that, and thank you." This was Tiv Garnet, the one DeShay promised he would introduce her to. After the hour they just spent talking, she understood why DeShay considered him a brother. This was the man she had a dying message for.

The noise level in Leba's small quarters continued to rise, and she found it difficult to hear everything Tiv was saying. She must have looked pretty foolish continually asking him to repeat a sentence or two.

He leaned close, putting his mouth to her ear. "I need to tell you something." Tiv grasped her hand. "Is there somewhere more private we can talk?" He raised her to her feet and pointed. "How 'bout back there?" Leba nodded. Tiv's hand was warm and strong, and he easily negotiated the crowd with her in tow.

Embarrassed by the disarray of her bedroom, Leba was glad the lights were still dimmed. Tiv shut the door. "Phew, thought my head would explode with all the noise." He stood in front of her and grasped both her arms and then gently slid down to her wrists then her hands, holding them gently.

"I need to apologize. I have an advantage over you." He scanned the room and returned to look at her. "You see, DeShay was very fond of you, and I heard all about you."

Is that good or bad? Leba's lower lip quivered, and she sniffled a few times, trying to hold back the tears.

Composing herself, she slipped her right hand out of his and fished in her pocket. Dangling the metal necklace from her hand, she took her left and cradled the medallion. Turning it over, she examined the inscription. "He wanted you to have this." Palms up, she offered Tiv the bequest. Tiv froze for a moment then carefully lifted it up. Silence prevailed for the longest time until Leba broke it. "Oh, that's right, he wanted me to tell you—'No worries, little brother.'" Tiv closed his hand tightly around the necklace, some of the chain still dangling, and rubbed the lower half of his face. Was he going to break down? Leba wasn't sure. Tiv sighed slowly and carefully placed it in his pants pocket and retook her hands.

She stared deeply into his face. His eyes seemed hollow and lost. Slowly he leaned toward her, his grip increased, his eyes closed, and he inclined his head. She rose slightly on her toes to meet him when Tiv's chrono alarm chirped, prompting him to pull away and curse. There was an urgent rapping at the bedroom door. Tiv cursed again.

"I could only arrange for Cathen to be gone for about an hour. My guess is that he'll be checking up on you fairly soon." The suddenness of his declaration startled her, but she knew he was right. She nodded, planting both feet back on the floor. Maybe this wasn't the right time. Maybe she should be mourning DeShay and not trying to start something with Tiv. What was this anyway? She barely knew this man, and yet they almost kissed.

"Okay, guys, we're out of here." Tiv Garnet announced as he emerged from the bedroom. One by one Defender Company filed out, thanking Leba for her service.

Tiv watched the rest of his people leave, making sure they cleaned up, leaving no traces they'd ever been there. As he was getting ready to leave, lingering a little until everyone else had left, Tiv's comm buzzed. "Tiv, JT here, Cathen's on his way there now. Move or you guys are busted."

Peering out the door and looking down the hallway, Tiv quickly backed up from the door, letting it slide shut. Grabbing Leba, Tiv doused the lights and put a finger to her lips. "Shhh," he whispered, "Cathen's on his way. Pretend like I'm not here."

Yeah, right. We're in my room, in the dark, I'm pressed up against your chest, and my heart's beating a thousand times per minute. When she opened her mouth to speak, Tiv's mouth met hers. He kissed her. Not one of those little pecks on the cheek, the kind that says "Thanks for a great evening," but... No, this kiss was different. It was long and deep and passionate. As he brought her closer, enveloping her in his arms, she could feel and hear his heart pounding in his chest too. He smelled good, so masculine and tasted, well, she wasn't sure. She would need further investigation. Until she heard boot steps outside her door, Leba momentarily forgot about Cathen. Tiv must have heard him too because he kissed her harder, his tongue exploring her mouth. Dizzy with emotion, her inner turmoil slowly giving way to her feelings, Leba explored his mouth too. Right now, all she wanted was Tiv.

The persistent door buzzer effectively broke their hold on each other. "Hang on," Leba responded, trying to catch her breath. "I'm coming." This time, her finger to his lips. Tiv kissed her finger. She shivered. With her other hand, she motioned Tiv toward the lavatory. He winked and let her go. As Cathen buzzed again, Leba pulled off her jacket and tossed it onto a chair. She ran to her bedroom, snatched her robe, and draped it over her uniform shirt. She hoped he would believe his intrusion awakened her. As she made her way to the door, she noticed Tiv's uniform jacket across the couch in plain sight. His jacket was a lot different than hers, decorated with a silver and blue braid and a silver shield signifying his rank of squad leader and his company designation. What to do? Grabbing her smaller and less decorated uniform jacket off the chair, she flung it over his, hoping to hide its presence. The door buzzed again, this time followed by thudding of an angry fist. "I'm coming, I'm coming!" she shouted.

"What took so long?" Cathen inquired.

"Lavatory." She yawned. "I was in the lavatory." Cathen could hear the plumbing running. Tiv had improvised by activating the facilities as Leba was answering the door.

"Just checking." Cathen handed her an envelope. "And this." While she unfolded the paper inside, Cathen scanned the room. What was he looking for? Did he know about Defender and their late-night visit? Worse yet, was he going to find its squad leader in her bathroom? Cathen shifted his eyes back and met her infuriated gaze.

"Inventory," she snapped. "I was supposed to be off for a few days after my next duty shift."

"Change of plans." Cathen steepled his fingers. "Unless you'd like to be reassigned from this deployment."

"No, sir." She stiffened to attention. "No, sir," she repeated. "Thank you, sir."

"That's better, Brader. I see some time in your room has improved your attitude."

"Yes, sir," she repeated. "Time in my room, sir, much better for it, sir." She wondered what Tiv was thinking in the other room. She hated being treated like a child, especially by a jerk like Cathen. Her parents would never treat her this way even if she had done something wrong.

"Good thing," Cathen returned. "Wouldn't want to have to send you packing, bad for our unit. But I think we understand who's in charge, don't we?" Leba hated this part. The military hierarchy had its place, but it was not always conducive to the team concept.

Leaders, good leaders, learned from and respected their subordinates. Leba realized when she signed on for this mission, she agreed to abide by the military system. Cathen outranked her. Despite her education and standing in the civilian community, here in the field, she was under his command and was sworn to obey his orders, be they legitimate or petty. His little show of power was demeaning at best.

Fifteen minutes later, Cathen left, seemingly pleased with himself. Didn't matter she was very well liked and respected among his unit. He showed her who was in charge. Tiv peeked out from behind the lavatory door. "He gone yet?" Leba nodded affirmatively. "I'd better get going too." He picked up a jacket from the couch and slung it over his shoulder. "Big day tomorrow: regroup, rethink, redeploy." He touched her arm. "Don't let him get to you."

She wanted to say "Will I see you again?" but was afraid of the answer. Heat of the moment, tensions of the day, maybe it was all too quick. Lustful, not meaningful. Well, meaningful in some sense but not that kind of meaningful. Leba stood at the door, looking down the hallway even after Tiv turned the corner. Leaning her head against the doorframe, she sighed. It was late, and in the course of one day, her life would never be the same.

About half an hour later, she sat on the end of her couch, wrapped in Tiv's jacket, slowly tracing its lines, trying to relive being in his arms. A knock broke her reflection. She smiled; her whole body tingled. Leba, head down, trying not to be too excited, opened the door and said, "I was wondering when you would figure out—" But stopped when she finally looked up. It wasn't Tiv. It was JT. Embarrassed, Leba tried to hide the fact she was wearing Tiv's jacket. She kept behind the door and could feel the flush creep up her face. "Hey, JT, what's up?"

Standing at her entryway door, JT said, "Aren't you going to invite me in?"

"I would." She dry swallowed. "But I'm on restriction."

"I heard." Pushing the door back, JT crossed the threshold. "I'm cleared." He made a three-sixty survey of the room and returned his attention to where Leba was hurriedly trying to unsuccessfully get her arms out of the larger jacket. "I told the duty officer I needed to run a medical problem by you." She closed the door with her freed hand and offered him a seat. "I think you might be missing this." JT removed her jacket where it was secreted beneath his coat. Leba felt a second blush come to her face. "Don't worry, your secret is safe with me," he promised.

Sitting comfortably on the couch, his legs splayed wide apart and his hand clasped behind his head, JT informed her, "Tiv's a good buddy of mine, and he asked me to retrieve his jacket and return yours. In fact, he asked me to keep Cathen busy for him while you two hooked up."

Leba fingered the jacket corners, running her hand up and down. Gingerly she finished taking her other arm out and held Tiv's jacket by the collar far enough away from JT that in order to grasp it, he had to come off the couch. She stared at him, not saying anything, until he got the message and headed for the door. She was not in a talkative mood.

"So we could hook up?" How wrong could she have been? Hook up, it sounded so cheap and dirty. What was she thinking, that maybe Tiv really liked her? How stupid was she? Disappointed, she felt totally used. She normally was a great judge of character, but with what JT had said... She played their encounter over and over in her mind, trying to figure out what she had missed. She needed some advice; she needed an expert. She needed Sendra. Sendra would be able to figure this out for her. Sendra knew men better than anyone else.

"Sendra, pick up. Please pick up," Leba begged.

"Slow down, Liebs, and stop crying and tell me what's wrong." Though sobbing and sniffling through most of the story, Leba recalled in gross and minute details the roller coaster of events that had taken place the preceding day. "Calm down, calm down," Sendra insisted. "Besides DeShay's death and all, I don't know what you're so upset about. I mean..."

"Huh," Leba said, her mind still not processing the emotional overload it was experiencing.

"Superanalytical Leba, the one with an answer to everybody's problems." Sendra giggled. "Can't figure out if a boy likes her or not."

Leba grumbled, "If I could figure it out myself, do you think I'd be calling you in the middle of the night?"

"The way I see it, Dr. Hobes is being a callous jerk who should mind his own business. This Tiv seems to be a good guy, and I think he probably likes you. DeShay, oh, sorry, anyway thought he was decent, right?"

"I guess so."

"If not, then you got kissed, really kissed, by what sounds like an incredibly hot guy. Remember that and move on. Things will play out one way or another. Deal with it, don't lose any sleep over it, like I am, and get on with your life. See, wasn't that simple?"

"Thanks, Sendra. I knew you could figure this out, I think."

"Now knowing you the way I do…" Sendra paused. "You will worry about it, think about it, analyze it, and make yourself sick over it, but that's just you."

"Thanks, Sendra. Sorry to wake you up."

"Don't be silly, that's what friends are for. You've been there for me when I'm having a crisis more often than I care to remember."

"Go back to sleep," Leba suggested. "Talk to you later."

"Leba, seriously, don't let this get to you. I'm sure everything will be different in the morning. Trust me. Good night." Leba carefully replaced the sat-phone in its cradle and waited for the sun to come up and, hopefully, the start of a better day.

JT walked back into his office, picking up his travel case and placing it on the desk. He shared this scantily furnished makeshift office with the other two docs assigned to the expeditionary deployment. There were two docs on any day, working staggered twelve-hour shifts: four days on, two days off, four nights on, two days off, four days on, and so on. Tonight was JT's first evening shift of the rotation. Leba would take over for him in a few hours, and Gordie would have the next two days off. Soon after relieving Gordie from his last night shift, Leba had been shuttled out to the field to triage and treat the unexpected casualties. Generally on scientific expeditionary deployments, the med units had a lot of downtime, treating cuts and bruises, the occasional bellyache or headache, and often spent time counting packages of suture material, reading, or playing games.

He and his team finished rebandaging the last head wound, retaping the last ankle, and rewarming the last frostbitten hand. His shift would be over in the next few hours, and besides his quick jaunt to Leba's quarters to return Tiv's jacket, he hadn't stopped working the entire shift. JT was exhausted. He flopped down into the rolling desk chair. Slowly, carefully he picked up a silver-framed picture. He gazed at her, the girl in the picture; those eyes, bright, blue, and beautiful, watching his every move. How long had he waited, needlessly waited, to have those eyes look back at him and only him. What he went through to prove himself to her. Why? He put the thought from his mind and placed the picture to his chest. "Don't worry, everything is right now," he mused. "Or at least it will be." He was certain of that. What he embarked on, the things he set into motion were taking on a life of their own. But it was only fair. He deserved to get a break. Soon, everything would be perfect, and he would have everything he ever wanted.

The sun was just barely peaking over the horizon. "You're earlier than usual," JT commented as Leba arrived to relieve him. "Couldn't sleep, huh?"

"Lots of things on my mind," she said, looking down at the desk and fingering some of the unfiled charts. She rubbed her forehead and finally looked up at him.

JT winked at her. "Know what you mean." After a brief signout, JT gathered up his things. "It's all yours. See you at 1900 hours."

CHAPTER 32

Base Commander Chalco Atacama sat staring at the multifaceted view screen in front of him. A burly man, his face lined and furrowed from years of military service. Although he was well seasoned, the thing he hated most was explaining to a civilian authority what went wrong with this mission. He swiveled in his chair to face the cadet who had just entered his inner sanctum. "Everyone's here, sir," the cadet began.

Atacama stroked his dark-bearded chin and then rose slowly from his chair. The cadet, who served as his aide, handed him a portfolio neatly organized with the commander's personal briefings and preplanned remarks. "Thank you," Atacama said. "Let's get this over with."

As per protocol, the cadet opened the door to the conference room and announced the base commander's entry. Everyone stood at attention, waited for the commander to sit, and then took their places at the conference table. The room was simple, four walls, no decorations, save for a closeted media board. The majority of the room was taken up by the meeting table, the only thing without military-straight corners. Atacama liked the thick oblong table where he could see all his charges at once, no place to hide. In his deep baritone, almost grandfatherly-like voice, Atacama began, "First, we lost a lot of good people yesterday, and I want to know why." He paused, slowly and individually eyeing everyone in the room, before proceeding. His brow was furrowed and his eyebrows knitted. "Second, this meeting is strictly confidential, and you will be told what you may and may not tell your subordinates." He paused again, repeating the same ritual of staring down his charges. "Third, only facts, concise and concrete. If I ask for speculation, then give it, otherwise stick to what we know." His gaze lingered on Luth Cathen for a moment. The man had a tendency to embellish, and Atacama had no stomach for it today. Cathen shrugged off the comment, opening his eyes wide as in disbelief. The majority of the troopers seated around the table were also seasoned veterans, not taken aback by his comments, but expecting them, and acknowledged the ground rules without hesitation. "Okay, then we may proceed." Despite what happened, Atacama realized how much of a toll this disaster inflicted on these younger troopers. Everyone expects there to be casualties but not to this degree and not during a scientific expedition on a supposedly sparsely inhabited moon. How could things have gone so wrong?

Tiv Garnet sat at the far end of the table, waiting for his turn to report. He was used to Atacama's briefings and knew what to expect. The past six months under his command had been rather low-key, but this debriefing was going to be different. Atacama, a stickler for protocol, always began with reports from the most forward unit, in this case, Explorer Company, and then worked his way through the backup units. Garnet's Company, Defender, was always last. They were the last line of defense, the unit expected to stand strong and hold the line. Once again they, his people, performed beyond his expectations. His unit was lucky yesterday, some morbidity, no mortality. He knew the slaughter some of the forward units experienced. Save for Cadet Raix not following his direct orders, Defender would have come through unscathed, and maybe DeShay would still be alive. *Dammit, DeShay, why did you countermand my order?* Garnet was pissed for more than Raix, though. Intelligence for this mission sucked. No one told them what they were really getting into. Someone knew. This wasn't the first deployment where Garnet served under Commander Atacama. The man was a stickler for details. By the concern on Atacama's face and the way Atacama had been taken so badly off guard by the devastating losses, Garnet wanted to believe Atacama was as in the dark as he was.

DeShay was dead and shouldn't be. He was a medic, a damn good one, and my friend. Someone would pay dearly for that. To be so overwhelmed by an enemy, or whatever did this to them, was unacceptable. He knew it, Chalco Atacama knew it, and in fact, the whole room knew it. Despite the anger fueling him, Tiv was tired, running on fumes. His own personal mission evaluation kept him up most of the night. Yesterday was so fraught with ups and downs the physical and mental ride he had been on in the last thirty-six hours was beginning to take a toll on him. He struggled to stay awake through the briefing.

The only bright spot was his chance meeting with DeShay's friend, the doctor who stayed behind. He should have stayed behind, been with DeShay in his final moments. When he looked down at his paper, he found her name scribbled in the margin. He traced the letters over and over until the name was etched into the pad. Feeling in his pocket for the medallion, Garnet fingered the links in the metal chain. The guilt was pervasive. She didn't seem to begrudge him, though, but understood his commitment to duty. His mind drifted for a moment to their meeting on the shuttle, to their toasting to DeShay's memory, to their kiss in her quarters.

A loud crash broke Garnet's reflection as Atacama slammed his portfolio down on the hardwood table. "Unacceptable!" Atacama shouted, "Absolutely unacceptable." Atacama singled out and severely chastised Overseer Company for neglecting to notify his office of an anomaly they picked up. Squad Leader Damond Fiorat made no apologies for his watch officer, who decided to sit on the information until the morning.

Explorer Company's squad leader was severely injured in the engagement and was already off-lifted to the hospital at planetary headquarters, so the remaining second in command priman assumed the unenviable task of describing his unit's horrific encounter on the front line when Atacama slammed his point home. The priman said shortly after being engaged by the opposing force, Overseer informed them of the anomaly. "Priman Henjin, how would you have deployed differently if you possessed intel earlier in the engagement?" Atacama questioned.

"Warres set us up to move out in an inverted chevron. If we'd known in advance, we probably would have gone diamond." Henjin cleared his throat, his swallow audible. "In retrospect, it probably wouldn't have mattered much anyway."

"How so?" Atacama questioned, ignoring Henjin's attempt at speculation.

"As soon as we cleared the perimeter, we were audibly assaulted. Our comm guy registered it in the ultrasonic range. Once it hit, it felt like a knife going through your brain. It was hard to think. Hell, it was hard to do anything but grab your ears to stop the noise. Until we switched modes, our helmet filters were no help either. Once we were essentially incapacitated, figuring out the adjustment took time. By then, we were being pelted with burning ice shards."

"Did you see them, son?" Atacama asked.

"No." Henjin grabbed the end of the table. "Warres ordered us to fall back, half our squad was down." Tears welled in Henjin's eyes. "We were paralyzed to do anything but get the hell out of there. I think Warres and Melpan got off a few covering shots but not much else. They tossed a few grenades, giving the rest us of time to retreat. Melpan didn't make it, and Warres took a lot of shrapnel." Henjin paused, collected himself and continued, "Warres caught up with us, and as we regrouped, we were able to get a call to base for reinforcements. He died before we got to the med station." Atacama studied him closely and listened further. "Striker Company was there in minutes, but they got slammed as well."

Atacama responded, "Thank you, Priman. Who's here from Striker?" He surveyed the room to find a talman from Striker.

"Me, sir," the young officer responded. "Talman Revo Ihew."

Atacama assessed him and asked, "Your squad leader?"

"Dead, sir," Ihew reported. "As well as both primans, our comm officer, and five of our cadets." Atacama could tell how shaken he was and gave him a few moments to compose himself.

Atacama wasn't one for wasting time, and Ihew was taking a little longer than expected with his report. "For the sake of time, Talman, let me walk you through the encounter," Atacama offered.

"No, sir," Ihew recoiled. "I'm ready to repot."

"By all means then, let's hear it." Atacama stared, interlocking his fingers over his portfolio.

"Squad Leader split us into two groups. We flanked Explorer Squad as they retreated and provided covering fire. Based on intel from Explorer Company, we adjusted our helmet filters to prevent the ultrasonic bursts. Our initial volleys seemed successful, and we were ordered to advance to try and repel the enemy."

"Had you seen any of them yet?" Atacama questioned. "Could you see what you were firing at?"

"We predicted where they were based on the trajectories of their weapons fire." Ihew inhaled and blew out hard. "As we fired on their positions, their projectile volleys tapered down to nothing. Squad Leader assumed we had them on the run." He lowered his head and rubbed his neck and then rested his hand on his forehead before finally looking up. "He was wrong. Within minutes, we were being assaulted from all sides, cut off from our fallback position." Ihew waited a moment, letting the room digest what he said.

"How did they get past you?" Atacama asked.

"I don't know," Ihew responded. "Squad Leader had our split company rejoin back-to-back to try and stave off a massacre. He asked me to take two cadets, try to get back and warn the others. He figured our best route was the way we came in. Our guys emptied their weapons to create a gap for us to get through. He told me not to look back…" His voice trailed off. "By the time Defender Company got there, it was too late."

Atacama leaned back in his chair, studied Ihew for a moment. "Thank you, Priman Ihew." Atacama was accustomed to giving battlefield promotions, and this seemed like as good a time as any. Morale was certainly low, given the devastation that had occurred, and promoting a brave young officer who followed orders would make the sacrifice of his company easier to swallow.

"Garnet, your report, please." Atacama turned to face Tiv.

Garnet straightened up in his chair, reopened the folder in front of him, and began, "Defender Company deployed on Vedax at 1100. We set up a temporary LZ a few clicks behind the scientific team's work facility. Going on the intel from the remaining members of Explorer and Striker Companies, we adjusted our helmet filters and deployed our stealth personnel transport vehicles. After ordering covering fire from the air, we inserted into the conflict zone. We locked in on Striker's signal and deployed in a hemi circumferential pattern, leaving a front door for the hostiles to enter. We sent out a gravitonic pulse to try and disrupt their forward position. This combined with the air cover seemed to shut down their ability to maneuver. We heard some distant explosions and their weapons systems powering down. Not wanting to let them regroup and redeploy and hit us again, we evac'd our guys and got out of there." Garnet paused, waiting for a response from Atacama, but none came. He finished by detailing the statistics of their rescue effort, citing the numbers of casualties, recoveries, and damages.

Atacama waited until Garnet closed his notebook before speaking. "As I stated at the beginning of this briefing, we lost a lot of good people yesterday. I don't plan to have that ever happen again, understood?"

The chorus of "Sir" rang out among those seated at the table.

Leba didn't like the small office she shared with the guys. Relatively speaking, JT and Gordie were messy. Before every shift, she had to right their wrongs, throwing out food wrappers, reshelving all the left out books, and refilling the remaining charts. They probably did it just to make her crazy. She dreaded coming to work after two days off because the mess would be twice as bad, inviting unwanted vermin to scrounge for crumbs. The day passed incredibly slowly. Morning rounds were uneventful with the remaining hospitalized troopers progressing as expected. There was Cadet Revil, from Explorer Company, recovering nicely from his collapsed lung; Talman Berkel, also from Explorer Company, recovering from his stab wound; and Two primans from Striker Two, Reserve Company, recovering from inhalation injuries. Explorer One and Striker One Companies lost a majority of their complement. Finally, in the last cubicle was a young neo, Methor, of Defender Company, getting therapy for his frostbitten hands and snow-blinded eyes.

"Don't worry, kid. You'll be good as new in no time," Leba encouraged him.

"Thanks, Doc, I hope so. I want to fly for Javel Squadron, like my father and grandfather before him. Your parents are pilots, aren't they?"

"I thought I recognized your name."

"Anzo Methor, just like my dad."

"I'm sure your father would be very proud of the way you risked your life to get your buddy to safety."

"Squad Leader said he'd put me in for a commendation, ma'am."

She carefully examined his reddened and stiff fingers. "Can you feel them yet?" she questioned.

"Some tingling and pain, but I guess that's better than nothing."

"Now keep your eyes closed while I check your progress." Leba closed the curtain to the cubicle and turned its overhead light from white to red. She peeled off the bandages, gently removing the opaque patch first from the right eye and then from the left eye. Using a microretinoscope, she evaluated each crop of rods and cones, noting their disruption and regeneration.

"Well, ma'am?" he questioned. "How's it look?"

"Yeah, Doc, how's it looking?"

Leba recognized the new voice before Methor chimed in excitedly, "Squad Leader!"

"Well, Doc, looks like Cadet Anzo Methor here is ready for duty."

"Cadet?" Anzo questioned his squad leader.

"Yeah, kid, your commendation brought with it an increase in rank. Congratulations."

"Congratulations, Cadet. Shouldn't be more than a day or two and you'll be as good as new." Leba tried to maintain her demeanor, not seem too excited at seeing Tiv Garnet again. But the tingles up her spine made her hands almost imperceptibly shake. "Your hands and eyes are making a great recovery. Let me redress your eyes and then let you two visit."

"Thanks, Doc," Tiv said, touching her hand, almost acknowledging her reaction to his presence. "I'll step out for a minute. Let me know when you're done." The corners of his mouth turned upward, and his eyebrows arched, momentarily flashing her. He stepped back behind the cubicle door.

She turned her attention back to Cadet Methor, glad he couldn't see the blush on her face Tiv's touch brought. After finishing repatching his eyes, she moved the curtain out of the way and returned the lights to their original status. She exited the cubicle. Her lips felt dry, and she moistened them with her tongue before facing Tiv. "He's all yours, Squad Leader."

Leba went back to her makeshift office, moved JT's stuff to one side, pulled up a chair, and began to review the latest lab results and scans from the hospitalized patients. It was hard to concentrate. The most difficult part wasn't trying to decipher JT and Gordie's illegible handwriting but trying to analyze Tiv's touching gesture. Did he like her, or was he just being polite?

When she returned to the ward to see the outpatient follow-ups, she was disappointed to find Tiv gone. Did she expect him to stop by and say good-bye? She didn't know what to expect. This stuff was Sendra's forte, not hers, and understanding the male brain and how it related to her was not one of her strong points. Of course, when the interaction was with a patient or a friend, she was usually on point. With a potential suitor, she was a jumbled mess.

As the long shift wound to a close, Leba was not surprised she had to wait for JT. Now that JT had a steady girlfriend, he was always late. To his credit, JT always had a great excuse, and Leba often cut him some slack. Gordie, however, did not. Gordie, an old married guy, had no time for JT's antics and told him in no uncertain terms that when his shift was over, JT better be there or else. Leba found it hard to be intolerant of JT's exploits, she envied how much he enjoyed life. He was not only a fun guy, but also a very skilled physician. When they were back at the clinic together, they worked well together, and she enjoyed his collegiality.

He'd been through a rough time lately, and Leba hoped his girlfriend, Nilsa, would continue to be a positive in his life. Leba knew JT was interested in Nilsa, a bright young military scientist, for quite some time. Unfortunately, Nilsa was obsessed with someone else. JT and Nilsa were friends early on, JT wanting more but settling for the confidant role when it was clear Nilsa set her sights on someone else. For a long time in their relationship, Nilsa would drift from guy to guy, never realizing the one who truly cared for her was right beside her all along. JT confided in Leba how much he cared for Nilsa and he'd do anything to make her happy. Instead of realizing that maybe Nilsa was at the heart of the problem, JT became more and more incensed with the men who broke her heart. One time Leba implied perhaps Nilsa was obsessive, she obviously couldn't see how great JT would be for her, JT took offense. Leba quickly apologized and changed the subject.

The last breakup had been very traumatic for Nilsa, at least the way she explained it to JT. This time when he spent long nights comforting her, she began to see JT differently. Leba was glad when JT announced he and Nilsa were a couple. All the energy JT spent picking up the pieces could now be redirected to building a lasting relationship with his dream girl. He took her to the Grand Octranian and even finagled her last-minute participation in this mission.

"I know I'm late," JT apologized as he walked into the office. "Guess you'll be back on nights in a few days."

"Cathen took my two days off and turned them into inventory," Leba remarked, gathering her belongings. JT flung his stuff into a newly cleaned corner, knocking a shelf clear in the process.

"Well, somebody has to do it, and better you than me," he teased and bent over to replace one of the fallen books.

"Thanks, JT, I'll remember your compassion next time I have to cover your lateness," Leba retorted. "Hope your girlfriend appreciates my dedication to duty."

"Ha, ha." JT remained crouched on the floor, his back toward the door. "See you in the morning."

Leba slung her rucksack over her shoulder and headed toward her quarters. She was tired, and it had been a long enough day without JT showing up late. All she wanted to do was take a hot shower, eat some food, and get into bed. No drama, no excitement.

Leba's alarm startled her out of bed. She hadn't remembered sleeping so soundly in such a long time. She stretched as she got out of bed, got dressed, and headed toward the med clinic's storeroom to spend the day cataloguing supplies. The shelves were floor to ceiling piled high with an assortment of medical necessities. This was not how she remembered it when they first set it up. Everything had a place and was labeled and ready for immediate use. What she should have done was vaporized the entire room and started from scratch. Rearranging the mess would be time-consuming, but Cathen said she needed to straighten up, and this would be a good way to understand the concept. Stopping by around lunchtime, Lord Cathen poked his head in to assess her progress. After making some gratuitous remark, he left. Seems everyone else decided she was to be the center of attention. Beginning with JT finishing his shift and Gordie beginning his shift until they switched at the end of the day, everyone who passed by felt it necessary to comment or give her advice. If she could get the majority of the work done on day one, then she could at least get some free time before the end of day two.

Inventory day one ended much in the same way as the night before except Leba found it hard to get to sleep. She began to wonder why she hadn't heard from Tiv. Not that Tiv gave her any indication he would want to spend more time with her, it bugged her he didn't. Maybe another call to Sendra would be in order. No, Leba knew what Sendra would say. "You have two choices, call him or don't." Although Leba did want to see Tiv again, she was afraid of what his response would be. She could ask JT in the morning. Tiv and JT were friends. No, Leba knew what JT would say. "You have two choices, call him or don't." Leba, practical Leba, sensible Leba, no-nonsense Leba, really stupid Leba would wait and see. If he contacted her, it would be a good sign. Maybe she would run into him in the clinic if he was visiting his cadet. *That's it. I'm sure I'll run into him tomorrow.* Once she reasoned out a course of action, she could fall asleep. She slept restlessly, but at least she slept.

"Morning, JT," Leba said as she walked into the clinic office early the next day. "Did I wake you?"

A drowsy JT straightened up in his chair and quickly removed his feet from the desk. "Slow night," JT began. "Oh, and by the way, I am supposed to tell you Cadet Methor said thanks for all your help.

I sent him out last evening." The smile on Leba's face faded slightly. "How much more do you have to do today?" JT questioned, oblivious to her change in demeanor.

"Couple of hours at best. I should be done before you come back tonight." Leba started out the door. "Remember, don't be late, or Cathen will have your head."

"I know," JT said. "I got an earful yesterday. Luckily he's more pissed at you than me. Cathen was about ready to come down on me for being late for shifts, but with your insubordination, I escaped his wrath. And you got my punishment. Thanks. Too bad for you, though." He made an exaggerated pout. "But my luck seems to be changing. I'm looking forward to finishing my last shift and getting a few days off." He smiled slyly. "Besides, I could never have done the job as well as you. I guess it all worked out for the best."

"That's it." Leba stared around the supply room. "Everything's labeled, counted, and recorded."

Gordie strode by, paused at the entry door, hands on hips, and looked top to bottom. "Wow. Never seen the place look so neat."

"Thanks, Gordie," Leba said, dusting herself off as she stood up. "If I can get Cathen to sign off on it, maybe I can get some time off."

"Big plans, huh," Gordie inquired.

"No, thought I'd catch up on some reading and see the Dologos game."

"What time's the simulcast?" Gordie asked. "I used to work sideline for the Crimson Warriors."

"Warriors versus Wildwings at 2100 hours," Leba answered. "My dad, being a pilot, had season tickets to the Wildwings games when we were growing up. My brother, sister, and I were on a rotation as to who got to go to the games." Approaching boot steps marched down the hall.

"Here comes your buddy now," Gordie said sarcastically as Cathen entered the clinic. "Good luck."

Right on schedule, Leba watched as Gordie made way for Cathen to occupy the doorframe. "Squad Leader, sir." She saluted.

"At ease, Brader," Cathen ordered. He stepped into the storage room and surveyed it. His pursed lips, which were now thin lines, framed the corners of his slightly downturned mouth. Leba knew he'd no choice but to acknowledge her effort. Cathen began slowly, his legs splayed, his chest pushed forward, and his arms rested behind his back. "Well, Brader, you did not disappoint." Leba waited for the *but*. "I suppose you can go. Take the rest of the afternoon off."

Leba smiled. "Thank you, sir."

"But, Brader." He sneered. "You're still on restriction until the end of this duty cycle."

"Understood, sir." She saluted. He turned and left. There was no way she was going to let him intimidate her. Cathen may win a battle or two but not the war.

After stopping at the commissary to pick up a few essentials, Leba returned to her quarters. She checked, no messages. Disappointed, Leba ate a late lunch, put on sweatpants and her indigo-and-silver Wildwings jersey over a black racer back T-shirt. She found her current novel where she left it, flipped to the turned-down page, and became engrossed in the story. By the time she finished the book, it was already dark. There was a knock on her door. Her chrono displayed 1830 hours. *Probably JT wants me to do his shift tonight so he can have three days off. That was just like JT to not think of anyone but himself when it came to spending time with Nilsa.* "I'll be right there," she responded to the second knock at the door. She wasn't thrilled at the prospect of having to cover for him again on such short notice, but she would; she always did. Getting to the door slowly was her small way to make him sweat.

Leba opened the door, expecting to see JT's big grin, but was pleasantly surprised by the face staring back. There was a day's worth of beard stubble on Tiv, but it added to his hardworking, now-ready-to-play mode. "Are you going to invite me in?" he questioned. "I brought dinner." Boy, did he look great in his uniform. Leba imagined he'd probably look even better out of it.

"Please," she said, trying not to smile too much or blush too much or anything too much. Her mouth was dry, and the lump in her throat pulsed faster. "What a pleasant surprise," she said. Then thought how stupid that sounded and tried again. "Come in, make yourself at home." What was she thinking? *Get a grip, girl. He's just a man. No, an incredibly hot man whose at my door with a big greasy bag. Don't stare.*

"I hope I didn't disturb you." Tiv noticed her wavy brown hair and how it laid in wisps around her shoulders. She circled her hair around her ears to get it out of her face. He had only seen her in the dim light before. Now he noticed her red highlights. She was in regular clothes and wondered how she'd look out of them. *Slow down, you're getting ahead of yourself.* With his self-imposed ban, it had been a while since he was with a woman. And although his ship was begging for full steam ahead after their encounter the other day, he needed to get a better feel of the situation before hitting the open ocean.

"No," she said, "I was just thinking about what to have for dinner and getting set to watch the game."

Cool, a girl who actually likes Dologos. So far, DeShay, right on target.

"Let me guess." Tiv grinned. "You must be an Indigo Wildwings fan."

"How'd you know?" Leba asked.

"The Wildwings hat and sweatshirt, for starters," he said, pointing at her striped jersey.

"Oh, yeah." She blushed, wrapping her arms across her chest and bowing her head. "Guess I'm still off from counting inventory all day."

I can help you take your mind off that.

"My little brother, Kyle, plays for the Warriors," Tiv said, walking farther into the room. "He's a defenseman, been with them two years now." Her quarters were tidy and smelled fresh. "I try to catch his games anytime I can." The greasy-bottomed bag he brought needed to be dealt with before the burgers came through, and Tiv put the bag down in the middle of her table. He picked up the small framed picture of her and DeShay.

"You're more than welcome to watch here with me if you can stand to be in the same room as a Wildwings fan," Leba teased. Tiv caught her looking at the bag, no, the picture he was holding. He placed it back on the table.

"I think I'll manage. I don't know about you, but I'm pretty hungry. Hope you like Commando Burgers." He lifted the bag, shaking its contents. Moving the framed remembrance to an end table, Leba cleared a place on the dining table and set out some plates and utensils. "You don't mind I stopped by and invited myself to dinner?"

"Not at all. In fact, I could use the company." She glanced at DeShay's picture. Tiv could see she was hurting too. Leba sat first. Digging his hand into the bag, Tiv removed two burgers and set one down on her plate and then his.

Let's test the waters. "DeShay told me you'd do almost anything for one of these." Smiling shyly, she adjusted her cap. He took a chair from the opposite end of the table and moved adjacent to her and sat. Their eyes locked for a moment. Tiv ripped the bag open, spilling the crisps out.

"It's been kinda lonely lately, being sent to my room and all," she said, her hand resting on her chin.

"Sometimes being naughty has its advantages." Tiv mirrored her. He noticed the little freckles dotting her cheeks and the bridge of her nose. *No makeup, kinda like that.* He reached over and offered her a crisp. She took a bite from it. After popping the rest of the crisp into his mouth, he stroked her face with his outstretched hand. Tiv pushed her plate aside, and fingered the brim of her hat. *This needs to go.* Tossing it aside, Tiv kissed her. Then he kissed her again. He took her hand and led her from the table.

On the couch, he slid an arm around her, moving himself on top of her. He kissed her again, this time longer and deeper. *Slow down.* DeShay joked about this being her maiden voyage. He just met her, and he really didn't have a sense for her yet. He felt her relax, the tension slipping away under his embrace. His jacket was already unzipped and off by the time she took a breath. The mainsail was trimmed and ready for hoisting. He moved from her mouth to her neck, exploring every inch. Her hands climbed up through his hair. His lips found the sweet spot at her jawline, where her pulse reflected his success in pushing the right buttons. Sliding his hands down her sides, he slipped them under her sweatshirt and slowly scrunched it upward. He moved south, and tiny droplets of perspiration salted his mouth as he tickled her navel with his tongue. He grasped the ends of her sweatshirt and was preparing to free her from its confines.

"Too fast," she whispered, righting herself. Her hands gently pushing him away.

Leba pulled her knees toward her chest and grasped them with her arms. Resting her chin on top, she didn't look at him. *Nice job, hotshot.* Tiv slowly backed away. "I'm sorry." Her lip quivered as tears welled in her eyes. "Things are moving way too fast for me." She rocked slowly back and forth, looking up momentarily to catch his glance. "Please don't be angry," she said, her lower lip pouted.

"No, I'm sorry." Tiv sighed. *Geez, DeShay, you could have told me. I didn't think you were serious about the maiden thing.* Grabbing her outer arm first and then the other, he pulled her close and held her. *I really thought the two of us connected before.* With her head tucked under his chin, he whispered, "Don't be upset." He gently kissed the top of her head. "No worries." *Blew it big time, and I wanted this to work.*

"Can we take things a little slower?" She looked up into his eyes. *Well, maybe I didn't screw it up too badly.*

"Of course," he said as he made his way off the couch and back to the table. "Hungry?" he asked while tucking in his shirt. Leba stretched out her legs, brushed the hair from her face, and made her way over to join him. Her face was still flushed and her cheeks tearstained. *This innocent stuff is kinda sexy, though.* He handed her a napkin, and she wiped her face. They finished the burgers and most of the crisps in relative silence. After his aggressive move, Leba would probably never want to see him again.

"So where do you want to start?" he asked. Maybe he could salvage the evening anyway.

"I'll make some tea, and you take your shirt off," Leba said as she went toward the kitchen area. "And your pants too."

"Huh." Tiv laughed. "I thought you wanted to take it slow."

"I do." The corners of her mouth slightly upturned, and her eyes smiled wide. "I'll show you. Just keep your shorts on."

Leba returned with a cup of tea. *What's this about?* She placed it on the table. Steam rose into the air, and Tiv watched as she slowly stirred in a syrupy yellow substance. "Drink this slowly," she advised. Interest piqued, Tiv did as he was told. "Now close your eyes."

Kinky, but I'm game.

"I thought you wanted to take it slow." She moved around the table to stand behind him and slowly dragged her finger across the top of his back. *What are you up to back there?*

She gave him a playful tap on the back of his head. "Close your eyes, Squad Leader." She put her hands on his shoulders. "I want you to relax. Release the tension in your muscles. Take in some deep breaths." Leba massaged his neck, using her fingers to work out the knots. Slowly and methodically moving down his shoulders and arms and back. "Now lie down on the floor, facedown," she instructed. *She puts on leather, pulls out a whip, and I'm hers forever.*

"I thought you wanted to take it slow? Not that I'm complaining or anything."

"Shh," she quieted him. "Relax and enjoy." She worked through each muscle group again, stretching and kneading. "Tiv," she whispered into his ear, "see how good taking it slow can feel?" Her warm breath made him shiver. He could get used to someone making him feel this way.

"Uh-huh." He moaned. Eyes closed and head down on the floor, he lay there until his chrono alarmed. He flipped over and stared up at her. Startled by his maneuver, Leba almost fell on top of him. "Game time in thirty minutes." He laughed, trying to steady her. "But I'm willing to miss it for more of this."

Leba bit her lower lip, winked, resumed straddling him, and began kneading his chest. "Won't your brother be disappointed you missed his performance?"

"I'd take your performance over his anytime." He placed both his hands on her shoulders and slid from underneath her. Now sitting in front of her, Tiv cupped her head in his hands. He wanted to kiss her, that red-lipped, pouty little face of hers, but didn't. "Anyway, if you trust me to behave, it's your turn." Not at all what he expected. No wonder DeShay liked her. All full of surprises. Getting to know her was going to be fun, lots of fun. "Drink this slowly," he mimicked her request. After sipping some tea, she pulled her Wildwings jersey over her head, revealing a sleek black tank top. He stared for a moment. "You know"–he exhaled through puffed cheeks—"I could get used to this slow stuff."

He proceeded to work on her muscles, mimicking her routine until Leba felt like jelly. To his delight, she turned over, slung her arms around his neck, and brought him down to the floor. This time, she kissed him. And not short and sweet. *Wow.* He helped her up from the floor, and the two of them sat back on the couch, his arm loosely draped over her shoulder, her head nestled against his chest, their four feet on the tabletop, touching ever so slightly, and watched the game. *I'm glad DeShay didn't tell me everything about you.*

"Your brother's very good, he's kept us from scoring all night long," she commented. Tiv watched the blush blossom on her face.

"Taught him everything he knows," Tiv boasted. He found her mouth and kissed her. "About scoring and all."

"You are so bad," she scolded him, playfully poking him in the side.

"Now I'm the bad influence. This from the girl who's restricted to quarters by her squad leader and dares to have a dinner date with a half-naked stranger. If I was your squad leader, I'd have you restricted to your room for a much longer time," he said in a serious voice.

"You'd like that, wouldn't you, soldier," she retorted with a pout. "Let me guess, you'd probably stand guard duty the entire time to make sure I didn't invite over any other half-naked men."

"Something like that." Up went his hands. "Score!" he yelled.

"Shh, or you'll have my watchdog barking at my door."

"Ah-ha." He grinned. "You'd like that, wouldn't you, and then you wouldn't have to pay up on the bet." *Time to get a status check.* She inclined her head and cocked an eyebrow at him. "You know, the bet where I get to choose our next date, 'cause your team stinks, and my Warriors won." This time he poked her side. They shared the laugh until his chrono alarm went off again.

"Damn." Tiv stared at the cracked face on his chrono. "Early day tomorrow." Tiv got up from the couch, gathered up his shirt and jacket. "I hate to leave, but…"

"Looking for these," she teased, holding his pants. "Don't believe you'll be going anywhere without these."

"Don't tempt me." He smiled, trying to take them from her, but she pulled away. "And who do you think would get in more trouble if I walked out of here without them?"

"Probably me," she grumbled. "Cathen would probably have me clean the med clinic floors with a toothbrush. You, on the other hand, would probably get a medal or something."

Tiv chuckled as she handed him his pants. "Thanks for a great evening." Tiv gathered her up in his arms and kissed her. "Pleasant dreams," he said and, with that, was out the door.

She watched him go down the hall until he slipped out of sight around the turn. The air was still rich with his cologne, and she inhaled deeply, lingering at the door for a moment or two before securing it closed and wondering whether she'd ever hear from him again. Was the next date line legit, or was he being nice? Pleasant dreams, she considered. If he only knew.

CHAPTER 33

The locker room was not big enough for the two of them. Shirt off and still glistening with sweat, Damond Fiorat stood in front of his open locker, toweling off. When Zach stood in the same position, there was a locker visible on both sides. Gathering up his nerve, with both fists clenched, he approached his squad leader. It was probably a good move to confront the man after his punishing workout. Maybe he would be too tired.

"What up, little man?" Fiorat seemed stunned by Kixon's aggressive approach.

Good, he knows I'm angry and mean business.

"You want I should beat your sorry ass into the ground or slap the crap out of you?" Zach retorted. He was taking a big chance challenging his squad leader this way, but there were some things a man had to do.

"I understand how you feel about Sendra Tohl, but she's way out of your league, little man," Fiorat shot back, turned, and looked in the mirror, and with both hands, dried his hair. *Don't turn your back on me.*

Zach repeated his question to his now really pissed squad leader. "Well, how do you want it?"

After wringing the towel, Fiorat slung it over the back of his neck. "Calm down, Cadet." His eyes narrowed, and his gaze zeroed in. "You're seriously close to being insubordinate or at the very least getting the hell knocked out of you," Fiorat cautioned.

"You shouldn't have treated her that way, you dumb pig," Zach spat out the words without thinking, his hands raised in an offensive posture. Then the lights went out. When Zach awoke, he was dizzy, his head hurt, and he was sitting propped up against his locker. Zach wiped the semi-dried blood from his nose with the back of his sleeve, leaving a distinctive reddish trail. "Damn," Zach cursed. "Now I'm gonna have to get my new jacket laundered." Not even considering how long he'd been there or what else might not function, he tried to stand, his legs unsupportive. His right hand hurt, and the knuckles were bluish and swollen. He looked left and then right. With no one else around, he got on all fours. Still somewhat wobbly, Zach supported himself against one of the nearby empty lockers and climbed hand over hand to a standing position. He opened the door and looked at the small mirror affixed on its inner surface. A black circle was forming under his right eye. Zach couldn't remember much after calling Fiorat a pig, but it really didn't matter. Right now he needed to find someone to fix his broken hand.

"It's not broken," the corpsman reassured him. "Nice shiner, though." The medic secured an ice pack over Zach's right hand and then put another in his left. "Here, hold this on your eye." The picture on the wall in the treatment room went in and out of focus. Zach's head hurt. "Take these." Zach swallowed the two caplets dry and screwed up his face. "What's the other guy look like?"

Zach couldn't answer because he didn't know.

———

"Can't believe I'm finally off restriction," Leba explained to Sendra on the sat-phone.

"Hasn't seemed to keep you out of trouble," Sendra teased. "Sneaking your boyfriend into your quarters sounds like something I'd do, not you."

"He's not really my official boyfriend," Leba opined.

"Right," snapped Sendra. "What do you need, an official announcement? Being an expert in men, I'd say he's pretty smitten with you even if you don't have a certificate on your wall declaring it."

"Okay, okay, enough about me, how's things at the clinic?" Leba chewed on her cuticle.

"Boring, the locum docs are insufferable. They know the medicine and all, but they're no fun. We actually have to work. And pathetic, where do they dig up these old geezers anyway? I've got no one to talk to except the old woman who greets patients as they come in. All she ever talks about is her animals. I don't think she even knows men exist. You know how bad it is without you here? Sometimes I even look forward to her cat stories."

"How's Damond?" Leba asked.

"Too long gone, as far as I'm concerned," Sendra responded, the unhappiness evident.

"You know what happened with Zach and Damond?" Leba inquired on a more serious note.

"Damond called and told me what went down. I guess I have to be more careful when I discuss things with Zach. I didn't realize he took what I said so seriously."

"He thinks he has to defend your honor," Leba explained. "If he can't have you, and he knows he can't, then the man who does better treat you right or Zach's going to take care of business."

"Damond was actually proud Zach stood up to him. Originally had some questions about his toughness, but not anymore. Damond was surprised he had it in him."

"I don't think they should continue to work in the same company," Leba proffered.

"You sound like Damond, but how do we arrange it?"

"Leave it to me. I have something in the works already," Leba reassured her.

"You always have a plan, and it doesn't hurt you're sleeping with a squad leader." She laughed.

"You know me better than that. I would never use my position with Tiv." She hesitated, thinking about her choice of words.

Sendra laughed out loud. "I know what you mean. I'm thinking it would be a lot less complicated if Zach was in Tiv's company and not Damond's. Even if you aren't sleeping with Tiv yet, maybe you could get Zach assigned to his company."

Leba made her thumb bleed. "I think Zach's avoiding me since it all went down. I guess he figured I'd notice his black eye."

"You are a doctor, you know."

"I'm sure Zach will come around to visit sooner or later, and I'll bring it up. Right now Zach's got other problems. Girl problems."

"Do tell," Sendra inquired. Leba detailed Zach's latest foray into the dating world. "Sounds like this one may be a keeper. I wouldn't want to be Zach explaining to her how he got hit defending the honor of another woman."

"He's a smart boy. He'll come up with something. Anyway, if he can stall about two weeks, his eye will be healed."

"What else is up?" Sendra asked. "How's your mom and dad?"

"They're doing fine. I hear from them at least once a week. My sibs are doing the same old things. How 'bout your family?"

"Nothing new, now let's talk more about Tiv, sounds really dreamy to me," Sendra ventured.

"Oh, got to go, someone's knocking at my door." Leba hurried to get off the phone.

"Probably your dreamy hunk. Can't wait to meet him. Make sure you give him a kiss for me."

The knock at the door got louder. "I'm coming, keep your pants on."

"Pants on or pants off. You girls can never make up your minds." Although Tiv liked to test the ground rules, Leba was more comfortable and less pressured in his presence. She wasn't sure how long that would remain. This more relaxed pace would hopefully give time for the relationship to grow. One day, though, it would have to progress further if she wanted to keep him around, but for right now, he seemed to understand.

"How was your day?" Leba asked, the question sounding like one-half of an old married couple.

"Great," Tiv said. His whole face was lit up. "That's why I came over early, to tell you." Tiv took off his jacket, went to the kitchen area, and poured a drink. Leba liked the fact Tiv was beginning to make himself at home.

"Don't keep me in suspense." She beckoned him over to where she had taken a seat on the couch.

"First things first," he said, kissing her gently on the lips. "Glad to see you." She returned his kiss, lingering a little bit, nuzzling his neck. "Now if you're gonna start that, I'm never gonna get around to telling you my news."

"If you insist," she teased. "So what's so spectacular that it couldn't wait for later?"

"My brother, Kyle, is coming to Pareq to play an exhibition game. He got us tickets to see him play. I told him about you, and I want you to meet him." Leba frowned and rubbed the lower half of her face. "You want to go, don't you?" Tiv questioned.

"Of course, I just hope I can live up to your description of me," she answered. "When is it?" she asked.

"Tonight," Tiv said.

"Tonight?" Leba repeated. "Unfortunately, I already have plans with this handsome soldier, but no problem, I'm sure he'll understand." She patted the side of his face with her hand.

Tiv reached behind, snatched a couch pillow, and threw it at her. "Listen, I've got to go tie up some loose ends with my company, but I'll pick you up at 1800 hours. I figure we'd take Kyle out to dinner after the game, if you can spare the time." Leba proceeded to throw the pillow back at him. He winked, slung his jacket over his shoulder, and left her quarters.

Meet the family. According to Sendra's rules about men and relationships, meet the family was a big step toward certified boyfriend-ness.

Fresh out of the shower, her hair still wet, Leba hunted for information on Kyle Garnet. She needed to figure out everything there was to know about Tiv's younger brother, but dripping on her keypad probably wasn't the smartest thing she'd ever done. She grasped up a handful of hair and squeezed it out over the carpet. That'll do for now.

Fortunately as one of the Dologos league's premier defensemen, information on Kyle Garnet was easy to find. Tiv's little brother was shorter and stockier, sporting a thin, well-trimmed black goatee, and with the same penetrating blue eyes. His favorite band, meal he ate before every game, and his reluctance to change his game day socks after a win were all common knowledge to the amassed fan database. Married to his academy sweetheart, he had two small boys. Tiv adored his nephews and how much he missed them when he was on an extraplanetary deployment. The fact Tiv hadn't seen his brother's family in such a long time spoke to his commitment to duty. Leba knew how close Tiv and Kyle were. Tiv was the best man at Kyle's wedding and the second parent to his nephews. Leba studied Kyle's performance statistics as a member of the Crimson Warriors. He'd been the undoing of many other teams' hopes for a championship.

Leba figured it mattered to Tiv to have his brother's approval. She hoped Kyle would like her too. If she were to become a part of Tiv's life, passing the brother test was a big step.

The door to the team room burst open. Tiv put down the stylus and looked up at Brit Belk. He was huffing and puffing, must have sprinted down the hall. Tiv rested his elbow on the desk and brought his palm up to support his head. Inclining toward Brit, Tiv waited for him to speak.

Brit leaned onto the desk, push-up position, and hooked his thumbs under the table lip. "So did you get us tickets to the game?" He drummed his fingers. "Well?" Brit leaned in, encroaching on Tiv's personal space.

You know how much that annoys me, but two can play that game. Tiv brought his supporting hand around to cover the lower half of his face and cocked an eyebrow. "I thought you had the watch tonight?"

Brit pushed up from the table until his elbows were almost at full extension. "Are you kidding? And miss a live Dologos game?" Not getting an immediate reply, Brit pushed farther back from the desk and straightened up. His feet shifted back and forth. "Don't make me beg."

Tiv leaned back in his chair and ran his hands through his hair. "Kyle could only get so many tickets. Besides, I thought you pulled watch."

"And what, you're not taking your best friend? C'mon, man, after all I do for you."

Well, there's someone that does more for me, and she'd like to go. "Some girls like Dologos too." Tiv scratched the side of his head.

"Granted, but it's not like you've got anyone special—" Brit stopped talking when Tiv momentarily closed his eyes. "As far as I knew, you swore off women." Tiv was silent but couldn't help hide his eyebrow raise when the corners of his mouth upturned. "What aren't you telling me?"

Wouldn't you like to know? Brit was like an old woman with his gossip and prided himself as the source for all interpersonal intel. This time, Tiv knew something Brit didn't. Picking up his stylus, Tiv turned back to his info-screen and began tapping away.

Brit rubbed his forehead. "Who is she?" Tiv didn't look up. Smoothing his goatee and rising slightly up and down on the balls of his feet, Brit wagered, "If I figure out who she is, this girl who's taking my seat at the game, you'll give me the tickets." There was a long silence until Brit, still bouncing on his toes, said, "And if I don't, then I'll cover your watch for an entire duty cycle, so you can spend all your free time with the mystery girl, no switches, I promise."

"Sounds fair." Tiv put out his hand. Brit shook it. There was no way he could know about Leba, nobody did, and Tiv liked it that way. At the beginning of a relationship, it was always better to be the only player in the game. Tiv didn't need anyone's advice or recommendations. Thinking too much never seemed to work. In fact, had he listened to his own head, he never would have dated Nilsa as long as he did, and technically, it wasn't very long at all; it just seemed that way, especially with DeShay telling him to give it a chance.

Brit grabbed a nearby chair, deftly flipped it around backward, and sat. Folding his arms on the back of the chair, Brit rested his chin on his hands. Tiv sat up straight and tapped his stylus. "I thought you'd make one guess and be done."

"It's not that easy. You're such a tough guy to figure." Brit shut his eyes and squeezed his temples. "I know, the hot blonde in supply? No. Maybe the fiery red in launch control? No, not her either." The guesses came in rapid succession and were just as quickly dismissed. Brit clasped his hands, his thumbs to his lips. "Nope, none are your type."

"What, so now I have a type?"

"Not every girl is willing to put up with you and your idiosyncrasies."

"What, that I'd like to know them more than five minutes before they are warming my bed?"

"What's that supposed to mean?" Brit narrowed his eyes and stared.

"You're a smart guy, figure it out." Exasperated, Tiv exhaled through puffed cheeks. "Is this going to take much longer? I've got a lot of work to do before the game." He patted his shirt pocket where the tickets were.

"Okay, let me think. Well, she'd probably have to be here on base, you're not into the locals."

Tiv smirked. *This is really getting us nowhere.* "How many guesses do you get?"

"I've noticed you seem attracted to dark-haired girls, so I'll bet she's a brunette." Rocking his head back and forth, Brit continued, "She'd have to have some smarts. You seem to attract the brainy types, although it hasn't turned out too well lately. Wasn't Nilsa some kind of environmental bioculturist?"

"Don't go there." Tiv pointed his stylus at Brit.

"And eyes, she'd have to have eyes."

Screwing up his face, Tiv said, "I would hope so."

"You know what I mean. She'd probably be athletic too. Someone who could go a couple of rounds with you." Brit paused.

"Okay, so your guess is a smart brown-haired athletic girl with eyes?"

"Give me a second, since we're sticking to girls close to home, I'd say maybe someone in Overseer or Explorer." Steepling his fingers, Tiv pursed his lips. Brit was going to owe him big time. "No, I've changed my mind."

"Good, I hope this one works better." Tiv grinned.

"Let's see, how 'bout something outside your comfort zone, maybe a nurse or something. Maybe Cathen's lady decided to jump ship."

"I told you, she was too clingy."

"Okay, but let's stick with the Medical Company." By this time, Tiv was beginning to suspect something. Brit was just being too Brit. "I know, I bet she's a doctor."

"Why would a doctor want to date me?"

"That's what I was thinking."

"Enough," Tiv said as he forcefully put his stylus on the table. "How'd you know?"

A big grin crossed Brit's face. "It's my job as your wingman to know."

Punching his fist into the other, he said, "JT, that son of a—"

Brit put up both hands. "Calm down, it's no big deal. She was DeShay's friend, right?"

Reaching into his shirt pocket with two fingers, Tiv pulled out two tickets and handed them to Brit. "I was going to give these to you anyway."

"Thanks, buddy." Brit turned the tickets over in his hand. "What about you? Isn't your lady going to be upset that she couldn't go?"

"Who said she wasn't going?" Tiv tucked his chin and peered at Brit. "Kyle got me box seats." *Despite the fact that I'm a grunt and he's world famous, even if he forgets sometimes, I am still his brother.*

Retaking his seat, Brit rested his chin again on the back of the chair. "What now?" Tiv asked.

"So … tell me about her. This girl you broke your ban for."

⌇

The stadium was actually a converted academy field house. The parking was makeshift at best, and Tiv decided they could walk the distance instead. The pair could have a conversation without being interrupted. After being dropped off by the base shuttle, Tiv grasped Leba's hand, and they headed toward the crowd entering the arena. What bothered him was his question to Brit. *Why would a doctor want to date me?*

"I didn't know Pareq had a Dologos team," Leba stated.

"Kyle said the Pareq Pioneers are looking to enter Official Dologos Play, and this exhibition game is to gauge fan support. I guess it doesn't hurt a base full of Warrior fans moved in down the street."

Leba looked at him, smirking. "One thousand nine hundred ninety-nine Warrior fans and one Wildwings fan."

Tiv laughed. "Thank goodness you left your fan wear at home."

"Thanks for the Warriors hat, I guess you didn't want me embarrassing you." She poked at him.

He slung his arm over her shoulder. "I'll make a Warriors fan of you yet, just give me time," he said, pushing the brim of her hat down over her eyes.

He let his shoulder embrace go and grabbed her hand. "Come on." He tugged. "If we get in early enough, maybe we can get an autograph or two for you."

She laughed and picked up the pace. "You're such a kid when it comes to your Warriors." He smiled, and they ran hand-in-hand for the entry gate.

Impressed by Leba's knowledge of the Warriors names and numbers and statistics, Tiv said, "I thought you were a die-hard Wildwings fan."

"I'm not only trying to impress you, but I want to impress your brother as well."

"Don't worry," he conceded, "I like you, and that's good enough for me." *I don't need Kyle's approval.* She smiled, put an arm around his neck, and brought his head down to hers. For a moment, as they gazed into each other's eyes, Tiv forgot about the crowd noises, the rabid fans, and even the game. They were the only two people in the universe, just Tiv and Leba, and he wanted it to stay that way. Finally he met someone more concerned about his happiness than hers. She wanted to impress him. He could get used to this.

The small café was far enough from the stadium; Tiv hoped they wouldn't be bothered. Kyle's fans could be persistent, especially if they were wasted. The Warriors' decisive win over the Pioneers was punctuated by his brother's goal from half-field. Defensemen who were able to score was a rarity, and being present at a live occurrence was even scarcer, but Tiv still thought it was not the greatest public relations move ever. But in front of so many of his military fans, Kyle didn't disappoint. Tiv excused himself for a moment, promising to be right back, leaving Kyle at the table with Leba. He was taking a chance but knew Leba could handle herself.

"I leave you alone for two minutes and you have my girlfriend crying." Tiv tousled his brother's hair.

"We were just talking about DeShay," Leba interjected.

Tiv took a seat next to Leba, facing Kyle. "Did you order yet?"

"The server said she would be right back," Kyle answered.

"So how's Cika and the boys? I bet they're getting big," Tiv asked.

"Cika's great, I think she wants to try for a girl, though. Sometimes being the only female in the house wears on her patience. Wyter and Little Kyle go through shoes faster than I go through impact pads. In fact, we signed them both up to play junior Dologos at the rec center. I may even volunteer to coach." Kyle leaned back in his chair, clasping his hands behind his head. "So, big brother, how long do you think you'll be out here, basking in the light of this gas giant?"

"Don't know yet," Tiv hedged. "There's a lot more to see out here, and we're just getting started." The arm around Leba squeezed.

"What have you done to my brother?" Kyle said after noticing his brother's move. "I don't think I've ever seen him this happy."

"Your brother's a great guy," Leba said. "He works incredibly hard and never takes any time for himself."

Kyle took out his billfold and removed a picture. "This is when Tiv took my boys camping. All they talk about is their uncle Tiv. Pity he's deployed for such long stretches." Tiv rolled his tongue around the inside of his mouth. Kyle's dig hit home. He hated being away, but besides his nephews, home was never particularly inviting. His relationship with his father was strained, and Tiv didn't like competing with Kyle. Leba was listening intently. Tiv studied Kyle's face, trying to predict the next line of questioning.

"Tiv tells me you're a doctor." Leba nodded. "He told me what you did for his friend DeShay. That's what really impressed him about you."

Why are you telling her this?

"The way you stayed with him, even risking your life to be there in his final moments."

Is that because I wasn't there for him and the fact she was makes me indebted to her? Is that what you think, little brother?

Frowning, Leba nodded again, but this time, her lip was quivering and her eyes welling up with tears. "It wasn't like Tiv didn't want to be there, he couldn't, and I'm grateful one of us was." Leba turned to look at Tiv. "In fact, I wouldn't be here if he didn't have his shuttle wait for me."

Coming to her rescue, Tiv shifted the focus to what Kyle liked to talk about the most, himself. "What about you, any ideas what you're going to do when you finish your Warrior career?"

"I thought maybe I'd help Dad out and run the company with him." Kyle drummed his fingers on the table. "He always planned for you to take it over one day, but since you're stuck, I thought maybe I should."

Tiv answered deliberately, "I'm sure Dad would be more than happy to hand you the helm when the time comes." *You know Dad took the company after Grandpa promised it to me.* Tiv, whose arm was still draped across Leba's shoulder, gave her another squeeze.

"Not to interrupt, but I'm getting hungry," Leba said. "Hasn't it been a while since we've seen a server?"

"You know, I think you're right," Tiv agreed. "Kyle, maybe you could use some of your star power to get us some food."

"No problem, be right back." Kyle got up from the booth and headed toward the servers' alcove.

"Thanks." Tiv looked at Leba. She nestled closer to him, slipped her arm around his waist, and gave him a hug. He didn't say anything else but knew she understood. He picked up her chin, studied her mouth for a moment, and gently kissed her.

He whispered, "Before my celebrity brother returns, I want to apologize for his brashness."

"It's okay. I'm used to standing in the shadows of such a bright star." He tilted his head and kissed her again.

Tiv helped Leba board the shuttle for the trip back to base. "It was nice of you to pick up the check."

"I may not make as much as he does—" Tiv hung his head.

"No, that's not what I was getting at." She took his hand. "I think you're great." Tiv noticed her blush as she tucked her chin to her chest. "And I'm glad you took me to the game."

It was late when Tiv finally got Leba back to her quarters. "Do you mind if I come in for a minute?" Tiv asked.

"Of course not." Leba entered her key code, and the door slid open. She reached behind him and activated the lights.

Tiv didn't even take off his jacket but sat on the end of the couch. "I need to talk to you about something."

Uh-oh, what did I do wrong? This can't be good. "Do you want something to drink?" Leba said, trying to stall.

"No," Tiv said.

He always wanted something to drink. This was really bad. I must have really screwed up. Leba exhaled slowly. She could feel her hands trembling as she made her way to sit on the couch. He pulled slightly back so they weren't touching. She framed her face with her hands. *I guess I failed the meet the family test.*

"You know we've being going out for a few weeks now, and…" He paused. Leba searched his face for clues as to what was coming next but couldn't seem to read him. The discomfort he was experiencing was evident, though. He reached for her hand but angled away from her. "I know you're pretty busy the next few weeks, and I was thinking that maybe I should…"

Should what? Find other people to date? Stop seeing each other? What?

"Maybe I should ask you now to make sure you're available for the formal in three weeks." The pounding in her chest resonated so loudly in her ears she almost didn't hear what he was asking. "I'd really like you to go with me. It would mean a lot." He wasn't dumping her at all. He wanted her to go to the annual Tal-Kari formal with him. *Yay!*

ABOUT THE AUTHOR

Lisa Pachino, MD, is a full-time practicing gastroenterologist. Currently training for her black belt at Masada Tactical, she lives in Maryland with her husband and three kids.

CPSIA information can be obtained
at www.ICGtesting.com
Printed in the USA
LVHW091506120220
646715LV00001B/11